# CHAMPION

# CHAMPION

A Legend Novel

# MARIE LU

G. P. PUTNAM'S SONS
An Imprint of Penguin Group (USA)

G. P. PUTNAM'S SONS
An imprint of Penguin Young Readers Group
Published by Penguin Group (USA), 375 Hudson Street, New York, NY 10014, USA

USA | Canada | UK | Ireland | Australia | New Zealand | India | South Africa | China
Penguin Books Ltd, Registered Offices: 80 Strand, London WC2R 0RL, England
For more information about the Penguin Group, visit penguin.com

Published simultaneously in Canada. Printed in the United States of America.
ISBN 978-0-399-25677-6
1 3 5 7 9 10 8 6 4 2

Text set in Adobe Caslon and Mercury.
Map illustration by Peter Bollinger.

The publisher does not have any control over and does not assume any responsibility
for author or third-party websites or their content.

*For my readers*

GREENLAND

CANADA

REPUBLIC

COLONIES

MEXICO

THE
EUROPEAN
UNION

SOUTH
AMERICA

Ross City

ANTARCTICA

RUSSIA

MONGOLIA

CHINA

Hei Cheng
(the Sea Cities)

THE
MIDDLE
EAST

INDIA

CONFEDERATE
NATIONS
OF
AFRICA

WEST
AUSTRALIA

EAST
AUSTRALIA

# SAN FRANCISCO, CALIFORNIA

## REPUBLIC OF AMERICA

POPULATION: 24,646,320

# DAY

OUT OF ALL THE DISGUISES I'VE WORN, THIS ONE might be my favorite.

Dark red hair, different enough from my usual white-blond, cut to just past my shoulders and pulled back into a tail. Green contacts that look natural when layered over my blue eyes. A crumpled, half-tucked collar shirt, its tiny silver buttons shining in the dark, a thin military jacket, black pants and steel-toed boots, a thick gray scarf wrapped around my neck, chin, and mouth. A dark soldier cap is pulled low over my forehead, and a crimson, painted tattoo stretches all over the left half of my face, changing me into someone unfamiliar. Aside from this, I wear an ever-present earpiece and mike. The Republic insists on it.

In most other cities, I'd probably get even more stares than I usually do because of that giant goddy tattoo—not exactly a subtle marker, I gotta admit. But here in San Francisco, I blend right in with the others. The first thing I noticed when Eden and I moved to Frisco eight months ago was the local trend: young people painting black or red patterns on their faces, some small and delicate, like Republic seals on their temples or something similar, others huge and sprawling, like giant patterns of the Republic's land shape. I chose a pretty generic tattoo tonight, because I'm not loyal enough to the Republic to stamp that loyalty right on my face. Leave that to June. Instead, I have stylized flames. Good enough.

My insomnia's acting up tonight, so instead of sleeping, I'm walking alone through a sector called Marina, which as far as I can tell is the hillier, Frisco equivalent of LA's Lake sector. The night's cool and pretty quiet, and a light drizzle is blowing in from the city's bay. The streets are narrow, glistening wet, and riddled with potholes, and the buildings that rise up on both sides—most of them tall enough to vanish into tonight's low-lying clouds—are eclectic, painted with fading red and gold and black, their sides fortified with enormous steel beams to counter the earthquakes that roll through every couple of months. JumboTrons five or six stories high sit on every other block, blaring the usual barrage of Republic news. The air smells salty and bitter, like smoke and industrial waste mixed with seawater, and somewhere in there, a faint whiff of fried fish. Sometimes, when I turn down a corner, I'll suddenly end up close enough to the water's edge to get my boots wet. Here the land slopes right into the bay and hundreds of buildings poke out half submerged along the horizon. Whenever I get a view of the bay, I can also see the Golden Gate Ruins, the twisted remnants of some old bridge all piled up along the other side of the shore. A handful of people jostle past me now and then, but for the most part the city is asleep. Scattered bonfires light alleyways, gathering spots for the sector's street folks. It's not that different from Lake.

Well—I guess there are *some* differences now. The San

Francisco Trial Stadium, for one, which sits empty and unlit off in the distance. Fewer street police in the poor sectors. The city's graffiti. You can always get an idea of how the people are feeling by looking at the recent graffiti. A lot of the messages I've seen lately actually *support* the Republic's new Elector. *He is our hope,* says one message scrawled on the side of a building. Another painted on the street reads: *The Elector will guide us out of the darkness.* A little too optimistic, if you ask me, but I guess they're good signs. Anden must be doing *something* right. And yet. Every now and then, I'll also see messages that say, *The Elector's a hoax,* or *Brainwashed,* or *The Day we knew is dead.*

I don't know. Sometimes this new trust between Anden and the people feels like a string . . . and *I* am that string. Besides, maybe the happy graffiti's fake, painted by propaganda officers. Why not?

You never know with the Republic.

Eden and I, of course, have a Frisco apartment in a rich sector called Pacifica, where we stay with our caretaker, Lucy. The Republic's gotta take care of its seventeen-year-old most-wanted-criminal-turned-national-hero, doesn't it? I remember how much I distrusted Lucy—a stern, stout, fifty-two-year-old lady dressed in classic Republic colors—when she first showed up at our door in Denver. "The Republic has assigned me to assist you boys," she told me as she bustled in to our apartment. Her eyes had settled immediately on Eden. "Especially the little one."

Yeah. That didn't sit well with me. First of all, it'd taken me two months before I could even let Eden out of my sight. We ate side by side; we slept side by side; he was *never* alone. I'd gone as far as standing outside his bathroom door, as if Republic soldiers would somehow suck him out through a vent, take him back to a lab, and hook him up to a bunch of machines.

"Eden doesn't need you," I'd snapped at Lucy. "He's got *me. I* take care of him."

But my health started fluctuating after those first couple of months. Some days I felt fine; other days, I'd be stuck in bed with a crippling headache. On those bad days, Lucy would take over—and after a few shouting matches, she and I settled into a grudging routine. She *does* make pretty awesome meat pies. And when we moved here to Frisco, she came with us. She guides Eden. She manages my medications.

When I'm finally tired of walking, I notice that I've wandered right out of Marina and into a wealthier neighboring district. I stop in front of a club with THE OBSIDIAN LOUNGE scored into a metal slab over its door. I slide against the wall into a sitting position, my arms resting on my knees, and feel the music's vibrations. My metal leg is ice-cold through the fabric of my trousers. On the wall across from me, graffiti scrawled in red reads, *Day = Traitor.* I sigh, take a silver tin from my pocket, and pull out a long cigarette. I run a finger across the SAN FRANCISCO CENTRAL HOSPITAL text imprinted down its length. Prescription cigarettes. Doctor's orders, yeah? I put it to my lips with trembling fingers and light it up. Close eyes. Take a puff. Gradually I lose myself in the clouds of blue smoke, waiting for the sweet, hallucinogenic effects to wash over me.

Doesn't take long tonight. Soon the constant, dull headache disappears, and the world around me takes on a blurry sheen that I know isn't only from the rain. A girl's sitting next to me. It's Tess.

She gives me the grin I was so familiar with back on the streets of Lake. "Any news from the JumboTrons?" she asks me, pointing toward a screen across the road.

I exhale blue smoke and lazily shake my head. "Nope. I mean, I've seen a couple of Patriot-related headlines, but it's like you guys vanished off the map. Where are you? Where are you going?"

"Do you miss me?" Tess asks instead of answering.

I stare at the shimmery image of her. She's how I remember from the streets—her reddish-brown hair tied into a messy braid, her eyes large and luminous, kind and gentle. Little baby Tess. What were my last words to her . . . back when we had botched the Patriots' assassination attempt on Anden? *Please, Tess—I can't leave you here.* But that's exactly what I did.

I turn away, taking another drag on my cigarette. Do I miss her? "Every day," I reply.

"You've been trying to find me," Tess says, scooting closer. I swear I can almost feel her shoulder against mine. "I've seen you, scouring the JumboTrons and airwaves for news, eavesdropping on the streets. But the Patriots are in hiding right now."

Of course they're in hiding. Why would they attack, now that Anden's in power and a peace treaty between the Republic and the Colonies is a done deal? What could their new cause possibly be? I have no idea. Maybe they don't have one. Maybe they don't even exist anymore. "I wish you would come back," I murmur to Tess. "It'd be nice to see you again."

"What about June?"

As she asks this, her image vanishes. She's replaced by June, with her long ponytail and her dark eyes that shine with hints of gold, serious and analyzing, always analyzing. I lean my head against my knee and close my eyes. Even the illusion of June is enough to send a stabbing pain through my chest. Hell. I miss her so much.

I remember how I'd said good-bye to her back in Denver, before Eden and I moved to Frisco. "I'm sure we'll be back," I'd told her over my mike, trying to fill the awkward silence between us. "After Eden's treatment is done." This was a lie, of course. We were going to Frisco for *my* treatment, not Eden's. But June didn't know this, so she just said, "Come back soon."

That was almost eight months ago. I haven't heard from her since. I don't know if it's because each of us is too hesitant to bother the other, too afraid that the other doesn't want to talk, or maybe both of us are just too damn proud to be the one desperate enough to reach out. Maybe she's just not interested enough. But you know how it goes. A week passes without contact, and then a month, and soon too much time has passed and calling her would just feel random and weird. So I don't. Besides, what would I say? Don't worry, doctors are fighting to save my life. Don't worry, they're trying to shrink the problem area in my brain with a giant pile of medication before attempting an operation. Don't worry, Antarctica might grant me access to treatment in their superior hospitals. Don't worry, I'll be just fine.

What's the point of keeping in touch with the girl you're crazy about, when you're dying?

The reminder sends a throbbing pain through the back of my head. "It's better this way," I tell myself for the hundredth time. And it *is*. By not seeing her for so long, the memory of how we'd originally met has grown dimmer, and I find myself thinking about her connection to my family's deaths less often.

Unlike Tess's, for some reason June's image never says a word. I try to ignore the shimmery mirage, but she refuses to go away. *So damn stubborn.*

Finally, I stand, stub my cigarette into the pavement, and step through the door of the Obsidian Lounge. Maybe the music and lights will shake her from my system.

For an instant, I can't see a thing. The club is pitch-black, and the sound's deafening. I'm stopped immediately by an enormous pair of soldiers. One of them puts a firm hand on my shoulder. "Name and branch?" he asks.

I have no interest in making my real identity known. "Corporal Schuster. Air force," I reply, blurting out a random name and the first branch that comes to mind. I always think of the air force first, mostly because of Kaede. "I'm stationed at Naval Base Two."

The guard nods. "Air force kids over in the back left, near the bathrooms. And if I hear you picking any fights with the army booths, you're out and your commander hears about it in the morning. Got it?"

I nod, and the soldiers let me pass. I walk down a dark hall and through a second door, then melt into the crowds and flashing lights inside.

The dance floor is jammed with people in loose shirts and rolled-up sleeves, dresses paired with rumpled uniforms. I find the air force booths in the back of the room. Good, there are several empty ones. I slide into a booth, prop up my boots against the cushioned seats, and lean my head back. At least June's image has disappeared. The loud music sends all my thoughts scattering.

I've only been in the booth for a few minutes when a girl cuts her way through the crowded dance floor and stumbles toward me. She looks flushed, her eyes bright and teasing; and when I glance behind her, I notice a cluster of laughing girls watching us. I force a smile. Usually, I like the attention in clubs, but sometimes, I just want to close my eyes and let the chaos take me away.

She leans over and presses her lips against my ear. "Excuse me," she shouts over the noise. "My girlfriends want to know if you're Day."

I've been recognized already? I shrink instinctively away and shake my head so the others can see. "You got the wrong guy," I reply with a wry grin. "But thanks for the compliment."

The girl's face is almost entirely covered in shadows, but

even so, I can tell she's blushing furiously. Her friends burst out laughing. None of them look like they believe my denial. "Want to dance?" the girl asks. She glances over her shoulder toward the flashing blue and gold lights, then back at me. This must be something her friends dared her to do too.

As I'm trying to think up some sort of polite refusal, I take in the girl's appearance. The club's too dark for me to get a good look at her, and all I see are glimpses of neon highlights on her skin and long ponytail, her glossy lips curved into a smile, her body lean and smooth in a short dress and military boots. My refusal fades on my tongue. Something about her reminds me of June. In the eight months since June first became a Princeps-Elect, I haven't felt excited about many girls—but now, with this shadowy doppelgänger beckoning me onto the dance floor, I let myself feel hopeful again.

"Yeah, why not?" I say.

The girl breaks into a wide smile. When I get up from the booth and take her hand, her friends all let out a gasp of surprise, followed by a loud cheer. The girl leads me through them, and before I know it, we've pushed our way into the crowds and carved out a tiny space right in the middle of the action.

I press myself against her, she runs a hand along the back of my neck, and we let the pounding beat carry us away. *She's cute*, I admit to myself, blinded in this sea of lights and limbs. The song changes, then changes again. I have no idea how long we're lost like this, but when she leans forward and brushes her lips over my own, I close my eyes and let her. I even feel a shiver run down my spine. She kisses me twice, her mouth soft and liquid, her tongue tasting of vodka and fruit. I flatten one hand against the small of the girl's back and pull her closer, until her body's solidly against mine. Her kisses grow more urgent. *She* is *June*, I tell myself, choosing to indulge in the fantasy. With my eyes closed, my mind still hazy from my cigarette's hallucinogens, I can believe it for a moment—I can picture *her* kissing me here, taking every last breath from my lungs. The girl probably senses the change in my movements, my sudden hunger and desire, because she grins against my lips. *She* is *June*. It is June's dark hair that brushes against my face, June's long lashes that touch my cheeks, June's arm wrapped around my neck, June's body sliding against mine. A soft moan escapes me.

"Come on," she whispers. Mischief laces her words. "Let's go get some air."

How long has it been? I don't want to leave, because it means I'll have to open my eyes and June will be gone, replaced with this girl that I don't know. But she pulls on my hand and I'm forced to look around. June is nowhere to be seen, of course. The club's lights flash and I'm momentarily blinded. She guides me through the throngs of dancers, down the club's dark hallway, and out an unmarked back door. We step into a quiet back alley. A few weak spotlights shine down along the path, giving everything an eerie, greenish glow.

She pushes me against the wall and drowns me in another kiss. Her skin is moist, and I feel her goose bumps rise beneath my touch. I kiss her back, and a small laugh of surprise escapes her when I flip us around and pin her against the wall.

*She's June,* I tell myself on repeat. My lips work greedily along her neck, tasting smoke and perfume.

Faint static sizzles in my earpiece, the sound of rain and frying eggs. I try to ignore the incoming call, even as a man's voice fills my ears. Talk about a buzzkill. "Mr. Wing," he says.

I don't answer it. *Go away. I'm busy.*

A few seconds later, the voice starts up again. "Mr. Wing, this is Captain David Guzman of Denver City Patrol Fourteen. I know you're there."

Oh, *this* guy. This poor captain's always the one tasked with trying to get hold of me.

I sigh and break away from the girl. "Sorry," I say breathlessly. I give her an apologetic frown and gesture at my ear. "Give me a minute?"

She smiles and smoothes down her dress. "I'll be inside," she replies. "Look for me." Then she steps through the door and back into the club.

I turn my mike on and start slowly pacing up and down the alley. "What do you want?" I say in an annoyed whisper.

The captain sighs over the earpiece and launches into his message. "Mr. Wing, your presence is requested in Denver tomorrow night, on Independence Day, at the Capitol Tower's ballroom. As always, you are free to turn down the request— as you usually do," he mutters under his breath. "However, this banquet is an exceptional meeting of great importance.

Should you choose to attend, we'll have a private jet waiting for you in the morning."

*An exceptional meeting of great importance?* Ever heard so many fancy words in one sentence? I roll my eyes. Every month or so, I get an invitation to some goddy capital event, like a ball for all the high-ranking war generals or the celebration they held when Anden finally ended the Trials. But the only reason they want me to go to these things is so they can show me off and remind the people, "Look, just in case you forgot, Day is on our side!" *Don't push your luck, Anden.*

"Mr. Wing," the captain says when I stay silent, as if he's resorting to some final argument, "the glorious Elector personally requests your presence. So does the Princeps-Elect."

The Princeps-Elect.

My boots crunch to a halt in the middle of the alley. I forget to breathe.

*Don't get too excited—after all, there are three Princeps-Elects, and he might be referring to any one of them.* A few seconds pass before I finally ask, "Which Princeps-Elect?"

"The one who actually matters to you."

My cheeks warm at the taunt in his voice. "June?"

"Yes, Ms. June Iparis," the captain replies. He sounds relieved to finally have my attention. "She wanted to make it a personal request this time. She would very much like to see you at the Capitol Tower's banquet."

My head aches, and I fight to steady my breathing. All thoughts of the girl in the club go out the window. June has not personally asked for me in eight months—this is the first time that she's requested I attend a public function. "What's this for?" I ask. "Just an Independence Day party? Why so important?"

The captain hesitates. "It's a matter of national security."

"What's *that* supposed to mean?" My initial excitement slowly wanes—maybe he's just bluffing. "Look, Captain, I've got some unfinished business to take care of. Try convincing me again in the morning."

The captain curses under his breath. "Fine, Mr. Wing. Have it your way." He mumbles something I can't quite make out, then goes offline. I frown in exasperation as my initial excitement fades away into a sinking disappointment. Maybe I should head home now. It's time for me to go back and check up on Eden, anyway. What a joke. Chances are he's probably lying about June's request in the first place, because if she'd really wanted me to go back to the capital that badly, she—

"Day?"

A new voice comes over my earpiece. I freeze.

Have the hallucinogens from the meds worn off yet? Did I just imagine her voice? Even though I haven't heard it in almost a year, I would recognize it anywhere, and the sound alone is enough to conjure the image of June standing before me, as if I'd run across her by chance in this alley. *Please, don't let it be her. Please, let it be her.*

Did her voice always have this effect on me?

I have no idea how long I was frozen like this, but it must've been a while, because she repeats, "Day, it's me. June. Are you there?" A shiver runs through me.

This is real. It's really her.

Her tone is different from what I remember. Hesitant and formal, like she's speaking to a stranger. I finally manage to compose myself and click my mike back on. "I'm here," I reply. My own tone is different too—just as hesitant, just as formal. I hope she doesn't hear the slight tremor in it.

There's a short pause on the other side before June continues. "Hi." Then a long silence, followed by, "How are you?"

Suddenly I feel a storm of words building up inside me, threatening to pour out. I want to blurt out everything: I've thought about you every day since that final farewell between us, I'm sorry for not contacting you, I wish you had contacted me. I miss you. I miss you.

I don't say any of this. Instead, the only thing I manage is, "Fine. What's up?"

She pauses. "Oh. That's good. I apologize for the late call, as I'm sure you're trying to sleep. But the Senate and the Elector have asked me to send this request to you personally. I wouldn't do it unless I felt it was truly important. Denver is throwing a ball for Independence Day, and during the event, we'll be having an emergency meeting. We need you in attendance."

"Why?" Guess I've resorted to one-word replies. For some reason, it's all I can think of with June's voice on the line.

She exhales, sending a faint burst of static through the

earpiece, and then says, "You've heard about the peace treaty being drafted between the Republic and the Colonies, right?"

"Yeah, of course." Everyone in the country knows about that: our precious little Anden's greatest ambition, to end the war that's been going on for who knows how long. And so far, things seem to be going in the right direction, well enough that the warfront has been at a quiet stalemate for the past four months. Who knew a day like that could come, just like how we'd never expected to see the Trial stadiums sitting unused across the country. "Seems like the Elector's on track to becoming the Republic's hero, yeah?"

"Don't speak too soon." June's words darken, and I feel like I can see her expression through the earpiece. "Yesterday we received an angry transmission from the Colonies. There's a plague spreading through their warfront cities, and they believe it was caused by some of the biological weapons we'd sent across their borders. They've even traced the serial numbers on the shells of the weapons they believe started this plague."

Her words are turning muffled through the shock in my mind, the fog that's bringing back memories of Eden and his black, bleeding eyes, of that boy on the train who was being used as a part of the warfare. "Does that mean the peace treaty is off?" I ask.

"Yes." June's voice falls. "The Colonies say the plague is an official act of war against them."

"And what does this have to do with me?"

Another long, ominous pause. It fills me with dread so icy cold that I feel like my fingers are turning numb. *The plague. It's happening. It's all come full circle.*

"I'll tell you when you get here," June finally says. "Best not to talk about it over earpieces."

# JUNE

I DESPISE MY FIRST CONVERSATION WITH DAY AFTER eight months of no communication. I *hate* it. When did I become so manipulative? Why must I always use his weaknesses against him?

Last night at 2306 hours, Anden came to my apartment complex and knocked on my door. Alone. I don't even think guards were stationed in the hallway for his protection. It was my first warning that whatever he needed to tell me had to be important—and secret.

"I have to ask a favor of you," he said as I let him in. Anden has almost perfected the art of being a young Elector (calm, cool, collected, a proud chin under stress, an even voice when angered), but this time I could see the deep worry in his eyes. Even my dog, Ollie, could tell that Anden was troubled, and tried reassuring him by pushing his wet nose against Anden's hand.

I nudged Ollie away before turning back to Anden. "What is it?" I asked.

Anden ran a hand through his dark curls. "I don't mean to disturb you so late at night," he said, leaning his head down toward mine in quiet concern. "But I'm afraid this is not a conversation that can wait." He stood close enough so that if I wanted to, I could tilt my face up and accidentally brush my lips against his. My heartbeat quickened at the thought.

Anden seemed to sense the tension in my pose, because he took an apologetic step away and gave me more room to breathe. I felt a strange mixture of relief and disappointment. "The peace treaty is over," he whispered. "The Colonies are preparing to declare war against us once again."

"What?" I whispered back. "Why? What's happened?"

"Word from my generals is that a couple of weeks ago, a deadly virus started sweeping through the Colonies' warfront like wildfire." When he saw my eyes widen in understanding, he nodded. He looked so weary, burdened with the weight of an entire nation's safety. "Apparently I was too late in withdrawing our biological weapons from the warfront."

*Eden.* The experimental viruses that Anden's father had used in attempts to cause a plague in the Colonies. For months, I'd tried to push that to the back of my mind—after all, Eden was safe now, under the care of Day and, last I heard, slowly adjusting to semblances of a normal life. For the last few months, the warfront had stood silent while Anden attempted to hash out a peace treaty with the Colonies. I'd thought that we would be lucky, that nothing would come out of that biological warfare. Wishful thinking.

"Do the Senators know?" I asked after a while. "Or the other Princeps-Elects? Why are you telling *me* this? I'm hardly your closest advisor."

Anden sighed and squeezed the bridge of his nose. "Forgive me. I wish I didn't have to involve you in this. The Colonies believe that we have the cure to this virus in our laboratories and are simply withholding it. They demand we share it, or else they put all of their strength behind a full-scale invasion of the Republic. And this time, it won't be a return to our old war. The Colonies have secured an ally. They struck a trade deal with Africa—the Colonies get military help, and in return, Africa gets half our land."

A feeling of foreboding crept over me. Even without him saying it, I could tell where this was going. "We don't have a cure, do we?"

"No. But we *do* know which former patients have the potential to help us find that cure."

I started shaking my head. When Anden reached out to touch my elbow, I jerked away. "Absolutely not," I said. "You can't ask this of me. I won't do it."

Anden looked pained. "I have called for a private banquet tomorrow night to gather all of our Senators. We have no choice if we want to put a stop to this and find a way to secure peace with the Colonies." His tone grew firmer. "You know this as well as I do. I want him to attend this banquet and hear us out. We need his permission if we're going to get to Eden."

*He's serious,* I realized in shock. "You'll never get him to do it. You realize that, don't you? The country's support for you is still soft, and Day's alliance with you is hesitant at best. What do you think he'll say to *this*? What if you anger him enough for him to call the people to action, to tell them to rebel against you? Or *worse*—what if he asks them to support the Colonies?"

"I know. I've thought through all of this." Anden rubs his temples in exhaustion. "If there was a better option, I'd take it."

"So you want *me* to make him agree to this," I added. My irritation was too strong to bother hiding. "I won't do it. Get the other Senators to convince Day, or try convincing him yourself. Or find a way to apologize to the Colonies' Chancellor—ask him to negotiate new terms."

"*You* are Day's weakness, June. He'll listen to you." Anden winced even as he said this, as if he didn't want to admit it. "I know how this makes me sound. I don't want to be cruel—I don't want Day to see us as the enemy. But I *will* do what it takes to protect the Republic's people. Otherwise, the Colonies will attack, and if that happens, you know it's likely the virus will spread here as well."

It was worse than that, even though Anden didn't say it aloud. If the Colonies attack us with Africa at their side, then our military might not be strong enough to hold them back. This time, they might win. *He'll listen to you.* I closed my eyes and bowed my head. I didn't want to admit it, but I knew that Anden was right.

So I did as he requested. I called Day and asked him to return to the capital. Just the thought of seeing him again leaves my heart pounding, aching from his absence in my life over these past months. I haven't seen or spoken to him for so long . . . and *this* is going to be how we reunite? What will he think of me now?

What will he think of the Republic when he finds out what they want with his little brother?

1201 HOURS.
DENVER COUNTY COURT OF FEDERAL CRIME.
72°F INDOORS.
SIX HOURS UNTIL I SEE DAY AT THE EVENING BALL.
289 DAYS AND 12 HOURS SINCE METIAS'S DEATH.

Thomas and Commander Jameson are on trial today.

I'm so tired of trials. In the past four months, a dozen for-mer Senators have been tried and convicted of participating in the plan to assassinate Anden, the plan that Day and I had barely managed to stop. Those Senators have all been executed. Razor has already been executed. Sometimes I feel like some-one new is convicted each week.

But today's trial is different. I know *exactly* who is being sentenced today, and why.

I sit in a balcony overlooking the courtroom's round stage, my hands restless in their white silk gloves, my body constantly shifting in my vest and black ruffled coat, my boots quietly tap-ping against the balcony pillars. My chair is made out of syn-thetic oak and cushioned with soft, scarlet velvet, but somehow I just can't make myself comfortable. To keep myself calm and occupied, I'm carefully entwining four straightened paper clips in my lap to form a small ring. Two guards stand behind me. Three circular rows of the country's twenty-six Senators sur-round the stage, uniform in their matching scarlet-and-black suits, their silver epaulettes reflecting the chamber's light, their voices echoing along the arched ceilings. They sound largely indifferent, as if they're meeting about trade routes instead of people's fates. Many are new faces that have replaced the traitor Senators, who Anden has already cleaned out. I'm the one who sticks out with my black-and-gold outfit (even the seventy-six soldiers standing guard here are clad in scarlet; two for each Senator, two for me, two for each of the other Princeps-Elects, four for Anden, and fourteen at the chamber's front and back entrances, which means the defendants—Thomas and Commander Jameson—are considered fairly high risk and could possibly make a sudden move).

I'm no Senator, clearly. I am a Princeps-Elect and need to be distinguished as such.

Two others in the chamber wear the same black-and-gold uniform that I do. My eyes wander over to them now, where they sit on other balconies. After Anden tapped me to train for the Princeps position, Congress urged him to select several others. After all, you cannot have only one person preparing to become the leader of the Senate, especially when that person is a sixteen-year-old girl without a shred of political experience. So Anden agreed. He picked out two more Princeps-Elects, both of them already Senators. One is named Mariana Dupree. My gaze settles on her, her nose turned up and her eyes heavy with sternness. Thirty-seven years old, Senator for ten years. She hated me the instant she laid eyes on me. I look away from her and toward the balcony where the second Princeps-Elect sits. Serge Carmichael, a jumpy thirty-two-year-old Senator and great political mind, who wasted no time showing me that he doesn't appreciate my youth and inexperience.

Serge and Mariana. My two rivals for the Princeps title. I feel exhausted just thinking about it.

On a balcony several dozen yards away, sitting flanked by his guards, Anden seems calm, reviewing something with one of the soldiers. He's wearing a handsome gray military coat with bright silver buttons, silver epaulettes, and silver sleeve insignias. He occasionally glances down toward the prisoners standing in the chamber's circle. I watch him for a moment, admiring his appearance of calm.

Thomas and Commander Jameson are going to receive their sentences for crimes against the nation.

Thomas looks tidier than usual—if that's possible. His hair is slicked back, and I can tell that he must've emptied an entire can of shoe polish onto each of his boots. He stands at attention in the center of the chamber and stares straight ahead with an intensity that would make any Republic commander proud. I wonder what's going through his mind. Is he picturing that night in the hospital alley, when he murdered my brother? Is he thinking of the many conversations he had with Metias, the moments when he had taken down his guard? Or the fateful night when he had chosen to betray Metias instead of help him?

Commander Jameson, on the other hand, looks slightly disheveled. Her cold, emotionless eyes are fixed on me. She has been watching me unflinchingly for the past twelve minutes. I stare back for a moment, trying to see some hint of a soul in her eyes, but nothing exists there except for an icy hatred, an absolute lack of conscience.

I look away, take deep, slow breaths, and try to focus on something else. My thoughts return to Day.

It's been 241 days since he visited my apartment and bid me good-bye. Sometimes I wish Day could hold me in his arms again and kiss me the way he did on that last night, so close that we could barely breathe, his lips soft against mine. But then I take back that wish. The thought is useless. It reminds me of loss, just like how sitting here and looking down on the people who killed my family reminds me of all the things I used to have; it reminds me too of my guilt, of all the things *Day* used to have that *I* took from him.

Besides, Day will probably never want to kiss me again. Not after he finds out why I've asked him to return to Denver.

Anden's looking in my direction now. When I catch his gaze, he nods once, excuses himself from his balcony, and a minute later he steps into my balcony. I rise and, along with my guards, snap to a salute. Anden waves a hand impatiently. "Sit, please," he says. When I've relaxed back into my chair, he bends down to my eye level and adds, "How are you holding up, June?"

I fight the blush as it spreads across my cheeks. After eight months without Day in my life, I find myself smiling at Anden, enjoying the attention, occasionally even hoping for it. "Doing fine, thanks. I've been looking forward to this day."

"Of course." Anden nods. "Don't worry—it won't be long before both of them are out of your life forever." He gives my shoulder a reassuring squeeze. Then he leaves as swiftly as he arrived, vanishing with the faint clink of medals and epaulettes, then reappearing moments later in his own balcony.

I lift my head in a vain attempt at bravery, knowing that Commander Jameson's icy eyes must still be upon me. As each of the Senators rises to cast aloud his vote on her verdict, I hold my breath and carefully push away each memory I have of her eyes staring me down, folding them into a neat compartment at the back of my mind. The voting seems to take forever, even though the Senators are all quick to say what they think will please the Elector. No one has the courage to risk crossing Anden after watching so many others convicted and executed. By the time my turn comes, my throat is parched. I swallow a few times, then speak up.

"Guilty," I say, my voice clear and calm.

Serge and Mariana cast their votes after me. We run through another round of voting for Thomas, and then we're done. Three minutes later, a man (bald, with a round, wrinkled face and scarlet floor-length robes he's clutching with his left hand) hurries into Anden's balcony and gives him a rushed bow. Anden leans toward the man and whispers in his ear. I watch their interaction in quiet curiosity, wondering whether I can predict the final verdict by their gestures. After a short deliberation, Anden and the messenger both nod. Then the messenger raises his voice to the entire assembly.

"We are now ready to announce the verdicts for Captain Thomas Alexander Bryant and Commander Natasha Jameson of Los Angeles City Patrol Eight. All rise for the glorious Elector!"

The Senators and I stand with a uniform clatter, while Commander Jameson simply turns to face Anden with a look of utter disdain. Thomas snaps to a sharp salute in Anden's direction. He holds the position as Anden stands up, straightens, and puts his hands behind his back. There's a moment of silence as we wait for his final verdict, the one vote that really matters. I fight back a rising urge to cough. My eyes dart instinctively to the other Princeps-Elects, something I now do all the time; Mariana has a satisfied frown on her face, while Serge just looks bored. One of my fists clenches tightly around the paper clip ring I'm working on. I already know it will leave deep grooves in my palm.

"The Senators of the Republic have submitted their individual verdicts," Anden announces to the courtroom, his words bearing all the formality of a traditions-old speech. I marvel at the way his voice can sound so soft, yet carry so well at the same time. "I have taken their joint decision into account, and now I give my own." Anden pauses to turn his eyes down toward where both of them are waiting. Thomas is still in full salute, still staring intently at the empty air in front of him. "Captain Thomas Alexander Bryant of Los Angeles City Patrol Eight," he says, "the Republic of America finds you *guilty . . .*"

The room stays silent. I fight to keep my breathing even. *Think about something. Anything.* What about all the political books I've been reading this week? I try to recite some of the facts I've learned, but suddenly I can't remember any of it. Most uncharacteristic.

". . . of the death of Captain Metias Iparis on the night of November thirtieth—of the death of civilian Grace Wing without the warrants necessary for execution—of the single-handed execution of twelve protesters in Batalla Square on the afternoon of—"

His voice comes in and out of the blur of noise in my head. I lean a hand against my chair's armrest, let out a slow breath, and try to prevent myself from swaying. *Guilty.* Thomas has been found guilty of killing both my brother and Day's mother. My hands shake.

"—and thereby sentenced to death by firing squad two days from today, at seventeen hundred hours. Commander Natasha Jameson of Los Angeles City Patrol Eight, the Republic of America finds you *guilty* . . ."

Anden's voice fades away into a dull, unrecognizable hum. Everything around me seems so slow, as if I'm living too quickly for it all and leaving the world behind.

A year ago I'd been standing outside Batalla Hall on a different sort of court stage, looking on with a huge crowd as a judge gave Day the exact same sentence. Now Day is alive, and a Republic celebrity. I open my eyes again. Commander Jameson's lips are set in a tight line as Anden reads out her death penalty. Thomas looks expressionless. *Is* he expressionless? I'm too far away to tell, but his eyebrows seem furrowed into a strange sort of tragedy. *I should feel good about this,* I remind myself. Both Day and I should be rejoicing. Thomas killed Metias. He shot Day's mother in cold blood, without a second's hesitation.

But now the courtroom falls away and all I can see are

memories of Thomas as a teenager, back when he and Metias and I used to eat pork *edame* inside a warm first-floor street stand, with the rain pouring down all around us. I remember Thomas showing off his first assigned gun to me. I even remember the time Metias brought me to his afternoon drills. I was twelve and had just begun my courses at Drake for a week—how innocent everything seemed back then. Metias picked me up after my classes that afternoon, right on time, and we headed over to the Tanagashi sector, where he was running his patrol through drills. I can still feel the warmth of the sun beating down on my hair, still see the swoosh of Metias's black half cape, the gleam of his silver epaulettes, and still hear the sharp clicks of his shining boots on the cement. While I settled down on a corner bench and turned my comp on to (pretend to) do some advance reading, Metias lined up his soldiers for inspection. He paused before each soldier to point out flaws in their uniforms.

"Cadet Rin," he barked at one of the newer soldiers. The soldier jumped at the steel in my brother's voice, then hung her head in shame as Metias tapped the lone medal pinned on the cadet's coat. "If I wore my medal like this, Commander Jameson would strip me of my title. Do you want to be removed from this patrol, soldier?"

"N-no, sir," the cadet stammered.

Metias kept his gloved hands tucked behind his back and moved on. He criticized three more soldiers before he reached Thomas, who stood at attention near the end of the line. Metias looked over his uniform with a stern, careful eye. Of course, Thomas's outfit was absolutely spotless—not a single thread out of place, every medal and epaulette groove polished to a bright shine, boots so flawless that I could probably see my reflection in them. A long pause. I put my comp down and leaned forward to watch more closely. Finally, my brother nodded. "Well done, soldier," he said to Thomas. "Keep up the good work, and I'll see that Commander Jameson promotes you before the end of this year."

Thomas's expression never changed, but I saw him lift his chin with pride. "Thank you, sir," he replied. Metias's eyes lingered on him for a second, and then he moved on.

When he finally finished inspecting everyone, my brother turned to face his entire patrol. "A disappointing inspection, soldiers," he called out to them. "You're under my watch now, and that means you're under Commander Jameson's watch. She expects a higher caliber from this lot, so you'd do well to try harder. Understood?"

Sharp salutes answered him. *"Yes, sir!"*

Metias's eyes returned to Thomas. I saw respect on my brother's face, even admiration. "If each of you paid attention to detail the way Cadet Bryant does, we'd be the greatest patrol in the country. Let him serve as an example to you all." He joined them in a final salute. "Long live the Republic!" The cadets echoed him in unison.

The memory slowly fades from my thoughts, and Metias's clear voice turns into a ghost's whisper, leaving me weak and exhausted in my sadness.

Metias had always talked about Thomas's fixation on being

the perfect soldier. I remember the blind devotion Thomas gave to Commander Jameson, the same blind devotion he now gives to his new Elector. Then I see Thomas and me sitting across from each other in an interrogation room—I remember the anguish in his eyes. How he'd told me that he wanted to protect me. What happened to that shy, awkward boy from Los Angeles's poor sectors, the boy who used to train with Metias every afternoon? Something blurs my vision and I quickly wipe a hand across my eyes.

I *could* be compassionate. I could ask Anden to spare his life and let him live out his years in prison, and give him a chance to redeem himself. But instead I just stand there with my closed lips and unwavering posture, my heart hard as stone. Metias would be more merciful in my position.

But I was never as good a person as my brother.

"This concludes the trial for Captain Thomas Alexander Bryant and Commander Natasha Jameson," Anden finishes. He holds a hand out in Thomas's direction and nods once. "Captain, do you have any words for the Senate?"

Thomas doesn't flinch in the slightest, doesn't show a single hint of fear or remorse or anger on his face. I watch him closely. After a heartbeat, he turns his eyes up to where Anden stands, then bows low. "My glorious Elector," he replies in a clear, unwavering voice. "I have disgraced the Republic by acting in a way that has both displeased and disappointed you. I humbly accept my verdict." He rises from his bow, then returns to his salute. "Long live the Republic."

He glances up at me when the Senators all voice their

agreement with Anden's final verdict. For an instant, our eyes meet. Then I look down. After a while, I look back up and he's staring straight ahead again.

Anden turns his attention to Commander Jameson. "Commander," he says, extending his gloved hand in her direction. His chin lifts in a regal gesture. "Do you have any words for the Senate?"

She doesn't flinch from looking at the young Elector. Her eyes are cold, dark slates. After a pause, she finally nods. "Yes, *Elector*," she says, her tone harsh and mocking, a stark contrast to Thomas's. The Senators and soldiers shift uneasily, but Anden raises a hand for silence. "I do have some words for you. I was not the first to hope for your death, and I won't be the last. You are the Elector, but you are still just a boy. You don't know who you are." She narrows her eyes . . . and smiles. "But *I* know. I have seen far more than you have—I've drained the blood from prisoners twice your age, I've killed men with twice your strength, I've left prisoners shaking in their broken bodies who probably have twice your courage. You think you're this country's savior, don't you? But I know better. You're just your father's boy, and like father, like son. He failed, and so will you." Her smile widens, but it never touches her eyes. "This country will go down in flames with you at the helm, and my ghost will be laughing at you all the way from hell."

Anden's expression never changes. His eyes stay clear and unafraid, and in this moment, I am drawn to him like a bird to an open sky. He meets her stare coolly. "This concludes today's trial," he replies, his voice echoing throughout the chamber.

"Commander, I suggest you save your threats for the firing squad." Then he folds his hands behind his back and nods at his soldiers. "Remove them from my sight."

I don't know how Anden can show so little fear in front of Commander Jameson. I envy it. Because as I watch the soldiers lead her away, all I can feel is a deep, ice-cold pit of terror. Like she's not done with us yet. Like she's warning us to watch our backs.

# DAY

WE TOUCH DOWN IN DENVER ON THE MORNING OF THE EMER-
gency banquet. Even the words themselves make me want to
laugh: emergency *banquet*? To me, a banquet still means a feast,
and I don't see how any emergency should be cause for a goddy
mountain of food, even if it *is* for Independence Day. Is that how
these Senators deal with crises—by stuffing their fat faces?

After Eden and I settle into a temporary government apartment and Eden dozes off, exhausted from our early morning
flight, I reluctantly leave him with Lucy in order to meet the
assistant assigned to prep me for tonight's event.

"If anyone tries to see him," I whisper to Lucy as Eden
sleeps, "for any reason, please call me. If anyone wants—"

Lucy, used to my paranoia, hushes me with a wave of her
hand. "Let me put your mind at ease, Mr. Wing," she replies.
She pats my cheek. "No one will see Eden while you're gone. I
promise. I'll call you in an instant if anything happens."

I nod. My eyes linger on Eden as if he'll disappear if I
blink. "Thanks."

To attend an event this fancy, I need to dress the part—
and to dress the part, the Republic assigns a Senator's
daughter to take me through the downtown district, where
the city's main shopping areas are clustered. She meets me
right where the train stops in the center of the district.
There's no mistaking who she is—she's decked out in a stylish

uniform from head to toe, her light brown eyes set against dark brown skin and thick black curls of hair tied up into a knotted braid. When she recognizes me, she flashes me a smile. I catch her looking me over, as if already critiquing my outfit. "You must be Day," she says, taking my hand. "My name is Faline Fedelma, and the Elector has assigned me to be your guide." She pauses to raise an eyebrow at my clothes. "We have some work to do."

I look down at my outfit. Trousers tucked into scuffed-up boots, a rumpled collar shirt, and an old scarf. Would've been considered luxurious on the streets. "Glad you approve," I reply. But Faline just laughs and loops an arm through mine.

As she leads me to a government clothing street that specializes in evening wear, I take in the crowds of people rushing around us. Well-dressed, upper-class folks. A trio of students pass, giggling about something or other, dressed in pristine military uniforms and polished boots. As we round a corner and step inside a shop, I realize that soldiers are standing guard up and down the street. A *lot* of soldiers.

"Are there usually this many guards downtown?" I ask Faline.

She just shrugs and holds up an outfit against me, but I can see the unease in her eyes. "No," she replies, "not really. But I'm sure it's nothing for you to worry about."

I let it drop, but a pulse of anxiety rushes through my mind. Denver's beefing up its defenses. June hasn't explained why she needed me to attend this banquet so badly, badly enough to contact me herself after so many months of no word. What the hell would she need from *me*? What does the Republic want this time?

If the Republic really is going back to war, then maybe I should find a way to get Eden out of the country. We have the power to leave now, after all. Don't know what's keeping me here.

Hours later, after the sun has set and fireworks for the Elector's birthday have already started going off in random parts of the city, a jeep takes me from our apartment toward Colburn Hall. I peer impatiently out the window. People travel up and down the sidewalks in dense clusters. Tonight each of them is dressed in very specific clothing—mostly red, with hints of gold makeup and Republic seals stamped prominently here and there, on the back of white gloves or on the sleeves of military coats. I wonder how many of these folks agree with the *Anden is our savior* graffiti and how many side with the *Anden is a hoax* message. Troops march up and down the streets. All the JumboTrons have images of enormous Republic seals on display, followed by live footage streaming from the festivities happening inside Colburn Hall. To Anden's credit, there's been a steady decline in Republic propaganda lately on the JumboTrons. Still no news about the outside world, though. Guess you can't have everything.

By the time we reach the cobbled steps of Colburn Hall, the streets are a mess of celebrations, throngs of people, and unsmiling guards. The onlookers let out a huge cheer when they see me step out of the jeep, a roar that shakes my bones and sends a spasm of pain through the back of my head. I wave hesitantly back.

Faline's waiting for me at the bottom of the steps that lead up to Colburn Hall. This time she's clad in a gold dress, and gold dust shimmers on her eyelids. We exchange bows before I follow behind her, looking on as she motions for others to clear a path. "You clean up nicely," she says. "Someone's going to be very pleased to see you."

"I don't think the Elector will be as excited as you think."

She smiles at me over her shoulder. "I wasn't talking about the Elector."

My heart jumps at that.

We make our way through the shouting mob. I crane my neck and stare at the elaborate beauty of Colburn Hall. Everything glitters. Tonight the pillars are each adorned with tall scarlet banners displaying the Republic seal, and hanging right in the middle of the pillars and above the hall's entrance is the largest portrait I've ever seen. Anden's giant face. Faline guides me down the corridor, where Senators are carrying on random conversations and other elite guests talk and laugh with one another like everything in the country is going great. But behind their cheerful masks are signs of nervousness, flickering eyes, and furrowed brows. They've gotta sense the unusual number of soldiers here too. I try to mimic the proper, precise way they have of walking and talking, but stop when Faline notices me doing it.

We wander the lush, open setting of Colburn Hall for several minutes, lost in the sea of politicians. The tassels of my epaulettes clink together. I'm looking for *her,* even though I don't know what I'll say when—*if*—I find her. How will I even catch a glimpse of her in the middle of all this goddy luxury? Wherever we turn, I see another flurry of colorful gowns and polished suits, fountains and pianos, waiters carrying skinny glasses of champagne, fancy people wearing their fake smiles. I feel a sudden sense of claustrophobia.

*Where am I? What am I doing here?*

As if on cue, the instant I ask myself these questions is the instant I finally see her. Somehow, in the midst of these aristocrats who blend into one blurry portrait, my eyes catch her silhouette and pause. *June.* The noise around me fades into a dull hum, quiet and uninteresting, and all of my attention turns helplessly to the girl I thought I'd be able to face.

She's dressed in a floor-length gown of deep scarlet, and her thick, shining hair is piled high on her head in dark waves, pinned into place with red, gem-studded combs that catch the light. She's the most beautiful girl I've ever seen, *easily* the most breathtaking girl in the room. She's grown taller in the eight months since I've seen her, and the way she holds herself—poised and graceful, with her slender, swanlike neck and her deep, dark eyes—is the image of perfection.

*Almost* perfection. At closer look, I notice something that makes me frown. There's an air of restraint about her, something uncertain and unconfident. Not like the June I know. As if powerless against the sight, I find myself guiding both Faline and me toward her. I only stop when the people around her move apart, revealing the man standing at her side.

It's Anden. Of course, I shouldn't be surprised. Off to the side, several well-dressed girls are trying in vain to catch his attention, but he seems focused only on June. I watch as he leans in to whisper something in her ear, then continues his relaxed conversation with her and several others.

When I turn silently away, Faline frowns at my sudden shift. "Are you okay?" she asks.

I attempt a reassuring smile. "Oh, absolutely. Don't worry." I feel so out of place among these aristocrats, with their bank accounts and posh manners. No matter how much money the Republic throws at me, I will forever be the boy from the streets.

And I'd forgotten that a boy from the streets is no match for the future Princeps.

# JUNE

I THINK I SEE DAY IN THE CROWD. A FLASH OF WHITE-gold hair, of bright blue eyes. My attention suddenly breaks from my conversation with Anden and the other Princeps-Elects, and I crane my neck, hoping to get a better look—but he's gone again, if he was ever there. Disappointed, I return my gaze to the others and give them my well-rehearsed smile. *Will* Day show up tonight? Surely Anden's men would have alerted us if Day had refused to get on the private jet sent for him this morning. But he'd sounded so distant and awkward over the mike that night, perhaps he just decided it wasn't worth coming out here after all. Maybe he hates me, now that we've had enough time apart for him to think clearly about our friendship. I scan the crowd again when the other Princeps-Elects are laughing at Anden's jokes.

A feeling in my stomach tells me Day *will* be here. But I am hardly a person who relies on gut instinct. I absently touch the jewels in my hair, making sure they're all still in the right places. They're not the most comfortable things I've ever worn, but the hairdresser had gasped at how the rubies stood out against my dark locks, and that reaction was enough for me to think they're worth the trouble. I'm not sure why I bothered to look so nice for tonight. It *is* Independence Day, I suppose, and the occasion is a large one.

"Miss Iparis is as precocious as we all assumed she would be," Anden's saying to the Senators now, turning his smile on me. His apparent happiness is all for show, of course. I've shadowed Anden for long enough now to know when he is tense, and tonight the nervousness reflects off every gesture he makes. I'm nervous too. A month from now, the Republic might have Colonies flags flying over her cities. "Her tutors say they've never seen a student progress so rapidly through her political texts."

"Thank you, Elector," I reply automatically to his compliment. The Senators both chuckle, but underneath their jolly expressions lies the lingering resentment they have against me, this *child* who has been tapped by the Elector to potentially become their leader one day. Mariana gives me a diplomatic, albeit stern, nod, but Serge doesn't look too pleased with the way Anden singles me out. I ignore the dark scowl that the Senator casts in my direction. His scowls used to bother me— now I'm just tired of them.

"Ah, well." Senator Tanaka of California tugs on the collar of his military jacket and exchanges a look with his wife. "That's wonderful news, Elector. Of course, I'm sure the tutors also know how much of a Senator's job is learned *outside* of texts and from years of experience in the Senate chamber. Like our dear Senator Carmichael here." He pauses to nod graciously at Serge, who puffs up.

Anden waves off his concern. "Of course," he echoes. "All in good time, Senator."

Beside me, Mariana sighs, leans over, and tilts her chin at Serge. "If you stare at his head long enough, it might sprout wings and take flight," she mutters.

I smile at that.

They steer off the topic of me and onto the topic of how to better sort students into high schools now that the Trials are discontinued. The political chatter grates on my nerves. I start scanning the crowd again for Day. After more futile searching, I finally put a hand on Anden's arm and lean over to whisper, "Excuse me. I'll be right back." He nods in return. When I turn away and start blending in with the crowd, I can feel his stare lingering on me.

I spend several minutes walking the ballroom in vain, greeting various Senators and their families as I go. Where is Day? I try to hear snatches of conversations, or notice where clusters of people might be gathering. Day is a celebrity. He must be attracting attention if he already arrived. I'm about to make my way across the other half of the ballroom when I'm interrupted by the loudspeakers. The pledge. I sigh, then turn back to where Anden has already taken his place on the front stage, flanked on both sides by soldiers holding up Republic flags.

"I pledge allegiance to the flag of the Republic of America . . ."

*Day.* There he is.

He's standing about fifty feet away, his back partially turned to me so that I can only see a tiny sliver of his profile, his hair loose and thick and perfectly straight, and on his arm is a girl in a shining gold dress. When I observe him more closely, I notice that his mouth isn't moving at all. He stays silent throughout the entire pledge. I turn my attention back to the front as applause fills the chamber and Anden begins his prepared speech. From the corner of my eye, I see Day turn to look over his shoulder. My hands tremble at this momentary glimpse of his face—have I really forgotten how beautiful he is, how his eyes reflect something wild and untamed, free even in the midst of all this order and elegance?

When the speech ends, I head straight in Day's direction. He's dressed in a perfectly tailored black military jacket and suit. Is he also thinner? He looks to have lost a good ten pounds since the last time I saw him. He's been ill recently. As I get closer, Day catches sight of me and pauses in his conversation with his date. His eyes widen a little. I can feel the heat rising on my cheeks, but force it down. This will be our first face-to-face meeting in months, and I refuse to make a fool of myself.

I stop a few feet away. My eyes wander to his date, a girl whom I recognize as Faline, the eighteen-year-old daughter of Senator Fedelma.

Faline and I exchange a quick nod. She grins. "Hi, June," she says. "You look gorgeous tonight."

She makes a genuine smile escape from me, a relief after all the practiced smiles I've been giving the other Princeps-Elects. "So do you," I reply.

Faline doesn't waste a single awkward second—she catches the slight blush on my cheeks and curtsies to both of us. Then she heads back into the crowd, leaving Day and me alone in the sea of people.

For a second, we just stare at each other. I break the silence before it stretches on for too long. "Hi," I say. I take in his face, refreshing my memory with every little detail. "It's good to see you."

Day smiles back and bows, but his eyes never leave me. The way he stares sends rivers of heat racing through my chest. "Thanks for the invite." *Hearing his voice in person again . . .* I take a deep breath, reminding myself of why I invited him here. His eyes dance across my face and to my dress—he seems ready to comment on it, but then decides against it and waves his hand at the room. "Nice little party you have here."

"It's never quite as fun as it looks," I reply in a hushed voice, so that the others can't hear me. "I think some of these Senators might burst from being forced to talk to people they don't like."

My teasing brings a small smile of relief to Day's lips. "Glad I'm not the only unhappy one."

Anden has already left the stage, and Day's comment reminds me that I should be escorting him to the banquet soon. The thought sobers me. "It's almost time," I say, motioning for Day to follow me. "The banquet is very private. You, me, the other Princeps-Elects, and the Elector."

"What's going on?" Day asks as he falls into step beside me. His arm brushes once against mine, sending shivers dancing across my skin. I struggle to catch my breath. *Focus, June.*

"You weren't exactly specific in our last conversation. I hope I'm putting up with all of these snobby Congress trots for a good reason."

I can't help my amusement at the way Day refers to the Senators. "You'll find out when we get there. And keep your insults to a minimum." I look away from him and toward the small corridor we're heading for, Jasper Chamber, a discreet hall branching away from the main ballroom.

"I'm not going to like this, am I?" Day mutters close to my ear.

Guilt rises in me. "Probably not."

We settle down in the private banquet room (a small, rectangular cherrywood table with seven seats), and after a while, Serge and Mariana filter in. They each take a seat on either side of Anden's reserved chair. I stay next to Day, as Anden had wished. Two servers go around the table, placing dainty plates of watermelon and pork salad before each seat. Serge and Mariana make polite small talk, but neither Day nor I says another word. Now and then, I manage to steal a glance at him. He's eyeing the lines of forks, spoons, and knives at his place setting with an uncomfortable frown, trying to figure them out without asking for help. *Oh, Day.* I don't know why this gives me a painful, fluttering feeling in my stomach, or why it pulls my heart to him. I'd forgotten how his long lashes catch the light.

"What's this?" he whispers to me, holding up one of his utensils.

"A butter knife."

Day scowls at it, running a finger along its blunt, rounded edge. "This," he mutters, "is *not* a knife."

Beside him, Serge notices his hesitation too. "I take it you're not accustomed to forks and knives where you're from?" he says coolly to him.

Day stiffens, but he doesn't miss a beat. He grabs a larger carving knife, purposely disturbing his place's careful setup, and gestures casually with it. Both Serge and Mariana edge away from the table. "Where I come from, we're more about efficiency," he replies. "A knife like this'll skewer food, smear butter, and slit throats all at the same time."

Of course Day's never slit a throat in his life—but Serge doesn't know that. He sniffs in disdain at the reply, but the blood drains from his face. I have to pretend to cough so that I don't laugh at Day's mock-serious expression. For those who don't know him well, his words actually sound intimidating.

I also notice something I hadn't earlier—Day looks pale. *Much* paler than I remember. My amusement wavers. Is his recent illness something more serious than I'd first assumed?

Anden arrives in the room a minute later, causing the usual stir as we all rise for him, and gestures for all of us to take our seats. He's accompanied by four soldiers, one of whom closes the door behind him and finally seals us in to our private meal.

"Day," Anden greets. He pauses to nod courteously in Day's direction. Day looks unhappy with the attention, but manages to return the gesture. "It's a pleasure to see you again, if under unfortunate circumstances."

"Very unfortunate," Day says in return. I shift uncomfortably in my seat, trying to imagine a more awkward scenario than this dinner setup.

Anden lets the stiff reply slide. "Let me catch you up on the current situation." He puts his fork down. "The peace treaty we've been working on with the Colonies is now shelved. A virus has hit the Colonies' southern warfront cities hard."

Beside me, Day crosses his arms and regards the crowd with a suspicious expression on his face, but Anden goes on. "They believe this virus was caused by us, and they are demanding that we send them a cure if we want to continue peace talks." Serge clears his throat and starts to say something, but Anden holds up a hand for silence. He then goes on to spill all the details—how the Colonies first sent a harsh message to the Republic, demanding info on the virus wreaking havoc amongst their troops, hastily withdrawing their affected soldiers, and then broadcasting their ultimatum to the warfront generals, warning of dire consequences if a cure was not delivered immediately.

Day listens to all of it without moving a muscle or uttering a word. One of his hands grips the edge of the table tightly enough to turn his knuckles white. I wonder whether he's guessed where this is going and what all this has to do with him, but he just waits until Anden has finished.

Serge leans back in his chair and frowns. "If the Colonies want to play games with our peace offer," he scoffs, "then let them. We've been at war long enough—we can handle some more."

"No, we can't," Mariana interjects. "Do you *honestly* think the United Nations will accept the news that our peace treaty fell apart?"

"Do the Colonies have any evidence that we caused it? Or are these empty accusations?"

"Exactly. If they think we're going to—"

Day suddenly speaks up, his face turned toward Anden. "Let's stop dragging our feet," he says. "Tell me why I'm here." He's not loud, but the ominous tone of his voice hushes the conversation in the room. Anden returns his look with an equally grave one. He takes a deep breath.

"Day, I believe this is the result of one of my father's bio-weapons—and that the virus came from your brother Eden's blood."

Day's eyes narrow. "And?"

Anden seems reluctant to continue. "There's more than one reason why I didn't want all my Senators in here with us." He leans forward, lowers his voice, and gives Day a humbled look. "I don't want to hear anyone else right now. I want to hear *you*. You are the heart of the people, Day—you always have been. You've given everything you have in order to protect them." Day stiffens beside me, but Anden goes on. "I fear for the people. I worry about their safety, that we'll be handing them over to the enemy just as we're starting to put the pieces together." He grows quieter. "I need to make some difficult decisions."

Day raises an eyebrow. "What kind of decisions?"

"The Colonies are desperate for a cure. They will *destroy* us to get it, everything both you and I care about. The only chance we have of finding one is to take Eden into temporary—"

Day pushes his chair from the table and rises. "No," he says. His voice is flat and icy, but I remember my old, heated argument with Day well enough to recognize the deep fury beneath his calmness. Without another word, he turns from the group and walks away.

Serge starts to get up, no doubt to shout at Day about his rudeness, but Anden shoots him a warning stare and motions for him to sit. Then Anden turns to me with a look that says, *Talk to him. Please.*

I watch Day's retreating figure. *He has every right to refuse, every right to hate us for asking this of him.* But I still find myself rising from my own chair, stepping away from the banquet table, and hurrying in his direction.

"Day, wait," I call out. My words send me a painful reminder of the last time we'd been in the same room together, when we had said our good-byes.

We head into the smaller corridor that leads out to the main ballroom. Day doesn't turn around, but he seems to slow his steps down in an attempt to let me catch up. When I finally reach him, I take a deep breath. "Look, I know—"

Day presses a finger to his lips, silencing me, and then grabs my hand. His skin is warm through the fabric of his glove. The feel of his fingers around mine is such a shock after all these months that I can't remember the rest of my sentence—everything about him, his touch, his closeness, feels *right*. "Let's talk in private," he whispers.

We head inside one of the doors lining the corridor, then close it behind us and turn the lock. My eyes do a categorical sweep of the room (private dining chamber, no lights on, one round table and twelve chairs all covered in white cloths, and a single large, arched window at the back wall that lets in a stream of moonlight). Day's hair transforms in here to a silver sheet. He turns his gaze back to me now.

Is it my imagination, or does he look as flustered as I am about our brief handhold? I feel the sudden tightness of the dress's waist, the air hitting my exposed shoulders and collarbone, the heaviness of the fabric and the jewels in my hair. Day's eyes linger on the ruby necklace sitting at the small of my throat. *His parting gift to me.* His cheeks turn a little pink in the darkness. "So," he says, "is this seriously why I'm here?"

Despite the anger in his voice, his directness is like a cool, sweet breeze after all these months of calculated political talk. I want to breathe it in. "The Colonies refuse to accept any other terms," I reply. "They're convinced that we have a cure for the virus, and the only one who might carry the cure is Eden. The Republic's already running tests on other former . . . experiments . . . to see whether they can find anything."

Day cringes, then folds his arms in front of his chest and regards me with a scowl. "Already running tests," he mutters to himself, looking off toward the moonlit windows. "Sorry I can't be more enthusiastic about this idea," he adds dryly.

I close my eyes for a moment. "We don't have much time," I admit. "Every day we don't hand over a cure further angers the Colonies."

"And what happens if we don't give them anything?"

"You know what happens. War."

A note of fear appears in Day's eyes, but he still shrugs. "The Republic and the Colonies have been at war forever. How will this be any different?"

"This time they'll win," I whisper. "They have a strong ally. They know we're vulnerable during our transition to a young new Elector. If we can't hand over this cure, we don't stand a chance." I narrow my eyes. "Don't you remember what we saw when we went to the Colonies?"

Day pauses for a heartbeat. Even though he doesn't say it aloud, I can see the conflict written clearly on his face. Finally, he sighs and tightens his lips in anger. "You think I'm going to let the Republic take Eden again? If the Elector believes that, then I really did make a mistake throwing my support behind him. I didn't help him out just to watch him toss Eden back into a lab."

"I'm sorry," I say. No use trying to convince him of how much Anden also hates the situation. "He shouldn't have asked you like this."

"He put you up to this, didn't he? I bet you resisted too, yeah? *You* know how this sounds." His tone turns more exasperated. "You *knew* what my answer would be. Why'd you still send for me?"

I look into his eyes and say the first thing that comes to mind. "Because I wanted to see you. Isn't that why you agreed too?"

This makes him pause for a moment. Then he whirls around, rakes both hands through his hair, and sighs. "What do *you* think, then? Tell me the truth. What would you ask me to do, if you felt absolutely no pressure from anyone else in this country?"

I tuck a strand of hair behind my ear. *Steel yourself, June.* "I'd . . . ," I begin, then hesitate. What would I say? Logically, I agree with Anden's assessment. If the Colonies do what they threaten, if they attack us with the full force of a superpower's help, then many innocent lives will be lost unless we take a risk with *one* life. There is simply no easier choice. Besides, we could ensure that Eden would be treated as well as possible, with the best doctors and the most physical comfort. Day could be present during all of the potential procedures—he could see exactly what was happening. But how do I explain that to a boy who has already lost his entire family, who saw his brother experimented on before, who has been experimented on *himself*? This is the part that Anden doesn't understand as well as I do, even though he knows Day's past on paper—he still doesn't know *Day*, hasn't traveled with him and witnessed the suffering he's gone through. The question is too complicated to be answered with simple logic.

Most importantly—*Anden's unable to guarantee his brother's safety.* Everything will come with a risk, and I know with dead certainty that nothing in the world could possibly make Day take *this* risk.

Day must see the frustration dancing across my face, because he softens and steps closer. I can practically feel the heat coming off him, the warmth of his nearness that turns my breath shallow. "I came here tonight for *you*," he says in a low voice. "There's nothing in the world they could've said to convince me, except that *you* wanted me here. And I can't turn down a request from you. They told me you had personally . . ." He swallows. There's a familiar war of emotions in his expression that leaves me with a sick feeling—emotions that I know are *desire*, for what we once had, and *anguish*, for desiring a girl who destroyed his family. "It's so good to see you, June."

He says it like he's letting go of a huge burden that's been holding him down. I wonder whether he can hear my heart pounding frantically against my ribs. When I speak, though, I manage to keep my voice steady and calm. "Are you okay?" I ask. "You look pale."

The weight returns to his eyes, and his brief moment of intimacy fades as he steps away and fiddles with the edge of his gloves. *He's always hated gloves,* I remember. "I've had a bad flu for the last couple of weeks," he replies, flashing me a quick grin. "Getting better now, though." (Eyes flickering subtly to the side, scratching the edge of his ear, stiffness of his limbs, timing slightly off between his words and his smile.) I tilt my head at him and frown.

"You're such a bad liar, Day," I say. "You might as well tell me what's on your mind."

"There's nothing to tell," he replies automatically. This time he points his eyes at the floor and puts his hands in his pockets. "If I seem off, it's because I'm worried about Eden. He's gotten a year of treatment for his eyes and he still can't see much. The doctors tell me that he may need some special contacts, and even then, he might never get his full eyesight back."

I can tell this isn't the real reason behind Day's exhausted appearance, but he knows that bringing Eden's recovery into this conversation will stop any questions from me. Well, if he really doesn't want to tell me, then I won't pressure him. I clear my throat awkwardly. "That's terrible," I whisper. "I'm so sorry to hear it. Is he doing okay, otherwise?"

Day nods. We fall back into our moonlit silence. I can't help recalling the last time we were alone in a room together, when he took my face in his hands, when his tears were falling against my cheeks. I remember the way he whispered *I'm sorry* against my lips. Now, as we stand three feet apart and stare at each other, I feel the full distance that comes with spending so much time apart, a moment filled with the electricity of a first meeting and the uncertainty of strangers.

Day leans toward me, as if drawn by some invisible force. The tragic plea on his face twists my stomach into painful knots. *Please don't ask this of me,* his eyes beg. *Please don't ask me to give up my brother. I would do anything else for you. Just not this.* "June, I . . . ," he whispers. His voice threatens to break with all the heartache he's keeping bottled inside.

He never finishes that sentence. Instead, he sighs and bows his head. "I can't agree to your Elector's terms," he says in a somber tone. "I'm not going to hand my brother to the Republic as another experiment. Tell him I'll work with him to find another solution. I understand how serious this all is—I don't want to see the Republic fall. I'd be glad to help and figure something else out. But *Eden* stays out of this."

And that's the end of our conversation. Day nods at me in

farewell, lingers for a few last seconds, and then steps toward the door. I lean against the wall in sudden exhaustion. Without him nearby, there's a lack of energy, a dulling of color, gray moonlight where moments earlier there had been silver. I study his paleness a final time, analyzing him from the corner of my eye. He avoids my gaze. Something is wrong, and he refuses to tell me what it is.

What am I missing here?

He pulls the door open. His expression hardens right before he steps out of the room. "And if for some reason the Republic tries to take Eden by force, I'll turn the people against Anden so fast that a revolution will be on him before he can blink."

# DAY

SERIOUSLY, I SHOULD BE USED TO MY NIGHTMARES BY NOW.

This time I dream about me and Eden at a San Francisco hospital. A doctor's fitting Eden with a new pair of glasses. We end up at a hospital at least once a week, so that they can monitor how Eden's eyes are slowly adjusting to medication, but this is the first time I see the doctor smile encouragingly at my brother. Must be a good sign, yeah?

Eden turns to me, grins, and puffs his chest out in an exaggerated gesture. I have to laugh. "How does it look?" he asks me, fiddling with his huge new frames. His eyes still have that weird, pale purple color, and he can't focus on me, but I notice that he can now make out things like the walls around him and the light coming in from the windows. My heart jumps at the sight. Progress.

"You look like an eleven-year-old owl," I reply, walking over to ruffle his hair. He giggles and bats my hand away.

As we sit together in the office, waiting for paperwork, I watch Eden busily folding pieces of paper together into some kind of elaborate design. He has to hunch close to the papers to see what he's doing, his broken eyes almost crossed with concentration, his fingers nimble and deliberate. I swear, this kid's always making something or other.

"What is it?" I ask him after a while.

He's concentrating too hard to answer me right away.

Finally, when he tucks one last paper triangle into the design, he holds it up and gives me that cheeky grin. "Here," he says, pointing to what looks like a paper leaf sticking out of the ball of paper. "Pull this."

I do as he says. To my amazement, the design transforms into an elaborate 3-D paper rose. I smile back at him in my dream. "Pretty impressive."

Eden takes his paper design back.

In that instant, an alarm blares throughout the hospital. Eden drops the paper flower and jumps to his feet. His blind eyes are wide open in terror. I glance to the hospital's windows, where doctors and nurses have gathered. Out along the horizon of San Francisco, a row of Colonies airships sail closer and closer to us. The city below them burns from a dozen fires.

The alarm deafens me. I grab Eden's hand and rush us out of the room. "We have to get out of here," I shout. When he stumbles, unable to see where we're going, I hoist him onto my back. People rush all around us.

I reach the stairwell—and there, a line of Republic soldiers stops us. One of them pulls Eden off my back. He screams, kicking out at people he can't see. I struggle to free myself from the soldiers, but their grip is ironclad, and my limbs feel like they're sinking into deep mud. *We need him,* some unrecognizable voice whispers into my ear. *He can save us all.*

I scream out loud, but no one can hear me. Off in the distance, the Colonies airships aim at the hospital. Glass shatters all around us. I feel the heat of fire. On the floor lies

Eden's paper flower, its edges crisping from flames. I can no longer see my brother.

He's gone. He's dead.

A pounding headache pulls me from my sleep. The soldiers vanish—the alarm silences—the chaos of the hospital disappears into the dark blue hue of our bedroom. I try to take a deep breath and look around for Eden, but the headache stabs into the back of my skull like an ice pick, and I bolt upright with a gasp of pain. Now I remember where I really am. I'm in a temporary apartment back in Denver, the morning after seeing June. On the bedroom dresser sits my usual transmission box, the station still tuned to one of the airwaves I thought the Patriots might've been using.

"Daniel?" In the bed next to mine, Eden stirs. Relief hits me, even in the midst of my agony. Just a nightmare. Like always. *Just a nightmare.* "Are you okay?" It takes me a second to realize that dawn hasn't quite arrived—the room still looks dark, and all I can see is my brother's silhouette against the bluish black of the night.

I don't answer right away. Instead, I swing my legs over the side of the bed to face him and clutch my head in both hands. Another jolt of pain hits the base of my brain. "Get my medicine," I mutter to Eden.

"Should I get Lucy?"

"No. Don't wake her," I reply. Lucy's already had two sleepless nights because of me. "Medicine."

The pain makes me ruder than usual, but Eden jumps out of

bed before I can apologize. He immediately starts fumbling for the bottle of green pills that always sits on the dresser between our beds. He grabs it and holds out the bottle in my general direction.

"Thanks." I take it from him, pour three pills into my palm with a shaking hand, and try to swallow them. Throat's too dry. I push myself up from the bed and stagger toward the kitchen. Behind me, Eden utters another "Are you sure you're okay?" but the pain in my head is so strong that I can hardly hear him. I can hardly even *see*.

I reach the kitchen sink and turn the faucet on, cup some water into my hands, and drink it down with the medicine. Then I slide down to the floor in the darkness, resting my back against the cold metal of the refrigerator door.

*It's okay*, I console myself. My headaches had worsened over the past year, but the doctors assured me that these attacks should last no longer than a half hour each time. Of course, they also told me that if any of them felt unusually severe, I should be rushed to the emergency room right away. So every time I get one, I wonder if I'm experiencing a typical day—or the last day of my life.

A few minutes later, Eden stumbles into the kitchen with his walking meter on, the device beeping whenever he gets too close to a wall. "Maybe we should ask Lucy to call the doctors," he whispers.

I don't know why, but the sight of Eden feeling his way through the kitchen sends me into a fit of low, uncontrollable laughter. "Man, look at us," I reply. My laughter turns into coughs. "What a team, yeah?"

Eden finds me by placing a tentative hand on my head. He sits beside me with his legs crossed and gives me a wry grin. "Hey—with your metal leg and half a brain, and my four left-over senses, we almost make a whole person."

I laugh harder, but it makes the pain of my headache that much worse. "When did *you* turn so sarcastic, little boy?" I give him an affectionate shove.

We stay hunched in silence for the next hour as the head-ache goes on and on. I'm now writhing in pain. Sweat soaks my white collar shirt and tears streak my face. Eden sits next to me and grips my hand in his small ones. "Try not to think about it," he urges under his breath, squinting at me with his pale purple eyes. He pushes his black-rimmed glasses farther up his nose. Bits and pieces of my nightmare come back to me, images of his hand getting yanked out of mine. Sounds of his screams. I squeeze his hand so tightly that he winces. "Don't forget to breathe. The doctor always says taking deep breaths is supposed to help, right? Breathe in, breathe out."

I close my eyes and try to follow my little brother's com-mands, but it's hard to hear him at all through the pound-ing of my headache. The pain is excruciating, all-consuming, a white-hot knife stabbing repeatedly into the back of my brain. *Breathe in, breathe out.* Here's the pattern—first there's a dull, numbing ache, followed shortly by the abso-lute worst pain you can ever imagine going into your head, a spear shoved through your skull, and the impact of it is so hard that your entire body goes stiff; it lasts for a solid three seconds, followed by a split second of relief. And then it repeats itself all over again.

"How long has it been?" I gasp out to Eden. Dim blue light is slowly filtering in from the windows.

Eden pulls out a tiny square com and presses its lone knob. "Time?" he asks it. The device immediately responds, "*Zero five thirty.*" He puts it away, a concerned frown on his face. "It's been almost an hour. Has it gone on this long before?"

*I'm dying. I really am dying.* It's times like this when I'm glad that I don't see much of June anymore. The thought of her seeing me sweating and dirty on my kitchen floor, clutching my baby brother's hand for dear life like some weepy weakling, while she's breathtaking in her scarlet gown and jewel-studded hair . . . You know, for that matter, in this moment I'm even relieved that Mom and John can't see me.

When I moan from another excruciating stab of pain, Eden pulls out his com again and presses the knob. "That's it. I'm calling the doctors." When the com beeps, prompting him for his command, he says, "Day needs an ambulance." Then, before I can protest, he raises his voice and calls out for Lucy.

Seconds later, I hear Lucy approach. She doesn't turn the light on—she knows that it only makes my headaches that much worse. Instead, I see her stout silhouette in the darkness and hear her exclaim, "Day! How long have you been out here?" She rushes over to me and puts one plump hand against my cheek. Then she glances at Eden and touches his chin. "Did you call for the doctors?"

Eden nods. Lucy inspects my face again, then clucks her tongue in worried disapproval and bustles off to grab a cool towel.

The last place I want to be right now is lying in a Republic hospital—but Eden's already placed the call, and I'd rather not be dead anyway. My vision has started to blur, and I realize it's because I can't stop my eyes from watering nonstop. I wipe a hand across my face and smile weakly at Eden. "Damn, I'm dripping water like a leaky faucet."

Eden tries to smile back. "Yeah, you've had better days," he replies.

"Hey, kid. Remember that time when John asked you to be in charge of watering the plants outside our door?"

Eden frowns for a second, digging through his memories, and then a grin lights up his face. "I did a pretty good job, didn't I?"

"You built that little makeshift catapult in front of our door." I close my eyes and indulge in the memory, a temporary distraction from all the pain. "Yeah, I remember that thing. You kept lobbing water balloons at those poor flowers. Did they even have any petals left after you were done? Oh man, John was so pissed." He was even madder because Eden was only four at the time and, well, how do you punish your wide-eyed baby brother?

Eden giggles. I wince as another wave of agony hits me.

"What was it that Mom used to say about us?" he asks. Now I can tell that he's trying to keep my mind on other things too.

I manage a smile. "Mom used to say that having three boys was kind of like having a pet tornado that talked back." The two of us laugh for a moment, at least before I squint my eyes shut again.

Lucy comes back with the towel. She places it against my forehead, and I sigh in relief at its cool surface. She checks my pulse, then my temperature.

"Daniel," Eden pipes up while she works. He scoots closer, his eyes still staring blankly off at a spot to the right of my head. "Hang in there, okay?"

Lucy shoots him a critical frown at what his tone implies. "Eden," she scolds. "More optimism in this house, please."

A lump rises in my throat, turning my breath shallower. John's gone, Mom's gone, Dad's gone. I watch Eden with a heavy ache in my chest. I used to hope that since he was the youngest of us boys, he might be able to learn from John's and my mistakes and be the luckiest out of us, maybe make it into a college or earn a good living as a mechanic, that we'd be around to guide him through the difficult times in life. What would happen to him if I were gone too? What happens if he has to stand alone against the Republic?

"Eden," I suddenly whisper to him, pulling him close. His eyes widen at my urgent tone. "Listen close, yeah? If the Republic ever asks you to go with them, if I'm ever not home or I'm in the hospital and they come knocking on our door, don't ever go with them. You understand me? You call me first, you scream for Lucy, you . . ." I hesitate. "You call for June Iparis."

"Your Princeps-Elect?"

"She's not my—" I grimace at another wave of pain. "Just do it. Call her. Tell her to stop them."

"I don't understand—"

"*Promise me.* Don't go with them, whatever you do. Okay?" My answer's cut short when a jolt of pain hits me hard enough to send me collapsing to the ground, curled up into a tight ball. I choke out a shriek—my head feels like it's being split in two. I even put a trembling hand to the back of my head as if to make sure my brain's not leaking out onto the floor. Somewhere above me, Eden is shouting. Lucy places another call to the doctor, this time frantic.

"Just hurry!" she yells. "*Hurry!*"

By the time the medics arrive, I'm fading in and out of consciousness. Through a cloud of haze and fog, I feel myself getting lifted off the kitchen floor and carried out of the apartment tower, then into a waiting ambulance that has been disguised to look like a regular police jeep. Is it snowing? A few light flakes drift onto my face, shocking me with pinpricks of coldness. I call out for Eden and Lucy—they respond from somewhere I can't see.

Then we're in the ambulance and pulling away.

All I see for a long time are blobs of color, fuzzy circles moving back and forth across my vision, like I'm peering through thick, bumpy glass. I try to recognize some of them. Are they people? I sure as hell hope so—otherwise I really *must* have

died, or maybe I'm floating in the ocean and debris is just drift-
ing all around me. That doesn't make any sense, though, unless
the doctors just decided to toss me right into the Pacific and
forget about me. Where's Eden? They must've taken him away.
Just like in the nightmare. They've dragged him off to the labs.

I can't breathe.

My hands try to fly up to my throat, but then someone
shouts something and I feel weight against my arms, pinning
me down. Something cold is going down my throat, choking me.

"Calm down! You're okay. Try to swallow."

I do as the voice says. Swallowing turns out to be more
difficult than I thought, but I finally manage a gulp, and
whatever the cold thing is slides right down my throat and
into my stomach, chilling me to my core.

"There," the voice goes on, less agitated now. "Should
help with any future headaches, I think." He doesn't seem
to be talking to me anymore—and a second later, another
voice chimes in.

"Seems to be working a little, Doctor."

I must've passed out again after that, because the next
time I wake up, the pattern on the ceiling's different and
late afternoon light is slanting into my room. I blink and look
around. The excruciating pain in my head is gone, at least for
now. I can also see clearly enough to know I'm in a hospital
room, the ever-present portrait of Anden on one wall and
a screen against another wall, broadcasting news. I groan,
then close my eyes and let out a sigh. Stupid hospitals. So
sick of them.

*"Patient is awake."* I turn to see a monitor near my bedside that recites the phrase. A second later, a real human's voice pops up over its speakers. "Mister Wing?" it says.

"Yeah?" I mutter back.

"Excellent," the voice replies. "Your brother will be in shortly to see you."

No sooner than her voice clicks off, my door bursts open and Eden comes running in with two exasperated nurses hot on his tail. "Daniel," he gasps out, "you're finally awake! Sure took you long enough." His lack of sight catches up with him—he stumbles against the edge of a drawer before I can warn him, and the nurses have to catch him in their arms to keep him from falling to the floor.

"Easy there, kid," I call out. My voice sounds tired, even though I feel alert and pain-free. "How long was I out? Where is . . . ?" I pause, confused for a moment. That's weird. What was our caretaker's name again? I grasp for it in my thoughts. *Lucy.* "Where's Lucy?" I finish.

He doesn't answer right away. When the nurses finally situate Eden beside me in bed, he crawls closer to me and flings his arms around my neck. To my shock, I realize that he's crying. "Hey." I pat his head. "Calm down—it's okay. I'm awake."

"I thought you weren't going to make it," he murmurs. His pale eyes search for mine. "I thought you were gone."

"Well, I'm not. I'm right here." I let him sob for a little while, his head buried against my chest, his tears blurring his glasses and staining my hospital gown. There's a coping mechanism I've started using recently where I pretend to retreat back into the shell of my heart and crawl out of my body, like I'm not really here and am instead observing the world from another person's perspective. *Eden's not my brother. He's not even real. Nothing is real. Everything is illusion.* It helps. I wait without emotion as Eden gradually composes himself, and then I carefully let myself back into my body.

Finally, when he's wiped away the last of his tears, he sits up and burrows in beside me. "Lucy's filling out paperwork up front." His voice still sounds a little shaky. "You've been out for about ten hours. They said they had to rush you out of our building through the main entrance—there just wasn't any time to try sneaking you out."

"Did anyone see?"

Eden rubs his temples in an attempt to remember. "Maybe. I don't know. I can't remember—I was too distracted. I spent all morning out in the waiting room because they wouldn't let me inside."

"Do you know . . ." I swallow. "Have you heard anything from the doctors?"

Eden sighs in relief. "Not really. But at least you're okay now. The doctors said you had a bad reaction to the medicine they put you on. They're taking you off it and trying something different."

The way Eden says this makes my heart beat faster. He doesn't fully grasp the reality of the situation—he still thinks that the only reason I'd collapsed like that wasn't because I'm getting worse, but because I just had a bad reaction. A sick, sinking feeling hits my stomach. Of course he'd be optimistic about it all; of course he thinks this is just a temporary setback. I'd been on that damn medication for the last two months after the first two rounds also stopped working, and with all the extra headaches and nightmares and nausea, I'd hoped that the pills had at least done *some* good, that they were successfully shrinking the problem spot in my hippocampus—their fancy word for the bottom of my brain. Apparently not. What if *nothing* works?

I take a deep breath and put on a smile for my brother. "Well, at least they know now. Maybe they'll try something better this time."

Eden smiles along, sweet and naïve. "Yeah."

Several minutes later, my doctor comes in and Eden moves back outside to the waiting room. As the doctor talks in a low voice to me about "our next options," what treatments they'll try to experiment with next, he also quietly tells me how small of a chance they have. Like I feared, my reaction wasn't just some temporary medicine issue. "The medication is slowly shrinking the affected area," the doctor says, but his expression stays grim. "Still, the area continues to fester, and your body has begun to reject the old medication, forcing us to search for new ones. We are quite simply racing against the clock, Day, trying to shrink it enough and pull it out before it can do its worst." I listen to it all with a straight face; his voice sounds like it's underwater, unimportant and out of focus.

Finally, I stop him and say, "Look, just tell me straight up. How much longer do I have? If nothing works out?"

The doctor purses his lips, hesitates, and then shakes his head with a sigh. "Probably a month," he admits. "Maybe two. We're doing the best we can."

A month or two. *Well, they've been wrong in the past—a month or two probably means more like four or five.* Still. I look toward the door, where Eden's probably pressed against the wood and trying in vain to hear what we're saying. Then I turn back to the doctor and swallow the lump in my throat. "Two months," I echo. "Is there any chance?"

"We might try some riskier treatments, although those have side effects that may be fatal if you react badly to them. A surgery before you're ready will likely kill you." The doctor crosses his arms. His glasses catch the cold fluorescent light and shine in a way that blocks out his eyes entirely. He looks like a machine. "I would suggest, Day, that you begin getting your priorities in order."

"My priorities in order?"

"Prepare your brother for the news," he replies. "And settle any unfinished business."

# JUNE

AT 0810 HOURS ON THE MORNING AFTER THE EMER-
gency banquet, Anden calls me. "It's Captain Bryant," he
says. "He has put in his last request, and his last request is to
see you."

I sit at the edge of my bed, blinking away a night of fitful
sleep, trying to work up the energy to understand what Anden
is telling me.

"Tomorrow we transfer him to a prison on the other side
of Denver to prepare for his final day. He's asked if he can see
you before then."

"What does he want?"

"Whatever he has to say, he wants it heard by your ears
alone," Anden replies. "Remember, June—you have the option
to refuse him. We don't have to grant this last request."

*Tomorrow, Thomas will be dead.* I wonder whether Anden
feels any guilt over sentencing a soldier to die. The thought
of facing Thomas alone in a jail cell sends a wave of panic
through me, but I steel myself. Maybe Thomas has something
to say about my brother. Do I want to hear it?

"I'll see him," I finally reply. "And hopefully this is the last
time."

Anden must hear something in my voice, because his words
soften. "Of course. I'll arrange for your escort."

## 0930 Hours.
### Denver State Penitentiary.

The hall where Thomas and Commander Jameson are being held is lit with cold, fluorescent light, and the sound of my boots echoes against the high ceiling. Several soldiers flank me, but aside from us, the hall feels empty and ominous. Portraits of Anden hang at sporadic intervals along the walls. My eyes stay focused on each of the cells we pass, studying them, details running through my mind in an effort to keep myself calm and focused. (32 × 32 feet in size, smooth steel walls, bulletproof glass, cams mounted outside of the cells instead of inside. Most of them are empty, and the ones that are filled hold three of the Senators who had plotted against Anden. This floor is reserved for prisoners associated specifically with Anden's attempted assassination.)

"If you experience any trouble at all," one of the soldiers says to me, tapping his cap in a polite bow, "just call us in. We'll have that traitor down on the ground before he can make a move."

"Thank you," I reply, my eyes still fixed on the cells as we draw closer. I know I won't need to do what he just said, because I know Thomas won't ever disobey the Elector and try to hurt me. Thomas is many things, but he isn't rebellious.

We reach the end of the hall where two adjacent cells sit, each one guarded by two soldiers.

Someone stirs in the cell closest to me. I turn toward the movement. I don't even have time to study the cell's interior before a woman raps her fingers against the steel bars. I jump, then swallow the cry that rises up in my throat as I stare into the face of Commander Jameson.

As she fixes her eyes on mine, she gives me a smile that makes me break out in a cold sweat. I remember this smile—she'd smiled like this on the night Metias died, when she approved me to become a junior agent in her patrol. There is no emotion there, nothing compassionate or even angry. Few things frighten me—but facing the cold, merciless expression of my brother's true killer is one of them.

"Well," she says in a low voice. "If it isn't Iparis, come here to see us." Her eyes flicker to me; the soldiers gather closer to me in a protective gesture. *Don't be afraid.* I straighten as well as I can, then clench my jaw and force myself to face her without flinching.

"You're wasting my time, Commander," I say. "I'm not here for you. And the next time I see you will be the day you stand before the firing squad."

She just smiles at me. "So brave, now that you have your handsome young Elector to hide behind. Isn't that so?" When I narrow my eyes, she laughs. "Commander DeSoto would've been a better Elector than that boy could ever be. When the Colonies invade, they'll burn this country to the ground. The people will regret ever putting their support behind a little boy." She presses against the bars, as if trying to edge as close to me as possible. I swallow hard, but even through my fear, my anger boils under the surface. I don't look away. It's strange, but I think I see a sheen of gloss across her eyes, something that looks disconcerting above her unstable smile.

"You were one of my favorites. Do you know why I was so interested in having you on my patrol? It's because I saw myself reflected in you. We're the same, you and I. I would've been Princeps, too, you know. I deserved it."

Goose bumps rise on my arms. A memory flashes through my mind of the night Metias died, when Commander Jameson escorted me to where his body lay. "Too bad that didn't work out, isn't it?" I snap. This time I can't keep the venom out of my words. *I hope they execute you as unceremoniously as they did Razor.*

Commander Jameson only laughs at me. Her eyes dilate. "Better be careful, Iparis," she whispers. "You might turn out just like me."

The words chill me to the bone, and I finally have to turn away and break my stare away from hers. The soldiers guarding her cell don't look at me; they just keep staring forward. I continue walking. Behind me, I can still hear her soft, low chuckle. My heart pounds against my ribs.

Thomas is being held inside a rectangular cell with thick glass walls, thick enough that I can't hear anything of what's happening inside. I wait outside, steadying myself after my encounter with Commander Jameson. For an instant I wonder whether I should have stayed away and turned down his final request; maybe that would have been for the best.

Still, if I leave now, I'll have to face Commander Jameson again. I might need a little more time to prepare myself for that. So I take a deep breath and step toward the steel bars lining Thomas's cell door. A guard opens it, lets two additional guards in after me, and then closes it behind us. Our footsteps echo in the small, empty chamber.

Thomas gets up with a clank of his chains. He looks more disheveled than I've ever seen him, and I know that if his hands were completely free, he'd go about ironing his rumpled uniform and combing his unruly hair right away. But instead, Thomas clicks his heels together. Not until I tell him to relax his stance does he look at me.

"It's good to see you, Princeps-Elect," he says. Is there a hint of sadness in his serious, stern face? "Thank you for indulging my final request. It won't be long now before you're rid of me entirely."

I shake my head, angry with myself, irritated that in spite of everything he has done, Thomas's unshakable loyalty to the Republic still stirs a drop of sympathy from me. "Sit down and make yourself comfortable," I tell him. He doesn't hesitate for a second—in a uniform motion, we both kneel down onto the cold cell floor, him leaning against the cell wall, me folding my legs underneath me. We stay like that for a moment, letting the awkward silence between us linger.

I speak up first. "You don't need to be so loyal to the Republic anymore," I reply. "You can let go, you know."

Thomas only shakes his head. "It's the duty of a Republic soldier to be loyal to the end, and I'm still a soldier. I will be one until I die."

I don't know why the thought of him dying tugs on my heartstrings in so many strange ways. I'm happy, relieved, angry, sad. "Why did you want to see me?" I finally ask.

"Ms. Iparis, before tomorrow comes . . ." Thomas trails off for a second before continuing. "I want to tell you the full details of everything that happened to Metias that night at the hospital. I just feel . . . I feel like I owe it to you. If anyone should know, it's you."

My heart begins to pound. Am I ready to relive all of that again—do I need to know this? Metias is gone; knowing the details of what happened will not bring him back. But I find myself meeting Thomas's gaze with a calm, level look. He *does* owe it to me. More importantly, I owe it to my brother. After Thomas is executed, *someone* should carry on the memory of my brother's death, of what really happened.

Slowly, I steady my heartbeat. When I open my mouth, my voice cracks a little. "Fine," I reply.

His voice grows quieter. "I remember everything about that night. Every last detail."

"Tell me, then."

Like the obedient soldier he is, Thomas begins his story. "On the night of your brother's death, I took a call from Commander Jameson. We were waiting with the jeeps outside the hospital's entrance. Metias was chatting with a nurse in front of the main sliding doors. I stood behind the jeeps some distance away. Then the call came."

As Thomas speaks, the prison around us melts away and is replaced by the scene of that fateful night, the hospital and the military jeep and the soldiers, the streets as if I were walking right beside Thomas, seeing all that he saw. Reliving the events.

"I whispered a greeting to Commander Jameson over my earpiece," Thomas continues. "She didn't bother greeting me back.

"'It has to be done tonight,' she told me. 'If we don't act now, your captain may plan an act of treason against the Republic, or even against the Elector. I'm giving you a direct order, Lieutenant Bryant. Find a way to get Captain Iparis to a private spot tonight. I don't care how you do it.'"

Thomas looks me in the eye now and repeats, *An act of treason against the Republic.* I tightened my jaw. I'd been dreading this inevitable call, ever since I'd first learned about Metias's hacking into the deceased civilians' databases. Keeping secrets from Commander Jameson was damn near impossible. My eyes darted to your brother at the entrance. 'Yes, Commander,' I whispered.

"'Good,' she said. 'Tell me when you're ready—I'll send in separate orders to the rest of your patrol to be at a different location during that time. Make it quick and clean.'

"That's when my hand began to shake. I tried to argue with the Commander, but her voice only turned colder. 'If you don't do it, *I* will. Believe me, I will be messier about it—and no one's going to be happy that way. Understood?'

"I didn't answer her right away. Instead I watched your brother as he shook hands with the nurse. He turned around, searching for me, and then spotted me by the jeeps. He waved me over, and I nodded, careful to keep my face blank. 'Understood, Commander,' I finally answered.

"'You can do it, Bryant,' she told me. 'And if you're successful, consider yourself promoted to captain.' The call cut off.

"I joined Metias and another soldier at the hospital entrance. Metias smiled at me. 'Another long night, eh? I swear, if we're stuck here until dawn again, I'll whine to Commander Jameson like there's no tomorrow.'

"I forced myself to laugh along. 'Let's hope for an uneventful night, then.' The lie felt so smooth.

"'Yes, let's hope for that,' Metias said. 'At least I have you for company.'

"'Likewise,' I told him. Metias glanced back at me, his eyes hovering for a beat, then looked away again.

"The first minutes passed without incident. But then, moments later, a ragged slum-sector boy dragged himself up to the entrance and stopped to talk to a nurse. He was a mess—mud, dirt, and blood smeared across his cheeks, dirty dark hair pulled away from his face, and a nasty limp. 'Can I be admitted, cousin?' he asked the nurse. 'Is there still room tonight? I can pay.'

"The nurse just continued scribbling on her notepad. 'What happened?' she finally asked.

"'Was in a fight,' the boy replied. 'I think I got stabbed.'

"The nurse glanced over at your brother, and Metias nodded to two of his soldiers. They walked over to pat down the boy. After a while, they pocketed something and waved the boy inside. As he staggered past, I leaned closer to Metias and whispered, 'Don't like the look of that one. He doesn't walk like someone who's been stabbed, does he?'

"Your brother and the boy exchanged a brief look. When the boy had disappeared inside the hospital, he nodded at me.

'Agreed. Keep an eye on that one. After our rotation's done, I'd like to question him a bit.'"

Thomas pauses here, searching my face, perhaps for permission to stop talking, but I don't give it.

He takes a deep breath and continues. "I blushed then at his nearness. Your brother seemed to sense it too, and an awkward silence passed between us. I'd always known about his attraction to me, but tonight it seemed particularly naked. Maybe it had something to do with his weary day, your university antics throwing him off, his usual air of command subdued and tired. And underneath my calm exterior, my heart hammered against my ribs. *Find a way to get Captain Iparis to a private spot tonight. I don't care how you do it.* This vulnerability would be my only chance."

Thomas looks briefly down at his hands, but carries on.

"So, sometime later, I tapped Metias on the shoulder. 'Captain,' I murmured. 'Can I speak to you in private for a moment?'

"Metias blinked. He asked me, 'Is this urgent?'

"'No, sir,' I told him. 'Not quite. But . . . I'd rather you know.'

"Your brother stared at me, momentarily confused, searching for a clue. Then he motioned for a soldier to take his place at the entrance and the two of us headed into a quiet, dark street near the back of the hospital.

"Metias immediately dropped some of his formal pretense. 'Something wrong, Thomas? You don't look well.'

"All I could think was *treason against the Republic.* He would never do it. Would he? We'd grown up together, trained together, grown close. . . . Then I remembered my commander's orders. I felt the sheathed knife sitting heavily at my waist. 'I'm fine,' I told him.

"But your brother laughed. 'Come on. You've never needed to hide anything from me before. You know that, right?'

*Just say it, Thomas,* I told myself. I knew I was teetering between the familiar and the point of no return. *Force the words out. Let him hear it.* Finally, I looked up and said, 'What is this between us?'

"Your brother's smile wavered. He grew very silent. Then he took a step back. 'What do you mean?'

"'You know what I mean,' I told him. 'This. All these years.'

"Now Metias was studying my face intently. Long seconds passed. '*This,*' he finally replied, emphasizing the word, 'can't happen. You're my subordinate.'

"Then I asked, 'But it means something to you, sir. Doesn't it?'

"Something joyful and tragic danced across Metias's face. He drew closer. I knew that a wall between us had finally formed a crack. 'Does it mean something to *you?*' he asked me."

Again, Thomas pauses. Then, in a softer voice, he says, "A blade of guilt twisted painfully in my chest, but it was too late to turn back. So I took a step forward, closed my eyes, and—I kissed him."

Another pause. "Your brother froze, like I thought he would. There was complete stillness. We drew apart, the silence heavy around us, and for a moment I wondered whether I'd made a huge mistake, whether I'd simply misread every signal from the past few years. Or perhaps, *perhaps* he knew what I was up to. I felt a strange sense of relief at that thought. *Maybe it'd be better if Metias figured out Commander Jameson's plans for him. Maybe there's a way to get out of this.*

"But then he leaned forward and returned the kiss, and the last of that wall crumbled away."

"Stop," I suddenly say. Thomas falls silent. He tries to hide his emotions behind some semblance of nobility, but the shame is plain on his face. I lean back, turn my face away from him, and press my hands to my temples. Grief threatens to overwhelm me. Thomas hadn't just killed Metias knowing that my brother loved him.

Thomas had *taken that knowledge and used it against him.*

*I want you to die. I hate you.* The tide of my anger grows stronger until finally I hear the whisper of Metias's voice in my head, the faint light of reason.

*It's going to be okay, Junebug. Listen to me. Everything is going to be okay.*

I wait, my heart beating steadily, until his gentle words bring me back. My eyes open, and I give Thomas a level stare. "What happened after that?"

It takes Thomas a long moment before he speaks again. When he does, his voice trembles. "There was no way out. Metias had no idea what was going on. He'd fallen into the plan with blind faith. My hand crept to the knife at my waist, but I couldn't bring myself to do it. I couldn't even breathe."

My eyes fill with tears. I want so desperately to hear every detail and at the same time for Thomas to stop talking, to shut this night away and never return again.

"An alarm cut through the air. We jumped apart. Metias

looked flushed and confused—only a second later did we both realize that the alarm came from the hospital.

"The moment broke. Your brother snapped back into captain mode and ran toward the hospital entrance. 'Get inside,' he shouted over his earpiece. He didn't look back. 'I want half of you in there—pinpoint the source. Gather the others at the entrance and wait for my command. *Now!*'

"I started running after him. My chance to strike had vanished. I wondered whether Commander Jameson had somehow been able to see my failure. *The Republic's eyes are everywhere. They know everything.* I panicked. I had to find another moment, another chance to get your brother alone. If I couldn't do it, then Metias's fate would fall into much harsher hands.

"By the time I caught up with him at the entrance, his face was dark with anger. 'Break-in,' he said. 'It was that boy we saw. I'm sure of it. Bryant, get five and circle east. I'll go the other way.' Already your brother was on the move, gathering his soldiers. 'He's going to have to get out of the hospital somehow,' he told us. 'We'll be waiting for him when he tries.'

"I did as Metias commanded—but the instant he was out of earshot, I ordered my soldiers to head east and then snuck away into the shadows. *I have to follow him. This is my last chance. If I fail, I'm as good as dead, anyway.* Sweat trickled down my back. I melted into the shadows, reminding myself of all the lessons Metias had taught me about subtlety and stealth.

"Then from somewhere in the night I heard glass shatter. I hid behind a wall as your brother raced past, alone and unguarded, toward the source of the sound. Then I followed.

The night's darkness swallowed me whole. For a moment, I lost Metias in the back alleys. *Where is he?* I whirled around in an alley, trying to figure out where your brother had gone.

"Just then, a call came through. Commander Jameson barked at me. 'You'd better find a second chance to take him down, Lieutenant. Soon.'

"Finally, minutes later, I found Metias. He was alone, struggling up from the ground with a knife buried in his shoulder, surrounded by blood and broken glass. A few feet from him lay a sewer cap. I rushed to his side. He smiled briefly at me, while clutching the knife in his shoulder.

"'It was Day,' he gasped. 'He escaped down the sewers.' Then he reached out to me. 'Here. Help me up.'

"*This is your chance,* I told myself. *This is your only chance, and if you can't do it now, it will never happen.*"

Thomas's voice falters as I search for my own. I want to stop him again, but I can't. I'm numb.

Thomas lifts his head and says, "I wish I could tell you all the images whirling through my mind—Commander Jameson interrogating Metias, torturing information out of him, tearing off his nails, slicing him open until he screamed for mercy, killing him slowly in the way that she did to all prisoners of war." As he speaks, the words come faster, tumbling from his mouth in a frantic jumble. "I pictured the Republic's flag, the Republic's seal, the oath I'd taken on the day Metias accepted me into a patrol. That I would forever remain faithful to my Republic and my Elector, until my dying day. My eyes darted to the knife buried in Metias's shoulder. *Do it. Do it now,* I told myself. I seized his collar, yanked the knife from his shoulder, and plunged it deep into his chest. Right up to the hilt."

I hear myself gasp. As if I expected a different ending. As if once I hear it enough times, the story will change. It never does.

"Metias let out a broken shriek," Thomas whispers. "Or perhaps it came from me—I can't remember anymore. He collapsed back onto the ground, his hand still clutching my wrist. His eyes were wide with shock.

"'I'm sorry,' I choked out." Thomas looks at me as he continues, his apology meant for both me and my brother. "I knelt over his trembling body. 'I'm sorry, I'm sorry,' I told him. 'I had no choice. You gave me *no choice!*'"

I can barely hear Thomas as he continues. "A spark of understanding appeared in your brother's eyes. With it came hurt, something that went beyond his physical pain, a bleeding moment of realization. Then revulsion. Disappointment. 'Now I know why,' he whispered. I didn't have to ask to know that he was referring to our kiss.

*"No! I meant it!* I wanted to scream. *It was a good-bye, the only one I could give. But I meant it. I promise.*

"Instead I said, 'Why did you have to cross the Republic? I warned you, over and over again. Cross the Republic too many times, and eventually they'll burn you. I *warned* you! I told you to listen!'

"But your brother shook his head. *It's something you'll never understand,* his eyes seemed to say. Blood leaked from his mouth, and his grip tightened on my wrist. 'Don't hurt June,' he said. 'She doesn't know anything.' Then a fierce, terrified light appeared in his eyes. *'Don't hurt her. Promise me.'*

"So I told him, 'I'll protect her. I don't know how, but I'll try. I promise.'

"The light gradually faded from his eyes, and his grip loosened. He stared at me until he couldn't stare anymore, and then I knew that he was gone. *Move. Get out of here,* I told myself. But I stayed crouched over Metias's body, my mind blank. His sudden absence hit me. Metias was gone, Metias was never coming back, and it was all my fault. No. *Long live the Republic.* That's what really mattered, I told myself, yes, yes, that was the important thing. This—whatever this was between Metias and me—wasn't real, could never have happened anyway. Not with Metias as my captain. Not with Metias as a criminal working against the country. It was for the best. *Yes. It was.*

"Eventually I heard shouts from approaching troops. I picked myself up. I wiped my eyes. I had to carry through now. I'd done it, I'd stayed faithful to the Republic. Some survival instinct kicked in. Everything seemed muted, like a fog had settled over my life. Good. I needed the strange calm, the absence of everything, that it brought. I folded my grief carefully back into my chest, as if nothing had happened, and when the first troops arrived on the scene, I placed a call to Commander Jameson.

"I didn't even need to say a word. My silence told her everything she needed to know. 'Fetch Little Iparis when you get a chance,' she said to me. 'And well done, Captain.'

"I didn't reply."

Thomas stays silent; the scene fades. I find myself back in his prison cell, my cheeks streaked with tears, my heart sliced open as if he had stabbed me in the chest as surely as he'd stabbed my brother.

Thomas stares at the floor between us with hollow eyes. "I loved him, June," he says after a moment. "I really did. Everything I did as a soldier, *all* my hard work and training, was to impress him." His guard is finally down, and I can see the true depth of his torture now. His voice hardens, as if he is trying to convince himself of what he's saying. "I answer to the Republic—Metias himself trained me to be what I am. Even *he* understood."

I'm surprised by how much my heart is breaking for him. *You could have helped Metias escape. You could have done something. Anything. You could have tried.* But even now, Thomas doesn't budge. He will never change, and he will never, ever know who Metias really was.

I finally realize the true reason he requested this meeting with me. He wanted to give a real confession. Just like during our conversation when he first arrested me, he is fishing desperately for my forgiveness, for something to justify—in any small way—what he did. He wants to believe what he did was warranted. He wants me to sympathize. He wants peace before he goes.

But he's wasted his efforts on me. I cannot give him peace, even on his final day. Some things cannot be forgiven.

"I feel sorry for you," I say quietly. "Because you're so weak."

Thomas tightens his lips. Still searching for some bit of validation he says, "I could've chosen Day's route. I could have become a criminal. But I didn't. I did everything *right,* you know. That was what Metias loved about me. He respected me. I followed *all* the rules, I obeyed *all* the laws, I worked my way up from where I started." He leans toward me; his eyes grow more desperate. "I took an oath, June. I am still bound by that oath. I will die with honor for sacrificing everything I have—*everything*—for my country. And yet, Day is the legend, while I am to be executed." His voice finally breaks with all his anguish and inner torment, the injustice he feels. "It makes no sense."

I stand up. Behind me, the guards move toward the cell door. "You're wrong," I say sadly. "It makes perfect sense."

"Why?"

"Because Day chose to walk in the light." I turn my back on him for the last time. The door opens; the cell's bars make way for the hall, a new rotation of prison guards, freedom. "And so did Metias."

## 1532 HOURS.

That afternoon, I head to Denver University's track with Ollie in an attempt to clear my thoughts. Outside, the sky looks yellow and hazy with the light of the afternoon sun. I try to picture the sky covered with the Colonies' airships, ablaze with the fire from aerial dogfights and explosions. Twelve days before we need to offer something to the Colonies. Without Day's help, how are we ever going to do that? The thought troubles me, but thankfully it helps keep the memories of Thomas and Commander Jameson out of my head. I pick up my pace. My running shoes pound against the pavement.

When I arrive at the track, I notice guards stationed at every entrance. At least four soldiers per gate. Anden must be doing his exercise routine somewhere out here too. The soldiers recognize me, let me through, and usher me into the stadium, where the track wraps around a large, open field. Anden's nowhere to be seen. Perhaps he's down in the stadium's underground lockers.

I do a quick round of stretches while Ollie waits impatiently, dancing from paw to paw, and then I begin making my way down the track. I run faster and faster along the curved path until I'm sprinting around the turns, my hair streaming out behind me, Ollie panting at my side. I imagine Commander Jameson sprinting after me, gun in hand. *Better be careful, Iparis. You might turn out just like me.* When I loop around to the side of the track with targets set up, I skid to a halt, whip out the gun at my belt, and shoot at each of the targets in rapid succession. Four bull's-eyes. Without pause, I loop around the track again and repeat my routine three times. Ten times. Fifteen times. Finally I stop, my heart beating a frantic tune against my chest.

I shift to a walk, slowly catching my breath, my thoughts whirling. If I had never met Day, could I have grown up to become Commander Jameson? Cold, calculating, merciless? Hadn't I turned into exactly that when I first figured out who

Day was? Hadn't I led the soldiers—led Commander Jameson *herself*—to his family's door, without a second thought for whether or not his family might be harmed? I reset my gun, then aim at the targets again. My bullets thud into the centers of the boards.

If Metias were alive, what would he have thought of what I did?

No. I can't think about my brother without remembering Thomas's confession from this morning. I fire my last bullet, then sit down in the middle of the track with Ollie and bury my head in my hands. I'm so tired. I don't know if I can ever outrun how I used to be. And now I'm doing it all over again—trying to persuade Day to give up his brother again, trying to use him to the Republic's advantage.

Finally I pick myself up, wipe the sweat from my brow, and head to the underground lockers. Ollie settles down to wait for me under the cool overhang near the doors; he laps hungrily at a pouch of water I set before him. I head down the stairs, then turn the corner. The air is humid from the showers, and the lone screen embedded at the end of the hall has a light film of mist over it. I walk down the corridor that splits off into the men's and women's locker rooms. A few voices echo from farther down the hall.

A second later, I see Anden emerge from the locker room with two guards walking alongside him. I blush in embarrassment at the sight. Anden looks like he just stepped out of the shower a few minutes ago, shirtless and still toweling off his damp hair, his lean muscles tense after his workout. He has a crisp collar shirt swung over one shoulder, the white of the fabric a startling contrast against the olive of his skin. One of the guards talks to him in hushed tones, and with a sinking feeling, I wonder whether it has something to do with the Colonies. A moment later, Anden glances up and finally notices me staring at them. The conversation pauses.

"Ms. Iparis," Anden says, a polite smile covering up whatever might have been bothering him. He clears his throat, hands his towel to one of the guards, and pulls one arm through the sleeve of his collar shirt. "I apologize for my half-dressed state."

I bow my head once, trying hard to look unfazed as all of their eyes fixate on me. "No worries, Elector."

He nods at his guards. "Go ahead. I'll meet you both at the stairs."

The guards bow in unison, then leave us alone. Anden waits until they've disappeared around the corner before turning back to me. "I hope your morning went well enough," he says as he starts buttoning up his shirt. His eyebrows furrow. "No trouble?"

"No trouble," I confirm, unwilling to dwell on my conversation with Thomas.

"Good." Anden runs a hand through his damp hair. "Then you've had a better morning than I. I spent several hours in a private conference with the President of Ross City, Antarctica—we've asked them for military help, in case of an invasion." He sighs. "Antarctica sympathizes, but they aren't easy to please. I don't know whether we can get around using Day's brother, and I don't know how to persuade Day to allow it."

"No one will be able to convince him," I reply, crossing my arms. "Not even me. You say that I'm his weakness, but his greatest weakness is his family."

Anden stays quiet for a moment. I study his face carefully, wondering what thoughts are going through his mind. The memory comes back to me of how merciless he can be when he chooses, how he didn't flinch when sentencing Thomas to death, how he'd thrown Commander Jameson's insult right back in her face, how he never hesitated to execute every single person who tried to destroy him. Deep underneath the soft voice and kind heart lies something cold. "Don't force him," I say. Anden looks at me in surprise. "I know that's what you're thinking."

Anden finishes buttoning his shirt. "I can only do what I have to do, June," he says gently. It almost sounds sad.

*No. I will never let you hurt Day like that. Not the way I've already hurt him.* "You're the Elector. You don't *have* to do anything. And if you care about the Republic, you won't risk angering the one person who the public believes in."

Too late, I bite my tongue. *The people believe in Day, but they don't believe in* you. Anden winces visibly, and even though he doesn't comment on it, I silently curse myself for my notorious turns of phrase. "I'm sorry," I murmur. "I didn't mean it like that."

A long pause drags on before Anden speaks again. "It's not as easy as it seems." He shakes his head. A tiny bead of water drops from his hair onto his collar. "You would do differently? Risk an entire nation instead of one person? I can't justify it. The Colonies will strike if we don't give them an antidote, and this whole mess stemmed from something that *I'm* responsible for."

"No, your father was responsible. That doesn't mean *you* are."

"Well, I'm my father's son," Anden replies, his voice suddenly stern. "What difference does it make?"

The words surprise both of us. I tighten my lips and decide not to comment on it, but my thoughts churn frantically. *It does make a difference.* But then I think back on what Anden had once told me about the Republic's founding, how his father and the Electors before him had been forced to act in those dark, early years. *Better be careful, Iparis. You might turn out just like me.*

Perhaps I'm not the only one who needs to be careful.

Something showing on the screen at the end of the hall distracts me. I look toward it. There's some news about Day; the footage shows some old video close-up of him and then a brief shot of the Denver hospital, but even though most of the video's cut off, I can catch glimpses of crowds gathered in front of the building. Anden turns to look at the screen too. Are they protesting? What could they be protesting?

```
Daniel Altan Wing admitted to hospital
for standard medical exam, to be released
tomorrow
```

Anden presses a hand to his ear. An incoming call. He glances briefly at me, then clicks on his mike and says, "Yes?"

Silence. As the screen's broadcast continues, Anden's face

turns pale. It reminds me for an instant of how pale Day had looked while at the banquet, and the two thoughts converge into a single, frightening thought. I suddenly know, beyond the shadow of a doubt, that *this* is the secret Day's been keeping from me. A horrible feeling builds in my chest.

"Who approved this footage's release?" Anden says after a moment, his voice now a whisper. I hear anger in it. "There won't be a next time. Inform me *first*. Is that understood?"

A lump rises in my throat. When his call finally ends, he drops his hand and gives me a long, grave look.

"It's Day," he says. "He's at the hospital."

"Why?" I demand.

"I'm so sorry." He bows his head in a tragic gesture, then leans forward to whisper in my ear. He tells me. And suddenly I feel light-headed, like the entire world has funneled into a blur of motion, like none of this is real, like I'm standing right back at the Los Angeles Central Hospital on the night I knelt before Metias's cold, lifeless body, staring into a face that I no longer recognized. My heartbeat slows to a stop. Everything stops. *This can't be real.*

How can the boy who stirred an entire nation be dying?

# DAY

THEY KEEP ME AT THE HOSPITAL OVERNIGHT BEFORE THEY release me to my apartment. By now, the news is out—bystanders had seen me wheeled out, had spread the word to other folks, and soon the wildfire was unstoppable, and the rumor's been uttered in every corner of the city. I've seen the news cycles try to hide it twice already. I was in the hospital for a standard checkup; I was in the hospital to visit my brother. All sorts of goddy stories. But no one's buying it.

I spend all day enjoying the luxury of a non-hospital bed, watching light, slushy snow falling outside our window, while Eden camps out on the bed by my feet and plays with a robotics kit we'd gotten from the Republic as a gift. He's piecing together some sort of robot now; he matches up a magnetic Light cube—a palm-size box with mini screens on its sides—with several Arm, Leg, and Wing cubes to create what's essentially a little flying JumboTron Man. He smiles in delight at it, then breaks the cubes apart and rearranges them into a pair of walking Legs that display JumboTron video feeds whenever they step down. I smile too, momentarily content that *he's* content. If there's one good thing about the Republic, it's that they indulge Eden's love for building stuff. Every other week we seem to get some new contraption that I've only ever seen upper-class kids own. I wonder if June's the one who put in this special request for Eden, knowing what she does. Or maybe Anden just feels guilty for all the stuff his father put us through.

I wonder if she's heard the news yet. She must have.

"Careful," I say as Eden climbs up onto my bed and leans over to stand his new creation up at the edge of the window. His hands fumble around, feeling for the windowsill and the glass pane. "If you fall and break something, we'll have to head back to the hospital, and I am *not* going to be happy about that."

"You're thinking about her again, aren't you?" Eden fires smoothly back. His blind eyes stay squinted at the blocks standing barely an inch from his face. "You always change your voice."

I blink at him in surprise. "What?"

He looks in my direction and raises an eyebrow at me, and the expression looks comical on his childlike face. "Oh, come on. It's so obvious. What's this June girl to you, anyway? The whole country gossips about you two, and when she asked you to come to Denver, you couldn't pack us up fast enough. You told me to call *her* in case the Republic ever comes to take me away. You're gonna have to spill sooner or later, yeah? You're always talking about her."

"I don't talk about her all the time."

"Uh-huh, right."

I'm glad Eden can't see my expression. I've yet to talk with him about June and her connection to the rest of our family—another good reason to stay away from her. "She's a friend," I finally reply.

"Do you like her?"

My eyes go back to studying the rainy scene outside our window. "Yeah."

Eden waits for me to say more, but when I remain silent, he shrugs and goes back to his robot. "Fine," he mutters. "Tell me whenever."

As if on cue, my earpiece blares out a second of soft static, warning me of an incoming call. I accept it. A moment later, June's whispered voice echoes in my ear. She doesn't say anything about my illness—she just suggests, "Can we talk?"

I knew it'd only be a matter of time before I heard from her. I watch Eden playing for a second longer. "We gotta do it somewhere else," I whisper back. My brother glances at me, momentarily curious at my words. I don't want to ruin my first day out of the hospital by breaking my depressing prognosis to an eleven-year-old.

"How about a walk, then?"

I glance out the window. It's dinnertime, and the cafés down on the street's ground level are crowded with patrons, almost all of them huddled under hats, caps, umbrellas, and hoods, keeping to themselves in this twilight slush. Might be a good time to walk around without attracting too much attention. "How about this. Come on over, and we'll head out from here."

"Great," June replies. She hangs up.

Ten minutes later, my doorbell rings and startles Eden to his feet—the new cube robot he built falls from my bed, three of its limbs snapping off. Eden turns his eyes in my direction. "Who's there?" he asks.

"Don't worry, kid," I reply, walking over to the door. "It's June."

Eden's shoulders relax at my words; a bright grin lights up his face, and he hops off the edge of the bed, leaving his block robot by the window. He feels his way toward the other end of the bed. "Well?" he demands. "Aren't you gonna let her in?"

It seems like during the time I'd spent living on the streets, I'd been missing out on seeing Eden blossom. Quiet kid turned stubborn and headstrong. Can't imagine how he inherited *that*. I sigh—I hate keeping things from him, but how do I explain *this* one? I'd told him over the past year who June is: a Republic girl who decided to help us out, a girl who's now training to be the country's future Princeps. I haven't figured out yet how to tell him the rest—so I just don't say anything about it at all.

June doesn't smile when I open the door. She glances at Eden, then back to me. "Is that your brother?" she says quietly.

I nod. "You haven't met him yet, have you?" I turn around and call out to him. "Eden. Manners."

Eden waves from the bed. "Hi," he calls out.

I step aside so that June can come in. She makes her way over to where Eden is, sits down next to him with a smile, and takes his small hand in hers. She shakes it twice. "Pleased to meet you, Eden," she says, her voice gentle. I lean against the door to watch the exchange. "How are you doing?"

Eden shrugs. "Pretty good, I guess," he replies. "Doctors say my eyes have stabilized. I'm taking ten different pills every day." He tilts his head. "But I think I've been getting stronger." He puffs out his chest a little, then strikes a mock pose by flexing his arms. His eyes are unfocused and pointing slightly to the left of June's face. "How do I look?"

June laughs. "I have to say, you look better than most people I see. I've heard a lot about you."

"I hear about you a lot too," Eden replies in a rush, "mostly from Daniel. He thinks you're really hot."

"Okay, that's enough." I clear my throat loud enough for him to hear, then shoot him a cranky look even though he's blind as a rock. "Let's head out."

"Have you eaten yet?" she asks as we head toward the door. "I was supposed to be shadowing Anden with the other Princeps-Elects, but he's been called to the Armor barracks for a quick briefing—something about food poisoning among the soldiers. So I had a couple of free hours." A faint blush touches her cheeks as she says this. "I thought maybe we could grab a bite."

I raise an eyebrow. Then I lean in toward her so that my cheek brushes against hers—to my excitement, I feel her shiver at my touch. "Why, June," I tease in a low, soft voice, smiling against her ear. "Are you asking me out on a *date*?"

June's blush deepens, but its warmth doesn't touch her eyes.

My moment of mischief ends. I clear my throat, then look over my shoulder at Eden. "I'll bring some food back for you. Don't go out on your own. Do what Lucy tells you to do."

Eden nods, already engrossed with the block robot again.

Minutes later, we head out of the apartment complex and into the thickening drizzle. I keep my head down and my face hidden under the shadow of a soldier cap; my neck's protected beneath my thick red scarf, and my hands are shoved deep into the pockets of my military coat. It's strange how much I've gotten used to Republic clothing. June pulls her coat collar high, and her breath billows out around her in clouds of steam. The slush has picked up some, sending fresh ice and water into my face and tickling my eyelashes. Bold red banners still hang from the windows of most high-rises, and the JumboTrons have a red-and-black symbol in the corners of their broadcasts in honor of Anden's birthday. Others along the street rush past in a blur of motion. We walk in comfortable silence, savoring the simple nearness of each other.

It's kind of weird, actually. Today's one of my better days, and I don't have a lot of trouble keeping up with June—today, it doesn't *feel* like I only have a couple of months to live. Maybe the new medicines they gave me are going to work this time.

We don't say a word until June finally stops us at a small, steaming café several blocks from my apartment. Right away I can see why she chose it—it's mostly empty, a tiny little spot on the first floor of a towering high-rise washed wet with slush, and not very well lit. Even though it's open to the air, like many other cafés in the area, it has a few dark nooks that are nice for us to sit at, and its only lights come from glowing, cube-shaped lanterns on each of its tables. A hostess ushers us inside, seating us at June's request in one of the shadowy corners. Flat plates of scented water sit scattered throughout the café. I shiver, even though our spot is pretty warm from our heat lantern.

*What are we doing here again?* A strange fog washes over me, then clears. *We're here for dinner, that's what we're doing.* I shake my head. I recall the brief struggle I'd had a few days ago, when I couldn't remember Lucy's name. A frightening thought emerges.

Maybe this is a new symptom. Or maybe I'm just being paranoid.

After we place our orders, June speaks up. The gold flecks in her eyes shine in the lantern's orange glow. "Why didn't you tell me?" she whispers.

I hold my hands against the lantern, savoring the heat. "What good would it have done?"

June furrows her eyebrows, and only then do I notice that her eyes look kind of swollen, like she's been crying. She shakes her head at me. "The rumors are all over the place," she continues in a voice I can barely hear. "Witnesses say they saw you being carried out of your apartment on a stretcher thirty-four hours ago—one of them apparently overheard a medic discussing your condition."

I sigh and put my hands up in defeat. "You know what, if this is all somehow causing riots in the street and more trouble for Anden, then I'm sorry. I was told to keep it a secret—and I *did*, as well as I could. I'm sure our *glorious* Elector will figure out a way to calm folks down."

June bites her lip once. "There must be some solution, Day. Have your doctors—"

"They're already trying everything." I wince as a painful spasm runs through the back of my head, as if on cue. "I've been through three rounds of experiments. Slow and painful progress so far." I explain to June what the doctors had told me, the unusual infection in my hippocampus, the medication that's been weakening me, sucking the strength out of my body. "Believe me, they're running through solutions."

"How long do you have?" she whispers.

I stay silent, pretending to be fascinated with the lantern. I don't know if I have the heart to say it.

June leans closer, until her shoulder bumps softly against mine. "How long do you have?" she repeats. "Please. I hope you still care about me enough to tell me."

I gaze back at her, slowly falling—as I always seem to do—back under her pull. *Don't make me do this, please.* I don't want to say it out loud to her; it might mean that it's actually true. But she looks so sad and fearful that I can't keep it in. I let out my breath, then run a hand through my hair and lower my head. "They said a month," I whisper. "Maybe two. They said I should get my priorities in order."

June closes her eyes—I think I see her sway slightly in her seat. "Two months," she murmurs vacantly. The agony on her face reminds me exactly why I didn't want to let her know.

After another long silence between us, June snaps out of her daze and reaches to pull something out of her pocket. She comes back up with something small and metallic in her palm. "I've been meaning to give this to you," she says.

I stare blankly at it. It's a paper clip ring, thin lines of wire pulled into an elegant series of swirls and closed into a circle, just like the one I'd once made for her. My eyes widen and dart up to hers. She doesn't say anything; instead, she looks down and helps me push it onto my right hand's ring finger. "I had a little time," she finally mutters.

I run a hand across the ring in wonder, my heartstrings pulled taut. A dozen emotions rush through me. "I'm sorry," I stammer out after a while, trying to put a more hopeful spin on everything. That's all I can say, after this gift from her? "They think there's still a chance. They're trying out some more treatments soon."

"You once told me why you chose 'Day' as your street name," she says firmly. She moves her hand so that it's over mine, hiding the paper clip ring from view. The warmth of her skin against mine makes my breath short. "Every morning, everything's possible again. Right?" A river of tingles runs up my spine. I want to take her face in my hands again, kiss her cheeks and study her dark, sad eyes, and tell her I'll be okay. But that would just be another lie. Half of my heart is breaking at the pain on her face; the other half, I realize guiltily, is swelling with happiness to know that she still cares. There's love in her tragic words, in the folds of that thin metal ring. Isn't there?

Finally, I take a deep breath. "Sometimes, the sun sets earlier. Days don't last forever, you know. But I'll fight as hard as I can. I can promise you that."

June's eyes soften. "You don't have to do this alone."

"Why should *you* have to bear it?" I mutter back. "I just . . . thought it would be easier this way."

"Easier for whom?" June snaps. "You, me, the public? You would rather just pass away silently one day, without ever breathing another word to me?"

"Yes, I would," I find myself snapping back. "If I'd told you that night, would you have agreed to become a Princeps-Elect?"

Whatever words sat on the tip of June's tongue go unspoken. She pauses at that, then swallows. "No," she admits. "I wouldn't have had the heart to do it. I would've waited."

"Exactly." I take a deep breath. "You think I wanted to whine to you about my health in that moment? To stand in the way of you and the position of a lifetime?"

"That was *my* choice to make," June says through clenched teeth.

"And *I* wanted you to make it without *me* in the way."

June shakes her head, and her shoulders slightly droop. "You really think I care so little about you?"

Our food arrives then—steaming bowls of soup, plates of dinner rolls, and a neatly wrapped package of food for Eden—and I lapse gratefully into silence. *It would've been easier for me,* I add to myself. *I'd rather step away than be reminded every day that I only have a few months left to be with you.* I'm ashamed to say this out loud, though. When June looks expectantly at me for an answer, I just shake my head and shrug.

And that's when we hear it. An alarm wails out across the city.

It's deafening. We both freeze, then look up at the speakers lining all the street's buildings. I've never heard a siren like this in my entire life—an endless and earsplitting scream that drenches the air, drowning out anything in its path. The JumboTrons have gone dark. I shoot June a bewildered look. *What the hell is that?*

But June's no longer looking at me. Her eyes are fixed on the speakers blaring out the alarm across the entire street, and her expression is stricken with horror. Together, we watch as the JumboTrons flare back to life—this time each screen is bloodred, and each has two gold words etched in bold across its display:

SEEK COVER

"What does it mean?" I shout.

June grabs my hand and starts to run. "It means that an air strike's coming. The Armor is under attack."

# JUNE

**"EDEN."**

It's the first word out of Day's mouth. The JumboTrons continue broadcasting their ominous scarlet notice as the alarm echoes across the city, deafening me with its rhythmic roar and blotting out all other sounds in the city. Along the street, others are peeking out of windows and pouring out from building entrances, as bewildered as we are over the unusual alarm. Soldiers are flooding into formation on the street, shouting into their earpieces as they see the approaching enemy. I run right beside him, thoughts and numbers racing through my mind as we go. (Four seconds. Twelve seconds. Fifteen seconds a block, which means seventy-five seconds until we reach Day's apartment if we keep up our pace. Is there a faster route? And *Ollie*. I need to get him out of my apartment and to my side.) A strange focus grips me, just like it had the moment I first freed Day from Batalla Hall all those months ago, like the moment Day climbed the Capitol Tower to address the people and I led soldiers off his trail. I may turn into a silent, uncomfortable observer in the Senate chamber, but out here on the streets, in the midst of chaos, I can think. I can act.

I remember reading about and rehearsing for this particular alarm back in high school, although Los Angeles is so far away from the Colonies that even those practice drills were rare. The alarm was to be used only if enemy forces attacked our city, if they were right at the city's borders and barging their way in. I don't know what the process is like in Denver, but I imagine it can't be that different—we are to evacuate immediately, then seek out the closest assigned underground bunker and board subways that will shuttle us to a safer city. After I entered college and officially became a soldier, the drill changed for me: Soldiers are to report immediately to a location their commanding officers give them over their earpieces. We must be ready for war at a moment's notice.

But I've never heard the alarm used for a real attack on a Republic city, because there hasn't been one yet. Most attacks were thwarted before they could reach us. Until now. And as I run alongside Day, I know exactly what must be going through his mind. It triggers a familiar guilt in my stomach.

Day has never heard the alarm before, nor has he ever gone through a drill for it. This is because he's from a poor sector. I was never sure before, and I admit that I never thought much about it, but seeing Day's confused expression makes it all very clear. The underground bunkers are only for the upper class, the gem sectors. The poor are left to fend for themselves.

Overhead, an engine screams by. A Republic jet. Then several more. Shouts rise up and mix with the alarm—I brace myself for a call from Anden at any moment. Then, far off along the horizon, I see the first orange glows light up along the Armor. The Republic is launching a counterattack from the walls. *This is really happening.* But it shouldn't be. The Colonies had given us *time,* however little, to hand over an antidote to them—and since that ultimatum, only four days have passed. My anger flares. Did they want to catch us off guard in such an extreme way?

I grab Day's hand and pick up my pace. "Can you call Eden?" I shout.

"Yeah," Day gasps out. Immediately I can tell that he doesn't have the stamina he used to have—his breathing is slightly labored, his steps slightly slower. A lump lodges in my throat. Somehow, this is the first evidence of his fading health that hits home, and my heart clenches. Behind us, another explosion reverberates across the night air. I tighten my hold on his hand.

"Tell Eden to be ready at your complex's entrance," I shout. "I know where we can go."

An urgent voice comes over my earpiece. It's Anden. "Where are you?" he says. I shiver as I detect a faint hint of fear in his words—another thing I rarely hear. "I'm at the Capitol Tower. I'll send a jeep to pick you up."

"Send a jeep to Day's apartment. I'll be there in a minute. And Ollie—my dog—"

"I'll have him sent to the bunkers immediately," Anden says. "Be careful." Then a click sounds out, and I hear static for a second before my earpiece goes dark. Beside me, Day repeats my instructions for Eden over his own mike.

By the time we reach the apartment complex, Republic jets are screaming by every other second, painting dozens of trails into the evening sky. Crowds of people have already started gathering outside the complex and are being guided in various directions by city patrols. A jolt of fear seizes me when I realize that some of the jets on the horizon are not Republic jets at all—but unfamiliar enemy ones. If they're this close, then they must've gotten past our longer range missiles. Two larger black dots hover at the end of the sky. Colonies airships.

Day sees Eden before I do. He's a small, golden-haired figure clutching the railings by the apartment complex's entrance door, squinting in vain at the sea of people around him. Their caretaker stands behind him with both of her hands firmly on his shoulders. "Eden!" Day calls out. The boy jerks his head in our direction. Day hops up the steps and scoops him into his arms, then turns back to me. "Where do we go?" he shouts.

"The Elector's sending a jeep for us," I reply in his ear, so that the others don't hear. Already a few people are casting us glances of recognition even as they stream past us in a haze of panic. I pull my coat collars as high up as they can go, then bow my head. *Come on,* I mutter to myself.

"June," Day says. I meet his eyes. "What's gonna happen to the other sectors?"

There's the question I've been dreading. *What will happen to the poor sectors?* I hesitate, and in that brief moment of silence, Day realizes the answer. His lips tighten into a thin line. A deep rage rises in his eyes.

The jeep's arrival saves me from answering right away. It screeches to a stop several feet from where the others have crowded around, and inside I see Anden wave once at me from the passenger's side. "Let's go," I urge Day. We make our way down the steps as a soldier opens the door for us. Day helps

Eden and their caretaker inside first, and when they're both buckled up, we climb in. The jeep takes off at breakneck pace as more Republic jets fly by overhead. Off in the distance, another bright orange cloud mushrooms up from the Armor. Is it me, or did that seem like a closer hit than before? (Perhaps closer by a good hundred feet, given the size of the explosion.)

"Glad to see you all safe," Anden says without turning around. He utters a quick greeting at each of us, then mumbles a command to the driver, who makes a sharp turn around the next block. Eden lets out a startled yelp. The caretaker squeezes his shoulders and tries to soothe him.

"Why take the slower route?" Anden says as we veer down a narrow street. The ground shakes from another far-off impact.

"Apologies, Elector," the driver calls back. "Word's that several explosions have gone off inside the Armor—our fastest route's not safe. They bombed a few jeeps on the other side of Denver."

"Any injuries?"

"Not too many, luckily. Couple jeeps overturned—several prisoners escaped, and one soldier's dead."

"Which prisoners?"

"We're still confirming."

A nasty premonition hits me. When I'd gone to see Thomas, there had been a rotation of guards standing in front of Commander Jameson's cell. When I left, the guards were different.

Anden makes a frustrated sound, then turns to glance back at us. "We're headed to an underground hold called Subterrain

One. Should you need to enter or leave the hold, my guards will scan your thumbs at its gateway. You heard our driver—it's not safe to head out on your own. Understand?"

The driver presses a hand to his ear, blanches, and looks at Anden. "Sir, we have confirmation on the escaped prisoners. There were three." He hesitates, then swallows. "Captain Thomas Bryant. Lieutenant Patrick Murrey. Commander Natasha Jameson."

My world lurches. I knew it. I knew it. Just yesterday I'd seen Commander Jameson securely behind bars, and talked to Thomas while he was withering away in prison. *They couldn't have gone far,* I tell myself. "Anden," I whisper, forcing my senses straight. "Yesterday, when I went to see Thomas, there had been a different rotation of guards. Were those soldiers supposed to be there?" Day and I exchange a quick look, and for an instant I feel as if the entire world is playing us for fools, weaving our lives into one cruel joke.

"Find the prisoners," Anden snaps into his mike. His own face has turned white. "Shoot them on sight." He glances back at me while he continues talking. "And get me the guards that were on duty. *Now.*"

I cringe as yet another explosion makes the ground tremble. *They couldn't have gone far. They'll be captured and shot by the end of the day.* I repeat these words to myself over and over. No, something else is at work here. My mind flits through the possibilities:

It's no coincidence that Commander Jameson managed to escape, that the Colonies' attack happened on the same day she was being transferred. There must be other traitors in the Republic's ranks, soldiers that Anden hasn't rooted out yet. Commander Jameson may have been passing information to the Colonies through them. After all, the Colonies somehow knew when our Armor soldiers would rotate shifts, and particularly that today we had fewer Armor soldiers stationed than usual due to the food poisoning. They knew to strike at our weakest moment.

If that's the case, then the Colonies may have been planning an attack for months. Perhaps even before the plague outbreak.

And Thomas. Was he in on the whole thing? Unless he was trying to warn me. That's why he asked for me yesterday. For his final request, but also in hopes that I would notice something off about the guards. My heartbeat quickens. But why wouldn't he just shout a warning?

"What happens next?" I ask numbly.

Anden leans his head against the seat. He's probably thinking through a similar list of possibilities about the escaped prisoners, but he doesn't say it aloud. "Our jets are all engaged right outside Denver. The Armor should hold for a good while, but there's a strong chance more Colonies forces are on their way. We're going to need help. Other nearby cities have been alerted and are sending their troops for reinforcement, but"— Anden pauses to look over his shoulder at me—"it might not be enough. While we keep funneling civilians underground, June, you and I need to have a private talk right away."

"Where are you evacuating the poor to, Elector?" Day pipes up quietly.

Anden turns in his seat again. He meets Day's hostile blue eyes with as level a look as he can manage. I notice that he avoids looking at Eden. "I have troops on their way to the outer sectors," he says. "They'll find shelter for the civilians and defend them until I give a command otherwise."

"No underground bunkers for them, I guess," Day replies coldly.

"I'm sorry." Anden lets out a long breath. "The bunkers were built a long time ago, before my father even became the Elector. We're working on adding more."

Day leans forward and narrows his eyes. His right hand grips Eden's tightly. "Then split the bunkers up between the sectors. Half poor, half rich. The upper class should risk their necks out in the open as much as the lower class."

"No," Anden says firmly, even though I hear regret in his words. He makes the mistake of arguing this point with Day, and I can't stop him. "If we were to do that, the logistics would be a nightmare. The outer sectors don't have the same evacuation routes—if explosions hit the city, hundreds of thousands more people would be vulnerable in the open because we wouldn't be able to organize everyone in time. We evacuate the gem sectors first. Then we can—"

"*Do* it!" Day shouts. "I don't care about your damn logistics!"

Anden's face hardens. "You *will* not talk back to me like that," he snaps. There's steel in his voice that I recognize from Commander Jameson's trial. "I am your Elector."

"And *I* put you there," Day snaps back. "Fine, you wanna talk logically? I'm game. If you don't make a bigger effort to protect the poor *right now,* I can practically guarantee that you'll have a full-on riot on your hands. Do you *really* want that while the Colonies are attacking? Like you said, you're the Elector. But you won't be if the rest of the country's poor hears about how you're handling this, and even I might not be able to stop them from starting a revolution. They already think the Republic's trying to kill me off. How long do you think the Republic can hold up against a war from both the outside *and* the inside?"

Anden's facing forward again. "This conversation's over." As always, his voice is dangerously quiet, but we can hear every single word.

Day lets out a curse and slumps back in his seat. I exchange a glance with him, then shake my head. Day has a point, of course, and so does Anden. The *problem* is that we don't have time for all this nonsense. After a moment of silence, I lean forward in my seat, clear my throat, and try an alternative.

"We should evacuate the poor into the wealthy sectors," I say. "They'll still be aboveground, but the wealthy sectors sit in the heart of Denver, not along the Armor where the fighting is happening. It's a flawed plan, but the poor will also see that we're making a concerted effort to protect them. Then, as the people in the bunkers are gradually evacuated to LA via underground subways, we'll have the time and space to start filtering everyone else underground as well."

Day mutters something under his breath, but at the same time he grunts in reluctant approval. He shoots me a grateful look. "Sounds like a better plan to me. At least the people'll have *something*." A second later, I figure out what it was that he'd muttered. *You'd make a better Elector than this fool.*

Anden's quiet for a moment as he considers my words. Then he nods in agreement and presses a hand against his ear. "Commander Greene," he says, then launches into a series of orders.

I meet Day's eyes. He still looks upset, but at least his eyes aren't burning in anger like they were a second ago. He turns his attention back on Lucy, who has an arm wrapped protectively around Eden. He's curled up in the corner of the jeep's seat with his legs tucked up and his arms wrapped around them. He squints at the scene blurring by, but I'm not sure how much of it he can actually make out. I reach across Day and touch Eden's shoulder. He tenses up immediately. "It's okay, it's June," I say. "And don't worry. We're going to be fine, do you hear?"

"Why did the Colonies break through?" Eden asks, turning his wide, purple-toned eyes on me and Day.

I swallow hard. Neither of us answers him. Finally, after he repeats his question, Day hugs him closer and whispers something in his ear. Eden settles down against his brother's shoulder. He still looks unhappy and scared, but the terror is at least tempered, and we manage to finish the rest of the ride without saying another word.

It feels like an eternity (in actuality the trip takes a mere two minutes and twelve seconds), but we finally arrive at a nondescript building near the heart of downtown Denver, a thirty-story high-rise covered with crisscrossing support beams on all four of its sides. Dozens of city patrols are mixed in with crowds of civilians, organizing them into groups at the entrance. Our driver pulls the jeep up to the side of the building, where patrols let us through the door of a makeshift fence. Through the window, I see soldiers click their heels together in sharp salutes as we pass by. One of them is holding Ollie on a leash. I slump in relief at the sight of him. When the jeep halts, two of them promptly open the doors for us. Anden steps out—immediately he's surrounded by four patrol captains, all feverishly updating him on how the evacuation is going. My dog pulls his soldier frantically to my side. I thank the soldier, take over the leash, and rub Ollie's head. He's panting in distress.

"This way, Ms. Iparis," the soldier who opens my door says. Day follows behind me in a tense silence, his hand still clutched tightly around Eden's. Lucy comes out last. I look over my shoulder to where Anden's now deep in conversation with his captains—he pauses to exchange a quick look with me. His eyes dart to Eden. I know that the thought he has must be the same thought running through Day's mind: *Keep Eden safe.* I nod, signaling to him that I understand, and then we move past a crowd of waiting evacuees and I lose sight of him.

Instead of dealing with the lineup of civilians at the entrance, soldiers escort us through a separate entrance and down a winding set of stairs, until we reach a dimly lit hallway that ends in a set of wide, steel double doors. The guards standing at the entrance shift their stance when they recognize me.

"This way, Ms. Iparis," they say. One of them stiffens at the sight of Day, but looks quickly away when Day meets his stare. The doors swing open for us.

We're greeted by a blast of warm, humid air and a scene of orderly chaos. The room we've stepped into seems like an enormous warehouse (half the size of a Trial stadium, three dozen fluorescents, and six rows of steel beams lining the ceiling), with a lone JumboTron on the left wall blasting instructions to the upper-class evacuees who mill all around us. Amongst them are a handful of poor-sector people (fourteen of them, to be exact), those who must have been the housekeepers and janitors of some of the gem-sector's homes. To my disappointment, I see soldiers separating them out into a different line. Several upper-class people cast them sympathetic looks, while others glare in disdain.

Day sees them too. "Guess we're all created equal," he mutters. I say nothing.

A few smaller rooms line the right wall. At the far end of the room, the end of a parked subway train rests inside a tunnel, and crowds of both soldiers and civilians have gathered along both of its platforms. The soldiers are attempting to organize the crowds of bewildered, frightened people onto the subway. Where it will take them, I can only guess.

Beside me, Day watches the scene with silent, simmering eyes. His hand stays clamped on Eden's. I wonder whether he's taking note of the aristocratic clothing that most of these evacuees are wearing.

"Apologies for the mess," a guard says to me as she escorts

us toward one of the smaller rooms. She taps the edge of her cap politely. "We are in the early stages of evacuations, and as you can see, the first wave is still in progress. We can have you, as well as Day and his family, on the first wave as well, if you don't mind resting for a moment in a private suite."

Mariana and Serge might already be waiting in rooms of their own. "Thank you," I reply. We walk past several doors, their long, rectangular windows revealing empty, blank rooms with portraits of Anden hanging on their walls. A couple look as if they have been reserved for high-ranking officials, while others appear to be holding people who must have caused trouble— detainees with sullen faces flanked by pairs of soldiers. One room that we pass by holds several people surrounded by guards.

It is *this* room that makes me pause. I recognize one of the people in there. Is it really her? "Wait," I call out, stepping closer to the window. No doubt about it—I see a young girl with wide eyes and a blunt, messy bob of a haircut, sitting in a chair beside a gray-eyed boy and three others who look more ragged than I recall. I glance at our soldier. "What are they doing in there?"

Day follows my lead. When he sees what I see, he sucks in a sharp breath. "Get us in there," he whispers to me. His voice takes on a desperate urgency. "*Please.*"

"These are prisoners, Ms. Iparis," the soldier replies, puzzled by our interest. "I don't recommend—"

I tighten my lips. "I want to see them," I interrupt.

The soldier hesitates, glances around the room, and then

nods reluctantly. "Of course," she replies. She steps toward the door and opens it, then ushers us in. Lucy stays right outside with her hand tightly gripping Eden's. The door closes behind us.

I find myself staring straight at Tess and a handful of Patriots.

# DAY

WELL, DAMN. THE LAST TIME I SAW TESS, SHE WAS STANDING in the middle of the alley near where we were supposed to assassinate Anden, her fists clenched and her face a broken picture. She looks different now. Calmer. Older. She's also gotten a good bit taller, and her once-round baby face has leaned out. Weird to see.

She and the others are all shackled to chairs. The sight doesn't help my mood. I recognize one of her companions immediately—Pascao, the dark-skinned Runner with a head of short curls and those ridiculously pale gray eyes. He hasn't changed much, although now that I'm close enough, I can see traces of a scar across his nose and another one near his right temple. He flashes me a brilliant white grin that drips sarcasm. "That you, Day?" he says, giving me a flirtatious wink. "Still as gorgeous as you've always been. Republic uniforms suit you."

His words sting. I turn my glare on the soldiers standing guard over them. "Why the hell are they prisoners?"

One of them tilts his nose up at me. Based on all the goddy decorations on his uniform, he must be the captain of this group or something. "They're former Patriots," he says, emphasizing his last word as if he's trying to make a jab at me. "We caught them along the edge of the Armor, where they were attempting to disable our military equipment and aid the Colonies."

Pascao shifts indignantly in his chair. "Bullshit, you blinder boy," he snaps. "We were camped out along the Armor because we were trying to help *your* sorry soldiers out. Maybe we shouldn't have bothered."

Tess watches me with a wary look that she's never used with me before. Her arms look so small and thin with those giant shackles clamped around her wrists. I clench my teeth; my gaze falls to the guns at the soldiers' belts. *No sudden moves,* I remind myself. *Not around these trigger-happy trots.* From the corner of my eye, I notice that one of the others is bleeding from the shoulder. "Let them go," I tell the soldier. "They're not the enemy."

The soldier glares at me with cold contempt. "Absolutely not. Our orders were to detain them until such time—"

Beside me, June lifts her chin. "Orders from whom?"

The soldier's bravado wavers a little. "Ms. Iparis, my orders came directly from the glorious Elector himself." His cheeks flush when he sees June narrow her eyes, and then he starts blabbing something about their tour of duty around the Armor and how intense the battle's been. I step closer to Tess and stoop down until we're at the same eye level. The guards shift their guns, but June snaps a warning at them to stop.

"You came back," I whisper to Tess.

Even though Tess still looks wary, something softens in her eyes. "Yes."

"Why?"

Tess hesitates. She looks over at Pascao, who turns his

startling gray eyes fully on me. "We came back," he replies, "because Tess heard you calling for us."

They'd heard me. All those radio transmissions I'd been sending out for months and months hadn't ended up lost somewhere in the dark—somehow, *they'd heard me.* Tess swallows hard before she works up enough courage to speak. "Frankie first caught you on the airwaves a few months ago," she says, nodding toward a curly-haired girl tied to one of the chairs. "She said you were trying to contact us." Tess lowers her eyes. "I didn't want to answer. But then I heard about your illness . . . and . . ."

So. The news has definitely gotten around.

"Hey now," Pascao interrupts when he catches my expression. "We didn't come back to the Republic just because we felt sorry for *you.* We've been listening to the news coming from both you and the Colonies. Heard about the threat of war."

"And you decided to come to our aid?" June pipes up. Her eyes are suspicious. "Why so generous all of a sudden?"

Pascao's sarcastic grin fades away. He regards June with a tilt of his head. "You're June Iparis, aren't you?"

The captain starts to tell him to greet June in a more formal way, but June just nods.

"So *you're* the one who sabotaged our plans and split up our crew." Pascao shrugs. "No hard feelings—not that, you know, I was a big fan of Razor or anything."

"Why are you back in the country?" June repeats.

"Okay, fine. We got kicked out of Canada." Pascao takes a deep breath. "We were hiding out there after everything fell apart during the"—he pauses to glance at the soldiers around them—"the, ah, you know. Our playdate with Anden. But then the Canadians figured out that we weren't supposed to be in their country, and we had to flee back south. A lot of us scattered to the winds. I don't know where half our original group is now—chances are that some of them are still in Canada. When the news about Day broke, little Tess here asked if she could leave us and head back to Denver on her own. I didn't want her to, well, *die*—so we came along." Pascao looks down for a moment. He doesn't stop talking, but I can tell that he's just babbling at this point, trying to give us any reason but their main one. "With the Colonies invading, I thought that if we tried helping out your war effort, then maybe we could get a pardon and permission to stay in the country, but I know your Elector probably isn't our biggest—"

"What is all this?"

All of us turn around at the voice, right as the soldiers in the room snap into salutes. I get up from my crouch to see Anden standing in the doorway with a group of bodyguards behind him, his eyes dark and ominous, his stare fixed first on June and me and then on the Patriots. Even though it hasn't been that long since we left him behind to talk with his generals, he has a fine layer of dust on the shoulders of his uniform, and his face looks bleak. The captain who'd been talking to us earlier now clears his throat nervously. "My apologies, Elector," he begins, "but we detained these criminals near the Armor—"

At that, June crosses her arms. "Then I'm guessing you *weren't* the one who approved this, Elector?" she says to Anden. There's an edge to her voice that tells me she and Anden aren't on the best of terms right now.

Anden regards the scene. Our argument from the car ride over is probably still stewing in his mind, but he doesn't bother looking in my direction. Well, good. Maybe I've given him something to think about. Finally, he nods at the captain. "Who are they?"

"Former Patriots, sir."

"I see. Who ordered this?"

The captain turns bright red. "Well, Elector," he replies, trying to sound official, "my commanding officer—"

But Anden has already turned his attention away from the lying captain and starts to leave the room. "Take those shackles off them," he says without turning back around. "Keep them in here for now, and then evacuate them with the final group. Watch them carefully." He motions for us to follow him. "Ms. Iparis. Mr. Wing. If you please."

I look back one more time at Tess, who's watching the soldiers unclip the shackles from her wrists. Then I head out with June. Eden rushes over to me, nearly colliding with me in his hurry, and I take his hand back in mine.

Anden stops us before a group of Republic soldiers. I frown at the sight. Four of the soldiers are kneeling on the ground with their hands on their heads. Their eyes stay downcast. One weeps silently.

The remaining soldiers in the group have their guns pointed at the kneeling soldiers. The soldier in charge addresses Anden. "These are the guards who were in charge of Commander Jameson and Captain Bryant. We found a suspicious communication between one of them and the Colonies."

No wonder he brought us out here, to see the faces of our potential traitors. I look back at the captured guards. The crying one looks up at Anden with pleading eyes. "Please, Elector," he begs. "I had nothing to do with their escape. I—I don't know how it happened. I—" His words cut off as a gun barrel cuffs him in the head.

Anden's face, normally thoughtful and reserved, has turned ice-cold. I look from the kneeling soldiers back to him. He's silent for a moment. Then he nods at his men. "Interrogate them. If they don't cooperate, shoot them. Spread the word to the rest of the troops. Let it be a lesson to any other traitors within our ranks. Let them know we *will* root them out."

The soldiers with the guns click their heels. "Yes, sir." They haul the accused traitors to their feet. A sick feeling hits my stomach. But Anden doesn't take back his words—instead, he looks on as the soldiers are dragged, shouting and pleading, out of the bunker. June looks stricken. Her eyes follow the prisoners.

Anden turns on us with a grave expression. "The Colonies have help."

A dull thud echoes from somewhere above us, and the ground and ceiling tremble in response. June peers closer at Anden, as if analyzing him. "What kind of help?"

"I saw their squadrons in the air, right beyond the Armor. They're not all Colonies jets. Some of them have African stars painted on their sides. My generals tell me that the Colonies are confident enough to have parked an airship and a squadron of jets less than a half mile from our Armor, setting up makeshift airfields as they go. They are ramping up for another assault."

My hand tightens around Eden's. He squints at the swarms of evacuees crowded near the subway, but he probably can't see anything more than a mass of moving blurs. I wish I could take that frightened look off his face. "How long is Denver gonna hold?" I ask.

"I don't know," Anden replies grimly. "The Armor is strong, but we can't fight a superpower for long."

"So what do we do now?" June says. "If we can't hold them off alone, then are we just going to lose this war?"

Anden shakes his head. "We need help too. I'm going to get us an audience with the United Nations or with Antarctica, see whether they're willing to step up to the plate. They might buy us enough time for . . ." He glances at my brother, quiet and calm beside me. A stab of guilt and rage hits me. I narrow my eyes at Anden—my hand clamps tighter on my brother's arm. Eden shouldn't have to be in the middle of this. I shouldn't have to choose between losing my brother and losing this damn country.

"Hopefully it won't come to that," I say.

As he and June launch into an in-depth conversation about Antarctica, I look back at the room where Tess and the Patriots are being held. Through the window, I can see Tess tending carefully to the girl with the bleeding shoulder while the soldiers look on with uneasy expressions. Don't know why all those trained killers should be scared of a little girl armed with a handful of bandages and rubbing alcohol. I shiver as I think of the way Anden ordered those accused soldiers out of the bunker and killed. Pascao looks frustrated, and for a moment, he meets my stare through the glass. Even though he doesn't move his mouth, I can tell what he's thinking.

He knows that trapping the Patriots inside a room during the middle of a battle, while civilians and soldiers alike are getting killed aboveground, is a total goddy waste.

"Elector," I suddenly say, turning back to face Anden and June. He pauses to stare at me. "Let them out of this bunker." When Anden stays silent, compelling me to go on, I add, "They can help your effort up there. I bet they can play the guerrilla game better than any of your soldiers, and since you won't be evacuating the poor sectors for a while, you might need all the help you can get."

June doesn't say anything about my little jab, but Anden folds his arms across his chest. "Day, I pardoned the Patriots as part of our original deal—but I haven't forgotten about my difficult history with them. While I don't want to see your friends shackled like prisoners, I have no reason to believe that they'll now help a country that they have terrorized for so long."

"They're harmless," I insist. "They have no reason to fight against the Republic."

"Three death-row prisoners just escaped," Anden snaps. "The Colonies have launched a surprise attack on our capital. And now my would-be assassins are sitting a dozen yards from me. I'm not in the most forgiving mood."

"I'm trying to help you," I fire back. "You just caught your traitors, anyway, didn't you? Do you really think the Patriots had anything to do with Commander Jameson's escape? Especially when she threw them to the dogs? Do you think I *like* the idea that my mother's killers are on the loose now? Unleash the Patriots, and they'll fight for you."

Anden narrows his eyes. "What makes you think they're so loyal to the Republic?"

"Let *me* lead them," I say. Eden jerks his head up at me in surprise. "And you'll get your loyalty." June shoots me a warning glare—I take a deep breath, swallow my frustration, and will myself to calm down. She's right. No point getting angry at Anden if I need him on my side. "Please," I add in a lower voice. "Let me help. You have to trust *someone*. Don't just leave people out there to die."

Anden studies my face for a long moment, and with a chill, I realize how much he looks like his father. The similarity is only there for an instant, though—and then it vanishes, replaced by Anden's serious, concerned gaze. As if he suddenly remembers who we are. He sighs deeply and tightens his lips. "Let me know what your plan is," he finally says. "And we'll see. In the meantime, I suggest you get your brother on a subway." When he sees my expression, he adds, "He'll be safe until you join him. You have my word."

Then he turns away and motions for June to accompany him. I let my breath out as I watch a soldier lead him and June toward a cluster of generals. June looks over her shoulder at me as they go. I know she's thinking the same thing I am. She's worried about what this war is doing to Anden. What it's doing to all of us.

Lucy interrupts my thoughts. "Perhaps we should get your brother on the evacuation train," she says. She gives me a sympathetic look.

"Right." I look down at Eden and pat his shoulder. I try my best to have faith in the Elector's promise. "Let's head over to the train and get the details on how to get you out of here."

"What about you?" Eden asks. "Are you really going to lead some kind of assault?"

"I'll meet up with you in Los Angeles. I swear."

Eden doesn't make a sound as we make our way over to the train platform and let the soldiers escort us toward the front. His expression has grown serious and sullen. When we're finally in front of the train's closed glass door, I bend to his eye level. "Look—I'm sorry I'm not going with you right away. I need to stay here and help, yeah? Lucy's got you. She'll keep you safe. I'll join up with you soon—"

"Yeah, fine," Eden grumbles.

"Oh." I clear my throat. Eden is sickly and tech-minded and occasionally obnoxious, but he's rarely angry like this. Even after his blindness, he's stayed optimistic. So his bluntness throws me off. "Well, that's good," I decide to respond. "I'm glad you're—"

"You're hiding something from me, Daniel," he interrupts. "I can tell. What is it?"

I pause. "No, I'm not."

"You're a terrible liar." Eden pulls himself out of my grasp and frowns. "Something's up. I could hear it in the Elector's voice, and then you said that weird thing to me the other day, about how you were afraid the Republic's soldiers would come knocking on our door . . . Why would they do that all of a sudden? I thought everything was fine now."

I sigh and bow my head. Eden's eyes soften a little, but his jaw stays firm. "What is it?" he repeats.

He's eleven years old. He deserves to know the truth.

"The Republic wants you back for experimentation," I reply, keeping my voice low so that only he can hear me. "There's a virus spreading in the Colonies. They think you have the antidote in your blood. They want to take you to the labs."

Eden stares in my direction for a long, silent moment. Above us, another dull thud shakes the earth. I wonder how well the Armor's holding up. Seconds drag by. Finally, I put a hand on his arm. "I won't let them take you away," I say, trying to reassure him. "Okay? You're going to be fine. Anden—the Elector—knows that he can't take you away without risking a revolution among the people. He can't do it without my permission."

"All those people in the Colonies are going to die, aren't they?" Eden mutters under his breath. "The ones with the virus?"

I hesitate. I never asked much about exactly what the plague's symptoms were—I stopped listening the instant they mentioned my brother. "I don't know," I confess.

"And then they're going to spread it to the Republic." Eden turns his head down and wrings his hands together. "Maybe they're spreading it right now. If they take over the capital, the disease will spread. Won't it?"

"I don't know," I repeat.

Eden's eyes search my face. Even though he's nearly blind, I can see the unhappiness in them. "You don't have to make all my decisions, you know."

"I didn't think I *was*. Don't you want to evacuate to LA? It's safer there, and I told you—I'll catch up with you there. I promise."

"No, not that. Why'd you decide to keep this a secret?"

*This* is why he's upset? "You're kidding, right?"

"Why?" Eden presses.

"You would've *agreed*?" I move closer to him, then glance around at the soldiers and evacuees and lower my voice. "I know I declared my support for Anden, but that doesn't mean I've forgotten what the Republic did to our family. To *you*. When I watched you get sick, when the plague patrols came to our door and dragged you out on that gurney, with blood blackening your eyes . . ." I pause, close my eyes, and shut the scene out. I've played it in my head a million times; no need to revisit it again. The memory makes the pain flare up at the back of my head.

"Don't you think I know that?" Eden fires back in a low, defiant voice. "You're my brother, not our mom."

I narrow my eyes. "I am now."

"No, you're not. Mom's dead." Eden takes a deep breath. "I remember what the Republic did to us. Of course I do. But the Colonies are invading. I want to help."

I can't believe Eden's telling me this. He doesn't understand the lengths the Republic will go to—has he really forgotten their experiments? I lean forward and put my hand on his tiny wrist. "It could kill you. Do you realize that? And they might not even find a cure using your blood."

Eden pulls away from me again. "It's *my* decision to make. Not yours."

His words echo June's from earlier. "Fine," I snap. "Then what's your decision, kid?"

He steels himself. "Maybe I want to help."

"You've gotta be kidding me. You want to help them out? Are you just doing that to go against what I'm saying?"

"I'm serious."

A lump rises in my throat. "Eden," I begin, "we've lost Mom and John. Dad is gone. You're all I have left. I can't afford to lose you too. Everything I've done so far, I've done for you. I'm not letting you risk your life to save the Republic—or the Colonies."

The defiance fades from Eden's eyes. He props his arms up

on the railing and leans his head against his hands. "If there's one thing I know about you," he says, "it's that you're not selfish."

I pause. Selfish. I *am* selfish—I want Eden to stay protected, out of harm's way, and screw whatever he thinks about that. But at his words, my guilt bubbles up. How many times had John tried to keep me out of trouble? How many times had he warned me against messing with the Republic, or trying to find a cure for Eden? I had never listened, and I don't regret it. Eden stares at me with sightless eyes, a disability the Republic handed to him. And now he's offering himself up, a sacrificial lamb to the slaughter, and I can't understand why.

No. I do understand. He is me—he's doing what I would've done.

But the thought of losing him is too much to bear. I put my hand on his shoulder and start steering him inside. "Get to LA first. We'll talk about this later. You better think this through, because if you volunteer for this—"

"I *did* think it through," Eden replies. Then he pulls out of my grasp and steps back through the balcony door. "And besides, if they came for me, do you really think we could stop them?"

And then his turn comes. Lucy helps him step onto the subway, and I hold his hand for a brief moment before he has to let go. Despite how upset he seems to be, Eden still clutches my hand hard. "Hurry up, okay?" he says to me. Without warning, he throws his arms around my neck. Beside him, Lucy gives me one of her reassuring smiles.

"Don't you worry, Daniel," she says. "I'll watch him like a hawk."

I nod gratefully at her. Then I hug Eden tight, squeeze my eyes shut, and take a deep breath. "See you soon, kid," I whisper. Then I reluctantly untangle his fingers from mine. Eden disappears onto the subway. Moments later, the train pulls away from the station and takes the first wave of evacuees toward the Republic's west coast, leaving only Eden's words behind, ringing in my mind.

*Maybe I want to help.*

I sit alone for some time after his train leaves, lost in thought, going over those words repeatedly. I'm his guardian now—I have every right to keep him from harm, and hell if I'm going to see him back in the Republic's labs after everything I've done to keep him from there. I close my eyes and bury my hands in my hair.

After a while, I make my way back to the room where the Patriots are being kept. The door's open. When I step inside, Pascao quits stretching out his arms and Tess looks up from where she's finishing the bandaging of the wounded girl's shoulder.

"So," I say to them, my eyes lingering on Tess. "You guys came back to town to give the Colonies some hell?" Tess drops her gaze.

Pascao shrugs. "Well, it won't matter if no one lets us back up there. Why? You have something in mind?"

"The Elector's given his permission," I reply. "As long as I'm in charge, he thinks we'll be good enough not to turn against the Republic." What a stupid fear, anyway. They still have my brother, don't they?

A slow smile spreads on Pascao's face. "Well. That sounds like it could be fun. What do you have in mind?"

I put my hands in my pockets and put my arrogant mask back on. "What I've always been good at."

# JUNE

51.5 HOURS SINCE MY FINAL CONVERSATION WITH THOMAS.
15 HOURS SINCE I LAST SAW DAY.
8 HOURS SINCE THE COLONIES' BOMBARDMENT OF
DENVER'S ARMOR CAME TO A LULL.

WE'RE ON THE ELECTOR'S PLANE HEADED TO ROSS
City, Antarctica.

I sit across from Anden. Ollie's lying at my feet. The other two Princeps-Elects are in an adjacent compartment, separated from us by glass (3 × 6 feet, bulletproof, Republic seal carved on the side facing me, judging from the edges of the cut). Outside the window, the sky is brilliant blue and a blanket of clouds pads the bottom of our view. Any minute now, we should feel the plane dip and see the sprawling Antarctican metropolis come into view.

I've stayed quiet for most of the trip, listening on as Anden takes a stream of endless calls from Denver about the battle. Only when we're almost over Antarctican waters does he finally fall silent. I watch how the light plays on his features, contouring the young face that holds such world-weary thoughts.

"What's the history between us and Antarctica?" I ask after a while. What I really want to say is, *Do you think they'll help us?*

but that question is just silly small talk, impossible to answer and thus pointless to ask.

Anden looks away from the window and fixes his bright green eyes on me. "Antarctica gives us aid. We've taken international aid from them for decades. Our own economy isn't strong enough to stand on its own."

It still unsettles me that the nation I once believed so powerful is in reality struggling for survival. "And what is our relationship with them now?"

Anden keeps his gaze steadily on me. I can see the tension in his eyes, but his face remains composed. "Antarctica has promised to double their aid if we can draft a treaty that can get the Colonies talking with us again. And they've threatened to halve their aid if we don't have a treaty by the end of this year." He pauses. "So we're visiting them not just to ask for help, but to try to persuade them not to withhold their aid."

We have to explain why everything has fallen apart. I swallow. "Why Antarctica?"

"They have a long rivalry with Africa," Anden replies. "If anyone with power will help us win a war against the Colonies and Africa, it'll be them." He leans forward and rests his elbows on his knees. His gloved hands are a foot away from my legs. "We'll see what happens. We owe them a lot of money, and they haven't been happy with us for the past few years."

"Has the President ever met you in person?"

"Sometimes I visited with my father," Anden replies. He offers me a crooked smile that sends unexpected flutters through my stomach. "He was a charmer during meetings. Do you think I have a chance?"

I smile back. I can sense the double meaning in his question; he's not just talking about Antarctica. "You're charismatic, if that's what you're asking," I decide to say.

Anden laughs a little. The sound warms me. He looks away and lowers his eyes. "I haven't been very successful at charming anyone lately," he murmurs.

The plane dips. I turn my attention to my window and take a deep breath, fighting down the pink rising on my cheeks.

The clouds grow nearer as we descend, and soon we are engulfed in swirling gray mist; after a few minutes we emerge from their underbelly to see a massive stretch of land covered in a dense layer of high-rises that come in a wild assortment of bright colors. I suck in my breath at the sight. One look is all I need to confirm just how much of a technological and wealth gap there is between the Republic and Antarctica. A thin, transparent dome stretches across the city, but we pass right through it as easily as we sliced through the clouds. Each building appears to have the ability to change colors on a whim (two have already shifted from a pastel green to a deep blue, and one changes from gold to white), and each building looks brand-new, polished and flawless in a way that very few Republic buildings are. Enormous, elegant bridges connect many of the towering skyscrapers, brilliantly white under the sun, each one linking one building's floor to its adjacent building and forming a honeycomb-like web of ivory.

The uppermost bridges have round platforms in their centers. When I look closer, I see what seem like aircraft parked on the platforms. (Another oddity: All of the high-rises have enormous silver holograms of numbers floating over their roofs, each ranging between zero and thirty thousand. I frown. Are they being beamed from a light at each rooftop? Perhaps they signify the population living in each skyscraper—although if that were the case, thirty thousand seems like a relatively low ceiling given the size of each building.)

Our pilot's voice rings out over the intercom to inform us of our landing. As the candy-colored buildings gradually fill our entire view, we zero in on one of the bridge platforms. Down below, I see people hurrying to prepare for our jet's landing. When we're finally hovering over the platform, an abrupt jolt jerks all of us sideways in our seats. Ollie lifts his head and growls.

"We're magnetically docked now," Anden tells me when he sees my startled expression. "From here on out, our pilot doesn't need to do a thing. The platform itself will pull us down for the landing."

We touch down so smoothly that I don't feel a thing. As we step out of the plane along with our entourage of Senators and guards, I'm shocked first by how nice the temperature is outside. A cool breeze, the warmth of the sun. Aren't we at the bottom of the earth? (Seventy-two degrees is my assumption, southwest wind, a breeze surprisingly light considering how high up from ground level we are.) Then I remember the thin, substance-less dome we passed through. It might be a way the Antarcticans control the climate in their cities.

Secondly, I'm shocked to see us immediately ushered into a plastic tent by a team of people in white biohazard suits and gas masks. (The news of the Colonies' plague must have spread here.) One of them quickly inspects my eyes, nose, mouth, and ears, and then runs a bright green light across my entire body. I wait in tense silence as the person (male or female? I can't be sure) analyzes the reading on a handheld device. From the corner of my eye, I can see Anden undergoing the same tests—being the Republic's Elector does not apparently exempt one from being possibly contaminated with plague. It takes a good ten minutes before we are all cleared for entry and led out from under the tarp.

Anden greets three Antarctican people (each dressed respectively in a green, black, or blue suit, cut in an unfamiliar style) waiting for us on the landing bridge with a few guards. "I hope your flight went well," one of them says as Mariana, Serge, and I approach. She greets us in English, but her accent is thick and lush. "If you prefer, we can send you home in one of our own jets."

The Republic is hardly perfect; that much I've known for a long time, and certainly ever since I met Day. But the Antarctican woman's words are so arrogant that I feel myself bristle. Apparently our Republic jets aren't good enough for them. I look at Anden to see what his reaction will be, but he simply bows his head and offers a beautiful smile to the woman.

"*Gracias,* Lady Medina. You are always so gracious," he replies. "I'm very grateful for your offer, but I certainly don't want to impose. We'll make do."

I can't help admiring Anden. Every day, I see new evidence of the burdens he shoulders.

After some argument, I reluctantly let one of the guards take Ollie away to the hotel quarters where I'll be staying. Then we all fall into a quiet procession as the Antarcticans lead us off the platform and along the bridge toward the connecting building (colored scarlet, although I'm not sure if it's in honor of our landing). I make a point of walking close to the bridge's edge, so that I can look down at the city. For once, it takes me a while to count the floors (based on the bridges branching out from every floor, this building has over three hundred floors—approximately three hundred twenty-seven, although eventually I look away to shake off a sense of vertigo). Sunlight bathes the uppermost floors, but the lower floors are also brightly illuminated; they must be simulating sunlight for those walking at ground level. I watch Anden and Lady Medina chat and laugh as if they are old friends. Anden falls so neatly into it that I can't tell whether he genuinely likes this woman or he is simply playing the role of an agreeable politician. Apparently our late Elector had at least trained his son well in international relations.

The building's bridge entrance, an archway framed with intricately carved swirls, slides open to greet us. We halt in a lavishly decorated lobby (thick ivory carpet that, to my fascination, bursts with swirls of color wherever I put my feet down; rows of potted palms; a curved glass wall displaying bright ads and what seem like interactive stations for things I don't understand). As we walk, the Antarcticans hand each of us a thin pair of glasses. Anden and many of the Senators immediately put them on as if they're used to this ritual, but the Antarcticans explain the glasses anyway. I wonder whether they know who I am, or whether they care. They certainly noticed my puzzlement at the glasses.

"Keep these on for the duration of your visit," Lady Medina tells us with her rich accent, although I know her words are directed at me. "They will help you see Ross City as it really is."

Intrigued, I put the glasses on.

I blink in surprise. The first thing I *feel* is a subtle tickle in my ears, and the first thing I *see* are the small, glowing numbers hovering over the heads of each of the Antarcticans. Lady Medina has *28,627: LEVEL 29*, while her two companions (who have yet to utter a sound) respectively have *8,819: LEVEL 11* and *11,201: LEVEL 13*. When I look around the lobby, I notice all sorts of virtual numbers and words—the green bulbous plant in the corner has *WATER: +1* hovering over it, while *CLEAN: +1* floats above a dark, half-circle side table. In the corner of my glasses, I see tiny, glowing words:

```
JUNE IPARIS
PRINCEPS-ELECT 3
REPUBLIC OF AMERICA
LEVEL 1
SEPT. 22. 2132
```

DAILY SCORE: 0
CUMULATIVE SCORE: 0

We've started walking again. None of the others seem particularly concerned about the onslaught of virtual text and numbers layered over the real world, so I'm left to my own intuition. (Although the Antarcticans aren't wearing glasses, their eyes occasionally flicker to virtual things in the world in a way that makes me wonder whether they have something embedded in their eyes, or perhaps in their brains, that permanently simulates all of these virtual things for them.)

One of Lady Medina's two companions, a broad-shouldered, white-haired man with very dark eyes and golden-brown skin, walks slower than the others. Eventually he reaches me near the end of the procession and falls into step beside me. I tense up at his presence. When he speaks, though, his voice is low and kind. "Miss June Iparis?"

"Yes, sir," I reply, bowing my head respectfully in the way Anden had done. To my surprise, I see the numbers in the corner of my glasses change:

SEPT. 22. 2132
DAILY SCORE: 1
CUMULATIVE SCORE: 1

My mind spins. Somehow, the glasses must have recorded my bowing action and added a point to this Antarctican scoring system, which means bowing is equal to one point. This is also when I realize something else: When the white-haired man spoke, I heard absolutely no accent—he's now speaking perfect English. I glance over to Lady Medina, and when I catch hints of what she's saying to Anden, I notice that her English now sounds impeccable too. The tickle I'd felt in my ears when I put on the glasses . . . maybe it's acting as some sort of language translation device, allowing the Antarcticans to revert to their native language while still communicating with us without missing a beat.

The white-haired man now leans over to me and whispers, "I am Guardsman Makoare, one of Lady Medina's newer bodyguards. She has assigned me to be your guide, Miss Iparis, as it seems you are a stranger to our city. It's quite different from your Republic, isn't it?"

Unlike Lady Medina, the way Guardsman Makoare speaks has no condescension in it at all, and his question doesn't rub me the wrong way. "Thank you, sir," I reply gratefully. "And, yes, I have to admit that these virtual numbers I see all over the place are strange to me. I don't quite understand it."

He smiles and scratches at the white scruff on his chin. "Life in Ross City is a game, and we are all its players. Native Antarcticans don't need glasses like you visitors do—all of us have chips embedded near our temples once we turn thirteen. It's a piece of software that assigns points to everything around us." He gestures toward the plants. "Do you see the words *Water— Plus One* hovering over that plant?" I nod. "If you decided to water that plant, for example, you would receive one point for doing so. Almost every positive action you make in Ross City will earn you achievement points, while negative actions subtract points. As you accumulate points, you gain levels. Right now, you are at Level One." He pauses to point up at the virtual number floating over his head. "I am at Level Thirteen."

"What's the point of reaching . . . levels?" I ask as we leave the hall and step into an elevator. "Does it determine your status in the city? Does it keep your civilians in line?"

Guardsman Makoare nods. "You'll see."

We step out of the elevator and head out onto another bridge (this time it's covered with an arched glass roof) that connects this building to another. As we walk, I begin to see what Guardsman Makoare is talking about. The new building we enter looks like an enormous academy, and as we peer through glass panels into classrooms lined with rows of what must be students, I notice that all of them have their own point scores and levels hovering over their heads. At the front of the room, a giant glass screen displays a series of math questions, each with a glowing point score over them.

```
CALCULUS SEMESTER 2
Q1: 6 PTS
Q2: 12 PTS
```

And so on. At one point, I see one of the students attempt to lean over and cheat from a neighbor. The point score over his head flashes red, and a second later the number decreases by five.

```
CHEATING: -5 PTS
1,642: LEVEL 3
```

The student freezes, then quickly returns to looking at his own exam.

Guardsman Makoare smiles when he sees me analyzing the situation. "Your level means everything in Ross City. The higher your level, the more money you make, the better jobs you can apply for, and the more respected you are. Our highest scorers are widely admired and quite famous." He points toward the back of the cheating student. "As you can see, our citizens are so engrossed in this game of life that most of them know better than to do things that will decrease their scores. We have very little crime in Ross City as a result."

"Fascinating," I murmur, my eyes still glued to the classroom even as we reach the end of the hallway and head out onto another bridge. After a while, a new message pops up in the corner of my glasses.

```
WALKED 1,000 METERS: +2 PTS
DAILY SCORE: 3
CUMULATIVE SCORE: 3
```

To my surprise, seeing the numbers go up gives me a brief thrill of accomplishment. I turn to Guardsman Makoare. "I can understand how this leveling system is good motivation for your citizens. Brilliant." I don't say my next thought aloud, but secretly I wonder, *How do they distinguish between good and bad actions?* Who decides that? What happens when someone speaks out against the government? Does her score go up or down? I marvel at the technology available here—it really makes clear, for the first time, exactly how far behind the Republic is. Have things always been so unequal? Were we ever the leaders?

We eventually settle inside a building with a large, semicircular chamber used for political meetings ("The Discussion Room," Lady Medina calls it). It's lined with flags from countries around the world. In the chamber's center is a long, mahogany wood table, and now the Antarctican delegates sit on one side while we sit on the other. Two more delegates who are at similar levels as Lady Medina join us as we begin our talks, but it's a third delegate who catches my attention. He's in his midforties, with bronze hair and dark skin and a well-trimmed beard. The text hovering over his head reads *LEVEL 202*.

"President Ikari," Lady Medina says as she introduces him to us. Anden and the other Senators bow their heads respectfully. I do the same. Although I don't dare turn my eyes away from the discussion, I can see the Republic's flag in my peripheral vision. With my glasses I see the virtual text *THE REPUBLIC OF AMERICA* above it in glowing letters. Right next to it is the Colonies flag, with its black and gray stripes and the bright gold bird in its center.

Some of the other countries' flags have the word *Ally* hovering under their names. But we don't.

From the beginning, our discussion is tense.

"It seems like your father's plans have backfired against you," the President tells Anden. He leans stiffly forward. "The United Nations is, of course, concerned that Africa has already given aid to the Colonies. The Colonies declined an invitation to talk with us."

Anden sighs. "Our scientists are hard at work on a cure," he continues. I notice he doesn't mention Day's brother in all this, and Day's lack of cooperation. "But the Colonies' forces are overwhelming with Africa's money and military supporting them. We need help to push them back, or we risk being over-run within the month. The virus could spread to us as well—"

"You speak with passion," the President interrupts. "And I have no doubt that you're doing great things as the Republic's new leader. But a situation like this . . . The virus must first be contained. And I've heard the Colonies have already breached your borders."

The President's honey-gold eyes are piercingly bright. When Serge tries to speak up, he silences him immediately, never taking his eyes off Anden. "Let your Elector respond," he says. Serge falls back into sullen silence, but not before I catch a smug look pass between the Senators. My temper rises. They—the Senator, the Antarctican President, even Anden's own Princeps-Elect—are all taunting Anden in their own subtle ways. Interrupting him. Emphasizing his age. I look at Anden, quietly willing him to stand up for himself. Mariana nods once at him.

"Sir?" she says.

I'm relieved when Anden first shoots a disapproving look at Serge, then lifts his chin and calmly replies. "Yes. We've managed to hold them off for now, but they are right at the outskirts of our capital."

The President leans forward and rests his elbows on the table. "So, there's a possibility that this virus has already crossed into your territory?"

"Yes," Anden replies.

The President is silent for a moment. Finally, he says, "What exactly do you want?"

"We need military support," Anden replies. "Your army is the best in the world. Help us secure our borders. But most of all, help us find a cure. They've warned us that a cure is the only way they'll retreat. And we need time to make that happen."

The President tightens his lips and shakes his head once. "No military support, money, or supplies. I'm afraid you're far too indebted to us for that. I *can* offer my scientists to help you find a cure for the disease. But I will *not* send my troops into an area infected with disease. It's too dangerous." When he sees the look on Anden's face, his eyes harden. "Please keep us updated, as I hope as much as you do to see a resolution for this. I apologize that we can't be of more help to you, Elector."

Anden leans on the table and laces his fingers together. "What can I do to persuade you to help us, Mr. President?" he says.

The President sits back in his chair and regards Anden for a moment with a thoughtful look. It chills me. He's been waiting for Anden to say this. "You're going to have to offer me something worth my while," he finally says. "Something your father never offered."

"And what's that?"

"Land."

My heart twists painfully at those words. Giving up land. In order to save our country, we'll have to sell ourselves to another nation. Something about it feels as violating as selling our own bodies. Giving up your own child to a stranger. Tearing away a piece of our home. I look at Anden, trying to decipher the emotions behind his composed exterior.

Anden stares at him for a long moment. Is he thinking about what his father would say in a situation like this? Is he wondering whether he's as good a leader to his people? Finally, Anden bows his head. Graceful, even in humility. "I'm open to discussion," he says quietly.

The President nods once. I can see the small smile at the corners of his lips. "Then we'll discuss," he replies. "If you find a cure to this virus, and if we agree to the land, then I promise you military support. Until then, the world will have to deal with this as we do with any pandemic."

"And what do you mean by that, sir?" Anden asks.

"We will need to seal your ports and borders, as well as the Colonies'. Other nations will need to be notified. I'm sure you understand."

Anden's silent. I hope the President doesn't see the stricken look on my face. The entire Republic is going to be quarantined.

# DAY

JUNE'S LEFT FOR ANTARCTICA. EDEN'S GONE TO LOS ANGELES
with the second wave of evacuees. The rest of us stay down
in this bunker, listening as the Colonies' assault continues.
This time the fighting sounds worse. Sometimes the earth
trembles so much that fine dust rains down on us from the
underground bunker's ceiling, coating lines of evacuees
with gray ash as they hurry onto the waiting trains. Rotat-
ing lights over the tunnel paint us all in flashes of red. I
wonder how other bunkers across the city are holding up.
The evacuations grow more urgent as each train leaves on
the hour and is replaced by a new one. Who knows how long
this tunnel will stay stable. Now and then I see soldiers
shoving civilians back into line when they get unruly. "Single file!" they bark out, hoisting their guns threateningly.
Their faces are hidden behind riot masks that I know all
too damn well. "Dissidents will be left behind, no questions
asked. Move along, people!"

I stay at one end of the bunker as the dust continues to
rain down, huddled with Pascao, Tess, and the other remaining Patriots. At first a few soldiers tried to hustle me onto
one of the trains, but they left me alone after I lashed
out at them with a string of curses. Now they ignore me. I
watch people load onto the train for a few seconds before
I return to my conversation with Pascao. Tess sits beside

me, although the unspoken tension between us makes her feel much farther away. My ever-present headache pounds a dull rhythm against the back of my head.

"You saw more of the city than I did," I whisper to Pascao. "How do you think the Armor is holding up?"

"Not great," Pascao responds. "In fact, with another country helping the Colonies, I wouldn't be surprised if the Armor breaks down in a matter of days with this kind of assault. It's not gonna hold for long, trust me."

I turn to see how many people are still waiting to board the trains. "How should we go about throwing the Colonies some curve balls?"

Another voice pipes up. It's one of the Hackers, Frankie, the girl with the wounded shoulder. "If we can get our hands on a few electrobombs," she says in a thoughtful voice, "I can probably rewire them to scramble some of the Colonies' weapons or something. We might be able to throw their jets off too."

Jets. That's right—Anden had mentioned the Colonies jets parked on a makeshift airfield outside the Armor's walls. "I can get my hands on some," I whisper. "And some grenades too."

Pascao clicks his tongue in excitement. "So we get to have fun with nitroglycerine in your plan? You get on that, then." He turns to address Baxter, who shoots me a cranky glare. His ear looks as mangled as ever. "Hey, Baxter boy. Back up Gioro and Frankie, make sure you give them cover while they're working their magic."

"Pascao," I say quietly. "You up for some decoy work?"

He laughs. "It's what Runners are best at, yeah?"

"Let's play with them a little—I want you to be my double while I'm heading toward their makeshift airfield."

"Sounds promising."

"Good." Despite the grimness of the situation, I smile. A note of haughtiness creeps into my voice. "This night'll end with a bunch of expensive, useless military machines."

"You're out of your mind, blinder boy," Baxter snaps at me. "The Republic itself can't even keep the Colonies out— you think *our* little group stands a chance at beating them?"

"We don't need to beat them. All *we* need to do is stall them. And I'm pretty sure we're good at that."

Baxter lets out a loud snort of irritation—but Pascao's grin grows wider. Next to me, Tess shifts uncomfortably. She's probably thinking back on my past crimes, how she'd had to witness them all and how she'd had to bandage me up after every single one. Maybe she's worried about me. Or maybe she's glad. Maybe she'd rather me not be here at all. But she had come back here because of me. That's what she said, isn't it? She must still care, at least on some level. I try to think of the right thing to say to her to fill this awkward silence, but instead I question the others. "You told me back in the room that you guys came back here because you wanted to be pardoned. But you could've tried escaping to a country other than the Republic, yeah? You wouldn't even have to help the Republic out. Anden—the Elector, that is—he would've pardoned you all anyway." My eyes fall on Pascao.

"You knew that, didn't you? Why'd you all really come back here? I know it's not just because you heard *my* plea."

Pascao's grin fades, and for a moment he actually looks serious. He sighs, then gazes around at our little group. It's hard to believe they used to be a part of something so much larger. "We're the Patriots, right?" he finally says. "We're supposed to be committed to seeing the United States return in some way or other. With the way things seem to be in the Colonies, I don't know if they'd be the right ones to bring that kinda change about. But I gotta admit, the new Republic Elector has potential, and after what Razor pulled on us, even *I* think Anden might be the answer we've been waiting for." Pascao pauses to nod at Baxter, who just shrugs. "Even Baxter boy here thinks so."

I frown. "So you guys came back here because you genuinely want to help the Republic win this war? You seriously want to help us defend ourselves?" Pascao nods again. "Why didn't you say that back in the room? Would've sounded pretty noble."

"No, it wouldn't." Pascao shakes his head. "They wouldn't have believed us. The Patriots, the terrorists who used to blow up Republic soldiers every chance they got? Yeah, right. I figured it'd be better for us if we played the pardon card instead. It'd seem like a more realistic answer for your Elector and your little Princeps-Elect."

I stay silent. When Pascao sees me hesitate, he dusts off his hands and stands up. "Let's get started," he says to me. "No time to waste, not with this hailstorm happening upstairs." He motions for the other Patriots to gather around and starts divvying up their individual tasks. I rise to a crouch.

Tess takes a deep breath, and when she catches my gaze again, she speaks to me for the first time since being in the room together. "I'm sorry, Day." She says it softly, so that the others can't hear.

I freeze where I am, resting my elbows on my crouched legs. "Why?" I reply. "You don't have anything to be sorry for."

"Yes, I do." Tess looks away. How did she grow up so quickly? She's still thin, still delicate, but her eyes belong to someone older than I remember. "I didn't mean to leave you behind, and I didn't mean to blame June for everything. I don't really believe she's bad. I *never* really believed that. I was just so . . . angry."

Her face pulls me to her like it always does, the way it did all the way back when I first saw her digging around in that dumpster. I wish I could hug her, but I sit back and wait, letting her make the call. "Tess . . . ," I say slowly, trying to figure out the best way to express what I'm feeling. Hell, I've said so many stupid things to her in the past. "I love you. No matter what happens between us."

Tess wraps her arms around her knees. "I know."

I swallow hard and look down. "But I don't love you the way you want me to. I'm sorry if I ever gave you the wrong impression. I don't think I've ever treated you as well as you deserve." My heart twists painfully as the words leave my mouth, striking her as they go. "So don't be sorry. It's my fault, not yours."

Tess shakes her head. "I know you don't love me that way. Don't you think I know that by now?" A note of bitterness enters her voice. "But you *don't* know how I feel about you. No one does."

I give her a level look. "Tell me, then."

"Day, you mean more to me than some *crush*." Her brows furrow as she tries to explain herself. "When the entire world turned its back on me and left me to die, *you* took me in. You were the one person who cared about what might happen to me. You were everything. *Everything*. You became my entire family—you were my parents and my siblings and my caretaker, my only friend and companion, you were both my protector and someone who needed protecting. You see? I didn't love you in the way you might've thought I did, although I can't deny that was part of it. But the way I feel goes beyond that."

I open my mouth to reply, but nothing comes out. I don't know what to say. All I can do is *see*.

Tess lets out a shaky breath. "So when I thought June might take you away, I didn't know what to do. I felt like she was taking everything that mattered to me. I felt like she was taking away from *you* all the things that I didn't have." She lowers her eyes. "That's why I'm sorry. I'm sorry because you shouldn't *have* to be everything to me. I had you, but I'd forgotten that I had myself too." She pauses to look over at the Patriots, who are deep in conversation. "It's a new feeling, something I'm still getting used to."

And just like that, we're both kids again. I see the younger us, dangling our feet over the edge of some broken high-rise, watching the sun dip every evening below the ocean's horizon. How much we've seen since then, how far we've come.

I reach over to tap her nose once, just like how I always have. She smiles for the first time.

The night has transitioned into the early hour before dawn, and the drizzle and slush has finally paused, leaving the city glistening under the moonlight. The evacuation alarm still echoes every now and then, and the JumboTrons continue their ominous red warning to seek cover, but a brief lull has hit the battle and the skies aren't full of jets and explosions. Guess both sides have to rest up or something. I rub the weariness from my eyes and try to ignore my headache—*I could use some rest.*

"It's not gonna be easy, you know," Pascao whispers to me as we both survey the morning. "They're probably on the lookout for Republic soldiers." We're perched on top of the Armor, watching the field just beyond the city's boundaries. It's not like people don't live outside the Armor, but unlike LA, which is just one large spread of buildings that melts right into its neighboring cities, Denver's population is sparser outside the safety of its walls. Small clusters of buildings sit here and there. They seem empty, and I wonder if the Republic saw the Colonies approaching from a distance and evacuated their people inside the Armor. Although the Colonies' airships have returned back to their own land in order to refuel, they've left a bunch of jets in the fields, and the areas they've occupied are well lit with floodlights. I'm kind of shocked by how repulsed I am at the thought of the Colonies taking us over. A year ago, I would be cheering at the top of my goddy lungs for this exact scenario. But now I just hear the Colonies' slogan over and over in my head. *A free state is a corporate state.* The ads I remember from their cities make me shiver.

It's hard to decide which I prefer, really: watch my brother grow up under the Colonies' rule, or watch him taken back for experimentation by the Republic?

"Yeah, they'll be on the lookout," I agree. Then I turn away from the Armor's edge and start making my way down the wall. Along the Armor's outer edge, Republic jets lie parked, manned, and ready. "But we're not Republic soldiers. If they can hit us with a surprise attack, then so can we."

Pascao and I are dressed exactly alike, in black from head to toe, with masks pulled over our faces. If it weren't for a little height difference, I don't think anyone would be able to tell us apart.

"You two ready?" Pascao mutters into his mike to our Hackers. Then he glances at me and gives a thumbs-up signal. If they're in place, then that means Tess is in place too. *Stay safe.*

We make our way down to the ground and then let

several Republic soldiers guide us around to a small, discreet underground passage. It leads outside the Armor and into dangerous territory. The soldiers nod a silent "good luck" to us before retreating back inside. I hope to hell this all works.

I look out at the field where Colonies jets are parked. When I first turned fifteen, I had set fire to a series of ten brand-new F-472 Republic fighter jets parked at the Burbank air force base in Los Angeles. It was the first stunt that landed me at the top of the most wanted list, and one of the crimes June herself actually made me confess to when I'd been arrested. I did it by first stealing gallons of highly explosive blue nitroglide from air force bases, then pouring the liquid into the jets' exhaust nozzles and across the tail end of the jets. The instant their engines turned on, their tails exploded into flames.

The memory comes back to me in sharp focus. The design of the Colonies jets looks different, with their strange, forward-swept wings, but at the end of the day they're still just machines. And this time, I'm not working alone. I've got the Republic's support. Most importantly, I've got their explosives.

"Ready to make your move?" I whisper to Pascao. "Got your bombs?"

"You think *I'd* forget to bring bombs? You should know me better than that." Pascao's voice turns taunting. "Day—no bull this time. Got it, pretty boy? If you suddenly think you wanna go rogue, you sure as hell better tell me first. Then at least I'll have time to sock you in the face."

I smile a little at the jab. "Yes, sir."

Our outfits blend us into the shadows. We creep forward without a sound, until we're past the short distance where the Armor's guns could protect us from the ground. Now we're out of range, and the Colonies' makeshift airfield looks within reach. Their soldiers stand guard along the edges of the field. Not far away are a couple rows of tanks. Their airships might not be here, but there sure as hell are enough war machines to start up another battle.

Pascao and I crouch behind a pile of rubble near the airfield. All I can see in this light is his silhouette. He nods his head once before whispering something into his mike.

We wait for a few tense seconds. Then the JumboTrons that line the outer edges of the Armor light up in unison. Displayed across the screens is a Republic flag, and over the city's loudspeakers, the pledge blares out across the night. The whole thing looks exactly like one of the Republic's typical propaganda reels—the JumboTrons start displaying generic videos of patriotic soldiers and civilians, war victories and prosperous streets. At the airfield, the soldiers' attention shifts to the JumboTrons' feed. At first they look alert and wary, but as the reel continues for a few seconds longer, the Colonies soldiers relax.

Good. They think the Republic's just broadcasting morale-boosting video. Nothing weird enough to put the Colonies on high alert, but something entertaining enough to hold their interest. I pick out an area where the soldiers are all watching the JumboTrons, then nod at Pascao. He motions at me. My turn to head out.

I squint harder to see where I can squeeze onto the airfield. There are four Colonies soldiers here, all of them focused on the broadcast; a soldier dressed like a pilot is the farthest away and has his back to me, and from here it looks like he's making fun of the broadcast with a pal of his. I wait until all of the guards are looking away from where I am. Then I scamper over the edge without a sound and hide behind the closest jet's back landing wheel. I tuck myself into a tight ball, letting my black outfit blend me in with the shadows.

One of the guards looks casually over his shoulder toward the jet. When he doesn't see anything interesting, though, he returns to surveying the Armor.

I wait for a few more seconds. Then I adjust my backpack and climb up inside the jet's exhaust nozzle. My heart pounds with anticipation at the déjà vu this gives me. I waste no time now—I pull a small metal cube out of my pack and attach it firmly to the inside of the nozzle. Its display panel gives off a very faint red glow, so dim I can barely see it. I make sure it's secure, and then shift to the edge of the nozzle. We won't have much longer before the guards lose interest in our little propaganda distraction. When the coast's clear, I hop out of the nozzle. My cushioned boots land without a sound. I melt back into the shadows cast by the jet's landing gear, watch for guards, and move to the next row of jets. Pascao should be doing the exact same work on the other side of the field. If this all goes down as planned, then one explosive per row should do plenty of damage.

By the time I make my way to the third row of jets and finish my work there, I'm soaked in sweat. Off in the distance, the JumboTrons' propaganda keeps running, but I can tell that some of the guards have already lost interest. Time to get out of here. I lower myself silently toward the ground again, dangle there in the shadows, and then pick the right moment to drop and rush toward the darkness.

Except it wasn't really the right moment. One of my hands slips and the metal edge of the exhaust nozzle slices my palm open. My weakened body doesn't land perfectly—I let out a grunt of pain and move too slowly into the landing gear's shadows. A guard spots me. Before I can stop him, his eyes widen and he lifts his gun at me.

He hasn't even had a chance to shout out when a shining knife comes flying out of the darkness and sinks itself in the soldier's neck. I watch for an instant, horrified. Pascao. I know it was him, saving my ass while drawing attention to himself. Already a couple of shouts have gone up on the other side of the airfield. He's pulling their focus away from me. I seize the opportunity, racing into the relative safety of the land outside the airfield.

I click my mike on and call Pascao. "Are you safe?" I whisper urgently.

"Safe as you, pretty boy," he hisses back, the sounds of heavy breathing and footsteps loud in my earpiece. "Just got out of the airfield's range. Give Frankie the okay—I gotta shake two more off my tail." He hangs up.

I contact Frankie. "We're ready," I tell her. "Let 'em go."

"You got it," Frankie answers. The JumboTrons suddenly stop their reel and go dark—the sound blasting across the city cuts short, plunging us all into an eerie silence. Colonies soldiers who'd probably been pursuing Pascao now look up at the blank JumboTrons in bewilderment, along with the others.

A few seconds of silence pass.

Then a bright, blinding explosion rips apart the center of the airfield. I steady myself. When I look back at the first line of soldiers on the street, I see them knocked off their feet and picking themselves slowly up in a daze. Sparks of electricity fill the air, jumping frantically back and forth between the jets. Soldiers farther down the street point their guns up at the buildings, firing randomly—but the ones along the front line discover that their guns no longer work. I keep running back toward the Armor.

Another explosion rocks the same area and an enormous golden haze engulfs everything in sight. Shouts of panic rise from the Colonies troops. They can't see what's happening, but I know that right now each bomb we'd planted is destroying the rows of jets, both crippling them and temporarily disabling the magnets in their guns. Some of them pull out their guns and fire randomly into the darkness, as if Republic soldiers are lying in wait. I guess they're not entirely wrong.

Right on cue, the Republic jets along the Armor take off into the sky. Their roars deafen me.

I switch my mike back to Frankie. "How are the evacuations going?"

"As smoothly as possible," she replies. "Probably two more waves of people left. Ready for your big moment?"

"Go for it," I whisper back.

The JumboTrons flare to life. This time, though, they're displaying my painted face on all of their screens. A prerecorded video we made. I smile widely for the Colonies, even as they scramble to what jets they still have, and in this instant, I feel like I'm looking into the face of a stranger, a face that's unfamiliar and terrifying behind its wide black stripe. For a moment, I can't even remember recording this video in the first place. The thought makes me scramble for the memory in a panic, until I finally recall it and breathe a sigh of relief. "My name is Day," my JumboTron video self says, "and I'm fighting for the Republic's people. If I were you, I'd be a little more careful."

Frankie cuts my feed again. Overhead, the Republic's jets scream across the sky—I see orange fireballs light up the airfield. With our stunt and half their jets gone, and the advantage of surprise, the Colonies soldiers scramble for a retreat. I bet the calls going back to their command are flying fast and furious now.

Frankie comes back online. She sounds elated. "The Republic's troops have gotten wind of our success," she says. In the background, I hear—to my relief—Pascao's line click on too.

"Nice job, Runners. Gioro and Baxter are already on their way." She sounds distracted. "We're heading back in now. Gimme a few seconds, and we'll be—"

She cuts off. I blink, surprised. "Frankie?" I say, reconnecting to her. Nothing. All I hear is static.

"Where'd she go?" Pascao says through the white noise. "Did she go offline for you too?"

"Yeah." I scramble onward, trying not to think the worst. The safety of the Armor isn't far away—I can make out the tiny side entrance we're supposed to return through—and here, in the midst of all the chaos, I see several Republic soldiers rushing through the dust to face off against any Colonies troops that might have followed us. Just a few yards from the door now.

A bullet sparks past me, narrowly missing my ear. Then I hear a scream that makes my blood run cold. When I whirl around, I see Tess and Frankie running behind me. They're leaning on each other. Behind them must be five or six Colonies soldiers. I freeze, then quickly change course. I yank a knife from my belt and throw it at the soldiers as hard as I can. It catches one of them clean in the side—he drops to his knees. The others notice me. Tess and Frankie barely make it to the door. I dash toward them. Behind me, the soldiers hoist their guns.

Just as Tess pushes Frankie through the entrance, a soldier steps out of the shadows near the door. I recognize him instantly. It's *Thomas,* a gun dangling from one hand.

His eyes are fixed on Tess and me, and his expression is

dark, deadly, and furious. For an instant, the world seems to go silent. I glance at his gun. He hoists it. *No.* Instinctively, I move toward Tess, shielding her with my body. *He's going to kill us.*

But even as this thought races through my mind, Thomas turns his back on us, facing the oncoming Colonies soldiers instead. His hand quivers with rage and tightens on the gun. Shock pulses through me, but there's no time to think about that now. "Go," I urge Tess. We stumble through the side door.

In that same moment, Thomas raises his gun—he fires one shot, then another, then another. He lets out a bloodcurdling yell as each bullet hurtles toward the enemy troops. It takes me a second to make out what he's screaming.

"Long live the Elector! Long live the Republic!"

He manages six shots before the Colonies soldiers return fire. I hug Tess to my chest, then cover her eyes. She lets out a cry of protest. "Don't look," I whisper in her ear. At that very moment, I see Thomas's head snap violently back and his entire body go limp. An image of my mother flashes before my eyes.

Shot through the head. He's been shot through the head. *Death by firing squad.*

The blast makes Tess jump—she utters a strangled sob behind my shielding hands. The door swings shut.

Pascao greets us the instant we're safely through. He's covered head to toe in dust, but he still has a half grin on his face. "The final evacuation wave is waiting for us," he says, nodding toward two parked jeeps ready to take us back to the bunker. Republic soldiers have already started toward us, but before any of us can feel relieved, I notice that Frankie has collapsed to the ground and Tess is hovering over her. Pascao's half grin vanishes. As soldiers seal off the side entrance, we gather around Frankie. Tess pulls out a kit of supplies. Frankie has started to convulse.

Her coat's stripped completely off, revealing a blood-soaked shirt beneath. Her eyes are open wide in shock, and she's struggling to breathe.

"She was shot as we were getting away," Tess says as she tears away the cloth of Frankie's shirt. Sweat beads along her brow. "Three or four times." Her trembling hands fly across Frankie's body, scattering powder and pressing ointment into the wounds. When she's done, she yanks out a thick wad of bandages.

"She's not gonna make it," Pascao mutters to Tess as she pushes him out of the way and pushes firmly down on one of Frankie's gushing wounds. "We have to move. Now."

Tess wipes her brow. "Just give me another minute," she insists through gritted teeth. "We have to control the bleeding."

Pascao starts to protest, but I silence him with a dangerous look. "Let her do it." Then I kneel beside Tess, my eyes helplessly drawn to Frankie's pitiful figure. I can tell that she's not going to make it. "I'll do whatever you say," I murmur to Tess. "Let us help."

"Keep pressure on her wounds," Tess replies, waving a hand at the bandages that are already more red than white. She rushes to make a poultice.

Frankie's eyelids flutter. She chokes out a strangled cry, then manages to look up at us. "You've—got—to go. The Colonies—they're—coming—"

It takes a whole minute for her to die. Tess keeps applying meds for a while longer, until I finally put a hand over hers to stop her. I look up at Pascao. One of the Republic soldiers approaches us again and gives us a stern frown. "This is your final warning," he says, gesturing toward the open doors of two jeeps. "We're heading out."

"Go," I tell Pascao. "We'll take the jeep right behind you."

Pascao hesitates for a second, stricken at the sight of Frankie, but then hops to his feet and disappears into the first jeep. It tears away, leaving a cloud of dust in its wake.

"Come on," I urge Tess, who stays hunched over Frankie's lifeless body. On the other side of the Armor, the sounds of battle rage. "We have to go."

Tess wrenches free of my grasp and flings her roll of bandages hard at the wall. Then she turns to look back at Frankie's ashen face. I stand up, forcing Tess to do the same. My bloody hand leaves prints on her arm. Soldiers grab both of us and lead us toward the remaining jeep. As we finally make our way inside, Tess turns her eyes up to mine. They're brimming with tears, and the sight of her anguish breaks my heart. We pull away from the Armor as soldiers load Frankie onto a truck. Then we turn a corner and speed toward the bunker.

By the time we arrive, Pascao's jeep has already unloaded and they've headed down to the train. The soldiers are tense. As they clear us past the bunker entrance's chain-link fence, another explosion from the Armor sends tremors through the ground. As if in a dream, we rush down the metal staircase and through the corridors flooded with dim red lights, the sound of pounding boots echoing dully from outside. Farther and farther down we go, until we finally reach the bunker and make our way onto the waiting train. Soldiers pull us on board.

As the subway flares to life and we pull away from the bunker, a series of explosions reverberate through the space, nearly knocking us off our feet. Tess clings to me. As I hold her close, the tunnel behind us collapses, encasing us in darkness. We speed along. Echoes of the explosions ring through the earth.

My headache flares up.

Pascao tries to say something to me, but I can no longer hear him. I can't hear anything. The world around me dulls into grays, and I feel myself spinning. *Where are we again?* Somewhere, Tess screams out my name—but I don't know what she says after that, because I lose myself in an ocean of pain and collapse into blackness.

# JUNE

ALL OF US HAVE SETTLED INTO OUR INDIVIDUAL HOTEL
rooms. Ollie's resting at the foot of my bed, completely
knocked out after an exhausting day. I can't imagine falling
asleep, though. After a while, I get up quietly, leave three treats
for Ollie near the door, and step out. I wander the halls with
my virtual glasses tucked into my pocket, relieved to see the
world as it really is again without the onslaught of hovering
numbers and words. I don't know where I'm going, but eventually I end up two floors higher and not far from Anden's room.
It's quieter up here. Anden might be the only one staying on
this floor, along with a few guards.

As I go, I pass a door that leads into a large chamber that
must be some public, central room on this floor. I turn back and
peer inside. The place looks whitewashed, probably because I
don't have my virtual glasses on and can't see all the simulations;
the room is partitioned into a series of tall cylinder-like booths,
each one a circle of tall, transparent slabs of glass. Interesting. I
have one of those cylinder booths in a corner of my hotel room,
although I haven't bothered trying it yet. I look around the hall,
then push gingerly on the door. It slides open without a sound.

I step inside and as soon as the door slides shut behind me, the room declares something in Antarctican that I can't understand. I take my virtual glasses out of my pocket and put them on. Automatically, the room's voice brightens and repeats her phrase, this time in English. "Welcome to the simulation room, June Iparis." I see my virtual score go up by ten points, congratulating me for using a simulation room for the very first time. Just as I suspected, the room now looks bright and full of colors, and the glass walls of the cylindrical rooms have all sorts of moving displays on them.

*Your access to the portal away from home!* one panel says. *Use in conjunction with your virtual glasses for a fully immersive experience.* Behind the text is a lush video depicting what look like beautiful scenes from around the world. I wonder whether their portal is their way of connecting to the Internet. Suddenly, my interest piques. I've never browsed the Internet outside of the Republic, never seen the world for what it was without the Republic's masks and filters. I approach one of the glass cylinder booths and step inside. The glass around me lights up.

"Hello, June," it says. "What can I find for you?"

What should I look up? I decide to try out the first thing that pops into my head. I hesitantly reply, wondering whether it'll just read my voice. "Daniel Altan Wing," I say. How much does the rest of the world know about Day?

Suddenly everything around me vanishes. Instead, I'm standing in a white circle with hundreds—thousands—of hovering rectangular screens all around me, each one covered with images and videos and text. At first I don't know what to do, so I just stay where I am, staring in wonder at the images all around me. Each screen has different info on Day. Many of them are news articles. The one closest to me is playing an old video of Day standing on top of the Capitol Tower balcony, rousing the people to support Anden. When I look at it long enough (three seconds), a voice starts talking. "In this video, Daniel Altan Wing—also known as Day— gives his support to the Republic's new Elector and prevents a national uprising. Source: The Republic of America's public archives. See whole article?"

My eyes flicker to another screen, and the voice from the first screen fades. This second screen comes to life as I look on, playing a video interviewing some girl I don't know, with light brown skin and pale hazel eyes. She sports a scarlet streak in her hair. She says, "I've lived in Nairobi for the past five years, but we'd never heard of him until videos of his strikes against the R-oh-A started popping up online. Now I belong to a club—" The video pauses there, and the same soothing voice from earlier says, "Source: Kenya Broadcasting Corporation. See whole video?"

I take a careful step forward. Each time I move, the rectangular screens rearrange around me to showcase the next circle of images for me to peruse. Images of Day pop up from when he and I were still working for the Patriots—I see one blurry image of Day looking over his shoulder, a smirk on his lips. It makes me blush, so I quickly glance away. I look through two more rounds of them, then decide to change my search. This time I search for something I've always been curious about. "The United States of America," I say.

The screens with videos and images of Day vanish, leaving me strangely disappointed. A new set of screens flip up around me, and I can almost feel a slight breeze as they shift into place. The first thing that pops up is an image that I instantly recognize as the full flag that the Patriots both use and base their symbol on. The voiceover says, "The flag of the former United States of America. Source: Wikiversity, the Free Academy. United States History One-oh-two, Grade Eleven. See full entry? For textual version, say 'Text.'"

"See full entry," I say. The screen zooms in toward me, engulfing me in its contents. I blink, momentarily thrown off by the rushing images. When I open my eyes again, I nearly stumble. I'm hovering in the sky over a landscape that looks both familiar and strange. The outline of it appears to be some version of North America, except there's no lake stretching from Los Angeles to San Francisco, and the Colonies' territory looks much larger than I remember. Clouds float by below my feet. When I reach a hesitant foot down, I smudge part of the clouds and can actually feel the cool air whistling beneath my shoes.

The voiceover begins. "The United States of America—also known as the USA, the United States, the US, America, and the States—was a prominent country in North America composed of fifty states held together as a federal constitutional republic. It first declared independence from England on July 4, 1776, and became recognized on September 3, 1783. The United States unofficially split into two countries on October 1, 2054 and officially became the western Republic of America and the eastern Colonies of America on March 14, 2055."

Here the voiceover pauses, then shifts. "Skip to a subtopic? Popular subtopics: the Three-Year Flood, the Flood of 2046, the Republic of America, the Colonies of America."

A series of bright blue markers appear over the west and east coasts of North America. I stare at them for a moment, my heart pounding, before I reach out and try to touch a marker near the southern coastline of the Colonies. To my surprise, I can feel the texture of the landscape under my finger. "The Colonies of America," I say.

The world rushes up at me with dizzying speed. I'm now standing on what feels like solid ground, and all around me are thousands of people huddled together in makeshift shelters in a flooded cityscape, while hundreds are launching an all-out attack against soldiers decked out in uniforms I don't recognize. Behind the soldiers are crates and sacks of what look like rations.

"Unlike the Republic of America," the voiceover starts, "where the government enforced rule through martial law in order to crack down on the influx of refugees into its borders, the Colonies of America formed on March 14, 2055 after corporations seized control of the federal government (the former United States, see higher index) following the latter's failure to handle debt accumulated from the Flood of 2046." I take a few steps forward—it's as if I'm right here in the middle of the scene, standing just a few dozen feet from where the people are rioting. My surroundings look shaky and pixilated, as if rendered from someone's personal videos. "In this civilian recording, the city of Atlanta stages a fifteen-day riot against the United States Federal Emergency Management Agency. Similar riots appeared in all eastern cities over the course of three months, after which the cities declared loyalty to the military corporation DesCon, which possessed funds the beleaguered government did not."

The scene blurs and clears, placing me in the center of an enormous campus full of buildings, each displaying a symbol I recognize as the DesCon logo. "Along with twelve other corporations, DesCon contributed its funds to aid the civilians. By early 2058, the United States government ceased to exist altogether in the east and was replaced with the Colonies of America, formed by a coalition of the country's top thirteen corporations and bolstered by their joint profits. After a series of mergers, the Colonies of America now consists of four ruling corporations: DesCon, Cloud, Meditech, and Evergreen. Skip to a specific corporation?"

I stay silent, watching the rest of the immersive video unfold until it finally pauses on the last frame, an unsettling image of a desperate civilian shielding his face from a soldier's hoisted gun. Then I remove my virtual glasses, rub my eyes, and step out of the now-blank and sterile-looking glass cylinder. My footsteps echo in the empty chamber. I feel dizzy and numb from the sudden lack of moving images.

How can two countries with such radically different philosophies ever reunite? What hope do we possibly have of transforming the Republic and the Colonies into what they once were? Or perhaps they're not as drastically different as I think they are. Aren't the Colonies' corporations and the Republic's government really the same thing? Absolute power is absolute power, no matter what it's called. Isn't it?

I exit the chamber, lost in thought, and as I turn the corner to head to my room, I almost bump right into Anden.

"June?" he blurts out when he sees me. His wavy hair is slightly disheveled, as if he's been raking his hands through it, and his collar shirt is crumpled, his sleeves rolled up to his elbows and the buttons near his neck undone. He manages to compose himself enough to offer me a smile and a bow. "What are you doing up here?"

"Just exploring." I return his smile. I'm too tired to mention all my online research. "I'm not sure what I'm doing here, to be honest."

Anden laughs softly. "Me either. I've been wandering the halls for over an hour." We pause for a moment. Then he turns back in the direction of his suite and gives me a questioning look. "The Antarcticans won't help us, but they've been kind enough to send a bottle of their best wine up to my room. Care to have a sip? I could use some company—and some advice."

Advice from his lowliest Princeps-Elect? I fall into step with him, all too aware of the closeness between us. "How very polite of them," I reply.

"Exceedingly polite," he murmurs under his breath so that I can barely hear him. "Next they'll be throwing us a parade."

Anden's suite is nicer, of course, than my own—at least the Antarcticans did him *that* courtesy. A curved glass window runs along half of the wall, giving us a breathtaking view of Ross City engulfed in thousands of twinkling lights. The Antarcticans must be simulating this nightfall too, considering how it's supposed to be summer down here—but the simulation seems flawless. I think back on the dome-like film we passed through as we descended into the city. Maybe it acts like a giant screen too. Streaks dance quietly across the sky in sheets of breathtaking color, turquoise and magenta and gold, all of them swirling together and vanishing and reappearing against a backdrop of stars. I catch my breath. Must be imitating the aurora australis. I'd read about these southern lights during our weekly lessons, although I hadn't expected them to look this beautiful, simulation or not.

"Nice view," I say.

Anden grins wryly, a small spark of amusement shining through his otherwise weary mood. "The useless advantages of being the Republic's Elector," he replies. "I've been reassured that we can see through this glass, but that no one from outside can see us. Then again, perhaps they're just messing with me."

We settle into soft chairs near the window. Anden pours us both glasses of wine. "One of the accused guards confessed about Commander Jameson," he says as he hands a glass to me. "Republic soldiers unhappy with my rule, paid off by the Colonies. The Colonies is taking advantage of Commander Jameson's knowledge of our military. She might even still be within our borders."

I sip my wine numbly. So, it was all true. I desperately wish

I could go back in time to when I'd visited Thomas in his cell, that I could have noticed the unusual setup in time. *And she could still be within our borders.* Where is Thomas?

"Rest assured," Anden says when he sees my expression, "that we're doing everything we can to find her."

Everything we can might not be enough. Not with our attention and soldiers spread out so thin, trying to fight a war on so many sides. "What do we do now?"

"We return to the Republic tomorrow morning," he replies. "That's what we do. And we'll push the Colonies back without the Antarcticans' help."

"Are you really going to give up some of our land to them?" I ask after a pause.

Anden swirls the wine in his glass before taking a sip. "I haven't turned them down yet," he says. I can hear the disgust with himself in his voice. His father must've seen such a move as the ultimate betrayal of his country.

"I'm sorry," I say quietly, unsure how to console him.

"I'm sorry too. The good news is I've received word that Day and his brother have both successfully evacuated to Los Angeles." He exhales a long breath. "I don't want to force him into anything, but I might be running out of options. He's keeping his word, you know. He'd agreed to help us in any way he could, short of giving up his brother. He's trying to help, in the hopes that it'll guilt me out of asking for Eden. I wish we'd brought him. I wish he could see the situation from my point of view." He looks down.

My heart squeezes again at the thought of Day being killed

in action, and settles in relief at the news that he has survived unscathed. "What if we persuade the Antarcticans to take Day in for his treatment? It might be his only chance at surviving his illness, and it might at least make him consider the risk of letting Eden undergo experimentation."

Anden shakes his head. "We have nothing to bargain with. Antarctica has offered as much help to us as they're willing. They won't trouble themselves with taking in one of our patients."

Deep down, I know this too. It's just a final, desperate idea from me. I understand, as well as he does, that Day would never hand over his brother in exchange for saving his *own* life. My eyes wander back to the display of light outside.

"I don't blame him, not at all," Anden says after a pause. "I should have stopped those bioweapons the instant they named me Elector. The very same day my father died. If I were smart, that's what I would've done. But it's too late to dwell on that now. Day has every right to refuse."

I feel a swell of sympathy for him. If he forcefully takes Eden into custody, Day will no doubt call the people to rise up in revolt. If he respects Day's decision, he risks not finding a cure in time and allowing the Colonies to take over our capital—and our country. If he hands over a piece of our land to Antarctica, the people may see him as a traitor. And if our ports are sealed, we won't be receiving any imports or supplies at all.

And yet, I can't blame Day either. I try to put myself in his shoes. The Republic tries to kill me as a ten-year-old; they experiment on me before I escape. I live the next few years in the harshest slums of Los Angeles. I watch the Republic poison my family, kill my mother and older brother, and blind my younger brother with their engineered plagues. Because of the Republic's experiments, I'm slowly dying. And now, after all the lies and cruelty, the Republic approaches me, begging for my help. Begging for me to allow them to experiment once again on my younger brother, experiments that can't guarantee his absolute safety. What would *I* say? I would probably refuse, just as he did. It's true that my own family suffered horrible fates at the hands of the Republic . . . but Day had been on the front lines, watching everything unfold from the time he was small. It's a miracle that Day had given his support to Anden in the first place.

Anden and I sip wine for four more minutes, watching the city lights in silence.

"I envy Day, you know," he says, his voice as soft as ever. "I'm jealous that he gets to make decisions with his heart. *Every* choice he makes is honest, and the people love him for it. He can *afford* to use his heart." His face darkens. "But the world outside of the Republic is so much more complicated. There's just no room for emotion, is there? All of our countries' relations are held together with a fragile web of diplomatic threads, and these threads are what prevent us from helping one another."

Something's broken in his voice. "There's no room for emotion on the political stage," I reply, putting my wineglass down. I'm not sure if I'm helping, but the words come out anyway. I don't even know if I believe them. "When emotion fails, logic will save you. You might envy Day, but you'll never be him and he'll never be you. He isn't the Republic's Elector. He's a boy protecting his brother. *You* are a politician. You have to make decisions that break your heart, that hurt and deceive, that no one else will understand. It's your duty." Even as I say this, though, I feel the doubt in the back of my mind, the seeds that Day has planted.

*Without emotion, what's the point of being human?*

Anden's eyes are heavy with sadness. He slouches, and for a moment I can see him as he really is, a young ruler standing alone against a tide of opposition and attempting to bear the burden of his country on his own shoulders, with a Senate cooperating only out of fear. "I miss my father sometimes," he says. "I know I shouldn't admit that, but it's true. I know the rest of the world sees him as a monster." He puts his wineglass down on the side table, then buries his head in his hands and rubs his face once.

My heart aches for him. At least I can grieve for my brother without fear of others' hatred. What must it be like to know that the parent you once loved was responsible for such evil acts?

"Don't feel guilty for your grief," I say softly. "He was still your father."

His gaze comes to rest on me, and as if pulled by some invisible hand, he leans forward. He wavers there, hovering precariously between desire and reason. He is so close now, close enough that if I were to move even a little, our lips might brush against each other. I feel his breath faintly against my skin, the warmth of his nearness, the quiet gentleness of his love. In this moment, I feel myself drawn to him.

"June . . . ," he whispers. His eyes dance across my face.

Then he touches my chin with one hand, coaxes me forward, and kisses me.

I close my eyes. I should stop him, but I don't want to. There is something electrifying about the bare passion in the young Elector of the Republic, the way he leans into me, his desire exposed even beneath his unfailing politeness. How he opens his heart for no one but me. How in spite of everything working against him, he still has the strength to step out every day with his chin up and his back straight. How he soldiers on, for the sake of his country. As do we all. I let myself succumb. He breaks away from my lips to kiss my cheek. Then the soft line of my jaw, right under my ear. Then my neck, just the softest whisper of a touch. A shiver sweeps through me. I can feel him holding back, and I know that what he really wants to do is to lace his fingers through my hair and drown himself in me.

But he doesn't. He knows, as much as I do, that this isn't real.

*I have to stop.* And with a pained effort, I pull away. I struggle to catch my breath. "I'm sorry," I whisper. "I can't."

Anden looks down, embarrassed. But not surprised. His cheeks flush a faint pink in the dim light of the room, and he runs a hand through his hair. "I shouldn't have done that," he murmurs. We fall silent for a few uncomfortable seconds, until Anden sighs and leans all the way back. I slouch a little, both disappointed and relieved. "I . . . know you care deeply for Day. I know I can't hope to compete with that." He grimaces. "That was inappropriate of me. My apologies, June."

I have a fleeting urge to kiss him again, to tell him that I *do* care, and to erase the pain and shame on his face that tugs at my heart. But I also know I don't love him, and I can't lead him on like this. I know the real reason we went so far is that I couldn't bear to turn him away in his darkest moment. That I wished, deep down . . . he were someone else. The truth fills me with guilt. "I should go," I say sadly.

Anden moves farther from me. He seems more alone than ever. Still, he composes himself and bows his head respectfully. His moment of weakness has passed, and his usual politeness takes over. As always, he hides his pain well. Then he stands up and holds a hand out to me. "I'll walk you back to your room. Get some rest—we'll leave in the early morning."

I stand too, but I don't take his hand. "It's fine. I can find my own way back." I avoid meeting his eyes; I don't want to see how everything I say only hurts him more. Then I turn toward the door and leave him behind.

Ollie greets me with a wagging tail when I return to my room. After a petting session, I decide to try out the Internet portal in my room while he curls up nearby and falls promptly asleep. I run a search on Anden, as well as on his father. My room's portal is a simplified version of the portals I used earlier, without interactive textures and immersive sounds attached, but it's still miles beyond anything I've seen in the Republic. I sift quietly through the search results. Most are staged photos and propaganda videos that I recognize—Anden having his portrait done as a young boy, the former Elector standing in front of Anden at official press events and meetings. Even the international community seems to have little information on the relationship between father and son. But the deeper I dig, the more I stumble across moments of something surprisingly genuine. I see a video of Anden as a four-year-old, holding his salute with a solemn young face while his father patiently shows him how. I find a photo of the late Elector holding a crying, frightened Anden in his arms and whispering something into his ear, oblivious to the crowd that surrounds them. I see a clip of him angrily shoving the international press away from his small son, of him clutching Anden's hand so tightly that his knuckles have turned white. I stumble across a rare interview between him and a reporter from Africa, who asks him what he cares about the most in the Republic.

"My son," the late Elector answers without hesitation. His expression never softens, but the edges of his voice shift slightly. "My son will always be everything to me, because someday he will be everything to the Republic." He pauses for a second to smile at the reporter. Inside that smile, I think I see glimpses of a different man who once existed. "My son . . . *reminds* me."

We had initially planned to return to the capital the next morning—but the news comes just as we board our jet in Ross City. It comes earlier than we thought it would.

Denver has fallen to the Colonies.

# DAY

"DAY. WE'RE HERE."

I open my eyes groggily to the gentle sound of Tess's voice. She smiles down at me. There's pressure on my head, and when I reach up to touch my hair, I realize that bandages are wrapped around my forehead. My cut hand is also now covered in clean white linen. It takes me another second to notice that I'm sitting in a wheelchair.

"Oh, come on," I immediately blurt out. "A goddy wheelchair?" My head feels foggy and light, the familiar sensation of coming off a dose of painkillers. "Where are we? What happened to me?"

"You'll probably need to stop at a hospital when we get off the train. They think all the commotion triggered a bad response in you." Tess walks beside me as some soldier pushes me down the length of the train car. Up ahead, I see Pascao and the other Patriots getting off the train. "We're in Los Angeles. We're back home."

"Where are Eden and Lucy?" I ask. "Do you know?"

"They've already settled into your temporary apartment in Ruby sector," Tess replies. She's quiet for a second. "Guess a gem sector's your home now."

Home. I fall silent as we exit the train and stream out onto the platform with the other soldiers. Los Angeles feels as warm as ever, a typical hazy day in late fall, and the yellowish light makes me squint. The wheelchair feels so for-eign and annoying. I have a sudden urge to bolt out of it and kick it onto the tracks. I am a Runner—I'm not supposed to be stuck in this cracked thing. Another bad response, this time triggered by commotion? I grit my teeth at how weak I've become. The doctor's last prognosis haunts me. *A month, maybe two.* The frequency of severe headaches has definitely been increasing.

The soldiers help me into a jeep. Before we leave, Tess reaches through my open car window and gives me a quick hug. The sudden warmth from her startles me. All I can do is hug her back, savoring the brief moment. We stare at each other until the jeep finally pulls away from the station and Tess's figure disappears around a bend. Even then, I keep turning around in my seat to see if I can spot her.

We stop at an intersection. As we wait for a group of evacuees to cross in front of our jeep, I study the streets of downtown Los Angeles. Some things appear unchanged: Lines of soldiers bark orders at unruly refugees; other civilians stand on the sidelines and protest the influx of new people; the JumboTrons continue to flash encouraging messages of the Republic's so-called victories on the warfront, reminding people: *Don't let the Colonies conquer your home! Support the cause!*

My conversation with Eden replays in my mind.

I blink, then look closer at the streets. This time, the scenes I'd thought were familiar take on new context. The lines of soldiers barking orders are actually handing out rations to the new refugees. The civilians protesting the new people are actually being *allowed* to protest—soldiers look on, but their guns stay tucked away at their belts. And the JumboTrons' propaganda, once images that looked so ominous to me, now seem like messages of optimism, a broadcast of hope in dark times, a desperate attempt to keep people's spirits up. Not far from where our jeep's stopped, I see a crowd of children evacuees surrounding a young soldier. He's knelt to their eye level, and in his hands is some sort of puppet toy that he's now using animatedly to tell the kids a story. I roll my window down. His voice is clear and upbeat. Now and then, the children laugh, their fear and confusion momentarily held at bay. Nearby, the parents look on with faces both exhausted and grateful.

The people and the Republic . . . are working together.

I frown at the unfamiliar thought. There's no question that the Republic has done some horrible things to us all, that they might *still* be doing those things. But . . . maybe I've also been seeing the things I *want* to see. Maybe now that the old Elector is gone, the Republic's soldiers have started to shed their masks too. Maybe they really *are* following Anden's lead.

The jeep takes me first to see the apartment where Eden's staying. He rushes out to greet me when we pull up, all unhappiness from our previous argument gone. "They said you caused a bunch of trouble out there," he says as he and Lucy join me in the jeep. A disapproving look creeps onto his face. "Don't ever scare me like that again."

I give him a wry smile and ruffle his hair. "Now you know how I feel about *your* decision."

By the time we end up outside the Los Angeles Central Hospital, word of our arrival has spread like wildfire and a huge crowd is waiting for my jeep. They're screaming, crying, chanting—and it takes two patrols of soldiers to form enough of a walkway for them to usher us inside the hospital. I stare numbly at the people as I pass by. A lot of them have the scarlet streak in their hair, while others hold up signs. They shout out the same thing.

## SAVE US.

I look away nervously. They've all seen and heard about what I did with the Patriots in Denver. But I'm not some invincible super-soldier—I'm a dying boy who's about to be stuck, helpless, in the hospital while an enemy takes over our country.

Eden leans over my wheelchair's handlebars. Even though he doesn't say a word, I take one look at his solemn face and know exactly what's running through his mind. The thought sends terror trickling down my spine.

*I can save them,* my little brother's thinking. *Let me save them.*

Once we're inside the hospital and the soldiers bar the doors, they wheel me up to the third-floor rooms. There, Eden waits outside while doctors strap a bunch of metal nodes and wires to me. They run a brain scan. Finally, they let me rest. Throughout it all, my head throbs continuously, sometimes so much that I feel like I'm moving even though I'm lying down on a bed. Nurses come in and give me some sort of injection. A couple of hours later, when I'm strong enough to sit up, a pair of doctors come to see me.

"What is it?" I ask before they can speak up. "Do I have three days left? What's the deal?"

"Don't worry," one of them—the younger, more inexperienced one—assures me. "You still have a couple of months. Your prognosis hasn't changed."

"Oh," I reply. Well, *that's* a relief.

The older doctor scratches uncomfortably at his beard. "You can still move around and do normal activities—whatever those are," he grumbles, "but don't strain yourself. As for your treatments . . ." He pauses here, then peers at me from the top of his glasses. "We're going to try some more radical drugs," the doctor continues with an awkward expression. "But let me be clear, Day—our greatest enemy is time. We are fighting hard to prepare you for a very risky surgery, but the time that your medication needs may be longer than the time you have left. There's only so much we can do."

"What *can* we do?" I ask.

The doctor nods at the dripping fluid bag hanging next to me. "If you make it through the full course, you might be ready for surgery a few months from now."

I lower my head. Do I have a few months left? They're sure as hell cutting it close. "So," I mutter, "I might be dead by the time the surgery comes around. Or there might not be a Republic left."

My last comment drains the blood from the doctor's face. He doesn't respond, but he doesn't need to. No wonder the other doctors had warned me to get my affairs in order. Even in the best of circumstances, I might not pull through in time. But I might actually live long enough to see the Republic fall. The thought makes me shudder.

The only way Antarctica will help is if we provide proof of a cure against this plague, give them a reason to call in their troops to stop the Colonies' invasion. And the only way to do *that* is to let Eden give himself over to the Republic.

The medicine knocks me out, and it's a full day before I come around. When the doctors aren't there, I test my legs by taking short walks around my room. I feel strong enough to go without a wheelchair. Still, I stumble when I try to stretch too thin and spring from one end of the room to the other. Nope. I sigh in frustration, then pull myself back into bed. My eyes shift to a screen on the wall, where footage from Denver is playing. I can tell that the Republic is careful about how much of it they show. I'd seen firsthand how it looked when the Colonies' troops started rolling in, but on the screen there are only faraway shots of the city. The viewer can just see smoke rising from several buildings and the ominous row of Colonies airships hovering near the edge of the Armor. Then it cuts to footage of Republic jets lining up on the airfield, preparing to launch into battle. For once, I'm glad that the propaganda's in place. There's just no point in scaring the hell out of the whole country. Might as well show that the Republic's fighting back.

I can't stop thinking about Frankie's lifeless face. Or the way Thomas's head snapped back when the Colonies soldiers shot him. I wince as it replays in my mind. I wait in silence for another half hour, watching as the screen's footage changes from the Denver battle to headlines about how I'd helped slow down the invading Colonies troops. More people are in the streets now, with their scarlet streaks and handmade signs. They really think I'm making a difference. I rub a hand across my face. They don't understand that I'm just a boy—I'd never meant to get involved so deeply in any of this. Without the Patriots, June, or Anden, I couldn't have done anything. I'm useless on my own.

Static suddenly blares out of my earpiece; an incoming call. I jump. Then, an unfamiliar male voice in my ear: "Mr. Wing," the man says. "I presume it's you?"

I scowl. "Who's this?"

"Mr. Wing," the man says, adding a flourish of cracked excitement that sends a chill down my spine. "This is the Chancellor of the Colonies. Pleased to make your acquaintance."

The Chancellor? I swallow hard. Yeah, right. "Is this some sort of joke?" I snap into the mike. "Some hacker kid—"

"Come now. This wouldn't be a very funny joke, now would it?"

I didn't know the Colonies could access our earpiece streams and make calls like this. I frown, then lower my voice.

"How'd you get in?" Are the Colonies winning in Denver? Did the city fall already, right after we finished evacuating it?

"I have my ways," the man replies, his voice dead calm. "It seems that some of your people have defected to our side. I can't say I blame them."

Someone in the Republic must have given up info to the Colonies to allow them to use our data streams like this. Suddenly my thoughts rush back to the job I'd done with the Patriots, where the Colonies soldiers had shot Thomas in the head—the image sends a violent shudder through me, and I force myself to push it away. *Commander Jameson.*

"I hope I'm not inconveniencing you," the Chancellor says before I can respond, "given your condition and such. And I'm sure you must be feeling a bit tired after your little escapade in Denver. I'm impressed, I must say."

I don't respond to that. I wonder what else he knows—whether he knows which hospital I'm currently lying in . . . or worse, where our new apartment is, where Eden's staying. "What do you want?" I finally whisper.

I can practically hear the Chancellor's smile over my earpiece. "I'd hate to waste your time, so let's get to the meat of this conversation. I realize that the Republic's current Elector is this young Anden Stavropoulos fellow." His tone is condescending. "But come now, both you and I know who really runs your country. And that's *you*. The people love you, Day. When my troops first went into Denver, do you know what they told me? 'The civilians have plastered posters of Day on the walls. They want to see him back on the screens.' They have been very stubborn to cooperate with my men, and it's a surprisingly tiresome process to get them to comply."

My anger slowly burns. "Leave the civilians out of it," I say through a clenched jaw. "They didn't ask for you to barge into their homes."

"But you forget," the Chancellor says in a coaxing voice. "Your Republic has done the exact same thing to them for decades—didn't they do it to your own family? We are invading the Republic because of what they did to *us*. This virus they've sent across the border. Exactly where do your loyalties lie, and *why*? And do you realize, my boy, how incredible your position is at your age, how you have your finger on the pulse of this nation? How much power you hold—"

"Your point, Chancellor?"

"I know you're dying. I also know you have a younger brother who you would love to see grow up."

"You bring Eden into this again, and this conversation's over."

"Very well. Just bear with me. In the Colonies, Meditech Corp handles all of our hospitals and treatments, and I can guarantee you they would do a much finer job dealing with your case than anything the Republic can offer. So here's the deal. You can slowly whittle away whatever's left of your life, staying loyal to a country that's not loyal to you—or you can do something for *us*. You can publicly ask the Republic's people to accept the Colonies, and help this country fall under the rule of something better. You can get treatment in a quality place. Wouldn't that be nice? Surely you deserve more than what you're getting."

A scornful laugh forces its way out of me. "Yeah, right. You expect me to believe that?"

"Well now," the Chancellor says, trying to sound amused, but this time I detect darkness in his words. "I can see this is a losing argument. If you choose to fight for the Republic, I'll respect that decision. I only hope that the best will happen for you and your brother, even after we establish our place firmly in the Republic. But I'm a businessman, Day, and I like to work with a Plan B in mind. So, let me ask you this instead." He pauses for a second. "The Princeps-Elect June Iparis. Do you love her?"

An icy claw grips my chest. "Why?"

"Well." The Chancellor lets his voice turn somber. "You have to see this situation from my point of view," he says gently. "The Colonies will win, inevitably, at this rate. Ms. Iparis is one of the people sitting at the heart of the losing government. Now, son, I want you to think about this. What do you suppose happens to the ruling government on the losing side of a war?"

My hands tremble. This is a thought that has floated in the dark recesses of my mind, something I've refused to think about. Until now. "Are you threatening her?" I whisper.

The Chancellor tsks in disapproval at my tone. "I'm only being reasonable. What do you think will happen to her once we declare victory? Do you *really* think we will let live a girl who is on track to become the leader of the Republic's

Senate? This is how all civilized nations work, Day, and it's been that way for centuries. For millennia. After all, I'm sure your Elector executed those who stood against him. Didn't he?" I stay silent. "Ms. Iparis, along with the Elector and his Senate, will be tried and executed. *That* is what happens to a losing government in a war, Day." His voice turns serious. "If you don't cooperate with us, then you might have to live with their blood on your hands. But if you *do* cooperate, I might find a way to pardon them of their war crimes. And what's more," he adds, "you can have all the comforts of a quality life. You won't need to worry for your family's safety ever again. You won't have to worry for the Republic's people either. They don't know any better; the common folk never know what's good for them. But you and I do, don't we? You know they're better off without the Republic's rule. Sometimes they just don't understand their choices—they need their decisions made for them. After all, you chose to manipulate the people yourself when you wanted them to accept your new Elector. Am I correct?"

Tried and executed. *June, gone.* Dreading the possibility is one thing; hearing it spelled out to me and then using it to blackmail me is another. My mind spins frantically for ways they could escape instead, to find asylum in another country. Maybe the Antarcticans can keep June and the others overseas and protected in case the Colonies overrun the country. There must be a way. But . . . what about the rest of us? What's to stop the Colonies from harming my brother?

"How do I know you'll keep your word?" I finally manage to croak.

"To show you my genuine nature, I give you my word that the Colonies have ceased their attacks as of this morning, and I will not resume them for three days. If you agree to my proposition, you just guaranteed the safety of the Republic's people . . . and of your loved ones. So, let the choice be yours." The Chancellor laughs a little. "And I recommend that you keep our conversation to yourself."

"I'll think about it," I whisper.

"Wonderful." The Chancellor's voice brightens. "Like I said, as soon as possible. After three days, I'll expect to hear back from you on making a public announcement to the Republic. This can be the start of a very fruitful relationship. Time is of the essence—I know you understand this more than anyone."

Then the call ends. The silence is deafening. I sit in the thick of our conversation for a while, soaking it in. Thoughts run endlessly through my mind . . . Eden, June, the Republic, the Elector. *Their blood on your hands.* The frustration and fear bubbling inside my chest threatens to drown me in its tide. The Chancellor's smart, I'll give him that—he knows exactly what my weaknesses are and he's going to try to use them to his advantage. But two can play at this. I have to warn June—and I'll have to do it quietly. If the Colonies find out that I've passed the word along instead of keeping my mouth shut and doing as the Chancellor says, then who knows what tricks they might try to pull. But maybe we can use this to our advantage. My mind whirls. Maybe we can fool the Chancellor at his own game.

Suddenly, a shriek echoes from the hallway outside that raises every hair on my skin. I turn my head in the sound's direction. Somebody's coming down the corridor against her will—whoever it is must be putting up a pretty damn good fight.

"I'm *not* infected," the voice protests. It grows louder until it's right outside my door, then fades as the sounds of the voice and gurney wheels travel farther down the hall. I recognize the voice right away. "Run your tests again. It's nothing. I'm *not infected*."

Even though I don't know exactly what's going on, I'm instantly sure of one thing—the sickness spreading through the Colonies has a new victim.

Tess.

# JUNE

FOR THE FIRST TIME IN THE REPUBLIC'S HISTORY, THERE is no capital to land in.

We touch down at an airfield located on the southern edge of Drake University at 1600 hours, not a quarter mile away from where I used to attend all of my Republic History classes. The afternoon is disconcertingly sunny. Has it really been less than a year since everything happened? As we step off the plane and wait for our luggage to unload, I look around in a dull stupor. The campus, both nostalgic and strange to me, is emptier than I remember—many of the seniors, I hear, have been pushed through graduation early in order to send them off to the warfront to fight for the Republic's survival. I walk in silence through the campus streets a few steps behind Anden, while Mariana and Serge, as part of their Senator nature, keep up a steady stream of chatter with their otherwise quiet Elector. Ollie stays close to my side, the hackles up on his neck. The main Drake quad, normally crowded with passing students, is now home to pockets of refugees brought over from Denver and a few neighboring cities. An unfamiliar, eerie sight.

By the time we reach a series of jeeps waiting for us and begin traveling through Batalla sector, I notice the various things throughout LA that have changed. Evacuation centers have popped up where Batalla sector meets Blueridge, where the military buildings give way to civilian high-rises, and many of the older, half-abandoned buildings along this poor sector have been hastily converted into evacuation centers. Large crowds of disheveled Denver refugees crowd the entrances, all hoping to be lucky enough to get a room assignment. One glance tells me that, naturally, the people waiting here are probably all from Denver's poor sectors.

"Where are we placing the upper-class families?" I ask Anden. "In a gem sector, I'm sure?" I find it difficult now to say something like this without a sharp edge in my voice.

Anden looks unhappy, but he calmly answers, "In Ruby. You, Mariana, and Serge will all have apartments there." He reads my expression. "I know what you're thinking. But I can't afford to have our wealthy families revolting against me for forcing them into evacuation centers in the poor sectors. I *did* set a number of spaces in Ruby to be allocated for the poor— they'll be assigned to them on a lottery system."

I don't answer, simply because I have nothing to argue against. What *is* there to do about this situation? It's not like Anden can uproot the entire country's infrastructure in the span of a year. As I look on through the window, a growing group of protesters gathers along the edge of a guarded refugee zone. MOVE TO THE OUTSKIRTS! One of their signs says, KEEP THEM QUARANTINED!

The sight sends a shiver down my spine. It doesn't seem so different from what had happened in the Republic's early years, when the west protested the people fleeing in from the east.

We ride in silence for a while. Then, suddenly, Anden presses his hand against his ear and motions to the driver. "Turn on the screen," he tells him, gesturing to the small monitor embedded into the jeep's seats. "General Marshall says the Colonies are broadcasting something onto our twelfth channel."

We all watch as the monitor comes to life. At first we only see a blank, black screen, but then the broadcast comes in, and I look on as the Colonies slogan and seal appear over an oscillating Colonies flag.

```
THE COLONIES OF AMERICA
CLOUD . MEDITECH . DESCON . EVERGREEN
A FREE STATE IS A CORPORATE STATE
```

Then, an evening landscape of a beautiful, sparkling city comes up, completely covered in thousands of twinkling blue lights. "Citizens of the Republic," a grandiose voice says. "Welcome to the Colonies of America. As many of you already know, the Colonies have overrun the Republic capital of Denver and, as such, have declared an unofficial victory over the tyrannical regime that has kept you all under its thumb. After over a hundred years of suffering, you are now free." The landscape changes to a top-down map of both the Republic and the Colonies—except this time, the line dividing the two nations is gone. A shiver runs down my spine. "In the weeks to come, you will all be integrated into our system of fair competition and freedom. You are a citizen of the Colonies. What does that mean, you might wonder?"

The voiceover pauses, and the imagery shifts to a happy

family holding a check in front of them. "As a new citizen, each of you will be entitled to at least five thousand Colonies Notes, equivalent to sixty thousand Republic Notes, granted from one of our four main corps that you decide to work for. The higher your current income, the higher we'll pay you. You will no longer answer to the Republic's street police but to DesCon's city patrols, your own private neighborhood police dedicated to serving *you*. Your employer will no longer be the Republic, but one of our four distinguished corps, where you can apply for a fulfilling career." The video shifts again to scenes of happy workers, proud, smiling faces hovering over suits and ties. "We offer you, citizens, the freedom of choice."

*The freedom of choice.* Images flash through my mind of what I'd seen in the Colonies when Day and I first ventured into their territory. The crowds of workers, the dilapidated slums of the poor. The advertisements printed all over the people's clothes. The commercials that covered every square inch of the buildings. Most of all, DesCon's police, the way they had refused to help the robbed woman who had missed her payments to their department. Is this the future of the Republic? And suddenly I feel nauseous, because I cannot say whether the people would be better off in the Republic or the Colonies.

The broadcast continues. "We only ask that you return a small favor to us." The video shifts again, this time to a scene of people protesting in solidarity. "If you, as a civilian, have grievances with the Republic, now is the time to voice them. If you are courageous enough to stage protests throughout your respective cities, the Colonies will pay you an additional five thousand Colonies Notes, as well as grant you a one-year discount on all of our Cloud Corp grocery goods. Simply send your proof of participation to any DesCon headquarters in Denver, Colorado, along with your name and mailing address."

So, this explains the various protests popping up around the city. Even their propaganda sounds like an advertisement. A dangerously tempting one. "Declaring victory a little too soon," I say under my breath.

"They're trying to turn the people against us," Anden murmurs in reply. "They announced a ceasefire this morning, perhaps as a chance to disseminate propaganda like this."

"I doubt it will be effective," I say, although I don't sound as confident as I should. All these years of anti-Colonies propaganda are going to be difficult for the Colonies to work around. Aren't they?

Anden's jeep finally slows to a halt. I frown, confused for a second. Instead of taking me back to a high-rise for my temporary apartment, we are now parked in front of the Los Angeles Central Hospital. The place where Metias died. I glance at Anden. "What are we doing here?" I ask.

"Day's here," Anden replies. His voice catches a little when he speaks Day's name.

"Why?"

Anden doesn't look at me. He seems reluctant to discuss it. "He collapsed during the evacuation to LA," he explains. "The series of explosions we used to knock out the underground tunnels apparently triggered one of his severe headaches. The doctors have started another round of treatment for him." Anden pauses, then gives me a grave stare. "There's another reason we're here. But you'll see for yourself."

The jeep comes to a halt. I climb out, then wait for Anden. A feeling of dread slowly creeps through me. What if Day's illness has gotten worse? What if he isn't going to pull through? Is that why he's here? There's no reason for Day to ever set foot inside this building again, not unless he was forced to, not after everything this hospital put him through.

Together, Anden and I head into the building with soldiers flanking us. We travel up to the fourth floor, where one of the soldiers swipes us inside, and then step into the Central Hospital's lab floor. The tense feeling in my stomach only tightens as we go.

Finally, we stop in front of a smaller series of rooms that line the side of the main lab floor. As we go through one of these doors, I see Day. He's standing outside a room with glass walls, smoking one of his blue cigarettes and looking on as someone inside gets inspected by lab technicians in full body suits. What makes me lose my breath, though, is that he's leaning heavily on a pair of crutches. How long has he been here? He looks exhausted, pale, and distant. I wonder what new drugs the doctors are trying on him. The thought is a sudden, stabbing reminder of Day's waning life, the few seconds he has left, slowly ticking by.

Standing beside him are a few lab techs with white jumpsuit gear and goggles dangling from their necks, each of them watching the room and typing away on their notepads. A short distance away, Pascao's deep in conversation with the other Patriots. They leave Day alone.

"Day?" I say as we approach.

He looks over to me—a dozen emotions flicker through his eyes, some that make my cheeks flush. Then he notices Anden. He manages to give the Elector a stiff bow of his head, then turns back to watching the patient on the other side of the glass. Tess.

"What's going on?" I ask Day.

He takes another puff of his cigarette and lowers his eyes. "They won't let me in. They think she might've come down with whatever this new plague is," he says. His voice is quiet, but I can hear an undercurrent of frustration and anger. "They've already run tests on me and the other Patriots. Tess is the only one who didn't come up clean."

Tess bats away one of the lab techs' hands, then stumbles backward as if she's having trouble keeping her balance. Sweat forms on her forehead and drips down her neck. The whites of her eyes have a sickly yellow tint to them, and when I look closely, I can tell that she's squinting in an effort to see everything around her—something that reminds me of her nearsightedness, the way she used to squint at the streets of Lake. Her hands are trembling. I swallow hard at the sight. The Patriots couldn't have been exposed for long to the Colonies soldiers, but apparently it was long enough for some soldier carrying the virus to pass it to one of them. It's also a very real possibility that the Colonies are purpose-fully spreading the disease right back to us, now that they're in our territory. My insides turn cold as I remember a line from Metias's old journals: *One day we'll create a virus that no one will be able to stop.* And that just might bring about the downfall of the entire Republic.

One of the lab techs turns to me and offers a quick explanation. "The virus looks like a mutation of one of our past plague experiments," she says, shooting Day a nervous glance (he must have given her a hard time about this earlier) before continuing. "As far as we can tell from the statistics the Colonies have released, the virus seems to have a low uptake rate among healthy adults, but when it does infect someone, the disease progresses rapidly and the fatality rate is very high. We're seeing infection-to-death times of about a week." She turns momentarily to Tess on the other side of the glass. "She's showing some early symptoms—fever, dizziness, jaundice, and the symptom that points us to one of our own manufactured viruses, temporary or possibly permanent blindness."

Beside me, Day clenches his crutches so hard that his knuckles look white. Knowing him, I wonder whether he's already had several fights with the lab techs, trying to force his way in to see her or scream at them to leave her alone. I know he must be picturing Eden right now, with his purple, half-blind eyes, and in this moment a deep hatred for the former Republic fills my chest. My father had worked behind those experimental lab doors. He had tried to quit once he found out what they were actually doing with all those local LA plagues, and he gave his life as a result. Is that country really behind us now? Can our reputation ever change in the eyes of the out-side world—or of the Colonies?

"She tried to save Frankie," Day whispers, his eyes still fixed on Tess. "She'd made it back inside the Armor right after we did. I thought Thomas was going to kill her." His voice turns bitter. "But maybe she's already marked for death."

"Thomas?" I whisper.

"Thomas is dead," he murmurs. "When Pascao and I were fleeing to the Armor, I saw him stand and face the Colonies soldiers alone. He kept firing at them until they shot him in the head." He flinches at this final sentence.

Thomas is dead.

I blink twice, suddenly numb from head to toe. I shouldn't be shocked. Why am I shocked? I was prepared for this. The soldier who had stabbed my brother through the heart, who had shot Day's mother . . . he's gone. And of course he would have died in this way—defending the Republic until the end, unwavering in his insane loyalty to a state that had already turned her back on him. I also understand right away why this has affected Day so much. *Shot through the head.* I feel empty at the news. Exhausted. Numb. My shoulders sag.

"It's for the best," I finally whisper through the lump in my throat. Images flash through my head of Metias, and of what Thomas had told me about his last night alive. I force my thoughts back to Tess. To the living, and those who still mat-ter. "Tess is going to be okay," I say. My words sound uncon-vincing. "We just have to find a way."

The lab techs inside the glass room stick a long needle into Tess's right arm, then her left. She lets out a choked sob. Day tears his eyes away from the scene, adjusts his grip on his crutches, and begins to make his way toward us. As he passes me, he whispers, "*Tonight.*" Then he leaves the rest of us behind and heads down the hall.

I watch him go in silence. Anden sighs, looks sadly toward Tess, and joins the other lab techs. "Are you sure Day is clean?" he says to the one who'd shared the virus information with us. She confirms it, and Anden nods at her in approval. "I want a second check run on all of our soldiers immediately." He turns to one of the other Senators. "Then I want a message sent right away to the Colonies' Chancellor, as well as their DesCon CEO. Let's see whether diplomacy can get us anywhere."

Finally, Anden gives me a long look. "I know I have no right to ask this of you," he says. "But if you can find it in your heart to ask Day again about his brother, I would be grateful. We might still have a chance with Antarctica."

1930 HOURS.
RUBY SECTOR.
73° F.

The high-rise I'm staying in is just a few blocks away from where Metias and I used to live. As the jeep I'm riding in approaches it, I look down the street and try to catch a glimpse of my old apartment complex. Even Ruby sector is now blocked off with segments of tape indicating which areas are for evacuees, and soldiers line the streets. I wonder where Anden's staying in the midst of all this mess; probably somewhere in Batalla sector. He'll definitely be up late tonight. Before I'd left for my assigned apartment, he had taken me aside in the lab hall. His eyes flickered unconsciously to my lips and then back up again. I knew he was dwelling on the brief moment we shared in Ross City, as well as the words that had come after it. *I know you care deeply for Day.*

"June," he said after an awkward pause. "We're meeting with the Senate tomorrow morning to discuss what our next steps should be. I want to give you the heads-up that this will be a conference where each of the Princeps-Elects will deliver some words to the group. It's a chance to experience what each of you would do if you were the official Princeps—but be warned, things may get heated." He smiled a little. "This war has left us all on edge, to put it lightly."

I'd wanted to tell him that I would sit this one out. Another meeting with the Senators—another four-hour-long session of listening to forty talking heads all battling to outdo one another, all attempting to either sway Anden to their side or embarrass him in front of the others. No doubt Mariana and Serge will lead the arguments to see which of them can come across as the better Princeps candidate. The mere idea of it drains me of all my remaining strength. But at the same time, the thought of leaving Anden to shoulder the burden alone in a room full of people who were so cold and distant was too hard to bear. So I smiled and bowed to him, like a good Princeps-Elect. "I'll be there," I replied.

Now the jeep pulls up to my assigned complex and stops, and I push the memory out of my mind. I get out of the jeep with Ollie, then watch it go until it turns a corner and disappears completely from sight. I head inside the high-rise.

I initially plan to stop by Day's room right after settling into my own, to see what he meant by his "tonight" comment. But as I reach my hall, I see that I don't have to.

Day is camped outside my door, sitting slouched against the wall and absently smoking a blue cigarette. His crutches are lying idly beside him. Even though he's not moving, some small piece of his manner—wild, careless, defiant—still shines through, and for an instant I flash back to when I'd first met him on the streets, with his bright blue eyes and quicksilver movements and unruly blond hair. That nostalgic image is so sweet that I suddenly feel my eyes watering. I take a deep breath and will myself not to cry.

He pulls himself to his feet when he sees me at the end of the hall. "June," he says as I approach. Ollie trots over to greet him, and he pats my dog once on the head. He still looks exhausted, but manages to give me a lopsided, if sad, grin. Without his crutches, he sways on his feet. His eyes are heavy with anguish, and I know it's because of our earlier stint in the lab. "From the look on your face, I'm guessing the Antarcticans weren't much help."

I shake my head, then unlock my door and invite him inside. "Not really," I reply as I close the door behind me. My eyes instinctively study the room, memorizing its layout. It resembles my old home a little too closely for comfort. "They've contacted the United Nations about the plague. They're going to seal off all of our ports to traffic. No imports or exports—no aid, no supplies. We're all under quarantine now. They've told us that they can help us out only after we show them proof of a cure, or if Anden hands over a chunk of Republic land to them as payment. Until then, they won't send any troops. All I know now is that they're monitoring our situation pretty closely."

Day says nothing. Instead, he wanders away from me and stands on the room's balcony. He leans against the railing. I put out some food and water for Ollie, then join him. The sun set a while ago, but with the glow from the city lights, we can see the low-lying clouds that block the stars, covering the sky in shades of gray and black. I notice how heavily Day has to lean on the railing to support himself, and I'm tempted to ask him how he's feeling. But the expression on his face stops me. He probably doesn't want to talk about it.

"So," he says after another puff on his cigarette. The light from distant JumboTrons paints a glowing line of blue and purple around his face. His eyes skim across the buildings, and I know he's instinctively analyzing how he would run each one of them. "Guess we're on our own now. Can't say I'm all that upset about it, though. The Republic's always been about closing off her borders, yeah? Maybe she'll fight better this way. Nothing motivates you like being alone and cornered on the streets."

When he lifts his cigarette to his lips again, I see his hand trembling. The paper clip ring gleams on his finger. "Day," I say gently. He just raises an eyebrow and glances at me sideways. "You're shaking."

He exhales a puff of blue smoke, squints at the city lights in the darkness, and then lowers his lashes. "It's strange being back in LA," he replies, his voice distracted and distant. "I'm fine. Just worried about Tess." A long pause follows. I know the name—Eden—that hangs at the tips of both of our tongues, although neither one of us wants to bring it up first. Day finally ends our silence, and when he does, he approaches the topic with slow and laborious pain. "June, I've been thinking about what your Elector wants from me. About, you know . . . about my brother." He sighs, then leans farther out on the railing and rakes a hand through his hair. His arm brushes past my own—even this small gesture sends my heart beating faster. "I had an argument with Eden about it all."

"What did he say?" I ask. Somehow, I feel guilty when I think back on Anden's request for me. *If you can find it in your heart to ask Day again about his brother, I would be grateful.*

Day puts his cigarette out on the metal railing. His eyes meet mine. "He wants to help," he murmurs. "After seeing Tess today, and after what you just told me, well . . ." He tightens his jaw. "I'll talk to Anden tomorrow. Maybe there's something in Eden's blood that can, you know . . . make a difference in all this. *Maybe.*"

He's still reluctant, of course, and I can hear the pain plainly in his voice. But he is also *agreeing.* Agreeing to let the Republic use his little brother to find a cure. A small, bittersweet smile tugs at the corners of my mouth. *Day, the champion of the people, the one who can't bear to see those around him suffer on his behalf, who would gladly give his life for those he loves.* Except it's not *his* life that we need in order to save Tess, but his brother's. Risking one loved one for the sake of another loved one. I wonder whether anything else made him change his mind. "Thank you, Day," I whisper. "I know how hard this is."

He grimaces and shakes his head. "No, I'm just being selfish. But I can't help it." He looks down, laying bare his weaknesses. "Just . . . tell Anden to bring him back. Please bring him back."

There's something else bothering him, something that's making his hands shake uncontrollably. I lean into him, then place one of my hands over his. He looks me in the eyes again. There's such deep sadness and fear in his face. It breaks my heart. "What else is wrong, Day?" I whisper. "What else do you know?"

This time, he doesn't look away. He swallows—and when he speaks, there's a slight tremor in his voice. "The Colonies' Chancellor called me while I was in the hospital."

"The Chancellor?" I whisper, careful to keep my voice low. You never know. "Are you sure?"

Day nods once. Then he tells me everything—the conversation he had with the Chancellor, the bribes, the blackmail and threats. He tells me what the Colonies have in store for me, should Day refuse them. All my unspoken fears. Finally, he sighs. The release of all this information seems to lighten the burden on his shoulders, if only by a hair. "There must be a way we can use this against the Colonies," he says. "Some way to trick them with their own game. I don't know what yet, but if we can find some way to make the Chancellor think that I'm going to help him out, then maybe we can take them by surprise."

If the Colonies really do win, they *will* come after me. We'll be killed, all of us. I try to sound as calm as he does, but I don't succeed. A tremor still manages to creep into my voice. "He'll expect you to react emotionally to all this," I reply. "It might be as good an opportunity as any to hit the Colonies with your own brand of propaganda. But whatever we do, we have to be careful about it. The Chancellor should know better than to trust you wholeheartedly."

"Things won't go well for you if they win," Day whispers, his voice pained. "I never took them to be some goddy compassionate softies—but maybe you should find a way to flee the country. Sneak off to a neutral place and seek asylum."

Flee the country, run away from this entire nightmare, and hole up in some faraway land? A small, tiny, dark voice in my head whispers agreement, that I will be safer that way . . . but I recoil from the thought. I draw myself up as well as I can. "No, Day," I reply gently. "If I flee, what will everyone else do? What about those who can't?"

"They will *kill* you." He draws closer. His eyes beg me to listen. "Please."

I shake my head. "I'm staying right here. The people don't need their morale crushed any further. Besides, you might need me." I give a little smile. "I think I know a few things about the Republic's military that could come in handy, wouldn't you say?"

Day shakes his head in frustration, but at the same time he

knows I won't budge. He knows, because he would do no differently in my position.

He takes my hand in his and pulls me toward him. His arms wrap around me. I'm so unused to his touch that this embrace sends an overwhelming wave of heat through my body. I close my eyes, collapse against his chest, and savor it. Has it really been so long since the last time we kissed? Have I really missed him this much? Have all the problems threatening to crush us both weakened us to the point where we are gasping for breath, clinging desperately to each other for survival? I've forgotten how right it feels to be in his arms. His collar shirt is rumpled and soft against my skin, and beneath it his chest is warm and pulses with the faint beating of his heart. He smells of earth, smoke, and wind.

"You drive me insane, June," he murmurs against my hair. "You're the scariest, most clever, bravest person I know, and sometimes I can't catch my breath because I'm trying so hard to keep up. There will never be another like you. You realize that, don't you?" I tilt my face up to see him. His eyes reflect the faint lights from the JumboTrons, a rainbow of evening colors. "Billions of people will come and go in this world," he says softly, "but there will *never* be another like you."

My heart twists until it threatens to break. I don't know how to respond.

Then he releases me abruptly—the coolness of the night is a sudden shock against my skin. Even in the darkness, I can see the blush on his cheeks. His breathing sounds heavier than usual. "What is it?" I say.

"I'm sorry," he replies, his voice strained. "I'm dying, June—I'm no good for you. And I do so well until I see you in person, and then everything changes again. I think I don't care about you anymore, that things will be easier once you're far away, and then all of a sudden I'm here again, and you're . . ." He pauses to look at me. The anguish in his expression is a knife cutting through my heart. "*Why* do I do this to myself? I see you and feel such—" He has tears in his eyes now. The sight is more than I can bear. He takes two steps away from me and then turns back like a caged animal. "Do you even love me?" he suddenly asks. He grips both of my shoulders. "I've said it to you before, and I still mean it. But I've never heard it from *you*. I can't tell. And then you give me this *ring*"—he pauses to hold his hand up—"and I don't know what to think anymore."

He draws closer, until I feel his lips against my ear. My entire body trembles. "Do you have *any idea*?" he says in a soft, broken, hoarse whisper. "Do you know how . . . how badly I *wish* . . ."

He pulls away long enough to look me desperately in the eyes. "If you don't love me, just say it—*you have to help me.* It'd probably be for the best. It'd make it easier to stay away from you, wouldn't it? I can let go." He says it like he's trying to convince himself. "I *can* let go, if you don't love me."

He says this as if he thinks I'm the stronger one. But I'm not. I can't keep this up any better than he can. "No," I say through gritted teeth and blurry vision. "I can't help you. Because I *do* love you." There it is, out in the open. "I'm in love with you," I repeat.

There's a conflicted look in Day's eyes, a joy and a grief, that makes him so vulnerable. I realize then how little defense he has against my words. *He loves so wholly. It is his nature.* He blinks, then tries to find the right response. "I—" he stumbles. "I'm so afraid, June. So afraid of what might happen to—"

I put two fingers against his lips to hush him. "Fear makes you stronger," I whisper. Before I can stop myself, I put my hands on his face and press my mouth to his.

Whatever shreds of self-restraint Day had now crumble into pieces. He falls into my kiss with helpless urgency. I feel his hands touch my face, one palm smooth and one still wrapped in bandages, and then he wraps his arms frantically around my waist, pulling me so close that I gasp aloud. No one compares to him. And right now, I want nothing else.

We make our way back inside, our lips never apart. Day stumbles against me, then loses his balance, and we collapse backward into my bed. His body knocks the breath out of me. His hands run along my jaw and neck, down my back, down my legs. I tug his coat off. Day's lips move away from mine and he buries his face against my neck. His hair fans out across my arm, heavy and softer than any silk I've ever worn. Day finally finds the buttons on my shirt. I've already loosened his, and underneath the fabric his skin is hot to the touch. The heat radiating from him warms me. I savor the weight of him.

Neither of us dares to say a word. We're afraid that words will stop us, that they'll tear apart the spell that binds us. He's trembling as much as I am. It suddenly occurs to me that he must be just as nervous. I smile when his eyes first meet mine and then lower in a bashful gesture. *Day is shy?* What a strange new emotion on his face, something out of place and yet so fitting. I'm relieved to see it, because I can feel the blush rising hot on my own cheeks. Embarrassed, I feel an urge to cover up my exposed skin. I've frequently imagined what this would be like, lying with Day for the first time. *I'm in love with him.* I tentatively test these new words again in my mind, amazed and frightened by what they might mean. He is here, and he is real, flesh and blood.

Even in his feverish passion, Day is gentle with me. It is a different gentleness from what I've felt around Anden, who is refinement and properness and elegance. Day is coarse, open, uncertain, and pure. When I look at him, I notice the subtle smile playing at the edges of his mouth, the smallest hint of mischief that only strengthens my desire for him. He nuzzles my neck; his touch sends shivers dancing along my spine. Day sighs in relief against my ear in a way that makes my heart pound, a sigh of freeing himself from all of the dark emotions that plague him. I fall into another kiss, running my hands through his hair, letting him know that I'm okay. He gradually relaxes. I suck in my breath as he moves against me; his eyes are so bright that I feel like I could drown in them. He kisses my cheeks, tucking a strand of my hair carefully behind my ear as he goes, and I slide my arms around his back and pull him closer.

No matter what happens in the future, no matter where our paths take us, this moment will be ours.

Afterward, we stay quiet. Day lies beside me with blankets

covering part of his legs, his eyes closed in a drowsy half sleep, his hand still entwined with mine as if for reassurance. I look around us. The blankets hang precariously off the corner of the bed. The sheets have wrinkles that radiate out, looking like a dozen little suns and their rays. There are deep indents in my pillow. Broken glass and flower petals litter the floor. I hadn't even noticed that we'd knocked a vase off my dresser, hadn't heard the sound of it shattering against the cherrywood planks. My eyes go back to Day. His face looks so peaceful now, free of pain in the dim glow of night. Even naïve. His mouth is no longer open, his brows no longer scrunched together. He's not trembling anymore. Loose hair frames his face, a few strands catching the city's lights from outside. I inch forward, run my hand along the muscles of his arm, and touch my lips to his cheek.

His eyes open; they blink at me sleepily. He stares at me for a long moment. I wonder what he sees, and whether all of the pain and joy and fear he had confessed earlier is still there, forever haunting him. He leans over to give me the gentlest, most delicate kiss. His lips linger, afraid to leave. I don't want to leave either. I don't want to think about waking up. When I pull him close to me again, he obliges, aching for more. And all I can think about is that I'm grateful for his silence, for not telling me that I am joining us together when I should be letting him go.

# DAY

IT'S NOT LIKE I HAVEN'T HAD MY SHARE OF MOMENTS WITH girls. I had my first kiss when I was twelve, when I locked lips with a sixteen-year-old girl in exchange for her not ratting me out to the street police. I've fooled around with a handful of girls in the slum sectors and a few from wealthy sectors—there was even one gem sector, high school freshman who I'd had a couple days' romance with back when I was fourteen. She was cute, with pixie-short, light brown hair and flawless olive skin, and we'd sneak off every afternoon to the basement of her school and, well, have a little fun. Long story.

But . . . *June.*

My heart's been torn wide open, just like I feared it would be, and I have no willpower to close it back up. Any barrier I might've succeeded in putting up around myself, any resistance I might've built up against my feelings for her, is now completely gone. Shattered. In the dim blue light of night, I reach out and run one hand along the curve of June's body. My breathing is still shallow. I don't want to be the first to say something. My chest is pressed gently against her back and my arm's resting comfortably around her waist; her hair drapes over her neck in a dark, glossy rope. I bury my face against her smooth skin. A million thoughts pour through my head, but like her, I stay silent.

There's simply nothing to say.

. . .

I jolt awake in bed, gasping. I can barely breathe—my lungs heave in an attempt to suck in air. I look around frantically. *Where am I?*

I'm in June's bed.

It was a nightmare, just a nightmare, and the Lake sector alley and street and blood are gone. I lie there a moment, trying quietly to catch my breath and slow the pounding of my heart. I'm completely drenched in sweat. I glance over at June. She's lying on her side and facing me, her body still rising and falling in a gentle, steady rhythm. Good. I didn't wake her. I hurriedly wipe tears from my face with the palm of my uninjured hand. Then I lie there for a few minutes, still trembling. When it's obvious that I'm not going to be able to fall back asleep, I slowly sit up in bed and crouch with my arms against my knees. I bow my head. My lashes brush against the skin of my arm. I feel so weak, like I just finished climbing up a thirty-story building.

This was easily the worst nightmare I've had yet. I'm even terrified to blink for too long, in case I have to revisit the images that danced under my eyelids. I look around the room. My vision blurs again; I angrily wipe the fresh tears away. What time is it? It's still pitch-black outside, with only the faint glow from distant JumboTrons and streetlights filtering into the room. I glance toward June, watching how the dim lights from outside splash color across her silhouette. This time, I don't reach out and touch her.

I don't know how long I sit there crouched like that, taking in one deep lungful of air after another until my breathing finally steadies. It's long enough for the sweat beading my entire body to dry. My eyes wander to the room's balcony. I stare at it for a while, unable to look away, and then I gingerly slide out of bed without a sound and slip into my shirt, trousers, and boots. I twist my hair up into a tight knot, then fit a cap snugly over it. June stirs a little. I stop moving. When she settles back down, I finish buttoning my shirt and walk over to the glass balcony doors. In the corner of the bedroom, June's dog gives me a curious tilt of his head. But he doesn't make a sound. I say a silent thanks in my head, then open the balcony doors. They swing open, then close behind me without a click.

I pull myself laboriously onto the balcony railings, perch there like a cat, and survey my surroundings. Ruby sector, a gem sector that's so completely different from where I came from. I'm back in LA, but I don't recognize it. Clean, manicured streets, new and shiny JumboTrons, wide sidewalks without cracks and potholes, without street police dragging crying orphans away from market stands. Instinctively, my attention turns in the direction of the city that Lake sector would be. From this side of the building, I can't see downtown LA, but I can *feel* it there, the memories that woke me up and whispered for me to come back. The paper clip ring sits heavily on my finger. A dark, terrible mood lingers at the back of my mind after that nightmare, something I can't seem to shake. I hop over the side of the balcony and work my way down to a lower ledge. I make my way silently, floor by floor, until my boots hit the pavement and I blend into the shadows of the night. My breaths come raggedly.

Even here in a gem sector, there are now city patrols guarding the streets, their guns drawn as if ready for a surprise Colonies' attack at any moment. I steer clear of them to avoid any questions, and go back to my old street habits, making my way through back alley mazes and shaded sides of buildings until I reach a train station where jeeps are lined up, waiting to give rides. I ignore the jeeps—I'm not in the mood to get chatty with one of the drivers and then have them recognize me as Day, and then hear rumors spreading around town the next morning about whatever the hell they think I was up to. Instead, I head into the train station and wait for the next automated ride to come and take me to Union Station in downtown.

Half an hour later, I step out of the downtown station and make my way silently through the streets until I'm close to my mother's old home. The cracks in all the slum sector roads are good for one thing—here and there I see patches of sea daisies growing haphazardly, little spots of turquoise and green on an otherwise gray street. On instinct, I bend down and pick a handful of them. Mom's favorite.

"You there. Hey, boy."

I turn to see who's calling. It actually takes me a few seconds to find her, because she's so small. An old woman's hunched against the side of a boarded-up building, shivering

in the night air. She's bent almost double, with a face completely covered in deep wrinkles, and her clothes are so tat-
tered that I can't tell where any of it ends or begins—it's
just one big mop of rags. She has a cracked mug sitting at
her dirty bare feet, but what really makes me stop is that her
hands are wrapped in thick bandages. Just like Mom's. When
she sees that my attention is on her, her eyes light up with a
faint glint of hope. I'm not sure if she recognizes me, but I'm
also not sure how well she can see. "Any spare change, little
boy?" she croaks.

I dig around numbly in my pockets, then pull out a small
wad of cash. Eight hundred Republic Notes. Not too long
ago, I would've put my life in danger to get my hands on this
much money. I bend down next to the old woman, then press
the bills into her shaking palm and squeeze her bandaged
hands with my own.

"Keep it hidden. Don't tell anyone." When she just continues to stare at me with shocked eyes and an agape mouth, I
stand up and start walking back down the street. I think she
calls out, but I don't bother turning around. Don't want to
see those bandaged hands again.

Minutes later, I reach the intersection of Watson and
Figueroa. My old home.

The street hasn't changed much from how I remember it,
but this time my mother's home is boarded up and abandoned, like many of the other buildings in the slum sectors.
I wonder if there are squatters in there, all holed up in our
old bedroom or sleeping on the kitchen floor. No light shines

from the house. I walk slowly toward it, wondering if I'm still lost in my nightmare. Maybe I haven't woken up at all. No more quarantine tape blocks the street off, no more plague patrols hang around outside the house. As I walk toward it, I notice an old bloodstain still visible, if only barely, on the broken concrete leading toward the house. It looks brown and faded now, so different from how I remember it. I stare at the bloodstain, numb and unfeeling, then step around it and continue on. My hand clings tightly to the thick bundle of sea daisies I brought.

When I approach the front door, I see the familiar red *X* is still there, although now it's faded and chipped, and several planks of rotting wood are nailed across the door frame. I stand there for a while, running a finger along the dying paint streaks. A few minutes later, I snap out of my daze and wander around to the back of the house. Half of our fence has now collapsed, leaving the tiny yard exposed and visible to our neighbors. The back door also has planks of wood nailed across it, but they're so rotten and crumbling that all I have to do is put a little weight on them and they come apart in a dull crackle of splinters.

I force the door open and step inside. I remove my cap as I go, letting my hair tumble down my back. Mom had always told us to take our hats off while in the house.

My eyes adjust to the darkness. I step quietly up a few steps and enter the back of our tiny living room. They may have boarded up the house as part of some standard protocol, but the furniture inside the house is untouched, different only in that it's all covered in a layer of dust. My family's few belongings are still here, in exactly the same condition as I'd last seen them. The old Elector's portrait hangs on the room's far wall, prominent and centered, and our little wooden dining table still has thick layers of cardboard tacked to one of its legs, still doing their job of holding the table up. One of the chairs is lying on the ground, as if someone had to get up in a hurry. *That had been John,* I now remember. I recall how we'd all headed into the bedroom to grab Eden, trying to get our little brother out before the plague patrols came for him.

The bedroom. I turn my boots in the direction of our narrow bedroom door. It only takes a few steps to reach it. Yeah, everything in here is exactly the same too, maybe with a few extra cobwebs. The plant that Eden had once brought home is still sitting in the corner, although now it's dead, its leaves and vines black and shriveled. I stand there for a moment, staring at it, and then head back into the living room. I walk once around the dining table. Finally, I sit in my old chair. It creaks like it always did.

I lay the bundle of sea daisies carefully on the tabletop. Our lantern sits in the middle of the table, unlit and unused. Usually, the routine went like this: Mom would come home around six o'clock every day, a few hours after I'd gotten back from grade school, and John would get home around nine or ten. Mom would try to hold off on lighting the table lantern each night until John returned, and after a while

Eden and I got used to looking forward to "the lantern lighting," which always meant John had just walked through the door. And *that* meant we'd get to sit down to dinner.

I don't know why I sit here and feel the familiar old expectation that Mom is going to come out from the kitchen and light the lantern. I don't know how I can feel a jolt of joy in my chest, thinking John is home, that dinner's served. Stupid old habits. Still, my eyes go expectantly to the front door. My hopes rise.

But the lantern stays unlit. John stays outside. Mom isn't home.

I lean my arms heavily against the table and press my palms to my eyes. "Help me," I whisper desperately to the empty room. "I can't do this." *I want to, I love her, but I can't bear it. It's been almost a year. What's wrong with me? Why can't I just move on?*

My throat chokes up. The tears come in a rush. I don't bother to stop them, because I know it's impossible. I sob uncontrollably—I can't stop, I can't catch my breath, I can't see. I can't see my family because they're not here. Without them, all this furniture is nothing, the sea daisies lying on the table are meaningless, the lantern is just an old, blackened piece of junk. The images from my nightmare linger, haunting me. No matter how hard I try, I can't push them away.

Time heals all wounds. But not this one. Not yet.

I DON'T STIR, BUT THROUGH MY HALF-LIDDED, SLEEPY eyes, I see Day sit up in bed beside me and bury his face in his arms. He's breathing heavily. Seven minutes later he gets up quietly, casts one last glance in my direction, and disappears out the balcony doors. He's as silent as ever, and if him waking up from his nightmare hadn't roused me, he would easily have left my room without my ever knowing.

But I *do* know, and this time I rise right after he leaves. I throw on some clothes, pull on my boots, and head out after him. The cool air washes over my face, and moonlight drenches the whole night in dark silver.

Even in his deteriorating condition, he's still fast when he wants to be. By the time I catch up with him at Union Station and follow him through the streets of downtown, my heart is pounding steadily in the way it does after a thorough workout. By now, I already know where he's going. He's returning to his family's old home. I look on as he finally reaches the intersection of Watson and Figueroa, turns the corner, and heads inside a tiny, boarded-up house with a faded *X* still painted on its door.

Just being back here makes me dizzy with the memory. I can't imagine how much worse it must be for Day. Gingerly I make my way over to the boarded windows, then listen intently for him. He goes in through the back door—I hear him shuffling around inside, his footsteps subdued and muffled, and then stop in the living room. I go from window to window until I finally find one that still has a crack between two of its wooden planks. At first I can't see him. But eventually I do.

Day is sitting at the living room table with his head in his hands. Even though it's too dark inside for me to make out his features, I can hear him crying. His silhouette trembles with grief, and his anguish is etched into every single crumpled, devastated muscle of his body. The sound is so foreign that it tears at my heart; I've seen Day cry, but I'm not used to it. I don't know whether I ever will be. When I reach up to my face, I realize that tears are running down my cheeks too.

*I did this to him* . . . and because he loves me, he can never really escape it. He'll remember the fate of his family every time he sees me, even if he loves me, *especially* if he loves me.

# DAY

I FINALLY RETURN, BLEARY-EYED AND EXHAUSTED, TO JUNE'S bedroom just before dawn. She's still there, apparently undisturbed. I don't try to crawl back into bed beside her; instead, I collapse onto her couch and fall into a deep, dreamless sleep until the light strengthens outside.

June's the one who shakes me awake. "Hey," she whispers. To my surprise, she doesn't comment on how red or puffy my eyes must look. She doesn't even seem shocked to wake up and find me lounging on her couch instead of in her bed. Her own eyes look heavy. "I've . . . informed Anden about what you decided. He says a lab team will be ready to pick you and Eden up in two hours, at your apartment." She sounds grateful, weary, and hesitant.

"I'll be there," I mutter. I can't help staring vacantly off into space for a few seconds—nothing seems real right now, and I feel like I'm swimming in a sea of fog where emotions and images and thoughts are all out of focus. I force myself off the couch and into the bathroom. There, I unbutton my shirt and splash water on my face and chest and arms. I'm afraid to look in the mirror this time. I don't want to see John staring back at me, with my own blindfold tight around his eyes. My hands are shaking so badly; the gash on my left palm is open again and bleeding, probably from the fact that I keep clenching that hand instinctively. Had June seen me leave? I shudder as I relive the memory of her standing there outside my mother's home, waiting at the head of a squadron of soldiers. Then I revisit the Chancellor's words to me, the precarious situation that June is in . . . that Tess is in, that Eden is in—that we're *all* in.

I splash water repeatedly on my face, and when that doesn't help, I jump in the shower and drown myself with scalding hot water. But it doesn't numb the images.

By the time I finally emerge from the bathroom, my hair still wet and my shirt half buttoned, I'm sickly pale and trembling. June watches me quietly as she sits on the edge of her bed, sipping a pale purple tea. Even though I know it's pointless to try hiding anything from her, I still give it a shot. "I'm ready," I say with as genuine of a smile as I can muster. She doesn't deserve to see this sort of pain on my face, and I don't want her to think that she's the one causing it. *She's not the one causing it,* I angrily remind myself.

But June doesn't comment on it. She studies me with those deep dark eyes. "I just got a call from Anden," she says, running a hand uncomfortably through her hair. "They have some new evidence that Commander Jameson's the one responsible for passing along some military secrets to the Colonies. It sounds like she's working for them now."

Underneath my tidal wave of emotions, a deep hatred wells up. If it weren't for Commander Jameson, maybe everything would have been better between June and me—and maybe our families would still be alive. I don't know. We'll *never* know. And now she's working for the enemy when she's supposed to be dead. I mutter a curse under my breath. "Is there any way to know exactly where she is? Is she actually in the Republic?"

"No one knows." June shakes her head. "Anden says they're trying to see if anything on her can be tracked, but she must have long changed out of her prison clothing, and her boots' tracking chips must be gone by now. She'll have made sure of that." When June sees the frustration on my face, she grimaces in sympathy. Both of us, broken by the same person. "I know." She puts her tea down and squeezes my uninjured hand.

Violent flashbacks flicker through my memory at her touch—I wince before I can stop myself. She freezes. For a second, I see the deep hurt in her expression. I quickly cover up my mistake by kissing her, trying to lose myself in the gesture as I did last night.

But I've never been the best liar, at least not around her. She takes a step away from me. "Sorry," she whispers.

"It's okay," I say in a rush, irritated with myself at dragging our old wounds back to the surface. "It's not—"

"Yes, it is." June forces herself to face me. "I saw where you went last night—I saw you in there. . . ." Her voice fades away as she looks down in guilt. "I'm sorry I followed you, but I had to know. I had to see that I was the one causing all of the grief in your eyes."

I want to reassure her that it's *not* all because of her, that I love her so desperately that I'm terrified of the feeling. But

I can't. June sees the hesitation on my face and knows it's a confirmation of her fear. She bites her lip. "It's my fault," she says, as if it's just simple logic. "And I'm not sure I will ever be able to earn your forgiveness. I *shouldn't.*"

"I don't know what to do." My hands dangle at my sides, helpless. Terrible images from our past flash through my mind again—my best attempts can't stop them. "I don't know how to do it."

June's eyes are glossy with tears, but she manages to hold them in. Can one mistake really destroy a lifetime together? "I don't think there's a way," she finally says.

I take a step toward her. "Hey," I whisper in her ear. "We'll be okay." I'm not sure if it's true, but it seems like the best thing to say.

June smiles, playing along, but her eyes mirror my own doubt.

The second day of the Colonies' promised ceasefire.

The last place I want to return to is the lab floor of the Los Angeles Central Hospital. It's hard enough being there and seeing Tess contained behind glass walls, with chemicals being injected into her bloodstream. Now I'll be back there with Eden at my side, and I'll have to deal with seeing the same thing happen to him. As we get ready to head down to the jeep waiting in front of our temporary apartment, I kneel in front of Eden and straighten his glasses. He stares solemnly back.

"You don't have to do this," I say again.

"I know," Eden replies. He brushes my hand impatiently away when I wipe lint off his jacket's shoulders. "I'll be fine. They said it wouldn't take all day, anyway."

Anden couldn't guarantee his safety; he could only promise that they would take every precaution. And coming from the mouth of the Republic—even a mouth that I've come to grudgingly trust—that little cracked bit of reassurance means almost nothing. I sigh. "If you change your mind at any point, you let me know, yeah?"

"Don't worry, Daniel," he says, shrugging off the whole thing. "I'll be fine. It doesn't seem that scary. At least you get to be there."

"Yeah. At least I get to be there," I echo numbly. Lucy fusses over his messy blond curls. More reminders of home, and of Mom. I shut my eyes and try to clear my thoughts. Then I reach out and tap Eden on the nose. "The sooner they start," I say to him, "the sooner it can all be over."

Minutes later, a military jeep picks me up while a medic truck transports Eden separately to the Los Angeles Central Hospital.

*He can do this,* I repeat to myself as I reach the fourth-floor laboratory. I'm escorted by technicians to a chamber with thick glass windows. *And if he can, then I can live through it.* But still, my hands are sweaty. I clench them again in an attempt to stop their endless trembling, and a stab of pain runs through my injured palm. Eden's inside this glass chamber. His pale blond curls are messy and ruffled in spite of

Lucy's efforts, and he's now wearing a thin red patient scrub. His feet are bare. A pair of lab technicians help him up onto a long, white bed, and one of them rolls up Eden's sleeves to take his blood pressure. Eden winces when the cool rubber touches his arm.

"Relax, kid," the lab tech says, his voice muffled by the glass. "Just take a deep breath."

Eden murmurs a faint "okay" in response. He looks so small next to them. His feet don't even touch the floor. They swing idly while he stares off toward the window separating us, searching for me. I clench and unclench my hands, then press them against the window.

The fate of the entire Republic rests on the shoulders of my kid brother. If Mom, John, or Dad were here, they'd probably laugh at how ridiculous this whole thing is.

"He's going to be okay," the lab tech standing next to me mutters in reassurance. He doesn't sound very convincing. "Today's procedures shouldn't cause him any pain. We're just going to take some blood samples and then give him a few medications. We've sent some samples to Antarctica's lab teams for analysis too."

"Is that supposed to make me feel better?" I snap at him. "*Today's* procedures shouldn't cause him any pain? What about tomorrow's?"

The lab tech holds his hands up defensively. "I'm sorry," he stammers. "It came out wrong—I didn't mean it like that. Your brother won't be in any pain, I promise. Some discomfort, perhaps, from the medicine, but we're taking every precaution we can. I, er, I hope you won't report this negatively to our glorious Elector."

So, that's what he's worried about. That if I'm upset, I'm going to run to Anden and whine. I narrow my eyes at him. "If you don't give me a reason to report anything bad, then I won't."

The lab tech apologizes again, but I'm not paying attention to him anymore. My eyes go back to Eden. He's asking one of the technicians something, although he's speaking quietly enough that I can't hear. The lab tech shakes his head at my brother. Eden swallows, looks back nervously in my direction, and then squeezes his eyes shut. One of the lab techs takes out a syringe, then carefully injects it into the vein of Eden's arm. Eden clenches his jaw tight, but he doesn't utter a sound. A familiar dull pain throbs at the base of my neck. I try to calm myself down. Stressing myself out and triggering one of my headaches at a time like this is not going to help Eden.

*He chose to do this,* I remind myself. I swell with sudden pride. When had Eden grown up? I feel like I blinked and missed it.

The lab tech finally removes the syringe, which is now filled with blood. They dab something on Eden's arm, then bandage it. The second technician then drops a handful of pills into Eden's open palm.

"Swallow them together," he tells my brother. Eden does

as he says. "They're a bit bitter—best to get it all over with at once."

Eden grimaces and gags a little, but manages to wash the pills down with some water. Then he lies down on the bed. The technicians wheel him over to a cylindrical machine. I can't remember what the machine's called, even though they told me less than an hour ago. They slowly roll him inside it, until all I can see of Eden are the balls of his bare feet. I slowly peel my hands off the window. My skin leaves prints on the glass. A minute later, my heart twists in my chest as I hear Eden crying from inside the machine. Something about it must be painful. I clench my teeth so hard that I think my jaw might break.

Finally, after what seems like an eternity, one of the lab techs motions for me to come inside. I immediately shove past them and enter the glass chamber to lean over Eden's side. He's sitting on the edge of the white bed again. When he hears me approach, he breaks into a smile.

"That wasn't so bad," he says to me in a weak voice.

I just take his hand and squeeze it in my own. "You did good," I reply. "I'm proud of you." And I am. I'm prouder of him than I've ever been of myself—I'm proud of him for standing up to me.

One of the lab techs shows me a screen with what looks like a magnified view of Eden's blood cells. "A good start," he tells us. "We'll work with this and try injecting Tess with a cure tonight. If we're lucky, she'll hang in there for another five or six days and give us some time to work with." The tech's eyes are grim, even though his words are pretty hopeful. The weird combination makes a chill run down my spine. I grip Eden's hand tighter.

"We don't have a lot of time left," Eden whispers to me when the lab techs leave us to talk in peace. "If they can't find a cure, what are we going to do?"

"I don't know," I admit. It's not something I really want to think about, because it leaves me feeling more helpless than I like. If we don't find a cure, there won't be any international military aid. If there's no aid, then we'll have no way to win against the Colonies. And if the Colonies overrun us . . . I recall what I saw when I was over there, and remember what the Chancellor had offered me. *If you choose, we can work together. The people don't know what's best for them. Sometimes you just have to help them along. Isn't that right?*

I need to find a way to stall them while we work on a cure. Anything to slow the Colonies down, to give the Antarcticans a chance to come to our aid. "We'll just have to fight back," I tell Eden, ruffling his hair. "Until we can't fight back anymore. That's the way it always seems to be, yeah?"

"Why can't the Republic win?" Eden asks. "I always thought their military was the strongest in the world. This is the first time I actually wish they were right."

I smile sadly at Eden's naïveté. "The Colonies have allies," I reply. "We don't." How the hell do I explain it all? How do I tell him exactly how helpless I feel, standing by like a broken puppet while Anden leads his army in a battle they just can't win? "They have a better army, and we just don't have enough soldiers to go around."

Eden sighs. His little shoulders slump in a way that chokes me up. I close my eyes and force myself to calm down. Crying in front of Eden at a time like this is way too embarrassing. "Too bad everyone in the Republic isn't a soldier," he mutters.

I open my eyes. *Too bad everyone in the Republic isn't a soldier.*

And just like that, I know what I need to do. I know how to answer the Chancellor's blackmail, and how to stall the Colonies. I'm dying, I don't have many days left—my mind is slowly falling apart, and so is my strength. But I do have enough strength for one thing. I have enough time to take one final step.

"Maybe everyone in the Republic *can* be a soldier," I reply quietly.

# JUNE

LAST NIGHT FEELS LIKE A DREAM, EVERY LAST DETAIL
of it. But this morning stands in stark contrast—there is no
mistaking the flinch I felt from Day when I touched his arm,
the violent shudder that went through him at just a brush of
my hand. My heart still hurts as I leave my apartment, headed
for a parked jeep that will be waiting for me. A morning spent
with the Senate. I try in vain to clear Day from my mind, but
it's impossible. A Senate meeting feels so trivial right now—
the Colonies are gradually pushing our country back with the
help of strong allies, Antarctica still refuses to help us, and
Commander Jameson is at large. And here I'll sit, talking politics when I could be—*should* be—out in the field, doing what
I'm trained to do. What am I going to say to all of them, anyway? Are any of them even going to listen?

What are we going to do?

No. I need to focus. I need to support Anden as he attempts,
yet again, to negotiate with the Colonies' Chancellor and
CEOs and generals. We both know that it won't get us anywhere. . . . The only thing that will make them budge is a cure.
And even then, it might not be enough to hold the Colonies
back. But still. We have to try. And perhaps he'll be up for
helping the Patriots with their plans, especially if he knows
how much Day will be involved in them.

The mere thought of Day brings back memories of last

night. My cheeks turn hot, and I know it's not because of the warm Los Angeles weather. *Stupid timing*, I chide myself, and push last night from my thoughts. All around me, the usually busy streets of Lake are eerily empty, as if we're preparing for an oncoming storm. I suppose that's not so inaccurate.

A prickling sensation suddenly travels up my spine. I stop for a moment, then frown. What was that? The streets still look deserted, but a strange premonition makes the hairs on the back of my neck stand up. *Someone is watching me.* Immediately the idea feels too far-fetched, but as I walk, I tighten my jaw and let my hand rest on my gun. Maybe I'm being ridiculous. Perhaps the warning that Day had given me—that the Colonies might use me against him or that they might have me in their sights—is starting to play tricks on my mind. Still, no reason to throw caution to the winds. I lean against the closest building so that my back is protected, and call Anden. The sooner this jeep arrives, the better.

And then I see her. I stop the call.

She wears a good disguise. (Weathered Republic attire that's supposed to be worn only by first-year soldiers, which means she looks unremarkable and easily missed; a soldier's cap pulled low over her face, with only a few dark red strands poking out from underneath it.) But even from this distance, I recognize her face—cold and hard.

Commander Jameson.

I look casually away and pretend to dig around in my pockets for something, but inside, my heart pounds at a furious pace. She's here in Los Angeles, which means she somehow managed to escape the fighting in Denver and avoided the Republic's clutches. Is it too big a coincidence that she is where I am? Perhaps she is here because she knew that *I* would be here? The Colonies. There must be other eyes here. My hands shake as she passes me by on the other side of the street. She gives no indication of seeing me, but I know that she's noticed. On such an empty block, I should be impossible to miss—and I'm not in disguise.

When her back is finally turned to me, I cross my arms, tilt my head slightly downward, and call Anden on my earpiece again. "I see her. She's here. Commander Jameson is in Los Angeles."

My voice sounds so quiet and mumbled that Anden has trouble making it out. "You see her?" he asks in disbelief. "She's on the same block as you?"

"Yes," I whisper. I'm careful to keep an eye on Commander Jameson's disappearing figure. "She might be here intentionally, looking for where my jeep will take me or perhaps trying to locate you." As she pulls farther away, an overwhelming desire rises up in me to tag along. For the first time in a long time, my agent skills are calling out to me. Gone are politics; suddenly I've been thrust back in the field. When she turns a corner, I immediately abandon my spot and start heading after her. Where is she going? "She's at Lake and Colorado," I whisper urgently to Anden. "Turning north. Get some soldiers out here, but don't let her know you're following along. I want to see where she's going." Before Anden can say anything else, I end the call.

I trail along the side of the buildings, careful to stay in the shadows as much as I can, and take a shortcut through one alley toward the street where I think Commander Jameson had gone. Instead of peering around the corner and potentially giving myself away, I instead huddle in the alley and calculate how much time has passed. If she kept up the same pace, and she stayed on this street, then she should have walked past this alley at least one minute ago. Carefully, I lean out until I can catch a quick glimpse of the street. Sure enough, she's already walked past me, and I can see the back of her figure hurrying away. This quick glimpse is also enough to tell me something else—she's talking into her own mike.

I wish Day were with me. He'd know instantly the best way to travel unseen through these streets. For a second I contemplate calling him, but for him to get here in time would be too much of a stretch.

Instead, I follow Commander Jameson. I tail her for a good four blocks, until we enter a strip of Ruby that borders part of Batalla, where two or three pyramid airship bases sit along the street. She makes a turn again. I hurry to turn with her—but by the time I look down the street, she's gone. Perhaps she knew someone was following her; after all, Commander Jameson is much more experienced in this sort of tracking than I am. I look to the roofs.

Anden's voice crackles in my earpiece. "We lost her," he confirms. "I've put out a silent alert to the troops there to search for her and report immediately back. She couldn't have gone far."

"That's true," I agree, but my shoulders sag. She'd disappeared without a trace. Who had she been talking to on her mike? My eyes scan the street, trying to figure out what she must have come here for. Maybe she's scouting. The thought unnerves me.

"I'm heading back," I finally whisper into my own mike. "If my suspicions are correct, then we might have—"

A whoosh of air—a blinding spark—something explodes before my eyes. I flinch and throw myself instinctively to the ground behind a nearby trash bin. *What was that?*

*A bullet.* I look to the wall where it hit. A small chunk of brick is missing. Someone tried to shoot me. My sudden turn to go back the way I came must have been the only thing that saved my life. I start placing another frantic call to Anden. Blood rushes through my ears like a tidal wave of noise, blocking out logic and allowing the panic in. Another bullet sparks against the metal of the trash bin. There's no question now that I'm under attack.

I click the call off. Where is Commander Jameson shooting from? Are there others with her? Colonies troops? Republic soldiers turned traitorous? I don't know. I can't tell. I can't hear and *I can't see—*

Through my rising panic, Metias's voice materializes. *Stay calm, Junebug. Logic will save you. Focus, think, act.*

I close my eyes, taking a deep, shuddering breath, and allow myself a second to still my mind, to concentrate on my brother's voice. This is no time to fall apart. I have never let emotions get the best of me, and I'm *not* about to start now. *Think, June. Don't be stupid.* After over a year of trauma, after months and months of political bargaining, after days of war and death, I am starting to suspect everything and everyone. This is how the Colonies could tear us apart . . . not with their allies or weapons, but with their propaganda. With fear and desperation.

My panic clears. Logic sweeps back in.

First, I yank my own gun out of its holster. Then I make an exaggerated gesture, like I'm about to dart out from behind the trash bin. Instead, I stay put—but my feint is enough to provoke another bullet. *Spark!* It ricochets off the brick wall that my back is pressed up against. Instantly I glance at the mark it leaves and pinpoint where it might have come from. (Not from the roofs—the angle isn't wide enough. Four, maybe five floors up. Not the building directly across from me, but the one right next to it.) I look over to the windows lining those floors. Several are open. At first I want to aim right back at those windows—but then I remind myself that I might hit someone unintentionally. Instead, I study the building. It looks like either a broadcast station or a military hall—it's close enough to the air bases that I wonder whether it's where the airships are being monitored from.

What is she up to that involves the air bases? Are the Colonies planning a surprise attack here?

I click my mike back on. "Anden," I whisper after I input his code. "Get me out of here. Use my gun's tracking."

But my call has no time to go through. A split second later, another bullet cracks right above my head—this time I flinch and flatten myself underneath the trash bin. When I open my eyes, I find myself staring straight into the cold eyes of Commander Jameson.

She grabs for my wrist.

I bolt out from under the trash bin before she can reach me. I twist around to aim my gun at her, but she's already darted away. Her own gun's raised. Right away I can tell that she's not aiming to kill. *Why?* The question runs through my mind at lightning speed. *Because the Colonies need me alive—because they need me to bargain with.*

She fires; I roll on the ground. A bullet misses my leg by inches. I hop onto my feet and aim at her again—this time I fire. I miss her by a hair. She ducks behind the trash bin. At the same time I try to put a call through again. I succeed. "Anden," I gasp into the mike as I turn tail and run. "Get me out!"

"Already on our way," Anden replies. I sprint around a corner right as I hear another shot fired behind me. It's the last one. Right on schedule, a jeep races toward me and screeches to a halt several feet away from me. A pair of soldiers pours out, shielding me while two others run out to the street toward Commander Jameson. I already know it's too late to catch her, though—she must've made a run for it too. It's all over as quickly as it began. I hop into the jeep with the soldiers' help, then collapse against the seat as we speed away. Adrenaline washes through me. My entire body trembles uncontrollably.

"Are you all right?" one of the soldiers asks, but his voice sounds far away. All I can think about is what the encounter meant. Commander Jameson had known I would wait at that block for my jeep; she must have lured me out in an attempt to capture me. Her presence at the airship bases was no coincidence. She's feeding information to the Colonies about our rotations and locations here. There are probably other Colonies soldiers hiding amongst us too—Commander Jameson is a wanted fugitive. She can't move around this easily without help. And with her experience, she could probably hold off a manhunt for her on these streets long enough for the Colonies to arrive. *For the Colonies to arrive.* They've targeted their next city, and it's going to be us.

Over my earpiece, Anden's voice comes on again. "I'm on my way," he says urgently. "Are you all right? The jeep will take you straight to Batalla Hall, and I'll have a full guard on you—"

"She's feeding them information about the ports," I breathe into the mike before he can finish. My voice shakes as I say it. "The Colonies are about to attack Los Angeles."

# DAY

I GET THE CALL ABOUT JUNE AS I'M SITTING WITH EDEN. After a morning of experimentations, he's finally fallen asleep. Outside, clouds blanket the entire city in a bleak atmosphere. Good. I wouldn't know how to feel if it were a bright, sunny day, not with this news about Commander Jameson and the fact that she'd tried to shoot June out in the open on the streets. Clouds suit my mood just fine.

While I wait impatiently for June to arrive at the hospital, I spend my time watching Tess through the glass of her room's window. The lab team still surrounds her, monitoring her vitals like a bunch of goddy vultures on an old nature show. I shake my head. I shouldn't be so hard on them. Earlier they let me put on a suit, sit inside next to Tess, and hold her hand. She was unconscious, of course, but she could still tighten her fingers around mine. She knows I'm here. That I'm waiting for her cure.

Now the lab team looks like they're injecting her with some sort of formula mixed from a batch of liquid made from Eden's blood cells. Hell if I know what'll happen next. Their faces are hidden behind reflective glass masks, turning them into something alien. Tess's eyes stay closed, and her skin's an unhealthy yellow.

*She has the virus that the Colonies spread,* I have to

remind myself. *No, that the* Republic *spread.* Damn this memory of mine.

Pascao, Baxter, and the other Patriots stay camped out at the hospital too. Where the hell else do they have to go, anyway? As the minutes drag on, Pascao takes a seat next to me and rubs his hands together. "She's hanging in there," he mutters, his eyes lingering on Tess. "But there have been reports of some other outbreaks in the city. Came mostly from some refugees. Have you seen the news on the JumboTrons?"

I shake my head. My jaw is tense with rage. *When* is June arriving? They said they were bringing her here over a quarter of an hour ago. "Haven't gone anywhere except to see my brother and to see Tess."

Pascao sighs, rubbing a hand across his face. He's careful not to ask about June. I'd apologize to him about my temper, but I'm too angry to care. "Three quarantine zones set up now in downtown. If you're still planning to execute your little stunt, we gotta move out within the next day."

"That's all the time we'll need. If the rumors we're hearing from June and the Elector are true, then this will be our best chance." The thought of parts of Los Angeles being cordoned off for quarantines sends a dark, uncomfortable nostalgia through me. Everything's so wrong, and I'm so tired. I'm so tired of worrying about it all, about whether or not the people I care about will make it through the night or survive the day. At the same time, I can't sleep. Eden's words from this morning still ring in my thoughts. *Maybe everyone in the Republic can be a soldier.* My fingers run along the paper clip ring adorning my finger. If June had gotten injured this morning, I wonder if the last shreds of my sanity would've vanished. I feel like I'm hanging on by a thread. I guess that's true in a pretty literal sense too—my headaches have been relentless today, and I've grown used to the perpetual pain pulsing at the back of my head. *Just a few months,* I think. *Just a few months, like the doctors said, and then maybe the medication will have worked enough to let me get that surgery. Keep hanging on.*

At my silence, Pascao turns his pale eyes on me. "It's gonna be dangerous, what you've told me," he says. He seems like he's treading carefully. "Some civilians will die. There's just no way around it."

"I don't think we have a choice," I reply, returning his look. "No matter how warped this country is, it's still their homeland. We have to call them to action."

Shouts echo from the hall beyond our own. Pascao and I both stop to listen for a second—and if I didn't know any better, I'd swear it was the Elector. Weird. I'm not exactly Anden's biggest fan, but *I've* never heard him lose his temper.

The double doors at the end of the hall swing open with a bang—suddenly, the shouts fill the hall. Anden storms in with his usual crowd of soldiers, while June keeps up beside him. *June.* Relief floods through my body. I hop to my feet. Her face lights up as I hurry over to her.

"I'm okay," she says, waving me off before I can even open

my mouth. She sounds impatient about it, like she's spent the entire day convincing everyone else of the same thing. "They're being overly cautious, bringing me here—"

I could care less if they're being overly cautious. I cut her off and pull her into a tight embrace. A weight lifts from my chest, and the rest of my anger comes flooding in. "You're the Elector," I snap at Anden. "You're the damn *Elector of the Republic*. Can't you make sure your own goddy *Princeps-Elect* isn't assassinated by a prisoner you guys can't even seem to keep imprisoned? What kind of bodyguards do you have, anyway—a pack of first-year cadets?"

Anden shoots me a dangerous look, but to my surprise, he stays silent. I pull away from June so I can hold her face in my hands. "You're okay, right?" I ask urgently. "You're completely okay?"

June raises an eyebrow at me, then gives me a quick, reassuring kiss. "*Yes*. I'm completely okay." She casts a glance over at Anden, but he's too distracted talking to one of his soldiers now.

"Find me the men assigned to retrieve the Princeps-Elect," he snaps at the soldier. Dark circles line the skin under his eyes, and his face looks both haggard and furious. "If luck hadn't been on our side, Jameson would have killed her. I've half a mind to label them all traitors. There's plenty of room in the firing squad yard for all of them." The soldier snaps to attention and rushes off with several others to do as Anden said. My own anger wanes, and a chill runs through me at how familiar his wrath feels. Like I'm looking at his father.

Now he faces me. His voice turns calmer. "The lab team tells me that your brother pulled through his experimentation so far very bravely," he says. "I wanted to thank you again for—"

"Don't lay it on too thick," I interrupt with a raised eyebrow. "This whole thing isn't over yet." After more days like today, where Eden's going to fade even faster from all the experiments, I might not be so polite. I lower my voice, making an effort to sound civil again. It's half working. "Let's talk in private. Elector, I have some ideas to run by you. With this recent news from Commander Jameson, we might just have an opportunity to stir up some trouble for the Colonies. You, me, June, and the Patriots."

Anden's eyes darken at that, and his mouth tightens in an uncertain frown as he scans his audience. Pascao's giant, ever-present grin doesn't seem to improve his mood. After a few seconds, though, he nods at his soldiers. "Get us a conference room," he says. "I want security cams off."

His soldiers scramble to do his bidding. As we fall into step behind him, I exchange a long glance with June. *She's okay, she's unharmed.* And yet, I'm afraid that she'll disappear if I'm careless enough to look away. I force myself to hold back on asking her about what happened until we're all in a private room—and from the look on her face, she's also waiting for the right moment. My hand aches to hold hers. I keep that to myself too. Our dance around each other always seems like it's doomed to repeat itself over and over again.

"So," Anden says once we've settled into a room and his patrol has disabled all of the cams. He leans back in one of the chairs and surveys me with a penetrating look. "Perhaps we should start with what happened to our Princeps-Elect this morning."

June lifts her chin, but her hands shake ever so slightly. "I saw Commander Jameson in Ruby sector. My guess is that she was in the area to scout locations—and she must have known where I would be." I marvel at how steady June sounds. "I tailed her for a while, until we reached the strip of airship bases that border Ruby and Batalla. She attacked me there."

Even this short of a summary is enough to make me see red. Anden sighs and runs a hand through his hair. "We suspect that Commander Jameson may have given some locations and schedules to the Colonies about Los Angeles airship bases. She may have also attempted to kidnap Ms. Iparis for bargaining power."

"Does that mean the Colonies are planning to attack LA?" Pascao asks. I already know his next thought. "But that would mean it's true, Denver has fallen . . ." He trails off at Anden's expression.

"We're receiving some early rumors," Anden replies. "The word is that the Colonies have a bomb that can level the entire city. The only thing holding them back from using it is an international ban. They wouldn't want to finally force Antarctica to get involved, now would they?" Since when did Anden become so sarcastic? "At any rate, if they attack now, we will be hard-pressed to have a cure ready to show Antarctica before the Colonies overwhelm us. We can defend against them. We can't defend against them *and* Africa."

I hesitate, then bring up the thoughts that have been churning in my mind. "I talked to Eden this morning, during his experimentation. He gave me an idea."

"And what's that?" June asks.

I look at her. Still as lovely as ever, but even June is starting to show the stress from this invasion, her shoulders slightly hunched. My eyes turn back to Anden. "Surrender," I say.

He hadn't expected *that*. "You want me to raise the white flag to the Colonies?"

"Yes, surrender." I lower my voice. "Yesterday afternoon, the Colonies' Chancellor made me an offer. He told me that if I could get the Republic's people to rise up in support of the Colonies and against the Republic soldiers, he'd make sure that Eden and I are protected once the Colonies win the war. Let's say that you surrender, and at the same time, I offer to meet the Chancellor to give him the answer to his request, that I'm going to ask the people to embrace the Colonies as their new government. You now have a chance to catch the Colonies off guard. The Chancellor already assumes you're going to surrender any day now, anyway."

"Faking a surrender is against international law," June mumbles to herself, although she studies me carefully. I can tell that she's not exactly against the idea. "I don't know whether the Antarcticans will appreciate that, and the whole point of this is to persuade them to help us out, isn't it?"

I shake my head. "They didn't seem to care that the Colonies broke the ceasefire without warning us, back when this all erupted." I glance at Anden. He watches me closely, his chin resting on his hand. "Now you get to return the favor, yeah?"

"What happens when you meet with the Chancellor?" he finally asks. "A false surrender can only last so long before we need to act."

I lean toward him, my voice urgent. "You know what Eden said to me this morning? 'Too bad everyone in the Republic can't be a soldier.' But they *can*."

Anden stays silent.

"Let me mark each of the sectors in the Republic, something that will let the people know that they can't just lie down and let the Colonies take over their homes, something that will ask them to wait for my signal and remind them what we're all fighting for. Then, when I make the announcement that the Colonies' Chancellor wants me to make, I won't call on the people to embrace the Colonies. I'll call them to action."

"And what if they don't respond to your call?" June says.

I shoot her a quick smile. "Have some faith, sweetheart. The people love me."

In spite of herself, June smiles back.

I turn to Anden. Seriousness replaces my flash of amusement. "The people love the Republic more than you think," I say. "More than *I* thought. You know the number of times I saw evacuees around here singing patriotic Republic songs? You know how much graffiti I've seen over the last few months that support both you and the country?" A note of passion enters my voice. "The people do believe in you. They believe in us. And they will fight back for us if we call on them— they'll be the ones ripping down Colonies flags, protesting in front of Colonies offices, turning their own homes into traps for invading Colonies soldiers." I narrow my eyes. "They'll become a million versions of me."

Anden and I stare at each other. Finally, he smiles.

"Well," June says to me, "while you're busy becoming the Colonies' most wanted criminal, the Patriots and I can join in your stunts. We'll pull them on a national level. If Antarctica protests, the Republic can just say they were the actions of a few vigilantes. If the Colonies want to play dirty, then let's play dirty."

# JUNE

1700 HOURS.
BATALLA HALL.
68° F.

I HATE SENATE MEETINGS. I HATE THEM WITH A PASSION—
nothing but a sea of bickering politicians and talking heads,
talking talking talking all the time when I could instead be
out in the streets, giving my mind and body a healthy workout. But after the plan that Day, Anden, and I have concocted,
there's no choice but to brief the Senate. Now I sit in the circular meeting chamber at Batalla Hall, my seat facing Anden
from across the room, trying to ignore the intimidating looks
from the Senators. Few events leave me feeling more like a
child than Senate meetings.

Anden addresses his restless audience. "Attacks against
our bases in Vegas have picked up since Denver fell," he says.
"We've seen African squadrons approaching the city. Tomorrow, I head out to meet my generals there." He hesitates here.
I hold my breath. I know how much Anden hates the idea of
voicing defeat to anyone, especially to the Colonies. He looks
at me—my cue to help him. He's so tired. We all are. "Ms.
Iparis," he calls out. "If you please, I hand the floor over to you
to explain your story and your advice."

I take a deep breath. Addressing the Senate: the one thing I hate more than attending Senate meetings, made even worse by the fact that I have to sell them a lie. "By now, I'm sure all of you have heard about Commander Jameson's supposed work for the Colonies. Based on what we know, it seems likely that the Colonies will hit Los Angeles with a surprise attack very soon. If they do, and the attacks on Vegas continue, we won't last for long. After talking with Day and the Patriots, we suggest that the only way to protect our civilians and to possibly negotiate a fair treaty is to announce our surrender to the Colonies."

Stunned silence. Then, the room bursts into chatter. Serge is the first to raise his voice and challenge Anden. "With all due respect, Elector," he says, his voice quivering with irritation, "you did not discuss this with your other Princeps-Elects."

"It was not something I had an opportunity to discuss with you before now," Anden replies. "Ms. Iparis's knowledge comes only because she was unfortunate enough to experience it firsthand."

Even Mariana, often on Anden's side, raises her voice against the idea. "This is a dangerous negotiation," she says. At least she speaks calmly. "If you are doing this to spare our lives, then I recommend you and Ms. Iparis reconsider immediately. Handing the people to the Colonies will not protect them."

The other Senators don't show the same restraint.

"A surrender? We have kept the Colonies off our land for almost a hundred years!"

"Surely we're not all that weakened yet? What have they done, aside from temporarily winning Denver?"

"Elector, this is something you should have discussed with all of us—even in the midst of this crisis!"

I look on as each voice rises higher than the next, until the entire chamber fills with the sound of insults, anger, and disbelief. Some spew hatred over Day. Some curse the Colonies. Some beg Anden to reconsider, to ask for more international help, to plead for the United Nations to stop sealing our ports. Noise.

"This is an outrage!" one Senator (thin, probably no more than a hundred and forty pounds, with a gleaming bald head) barks, looking at me as if I'm responsible for the entire country's downfall. "Surely we're not taking direction from a little girl? And from *Day*? You must be joking. We'll hand the country over based on the advice of some damn boy who should still be on our nation's criminal list!"

Anden narrows his eyes. "Careful how you refer to Day, Senator, before the people turn their backs on you."

The Senator sneers at Anden and raises himself up as high as he can. "*Elector*," he says, his tone exaggerated and mocking. "*You* are the leader of the Republic of America. You have power over this entire country. And here you are, held hostage to the suggestions of someone who tried to have you *killed*." My temper has begun to rise. I lower my head so that I don't have to look at the Senator. "In my opinion, *sir*, you need to do something before your entire government—and your entire *population*—sees you as nothing but a cowardly, weak-willed, backroom-negotiating pushover bowing to the demands of a teenage girl and a criminal and a ragtag team of terrorists. Your father would have—"

Anden jumps to his feet and slams his hand down on the table. Instantly the chamber turns silent.

"Senator," Anden says quietly. The man stares back, but with less conviction than he had two seconds ago. "You are correct about only one thing. As my father's son, *I* am the Elector of the Republic. *I* am the law. Everything *I* decide directly affects who lives or dies." I study Anden's face with a growing sense of worry. His gentle, soft-voiced self is slowly disappearing behind the veil of darkness and violence inherited from his father. "You'd do well to remember what happened to those Senators who *actually* plotted my failed assassination."

The chamber falls so quiet I feel like I can hear the beads of sweat rolling down the Senators' faces. Even Mariana and Serge have turned pale. In the midst of them all stands Anden, his face a mask of fury, his jaw tense, and his eyes a deep, brooding storm. He turns to me—I feel an awful, electric shudder run through my body, but I keep my gaze steady. I am the only one in the chamber willing to look him in the eye.

Even if our surrender is a fake one, one that the Senators aren't meant to understand, I wonder how Anden will deal with this group once it's all over.

Maybe he won't have to. Maybe we'll belong to a different country, or maybe Anden and I will both be dead.

In this moment, sitting amongst a divided Senate and a

young Elector struggling to hold them together, I finally see my path clearly. *I don't belong. I shouldn't be here.* The realization hits me so hard, I find it suddenly hard to breathe.

Anden and the Senators exchange a few more tense words, but then it's all over, and we file out of the room, an uneasy crowd. I find Anden—his deep red uniform a bright marker against the Senators' black—in the hall and pull him aside. "They'll come around," I say, trying to offer reassurance in a sea of hostility. "They don't have a choice."

He seems to relax, if only for a second. A few simple words from me are enough to dissipate his anger. "I know. But I don't want them to have *no* choice. I want them solidly behind me of their own will." He sighs. "Can we speak in private? I've something to discuss with you."

I study his face, trying to guess at what he wants to say, dreading it. Finally, I nod. "My apartment's closer."

We head out to his jeep and drive in silence, all the way to my high-rise in Ruby sector. There, we make our way upstairs and enter my apartment without a word. Ollie greets us, as enthusiastic as ever. I close the door behind me.

Anden's temper has long vanished. He looks around with a restless expression, then turns back to me. "Do you mind if I sit?"

"Please," I reply, taking a seat myself at the dining table. The Elector Primo, asking for permission to sit?

Anden takes the seat beside me with all of his signature grace, and then rubs his temples with weary hands. "I have some good news," he says. He tries to smile, but I can see how heavy it is. "I've made a deal with Antarctica."

I swallow hard. "And?"

"They've confirmed that they will send military support—some air support for now, more ground support when we prove we've found a cure," Anden replies. "And they will agree to treat Day." He doesn't look at me. "In exchange for Dakota. I had no choice. I'm giving them our largest territory."

My heart jumps with an overwhelming sense of joy and relief—and at the same time, it sinks with sympathy for Anden. He's been forced to fragment the country. Giving up our most precious resource; *everybody* in the world's most precious resource. It was inevitable. Every win comes with a sacrifice. "Thank you," I say.

"Don't thank me yet." His wry smile quickly turns into a grimace. "We are hanging by a thread. I don't know if their help will come fast enough. The word from the warfront is that we're losing ground in Vegas. If our plans with this phony surrender fail, if we don't find a cure soon, this war will be over before Antarctica's support ever arrives."

"Do you think finding a cure will make the Colonies stop?" I ask quietly.

Anden shakes his head. "We don't have many options," he replies. "But we have to hang on until help arrives." He falls silent for a moment. "I head to the warfront in Vegas tomorrow. Our troops need it."

Right into the thick of war. I try to stay calm. "Are your Princeps-Elects going too?" I ask. "Your Senators?"

"Only my generals will join me," Anden replies. "You're not

going to come, and neither are Mariana and Serge. Someone needs to hold firm in Los Angeles."

And here's the meat of what he wants to tell me. My mind spins over what I know he'll say next.

Anden leans on the table and threads his gloved fingers together. "Someone needs to hold firm in Los Angeles," he repeats, "which means one of my Princeps-Elects will need to take my place as an acting Elector. She would need to control the Senate, keep them in check while I'm away with the troops. I would select this person, of course, and the Senate would confirm it." A small, sad smile plays at the edges of his lips, as if he already knows what my answer will be. "I've already spoken individually with Mariana and Serge about this, and they are both eager for my appointment. Now I need to know whether *you* are, as well."

I turn my head away and look out the apartment window. The thought of becoming an acting Elector of the Republic— even though my chances of being chosen pale in comparison to that of Mariana and Serge—should excite me, but it doesn't.

Anden watches me carefully. "You can tell me," he finally says. "I realize what a turning point this decision is, and I've sensed your discomfort for quite some time." He gives me a level stare. "Tell me the truth, June. Do you *really* want to be a Princeps-Elect?"

I feel a strange emptiness. I had been contemplating this for a long time, my disinterest and weariness with the politics of the Republic, the bickering in the Senate, the fighting among Senators and the Princeps-Elects. I'd thought this would be hard to say to him. But now that he's here, waiting for my answer, the words come easily, calmly.

"Anden, you know that the role of a Princeps-Elect has been a huge honor for me. But as time goes on, I can tell that something's missing, and now I know what it is. You get to head off and lead your army against our enemies, while Day and the Patriots are fighting back against the Colonies in their own guerilla way. I *miss* being out in the field, working as a junior agent and relying on myself. I miss the days when things were straightforward instead of political, when I could easily sense the right path and what I should do. I . . . miss doing what my brother helped train me to do." I hold my gaze steady. "I'm sorry, Anden, but I don't know whether I'm cut out to be a politician. I'm a *soldier*. I don't think you should consider me as a temporary Elector in your absence, and I'm not sure whether I should continue on as your Princeps-Elect."

Anden searches my eyes. "I see," he finally says. Although there's a twinge of sadness in his voice, he seems to agree. If there's one thing Anden excels at, even more than Day, it's understanding where I'm coming from.

A moment later, I see another emotion in his eyes—envy. He's envious that I have the choice to step away from the world of politics, that I can turn to something else, when Anden will forever and always be our Elector, someone the country needs to lean on. He can never step away with a clean conscience.

He clears his throat. "What do you want to do?"

"I want to join the troops in the streets," I reply. I'm so sure of my decision this time, so excited by the prospect, that I can hardly bear it. "Send me back out there. *Let me fight.*" I lower my voice. "If we lose, then none of the Princeps-Elects will matter anyway."

"Of course," Anden says, nodding. He looks around the room with an uncertain expression, and behind his brave front I can see the boy king in him struggling to hold on. Then he notices a rumpled coat hanging at the foot of my bed. He lingers on it.

I'd never bothered to put Day's coat away.

Anden finally looks away from it. I don't need to tell him that Day had spent the night—I can already see the realization on his face. I blush. I have always been good at hiding my emotions, but this time I'm embarrassed that something about that night—the heat of Day's skin against mine, the touch of his hand smoothing my hair away from my face, the brush of his lips against my neck—will show up in my eyes.

"Well," he says after a long pause. He gives me a small, sad smile, then rises. "You *are* a soldier, Ms. Iparis, through and through—but it has been an honor to see you as a Princeps-Elect." The Elector of the Republic bows to me. "Whatever happens from here, I hope you remember that."

"Anden," I whisper. The memory of his dark, furious face in the Senate chamber comes back to me. "When you're in Vegas, promise me that you'll stay yourself. Don't turn into someone you're not. Okay?"

He may not have been surprised by my answer, or by Day's

coat. But this seems to catch him off guard. He blinks, confused for a second. Then he understands. He shakes his head. "I have to go. I have to lead my men, just like my father did."

"That's not what I mean," I say carefully.

He struggles for a moment to find the next words. "It's no secret how cruel my father was, or how many atrocities he committed. The Trials, the plagues . . ." Anden trails off a little, the light in his green eyes turning distant as he dwells on memories of someone few of us had ever come to know. "But he *fought* with his men. You understand this, perhaps more than anyone. He didn't hang back in a Senate chamber while he sent his troops off to die. When he was young and brought the country from a lawless mess to strict martial law, he was out in the streets and in front of his squadrons. He fought at the warfront itself, shooting down Colonies jets." Anden pauses to give me a quick look. "I'm not trying to defend anything he did. But if he was anything, he was *unafraid*. He won his military's loyalty through action, however ruthless. . . . I want to boost our troops' morale too, and I can't do it while hiding out in LA. I'm—"

"You are not your father," I say, holding his gaze with my own. "You're Anden. You don't have to follow in his footsteps; you have your own. You're the Elector now. You don't have to be like him."

I think back on my own loyalty to the former Elector, of all the video footage of him shouting orders from the cockpit of a fighter jet, or heading up tanks in the streets. He was always on the front lines. He *was* fearless. Now, as I look at Anden,

I can see that same fearlessness burning steadily in his eyes, his need to assert himself as a worthy leader of his country. When his father was young, perhaps he had also been like Anden—idealistic, full of hopes and dreams, of the noblest intentions, brave and driven. How had he slowly twisted into the Elector who created such a dark nation? What path had he chosen to follow? Suddenly, for however brief a second, I feel like I understand the former Republic. And I know that Anden won't go down that same road.

Anden returns my look, as if hearing my unspoken words . . . and for the first time in months, I see some of that dark cloud lift from his eyes, the blackness that gives birth to his moments of furious temper.

Without his father's shadow in the way, he's beautiful.

"I'll do my best," he whispers.

# DAY

WELL, NO POINT IN RETURNING HOME TONIGHT. PASCAO and I are gonna run through Los Angeles, marking doors and walls and alerting the people quietly to our cause, and we might as well do it from a central location like the hospital. Besides, I needed to sit with Eden for a while. An evening of blood tests haven't treated him well—he's thrown up twice since I've been here. While a nurse rushes out of the room with a bucket in hand, I pour a glass of water for my brother. He guzzles it down.

"Any luck?" he asks weakly. "Do you know if they've found anything yet?"

"Not yet." I take the empty glass from him and set it back on a tray. "I'll check in with them in a little bit, though. See how they're doing. Better be worth all this."

Eden sighs, closes his eyes, and leans his head against the mountain of pillows stacked on his bed. "I'm fine," he whispers. "How's your friend? Tess?"

Tess. She hasn't woken up yet, and now I find myself wishing that we could go back to when she was still able to shove the lab team around. I swallow hard, trying to replace my mental image of her sickly appearance with the sweet, cheery face I've known for years. "She's asleep. Lab says her fever hasn't broken."

Eden grits his teeth and looks back at the screen monitoring his vitals. "She seems nice," he finally says. "From everything I've heard."

I smile. "She is. After all this is over, maybe the two of you can hang out or something. You'd get along." *If we all pull through this,* I add to myself, and then hurriedly banish the thought. Damn, every day it's getting harder and harder to keep my chin up.

Our conversation ends after that, but Eden keeps one hand gripped tightly in my own. His eyes stay closed. After a while, his breathing changes into the steady rhythm of sleep, and his hand falls away to rest on his blanket. I pull the blanket up to cover him to his chin, watch him for a few more seconds, and then stand. At least he can still sleep pretty soundly. I don't. Every hour or so, for the last two days, I shake myself out of some gruesome nightmare and have to walk it off before attempting to sleep again. My headache stays with me, a constant, dull companion, reminding me of my ticking clock.

I open the door and sneak out as quietly as I can. The hall's empty except for a few nurses here and there. And Pascao. He's been waiting for me on one of the hall's benches. When he sees me, he gets up and flashes me a brief grin.

"The others are getting into position," he says. "We've got about two dozen Runners, all in all, already out there and marking the sectors. I think it's about time for the two of us to head out too."

"Ready to rouse the people?" I say, half joking, as he leads me down the hall.

"The excitement of it all is making my bones ache." Pascao pushes open a set of double doors at the hall's end, ushers us into a larger waiting room, and then into an unused hospital room with the lights still turned off. He flicks them on. My eyes go immediately to something lying on the bed. It looks like a pair of suits, dark with gray outlines, both laid out neatly on top of the sterile blankets. Beside the suits is some kind of equipment that looks a little like guns. I glance at Pascao, who shoves his hands into his pockets. "Check these out," he says in a low voice. "When I was throwing ideas around this afternoon with Baxter and a couple of Republic soldiers, they loaned out these suits for us Runners. It should help you in particular. June says she uses suits and air launchers like these to get around the city quickly, without being detected. Here." He tosses me one. "Throw this one."

I frown at the suit. It doesn't look like anything particularly special, but I decide to give Pascao the benefit of the doubt.

"I'll be in the next room," Pascao says as he swings his own suit over his shoulder. He nudges my shoulder as he passes. "With these things, we should have no trouble covering Los Angeles tonight."

I start to warn him that, with my recent headaches and

medications, I'm probably not strong enough to keep up with him around the entire city—but he's already out the door, leaving me alone in the room. I study the suit again, then unbutton my shirt.

The suit's surprisingly featherweight, and fits comfortably from my feet all the way to my zipped-up neck. I adjust it around my elbows and knees, then walk around for a bit. To my shock, my arms and legs feel stronger than usual. Much stronger. I try a quick jump. The suit absorbs almost all of my weight's force, and without much effort I'm able to jump high enough to clear the bed. I bend one arm, then the other. They feel strong enough to lift something heavier than what I've been used to for the past several months. A sudden thrill rushes through me.

I can run in this.

Pascao raps on my door, then comes back in with his own suit on. "How's it feel, pretty boy?" he asks, looking me over. "Fits you nicely."

"What are these for?" I reply, still testing my new physical limits.

"What do you think? The Republic usually issues these to their soldiers for physically taxing missions. There are special springs installed near joints—elbows, knees, whatever. In other words, it'll make you a little acrobatic hero."

Incredible. Now that Pascao's mentioned it, I can feel the very slight push and pull of some sort of spring along my elbows, and the subtle lift the springs give my knees whenever

I bend them. "It feels good," I say, while Pascao watches me with a look of approval. "Really good. It feels like I can scale a building again."

"Here's what I'm thinking," Pascao says, his voice lowering again to a whisper. His lighthearted attitude fades. "If the Colonies land their airships here in LA after the Elector announces a surrender, the Republic will get its troops into position to stage a surprise attack on those airships. They can cripple a hell of a lot of them before the Colonies even realize what we're up to. I'll lead the Patriots in with the Republic's teams, and we'll wire up some of the airship bases to blow up ships that are docked on them."

"Sounds like a plan." I flex one of my arms gingerly, marveling at the strength that the suit gives me. My heart hammers in my chest. If I don't carry out this plan just right, and the Chancellor figures out what we're really up to, then the Republic will lose the advantage of our fake surrender. We only get one shot at this.

We slide open the hospital room's glass doors and head out onto the balcony. The night's cool air refreshes me, taking away some of the grief and stress of the last few days. With this suit, I feel a little like myself again. I glance up at the buildings. "Should we test these things out?" I ask Pascao, hoisting the air launcher on my shoulder.

Pascao grins, then tosses me a can of bright red spray paint. "You took the words right out of my mouth."

So off we go. I scale down to the first floor so fast that

I nearly lose my footing, and then make my way effortlessly to the ground. We split up, each covering a different section of the city. As I run my sector, I can't help but smile. I'm free again, I can taste the wind and touch the sky. In this moment, my troubles melt away and once again I'm able to run away from my problems—I'm able to blend right in with the rust and rubble of the city, changing it into something that belongs to me.

I make my way through Tanagashi sector's dark alleys until I come across landmark buildings, places where I know most people will have to pass by, and then take out my spray paint can. I write the following on the wall:

## LISTEN FOR ME.

Below that, I draw the one thing I know everyone will recognize as coming from me—a red streak painted onto an outline of a face.

I mark everything I can think of. When I'm finished, I use the air launcher to travel to a neighboring sector, and there, I repeat the entire process. Hours later, my hair drenched in sweat and my muscles aching, I make my way back to the Central Hospital. Pascao's waiting outside for me, a sheen of sweat across his own face. He gives me a mock salute.

"Care to race back up?" he asks, flashing me a grin.

I don't reply. I just start climbing, and so does he. Pascao's figure is nearly invisible in the darkness, a shapeless form that leaps and bounds each story with the ease of a natural Runner. I dash after him. Another story, and then another.

We make it back to the balcony that runs all along the tower's fourth floor. Inside lies the hospital wing we'd left from. Even though I'm out of breath and my head is pounding again, I made the run almost as fast as Pascao did. "Hell," I mutter to him as we both lean against the railing in exhaustion. "Where was this equipment when I was at my healthiest? I could've single-handedly destroyed the Republic without breaking a sweat, yeah?"

Pascao's teeth shine in the night. He surveys the cityscape. "Maybe it's a good thing you didn't have it. Otherwise there'd be no Republic for us to save."

"Is it worth it?" I ask after a while, enjoying the cool winds. "Are you really willing to sacrifice your life for a country that hasn't done much of anything for you?"

Pascao stays silent for a moment, then lifts one arm and points toward some spot on the horizon. I try to make out what he wants me to see. "When I was little," he replies, "I grew up in Winter sector. I watched two of my little sisters fail the Trial. When I went to the stadium myself and had to take my own Trial, I almost failed too. I stumbled and fell on one of the physical jumps, you know. Ironic, don't you think? Anyway, one of the soldiers saw me fall. I'll never forget the look in his eyes. When I realized that no one else had seen me except for him, I begged him to let it go. He looked damn tortured, but he didn't record my fall. When I whispered my thanks, he told me that he remembered my two sisters. He said, 'I think two deaths in your family's enough.' " Pascao pauses for a moment. "I've always hated the Republic for what they did to the people I loved, to *all* of us. But sometimes I wonder whatever happened to that soldier, and what his life was like, and who he cared about, and whether or not he's even still alive. Who knows? Maybe he's already gone." He shrugs at the thought. "If I look the other way and decide to let the Republic handle its own business, and then it falls, I guess I could just leave the country. Find a way to live somewhere else, hide out from the government." He looks at me. "I don't really know why I want to stand on the hill with them now. Maybe I have a little bit of faith."

Pascao wants to explain himself further, like he's frustrated that he doesn't know how to put his answer into the right words. But I understand him already. I shake my head and stare out toward the Lake sector, remembering June's brother. "Yeah. Me too."

After a while, we finally head back inside the hospital. I take off the suit and change back into my own clothes. Plan's supposed to kick into effect starting with Anden's surrender announcement. After that, it's all one day at a time. Anything could change.

While Pascao heads off to get some rest, I retrace my steps down the hall and back toward Eden's room, wondering if the lab teams have sent up any new results for us to look at. As if they've read my mind, I see a few of them clustered outside

Eden's door when I arrive. They're talking in hushed tones. The serenity I'd felt during our brief night run fades away.

"What is it?" I ask. I can already see the tension in their eyes. My chest knots up at the sight. "Tell me what's happened."

From behind the clear plastic of his hood, one of the lab techs tells me, "We received some data from the Antarctican lab team. We think we've managed to synthesize something from your brother's blood that can almost act as a cure. It's working—to a degree."

A cure! A rush of energy courses through me, leaving me dizzy with relief. I can't help letting a smile spill onto my face. "Have you told the Elector yet? Does it work? Can we start using it on Tess?"

The lab tech stops me before I can go on. "*Almost* act as a cure, Day," he repeats.

"What do you mean?"

"The Antarctican team confirmed that the virus has likely mutated from the original one Eden developed immunity to, or that it may have combined its genome with another genome along the way. Your brother's T cells have the ability to shift along with this aggressive virus; in our samples, one of the cures we've developed seems to work partially—"

"So I can understand you," I say impatiently.

The lab tech scowls at me, as if *I* might infect *him* with my attitude. "We're missing something," he says with an indignant sigh. "We're missing a component."

"What do you mean, you're missing something?" I demand. "What are you missing?"

"Somewhere along the way, the virus that's causing our current outbreaks mutated from its original Republic plague virus and combined with another virus. There's something missing along the way, as a result. We think it may have mutated in the Colonies, perhaps quite a while ago. Months ago, even."

My heart sinks as I realize what they're trying to tell me. "Does that mean the cure won't work yet?"

"It's not only that the cure won't work yet. It's that we don't know if we can ever get it to work. Eden's not Patient Zero for this thing." The lab tech sighs again. "And unless we can find the person who this new virus mutated from, I'm not sure we'll ever create a cure."

# JUNE

I AWAKE TO THE SOUND OF A SIREN WAILING ACROSS our apartment complex. It's the air raid alarm. For a second, I'm back in Denver, sitting with Day at a little lantern-lit café while sleet falls all around us, listening to him tell me that he's dying. I'm back in the panicked, chaotic streets as the siren shrieks at us—we're holding hands, running for shelter, terrified.

Gradually, my room fades into reality and the siren wails on. My heart begins to pound. I jump out of bed, pause to comfort a whining Ollie, then rush to turn on my screen. News headlines blare out, fighting with the siren—and running along the bottom of the screen is an angry, red warning.

SEEK COVER

I scan the headlines.

ENEMY AIRSHIPS APPROACHING LOS ANGELES'S LIMITS

ALL TROOPS TO REPORT TO THEIR LOCAL HEADQUARTERS

ELECTOR PRIMO TO MAKE EMERGENCY ANNOUNCEMENT

They'd predicted that the Colonies would still take three more days before making a move on Los Angeles. It looks like they're ahead of schedule and preparing for the end of the three-day ceasefire, which means we need to put our plan ahead of schedule. I cover my ears from the siren, rush over to the balcony, and look out at the horizon. The morning light is still weak, and the cloudy sky makes it difficult for me to see properly, but even so, the dots lining up above California's mountain skyline are unmistakable. My breath catches in my throat.

Airships. Colonies, African—I can't quite tell from this distance, but there is no mistaking the fact that they are not Republic ships. Based on their position and speed, they will be hovering right over central Los Angeles before the hour's over. I click my mike on, then rush into the closet to throw on some clothes. If Anden's preparing to make an announcement soon, then it will undoubtedly be the surrender. And if that's the case, I'll need to join Day and the Patriots as quickly as I can. A fake surrender will only work for so long before it turns into a real one.

"Where are you guys?" I shout when Day comes onto the line.

His voice sounds as urgent as mine. The echo of the siren sounds out from his side too. "Eden's hospital room. You see the ships?"

I glance again at the horizon before lacing up my boots. "Yes. I'm in. I'll be there soon."

"Watch the sky. Stay safe." He hesitates for two seconds. "And hurry. We've got a problem." Then our call cuts off, and

I'm out the door with Ollie close at my side, galloping like the wind.

By the time we reach the Central Hospital's lab floor in the Bank Tower and are ushered in to see Day, Eden, and the Patriots, the sirens have stopped. The sector's electricity must have been switched off again, and aside from the main government buildings like the Bank Tower, the landscape outside looks eerily black, swallowed nearly whole by damp morning shadows. Down the hall, the screens show an empty podium where Anden will be standing any minute now, poised to give a live national address. Ollie stays glued to my side, panting his distress. I reach down and pat him several times, and he rewards me with a lick of my hand.

I meet Day and the others in Eden's room right as Anden appears onscreen. Eden looks exhausted and half conscious. He still has an IV hooked up to his arm, but aside from that, there are no other tubes or wires. Beside the bed, a lab tech is typing notes onto a notepad.

Day and Pascao are wearing what look like dark Republic suits meant for physically demanding missions—it's the same sort of suit I'd once worn back when I first needed to break Day out of Batalla Hall, when I spent a late night skimming building roofs in search of Kaede. Both of them are talking to a lab tech, and based on their expressions, they're not getting good news. I want to ask them for details, but Anden has stepped up to the podium already, and my words fade away as we turn our attention to the screen. All I hear is the sound of our breathing and the ominous, distant hum of approaching airships.

Anden looks composed; and even though he's only a year older than the first time I met him, the weight and gravity on his face make him look much more mature than he actually is. Only the slight clench of his jaw reveals a hint of his real emotions. He's dressed in solid white, with silver epaulettes on his shoulders and a gold Republic seal pinned near the collar of his military coat. Behind him are two flags: One is the Republic's, while the other is blank, white, devoid of color. I swallow hard. It's a flag I know well from all my studies, but one that I've never seen used. We all knew this was coming, we had planned this and we *know* it's not real—but even so, I can't help feeling a deep, dark sense of grief and failure. As if we are truly handing our country over to someone else.

"Soldiers of the Republic," Anden begins addressing the soldiers surrounding him at the base. As always, his voice is at once soft and commanding, quiet but clear. "It is with a heavy heart that I come to you today with this message. I have already relayed these same words to the Chancellor of the Colonies." He pauses for a moment, as if gathering his strength. I can only imagine that for him, even faking such a gesture must weigh on him far more than it already does on me. "The Republic has officially surrendered to the Colonies."

Silence. The base, filled with noise and chaos only a few minutes ago, is now suddenly still—every soldier frozen, listening in disbelief.

"We are now to cease all military activity against the Colonies," Anden continues, "and within the next day, we will meet with the Colonies' leading officials to draft official surrender terms." He pauses, letting the weight settle over the entire base. "Soldiers, we will continue to update you on information regarding this as we proceed." Then the transmission stops. He doesn't end with *Long live the Republic.* A chill runs through me when the screens are replaced with an image of, not the Republic flag, but the Colonies'.

They are doing a stellar job of making this surrender look convincing. I hope the Antarcticans are going to keep their word. I hope help is on the way.

"Day, we don't have much time to get these bases ready to blow," Pascao mutters to us as the address stops. The three Republic soldiers with us are geared up in a similar fashion, all ready to guide them to where the air bases will be wired. "You're gonna have to buy us some time. News is that the Colonies will start landing their airships at our bases in a few hours."

Day nods. As Pascao turns away to rattle off some directions to the soldiers, Day's eyes flicker to me. In them, I see a strained sense of fear that makes my stomach churn. "Something's gone wrong with the cure, hasn't it?" I ask. "How's Eden doing?"

Day sighs, running a hand through his hair, and then looks down at his brother. "He's hanging in there."

"But . . . ?"

"But the problem is that he isn't Patient Zero. They said they're missing something from his blood."

I look at the fragile boy in the hospital bed. Eden isn't Patient Zero? "But what? What are they missing?"

"It'd be easier to show you than try to explain it. Come on.

This is something we'll need to alert Anden about. What's the point of staging this whole surrender if we won't be able to get help from Antarctica?" Day leads us out and down the hall. We walk in a tense silence for a while, until we finally stop in front of a nondescript door. Day opens it.

We step inside a room full of comps. A lab tech monitoring the screens rises when he sees us, then ushers us over. "Time to update Ms. Iparis?"

"Tell me what's going on," I reply.

He sits us down in front of a comp and spends several minutes loading up a screen. When he finally finishes, I see two side-by-side comparisons of some slides of what I assume are cells. I peer more closely at them.

The lab tech points to the one on the left, which looks like a series of small, polygonal particles grouped around a large central cell. Attached to the particles are dozens of little tubes sticking out of the cell. "This," the lab tech says, circling the large cell with his finger, "is a simulation of an infected cell that we're trying to target. The cell has a red hue to it, indicating that viruses have taken hold inside. If no cure's involved, this cell lyses—bursts open—and dies. Now, see these little particles around it? Those are simulations of the cure particles that we need. They attach to the outside of the infected cell." He taps the screen twice where the large cell is, and a short animation plays, showing the particles latching on to the cell; eventually, the cell shrinks in size and the color of it changes. "They save the cell from bursting."

My eyes shift over to the comparison on the right, which

also has a similarly infected cell surrounded by little particles. This time, I don't see any tubes for the particles to attach to. "This is what's *actually* happening," the lab tech explains. "We're missing something from our cure particles that can attach to the cell's receptors. If we don't develop that, the rest of the particles can't work. The cell can't come in direct contact with the medicine, and the cell dies."

I cross my arms and exchange a frown with Day, who shrugs helplessly. "How can we figure out the missing piece?"

"That's the thing. Our guess is that this particular attaching feature wasn't a part of the original virus. In other words, someone specifically altered this virus. We can see traces of that marker on it when we label the cell." He points to tiny glowing dots scattered across the cell's surface. "This might mean, Ms. Iparis, that the Colonies actually physically altered this virus. The Republic certainly has no records of tampering with this one in this specific fashion."

"Wait a minute," Day interrupts. "This is news to me. Are you saying that the Colonies *created* this plague?"

The lab tech gives us a grim look, then returns to the screen. "Possibly. Here's the curious thing, though. We think this additional piece—the attaching feature—originally came out of the Republic. There's a similar virus that came out of a small Colorado town. But the tracers tell us that the altered virus came out of Tribune City, which is a warfront city on the Colonies side. So somewhere along that line, Eden's virus somehow came in contact with something else in Tribune City."

This is when the pieces of the puzzle finally fall into place for me. The color drains from my face. Tribune City: the city that Day and I had originally stumbled into when we first fled into the Colonies. I think back to when I'd gotten ill during my arrest in the Republic, how sick and feverish I'd been when Day carried us through that underground tunnel from Lamar all the way into the Colonies' territory. I'd been in a Colonies hospital for a night. They'd injected medicine into me, but I never considered the fact that they might have been using me for a different purpose. Had I been a part of an experiment without even realizing it? Am I the one holding the missing piece of the puzzle in my bloodstream?

"It's me," I whisper, cutting the lab tech short. Both he and Day give me a startled look.

"What do you mean?" the lab tech asks, but Day stays silent. A look of realization washes over his face.

"It's me," I repeat. The answer is so clear that I can hardly breathe. "I was in Tribune City eight months ago. I'd gotten ill while under arrest in Colorado. If this other virus you're talking about originated first in the Republic and then came back from Tribune City in the Colonies, then it's possible that the answer to your puzzle is *me*."

JUNE'S THEORY CHANGES EVERYTHING.

Immediately she joins the lab team in a separate hospital room, where they strap several tubes and wires to her and take a sample of her bone marrow. They run a series of scans that leave her looking nauseous, scans I've already seen being run on Eden. I wish I could stay. Eden's tests are over, thankfully, but the risk has now shifted to June, and in this moment all I want to do is stay here and make sure everything goes smoothly.

*For chrissakes,* I tell myself angrily, *it's not like you being here is going to help anything.* But when Pascao finally ushers us out the door and out of the hospital to join the others, I can't help but glance back.

If June's blood holds the missing piece, then we have a chance. We can contain the plague. We can save everyone. *We can save Tess.*

As we take a train from the hospital toward Batalla's airship bases with several Republic soldiers in tow, these thoughts build in my chest until I can barely stand to wait around. Pascao notices my restlessness and grins. "You ever been to the bases before? I seem to recall you doing a few stunts there."

His words trigger some memories. When I turned fourteen, I broke into two Los Angeles airships that were set to head out for the warfront. I got in—not unlike my stunt with the Patriots back in Vegas—by sneaking in through the ventilation system, and then navigating the entire ship undetected by weaving my way through their endless air vents. I was still halfway through my growth spurt back then; my body was thinner and smaller, and I had no trouble squeezing my way through their myriad of tunnels. Once inside, I stole as much canned food from their kitchens as I could, then set fires in their engine rooms that destroyed the ships enough to ultimately cripple them from serving the Republic for years, maybe forever. It was this particular stunt that first landed me on top of the Republic's most wanted list. Not too bad a job, if I do say so myself.

Now I think back on the bases' layouts. Aside from some airship bases in Batalla sector, the four main naval bases in LA occupy a thin strip of land along the city's west coastline that sits between our enormous lake and the Pacific Ocean. Our battleships stay there, unused for the most part. But the reason that the Patriots and I head there now is that all of LA's airship docks are there too, and it's where the Colonies will dock their airships if—when—they try to occupy the city after our surrender.

It's the third and final day of the Colonies' promised ceasefire. As the train speeds through the sectors, I can see groups of civilians crowding around JumboTrons that are now running Anden's surrender notice on repeat. Most look stricken with shock, clinging to one another. Others are furious—they throw shoes, crowbars, and rocks up at the screens and rage against their Elector's betrayal. Good. Stay angry, use that anger against the Colonies. I need to play out my part soon.

"All right, kids, listen up," Pascao says as our train nears the bridges leading to the naval bases. He holds out his palms to show us a series of small, metal devices. "Remember, six per dock." He points to a small red trigger in the center of each device. "We want clean, contained explosions, and the soldiers'll point out the best spots for us to plant these things. If done right, we'll be able to cripple any Colonies airship using our landing docks, and an airship with a messed-up landing bay is useless. Yeah?" He grins. "At the same time, let's not screw up the landing docks *too* much. *Six* per dock."

I look away and back out the window, where the first naval base draws near on the horizon. Enormous pyramid landing bases loom in a row, dark and imposing, and I instantly think of the first time I'd seen them in Vegas. My stomach twists uneasily. If this plan fails, if we're unable to hold the Colonies back and the Antarcticans never come to our rescue, if June *isn't* what we need for the cure—what will happen to us? What will happen when the Colonies finally get their hands on Anden, or June, or myself? I shake my head, forcing the images out of my mind. There's no time to worry about that. It'll either happen or it won't. We've already chosen our course.

When we arrive at the first landing dock of Naval Base

One, I can see enough of the inner city to notice the tiny, dark specks in the sky. Colonies troops—airships, jets, something—are hovering not far from the outskirts of Los Angeles, preparing to strike. A low, monotonous hum fills the air—guess we can already hear their ships' steady approach. My eyes turn up toward the JumboTrons lining the streets. Anden's announcement continues on, accompanied with a bright red *Seek Cover* warning running along the bottom of each screen.

Four Republic soldiers join up with us as we hurry out of the jeep and inside the pyramid base. I keep close to them as they usher us up the elevators toward the looming inner roof of the base, where airships take off and dock on. All around us is the deafening sound of soldiers' boots on echoing floors, rushing to their stations and preparing to take off against the Colonies. I wonder how many troops Anden had been forced to send off to Denver or Vegas for reinforcement, and I can only hope that we have enough left behind to protect us.

*This isn't Vegas,* I remind myself, trying not to think about the time when I'd let myself get arrested. But it doesn't help. By the time we've ridden our way up to the top of the base and climbed a flight of stairs up to the open top of the pyramid, my heart's pounding up a storm that's not all because of the exercise. Well, if *this* doesn't bring back memories of when I'd first start working for the Patriots. I can't stop studying the metal beams crisscrossing the interior underbelly of the base, all the little interlocking parts that will bind with an airship once it lands. The dark suit I'm wearing feels as light as air. Time to plant some bombs.

"Do you see those beams?" one Republic captain says to Pascao and me, pointing up to the shadows of the ceiling at one, two, three crevices that look particularly difficult to reach. "Max damage to the ship, minimal damage to the base. We'll have you two hit those three spots at each of the bases. We'd be able to get to them ourselves if we set up our cranes, but we don't have time for that." He pauses to give us a forced smile. Most of these goddy soldiers still don't seem entirely comfortable working alongside us. "Well," he says after an awkward pause, "does that look doable? Are you guys fast enough?"

I want to snap at the captain that he's forgotten my reputation, but Pascao stops me by letting out one of his loud, sparkling laughs. "You don't have enough faith in us, do you?" he says, nudging the captain playfully in the ribs and smirking at the indignant blush that he gets back.

"Good," the captain replies stiffly before moving on with the other Patriots and his own patrol. "Hurry. We don't have long." He leaves us to our work, then starts dictating bomb-planting spots to the others.

Once he's gone, Pascao drops his giant grin and concentrates on the crevices that the captain had pointed out. "Not easy to reach," he mutters. "You sure you're up for this? You strong enough, seeing as how you're dying and all?"

I cast him a withering glare, then study each of the crevices in turn. I test my knees and elbows, trying to gauge how much strength I have. Pascao's a bit taller than me—he'll be able to handle the first two crevices best, but the third crevice is wedged in such a tight position that I know only I can get to it. I can also see right away why the captain pointed that spot out. Even if we didn't plant six bombs along this side of the base, we'd probably disable any airship with a single bomb on *that* location. I point to it.

"I'll take that one," I say.

"You sure?" Pascao squints at it. "I don't want to watch you fall to your death on our very first base."

His words coax a sarcastic smile out of me. "Don't you have any faith in me at all?"

Pascao smirks. "A little."

We get to work. I take a flying leap from the stairs' ledge to the closest crisscrossing beam, and then weave myself seamlessly into the maze of metal. What a feeling of déjà vu. The springs embedded in my suit's joints take a little getting used to—but after a few jumps I grow into them. I'm fast. Really fast with their help. In the span of ten minutes, I've crossed a quarter of the base's ceiling and am now within striking distance of that crevice. Thin trickles of sweat run down my neck, and my head pulses with familiar pain. Below, soldiers pause to watch us even as all of the base's electronic tickers continue to run the surrender notice. They have no goddy clue what we're doing.

I pause at the final leap, then make my jump. My body hits

the crevice and slides snugly in. Instantly I pull out the tiny bomb, open its clip, and plant it firmly into place. My head-ache makes me dizzy, but I force it away.

Done.

I slowly make my way back along the beams. By the time I swing down onto the stairs again, my heart's pounding from adrenaline. I spot Pascao along the beams and give him a quick thumbs-up.

*This is the easy stuff,* I remind myself, my excitement giving way to an ominous anxiety. The hard part's going to be pulling off a convincing lie to the Chancellor.

We finish with the first base, then move on to the next. By the time we're done with the fourth base, my strength is starting to give way. If I was fully in my element, this suit could've made me damn near unstoppable—but now, even with its help, my muscles ache and my breaths sound strained. As the soldiers now guide me into a room in the air base and prepare me to make my call and my broadcast, I'm silently grateful that I don't need to run any more ceilings.

"What happens if the Chancellor doesn't buy you?" Pas-cao asks while the soldiers file out of the room. "No offense, pretty boy, but you don't exactly have the best reputation for keeping your promises."

"I didn't promise him anything," I reply. "Besides, he'll see my announcement go out to the entire Republic. He's going to think that everyone in the country will see me switch alle-giances to the Colonies. It won't last. But it'll buy us some time." Silently, I hope to hell that we can figure out the final cure before the Colonies realize what we're doing.

Pascao looks away and out the room's window, where we can see Republic soldiers finishing up the last few bomb placements on the base's ceiling. If this fails, or if the Colonies realize the surrender's fake before we have time to do anything about it, then we're probably done.

"Time for you to make your call, then," Pascao mutters. He locks the door, finds a chair, and pulls it off to one corner. Then he settles down with me to wait.

My hands tremble slightly as I click my mike on and call the Colonies' Chancellor. For a moment, all I hear is static, and a part of me hopes that it somehow can't trace the name that had called me before, and that somehow I'll have no way of reaching him. But then the static ends, the call clears, and I hear it connect. I greet the Chancellor.

"This is Day. Today is the last day of your promised cease-fire, yeah? And I have an answer to your request."

A few seconds drag by. Then, that crisp, businesslike voice comes on the other end. "Mr. Wing," the Chancellor says, as polite and pleasant as ever. "Right on time. How lovely to hear from you."

"I'm sure you've seen the Elector's announcement by now," I reply, ignoring his niceties.

"I have, indeed," the man replies. I hear some shuffling of papers in the background. "And now with your call, this day is looking to be full of good surprises. I'd been wondering when you would contact us again. Tell me, Daniel, have you given some thought to my proposal?"

From across the room, Pascao's pale eyes lock on to mine. He can't hear the conversation, but he can see the tension on my face. "I have," I reply after a pause. Gotta make myself sound realistic and reluctant, yeah? I wonder if June would approve.

"And what have you decided? Remember, this is entirely up to you. I won't force you to do anything you don't wish to do."

Yeah. I don't have to do anything—I'll just have to stand by and watch while you destroy the people I love. "I'll do it." Another pause. "The Republic's already surrendered. The people aren't happy about your presence, but I don't want to see them harmed. I don't want to see *anyone* harmed." I know I don't have to mention June by name for the Chancellor to understand. "I'll make a citywide announcement. We got access to the JumboTrons through the Patriots. It won't be long before that announcement hits all the screens in the entire Republic." I kick in a little more attitude to keep my lie authentic. "That good enough for you to keep your goddy hands off June?"

The Chancellor claps his hands once. "Done. If you're willing to become our . . . spokesman, so to speak, then I assure you that Ms. Iparis will be spared the trials and executions that come with an overturning of power."

His words send a chill through me, reminding me that if we

do fail, then what I'm going to do isn't going to save Anden's life. In fact, if we fail, the Chancellor will probably figure out that I'm behind all this too, and there goes June's . . . and probably Eden's . . . chances at safety. I clear my throat. Across the room, Pascao's face has turned stony with tension. "And my brother?"

"You need not worry about your brother. As I mentioned to you before, I am not a tyrant. I will not hook him up to a machine and pump him full of chemicals and poisons—I will not experiment on him. He—and you—will live a comfortable, safe life, free from harm and worry. This, I can guarantee you." The Chancellor's tone changes to what he thinks is soothing and gentle. "I can hear the unhappiness in your voice. But I do nothing except what is necessary. If your Elector imprisoned me, he would not hesitate to execute me. This is the way of the world. I am not a cruel man, Daniel. Remember, the Colonies are *not* responsible for your lifetime of suffering."

"Don't call me Daniel." My voice comes out low and quiet. *I am not Daniel to anyone outside of my family. I am Day. Plain and simple.*

"My apologies." He actually sounds genuinely sorry. "I hope you understand what I'm saying, Day."

I remain silent for a moment. Even now, I can still feel the pull against the Republic, all of the dark thoughts and memories that whisper to me to turn my back, to let it all crumble to pieces. The Chancellor can gauge me better than I would've thought. A lifetime of suffering is hard to leave behind. As if she can sense the dangerous pull of the Chancellor's spell, I hear June's voice cut through this train of thoughts and whisper something to me. I close my eyes and cling to her, drawing strength from her.

"Tell me when you want me to make this announcement," I say after a while. "Everything's wired up and ready to go. Let's get this whole thing over with."

"Wonderful." The Chancellor clears his throat, suddenly sounding like a businessman again. "The sooner, the better. I will land with my troops at the outer naval bases of Los Angeles by early afternoon. Let's arrange for you to speak at that time. Shall we?"

"Done."

"And one more thing," the Chancellor adds as I'm about to hang up. I stiffen, my tongue poised to click my mike off. "Before I forget."

"What?"

"I want you to make the announcement from the deck of my airship."

Startled, I glance at Pascao, and even though he has no idea what the Chancellor just said, he frowns at the way my face has just drained of color. From the Chancellor's airship? Of course. How could we think he'd be that easy to fool? He's taking precautions. If something goes wrong during the announcement, then he'll have me in his grip. If I make an announcement that's anything other than telling the Republic people to bow down to the Colonies, he could kill me right there on the airship's deck, surrounded by his men.

When the Chancellor speaks again, I can sense the satisfaction in his voice. He knows exactly what he's doing. "Your words will be more meaningful if given right from a Colonies airship, don't you agree?" he says. He claps his hands once again. "We'll expect you at Naval Base One in a few hours. Looking forward to meeting you in person, Day."

# JUNE

**THE REVELATION ABOUT MY CONNECTION TO THIS PLAGUE** changes all of my plans.

Instead of heading out with the Patriots and helping Day set up the airship bases, I stay behind at the hospital, letting the lab teams hook me up to machines and run a series of tests on me. My daggers and gun lie on a nearby dresser, so that they won't get in the way of all the wires, and only one knife stays tucked along my boot. Eden sits in bed beside me, his skin sickly pale. Several hours in, and the nausea has begun to hit.

"The first day's the worst," Eden says to me with an encouraging smile. He speaks slowly, likely from the medication the lab team gave him to help him sleep. "It gets better." He leans over and pats my hand, and I find myself warming to his innocent compassion. This must be what Day was like when he was young.

"Thanks," I reply. I don't speak the rest of my thoughts aloud, but I cannot believe that a child like Eden was able to tolerate this sort of testing for days. Had I known, I might have done what Day originally wanted and refused Anden's request altogether.

"What happens if they find out that you match?" Eden asks after a while. His eyes have started to droop, and his question comes out slurred.

What happens, indeed? We have a cure. We can present

the results to Antarctica and prove to them that the Colonies deliberately used this virus; we can present it to the United Nations and force the Colonies back. We'll have our ports opened up again. "The Antarcticans promise that help is on the way," I decide to say. "We might win. Just maybe."

"But the Colonies are already at our doorstep." Eden glances toward the windows, where our enemy's airships are now dotting the sky. Some have already docked at our bases, while others loom overhead. A shadow cast across our own Bank Tower building tells me that one is hovering over us right now. "What if Daniel fails?" he whispers, fighting back sleep.

"We just have to play it all carefully." But Eden's words make my gaze linger on the cityscape too. What if Day does fail? He told me as he left that he would contact us before his broadcast to the public. Now, seeing how close the Colonies' airships are, I feel an overwhelming sense of frustration that I can't be out there with them. What if the Colonies realize that the airship bases are all rigged? What if they don't come back?

Another hour passes. While Eden falls into a deep slumber, I stay awake and try to will away the nausea rolling over me in waves. I keep my eyes closed. It seems to help.

I must have fallen asleep, because suddenly I'm awakened by the sound of our door opening. The lab techs have finally returned. "Ms. Iparis," one of them says, adjusting his MIKHAEL name tag. "It wasn't a perfect match, but it was close—close enough that we were able to develop a solution. We're testing the cure on Tess now." He's unable to keep a grin from crossing his face. "You were the missing piece. Right under our noses."

I stare at him without saying a word. *We can send results to Antarctica*—the thought rushes through my mind. *We can ask for help. We can stop the plague's spread. We have a chance against the Colonies.*

Mikhael's companions start unhooking me from my tangle of wires, and then help me to my feet. I feel strong enough, but the room still sways. I'm not sure whether my unsteadiness is from the tests' side effects or the thought that this might all have worked. "I want to see Tess," I say as we start heading for the door. "How quickly will the cure start working?"

"We're not sure," Mikhael admits as we enter a long hall. "But our simulations are solid, and we ran several lab cultures with infected cells. We should start seeing Tess's health improve very soon."

We stop at the long glass windows of Tess's room. She lies in a delirious half sleep on her bed, and all around her are lab techs rushing about in full suits, monitors dictating her vital signs, charts and graphs beamed against the walls. An IV's injected into one of her arms. I study her face, searching for some sign of consciousness, and fail to find it.

Static in my earpiece. An incoming call. I frown, press a hand to my ear, and then click my mike on. A second later, I hear Day's voice. "Are you okay?" His first thought. Of course it is. The static is so severe that I can hardly understand what he's saying.

"I'm fine," I reply, hoping he can hear me. "Day, listen to me—we've found a cure."

No reply, just static, loud and unrelenting. "Day?" I say

again, and on the other side I hear some crackling, something like the desperation to communicate with me. But I can't get us hooked up. Unusual. The reception on these military bands is usually crystal clear. It's as if something else is blocking all of our frequencies. "Day?" I try again.

I finally catch his voice again. It holds a tension that reminds me of when he'd chosen to walk away from me so many months ago. It sends a river of dread through my veins. "I'm giving—announcement on board a Colonies airship—ellor won't have it any other way—"

On board a Colonies airship. The Chancellor would hold all the cards in that case—if Day were to make a sudden move, or make an announcement that went against what they agreed to, the Chancellor could have him arrested or murdered right on the spot. "Don't do it," I whisper automatically. "You don't have to go. We've found the cure, I was the missing piece of the puzzle."

"—June?—"

Then no answer, just more static. I try again twice more before I click my mike off in frustration. Beside me, I can see the lab tech also trying in vain to make a call.

And then I remember the shadow cast across the building we're in. My frustration fades immediately, followed by waves of terror and comprehension. *Oh no.* The Colonies. They're blocking our frequencies—they've taken them over. I had not thought that they would make their move so quickly. I rush over to the window looking out at Los Angeles's cityscape, then turn my eyes skyward. I can see the enormous Colonies airship that hovers overhead—and when I look more closely, I notice that smaller planes are leaving its deck and circling lower.

Mikhael joins me. "We can't reach the Elector," he says. "It seems all the frequencies are jammed."

Is this in preparation for Day's announcement? *He's in trouble. I know it.*

Just as this thought crosses my mind, the doors at the end of the hall swing open. Five soldiers come marching in, their guns hoisted, and in a flash I can see that these are not Republic soldiers at all—but Colonies troops, with their navy blue coats and gold stars. Panic rushes through me from head to toe. Instinctively I move toward Eden's room, but the soldiers see me. Their leader waves his gun at me. My hand flies to my gun strapped to my waist—and then I remember that all of my weapons (save for one ankle knife) are lying useless back in Eden's room.

"With the Republic's surrender," he says in a grandiose voice, "all reins of power have been transferred to Colonies' officials. This is your commander telling you to stand aside and let us pass, so that we can run a thorough search."

Mikhael throws up his hands and does as the official says. They draw closer. Memories whirl in my mind—they're all lessons from my days at Drake, a stream of maneuvers that run through my head at the speed of light. I gauge them carefully. A small team sent up here to accomplish some specific task. Other teams must be swarming each of the floors, but I know these soldiers must have been sent up to us for something in particular. I brace myself, ready for a fight. It's me they're after.

As if he read my mind, Mikhael nods once at the soldiers. His arms stay up high in the air. "What do you want?"

The soldier answers, "A boy named Eden Bataar Wing."

I know better than to suck in my breath and thus give away that Eden's on this floor—but a tidal wave of fear washes over me. I was wrong. They're not after me. They want Day's brother. If Day's forced to give his announcement on board the Chancellor's airship, alone, he'll be helpless if the Chancellor decides to take him hostage—and if he gets his hands on Eden, he'll be able to control Day at his every whim. My thoughts rush even further. If the Colonies truly succeed in taking over the Republic today, then the Chancellor could use Day indefinitely as his own weapon, as a manipulator of the Republic's people, for as long as the people continue to believe in Day as their hero.

I open my mouth before Mikhael can. "This floor just houses plague victims," I say to the soldier. "If you're looking for Day's brother, he'll be on a higher floor."

The soldier's gun swivels to me. He narrows his eyes in recognition. "You're the Princeps-Elect," he says. "Aren't you? June Iparis."

I lift my chin. "One of the Princeps-Elects, yes."

For a moment, I think he might believe what I said about Eden. Some of his men even start shifting back toward the stairs. The soldier watches me for a long time, studying my eyes, and then looks down the hallway behind me, where Eden's room lies. I don't dare flinch.

He frowns at me. "I know your reputation." Before I can

think of anything else to say in order to throw him off, he tilts his head at his troops and uses his gun to gesture at the hall. "Do a thorough search. The boy should be on this floor."

Too late to lie now. If I owe Day anything, I owe him this. I shift into the space between the soldiers and the hallway. Calculations rush through my head. (The hallway is a little over four feet wide—if I move into it, I can prevent the soldiers from attacking me all at once and break up my opponents into two smaller waves instead of one large one.) "Your Chancellor won't want me dead," I lie. My heart pounds furiously. Beside me, the lab tech looks on with stricken eyes, unsure of what to do. "He'll want me alive, and tried. You know this."

"Such big lies out of such a small mouth." The soldier hoists his gun. I hold my breath. "Move out of the way, or I shoot."

If I didn't see the hint of hesitation on his face, I would've done as he asked. No use to Day or Eden if I'm just dead and gunned down. But the soldier's flash of uncertainty is all I need. I hold my arms up slowly and carefully. My eyes stay fixed on him. "You don't want to shoot me," I say. I'm shocked at how firm my voice sounds—not a ripple of fear in it, despite the adrenaline rushing through my veins. My legs sway a little, still a touch unsteady from the experiments. "Your Chancellor doesn't sound like a forgiving man."

The soldier hesitates again. He doesn't know what the Chancellor has in mind for me. He has to give me the benefit of the doubt.

We hold our standoff for several long seconds.

Finally he spits out a curse and lowers his gun. "Get her," he snaps at his soldiers. "Don't shoot."

The world zooms in at me—everything fades, except for the enemy. My instincts kick into overdrive.

*Let's play. You have no idea who you're dealing with.*

I crouch into a fighting stance as the soldiers rush at me all at once. The narrowness of the hallway works instantly to my advantage—instead of dealing with five soldiers at the same time, I only deal with two. I duck the first soldier's swing, rip my knife out from my boot, and slash his calf as viciously as I can. The blade tears effortlessly through both his pant leg and his tendon. He shrieks. Instantly his leg buckles, taking him to the floor in a thrashing heap. The second soldier rushing at me trips right over his falling comrade. I kick out at the second soldier's face, knocking him out, and step off from his back to lunge at the third soldier. He tries to punch me. I block his blow with one arm—my other hand shoots up toward his face and smashes into his nose so hard that I feel the crunch of breaking bone. The soldier staggers backward once and falls, clutching his face in agony.

Three down.

My advantage of surprise vanishes—the last two soldiers take me on more warily. One of them shouts into his mike for backup. Behind them, Mikhael starts sneaking away. Even though I don't dare glance in his direction, I know that he must be moving to lock down the corridors in the stairwell, making it impossible for more Colonies soldiers to come swarming up. One of the remaining soldiers lifts his gun and points it at my legs. I kick out at him. My boot hits the barrel of his gun right as he fires it, sending a bullet ricocheting wildly over my shoulder. An alarm blares across the entire building's intercoms—the stairwells are locked down, an alert's been sent out. I kick the gun again so that it arcs backward, hitting the soldier hard in the face. It stuns him momentarily. I spin and strike him hard in the jaw with my elbow—

—but then something hits me hard in the back of my head. Stars explode across my vision. I stumble, falling to one knee, and struggle to swim up through my blindness. The second soldier must've struck me from behind. I swing out again, trying my best to guess at where the soldier is, but I miss and fall again. Through my hazy vision, I see the soldier raise the butt of his gun to strike me again in the face. *The blow will knock me unconscious.* I try in vain to roll away.

The strike doesn't come. I blink, struggling to my feet. What happened? When my vision clears a bit, I notice the last soldier lying on the ground and lab techs rushing over to tie their hands and feet. Suddenly there are people everywhere. Standing over me is Tess, pale and sickly and breathing hard, clutching a rifle from one of the other fallen soldiers. I had not noticed her leaving her room.

She manages a weak smile. "You're welcome," she says, extending a hand to help me up.

I smile back. She pulls me, trembling, to my feet. When I sway on uncertain legs, she offers me her shoulder to lean on. Neither of us is very steady, but we don't fall.

"Ms. Iparis," Mikhael gasps out as he hurries over to us. "We've managed to reach the Elector—we've told him about the cure. But we also just received a warning to evacuate the Bank Tower. They say the fake surrender will end very soon and that one of the Colonies' first targets of retaliation will be—"

A shudder shakes the hospital. We all freeze where we are. I glance at the horizon—at first the shudder felt a bit like an earthquake, or the rumble of a passing airship, but the shaking is set off in short, regular intervals instead of the sharp roll of a seismic wave or the low, steady hum of airships—and an instant later, I realize that the airship bases' bombs must have begun going off. I run to the window with Tess, where we look on as bright plumes of orange and gray billow up from the bases lining the horizon. Panic takes hold of me. Day must have made his announcement. Whether or not he survived it, I have no idea.

The phony surrender's over; the ceasefire has ended. The final fight for the Republic has begun.

# DAY

WHEN I WAS FIFTEEN, I BROKE INTO A BANK IN LOS ANGELES after guards standing at its back entrance didn't believe I could do it in ten seconds. The night before, I had made a detailed mental checklist of the layout of that bank, noting every foothold and window and ledge, and guesstimated every floor inside. I waited until its guards rotated at midnight, and then I snuck into the building's basement. There, I set a tiny explosive on the vault's lock. There was no way I could break in at night without triggering their alarms . . . but the next morning, when guards headed down to the vault to check on the inventory, most of the laser-guided alarms throughout the building would be off. I timed my entrance the next day to coincide. As I taunted the guards at the bank's back entrance, the guards inside the bank were opening the vault door. And the explosive went off. At the same time, I leaped through the bank's second floor window, then down the steps, then into the vault through smoke and dust, and made my way out of the building by hooking the bank's waiting line chains to myself and swinging out of the top floor. You should've seen me.

Now, as I walk straight up the inner ramps of a pyramid dock and toward the entrance of my very first Colonies airship, flanked on both sides by Colonies soldiers, I run through my old bank stunt and feel an overwhelming urge to flee. To swing onto the side of the ship, lose the troops tailing me, and weave into its vents. My eyes sweep the ship and try to map out the best escape routes, the closest hiding places, and most convenient footholds. Walking straight up to it like this leaves me feeling way too open and vulnerable. Still, I don't show it on my face. When I reach the entrance and a pair of lieutenants ushers me inside, then pats me down thoroughly for any weapons, I just smile politely at them. If the Chancellor wants to see me intimidated, he might be disappointed.

The soldiers don't catch the tiny, coin-size round discs sewn into my boots. One is a recorder. If there's any conversation I want to have to use against the Colonies, it's this one, to be shown to the entire public. The others are tiny explosives. Outside, somewhere beyond the airship base and hidden in the buildings' shadows, are Pascao and several other Patriots.

I hope the people are ready for my signal. I hope they're listening for my final step, watching and waiting.

It's the first time I've been in an airship that has no portraits of the Elector hanging on its walls. Instead, interspersed between swallowtail-shaped blue-and-gold flags are ads, screens as high as the walls that advertise everything from food to electronics to houses. I get an uncomfortable sense of déjà vu, recalling the time June and I had stumbled into the Colonies, but when the lieutenants glance my way, I just shrug at them and keep my eyes down. We make our way through the corridors and up two flights of stairs before they finally usher me into a large chamber. I stand there for a moment, unsure of what to do next. This looks like some sort of observation deck, with a long glass window that gives me a view of Los Angeles.

A lone man stands by the window, the city's light painting his silhouette black. He waves me over. "Ah, you're finally here!" he exclaims. Instantly I recognize the smooth, coaxing voice of the Chancellor. He looks nothing like how I pictured him: He's short and small, *frail*, his hair receded and gray, his voice way too big for his body. There's a slight hunch to his shoulders, and his skin looks thin and translucent in some areas, like it's made of paper and might crumple if I were to touch it. I can't keep the surprise off my face. This is the man who rules over corps like DesCon, who threatens and bullies an entire nation and negotiates with manipulative precision? A little anticlimactic, to be honest. I almost write him off before I get a good look at his eyes.

And that's where I recognize the Chancellor I've spoken to before. His eyes calculate, analyze, and deduce me in a way that chills me to the bone. Something is incredibly wrong about them.

Then I realize why. His eyes are mechanical.

"Well, don't just stand there," he says. "Come on over. Enjoy the view with me, son. This is where we'll have you make your announcement. A nice vantage point, isn't it?"

A retort—"The view's probably better without all the Colonies airships in the way"—is on the tip of my tongue, but I swallow it with some effort and do as he says. He smiles as I stop beside him, and I do my best not to look into his false eyes.

"Well, look at you, all young and fresh faced." He claps me on the back. "You did the right thing, you know, coming here." He gazes back at Los Angeles. "Do you see all that? What's the point of staying loyal to that? You're a Colonian now, and you won't have to put up with the Republic's twisted laws anymore. We'll treat you and your brother so well that you'll soon wonder why you ever hesitated to join us."

From the corner of my eyes, I make note of possible escape routes. "What'll happen to the people in the Republic?"

The Chancellor taps his lips in a display of thoughtfulness. "The Senators, unfortunately, might be less happy about the whole thing—and as for the Elector himself . . . well, you can only have one real ruler for one country, and I am already here." He offers me a smile that borders on kindness, a startling contrast to his actual words. "He and I are more alike than you might think. We are not cruel. We are simply practical. And you know how tricky it can be to deal with traitors."

A shiver runs down my spine. "And the Princeps-Elects?" I repeat. "What about the Patriots? This was part of our deal, remember?"

The Chancellor nods. "Of course I remember. Day, there are things you'll learn about people and society when you get older. Sometimes, you just have to do things the hard way. Now, before you work yourself up into a panic, know that Ms. Iparis will be unharmed. We already have plans to pardon her for your sake, given that you'll be helping us out.

Part of our deal, just like you said, and I do not go back on my word. The other Princeps-Elects will be executed along with the Elector."

Executed. So easy, just like that. I get a nauseous feeling in my stomach at the memory of Anden's botched assassination. This time he might not be so lucky. "As long as you spare June," I manage to choke out, "and as long as you don't hurt the Patriots or my brother. But you still haven't answered my first question. What will happen to the people of the Republic?"

The Chancellor eyes me, then leans closer. "Tell me, Day, do you think the masses have the right to make decisions for an entire nation?"

I turn to stare at the city. It's a long drop from here to the bottom of the naval base; I'll have to find a way to slow myself down. "The laws that affect an entire nation will also affect that nation's individuals, yeah?" I reply, goading him. I hope my recorder's picking all this up. "So of course the people have a right to contribute to those decisions."

The Chancellor nods. "A fair answer. But fairness does not power nations, Day, does it? I have read histories about nations where every person is given an equal start in life, where everyone contributes to the greater good and no one is richer or poorer than anyone else. Do you think that system worked?" He shakes his head. "Not with people, Day. That's something you'll learn when you grow up. People by nature are unjust, unfair, and conniving. You have to be careful with them—you have to find a way to make them *think* that you are catering to their every whim. The masses can't function on their own. They need help. They don't know what's good for them. And as for what will happen to the people of the Republic? Well, Day, I'll tell you. The people as a whole will be thrilled to be integrated into our system. They will know everything that they need to know, and we will make sure they are all put to good use. It will be a well-oiled machine."

"Everything they *need* to know?"

"Yes." He folds his hands behind his back and sticks his chin up. "Do you really believe that the people can make all of their own decisions? What a frightening world. People don't always know what they really want. You should know that better than anyone, Day, what with your announcement so long ago in favor of the Elector, and with the announcement you'll give us today." He tilts his head a little as he talks. "You do what you need to do."

*You do what you need to do.* Echoes of the philosophy of the Republic's own former Elector—echoes of something that, no matter what country I'm in, never seems to change. On the surface, I just nod, but inside, I feel a sudden hesitation to go through with my plan. *He's baiting you,* I remind myself, lost in the struggle. *You are not like the Chancellor. You fight for the people.*

*You are fighting for something real. Aren't you?*

I've got to get out of here, before he works his way deeper into my mind. My muscles tense up, ready for the announcement. I study the room from my peripheral vision. "Well," I say stiffly, "let's get this over with."

"More enthusiasm, my boy," the Chancellor says, clicking his tongue in mock disapproval, and then gives me a serious look. "We thoroughly expect you to sell your point to the people."

I nod. I step forward toward the window, then let two soldiers hook my mike up to broadcast from the airship. A transparent, live video of me suddenly appears on the glass. Shivers run down my entire body. There are Colonies soldiers all over the place, and they've ensured that if I don't make my move just right, I'll have sentenced myself and most likely all of my loved ones to death. This is it. There is no turning back from here.

"People of the Republic," I begin. "Today, I stand here with the Chancellor of the Colonies, on board his very own airship. I have a message for all of you." My voice sounds hoarse, and I have to clear my throat before continuing. When I shift my toes, I can feel the bump of the two tiny explosives on the bottom of my boots' soles, ready for my next move. I hope to hell that the markers that Pascao, the other Runners, and I left across the city have done their work, and that the people are prepared.

"We've been through a lot together," I continue. "But few things have been more trying than the last few months in the Republic. Believe me, I know. Adjusting to a new Elector, seeing the changes that have come around . . . and as you all know by now, I haven't been doing so well myself." My headache throbs as if in response. Outside the airship, my voice echoes across the city from the video feed playing from dozens of Colonies airships and hundreds of Los Angeles

JumboTrons. I take a deep breath, as if this might be the last time I ever speak to the people. "You and I will probably never get a chance to meet. But I know you. You have taught me about all the good things in my life, and why I've fought for my family all these years. I hope for great things for your own loved ones, that they can go through life without suffering the way mine have." I pause here. My eyes turn to face the Chancellor, and he nods once, coaxing me on. My heart is beating so loudly that I can barely hear my own voice.

"The Colonies have much to offer you," I say, my voice growing stronger. "Their ships are now in our skies. It will not be long before you see Colonies banners flying above your children's schools and over your homes. People of the Republic, I have one final message for you, before you and I say farewell to each other."

It's time. My legs tense, and my feet shift ever so slightly. The Chancellor looks on.

"The Republic is weak and broken." I narrow my eyes. "But it is still *your country*. Fight for it. *This is your home, not theirs.*"

In the same moment that I see the Chancellor's enraged expression, I spring from where I'm standing and kick at the glass as hard as I can. Colonies soldiers rush toward me. My boots hit the window—the explosives embedded in my soles give two brief pops, sending tremors through my feet. The glass shatters.

And now I'm midair, sailing through the open space. My arms whip up and grab the top edge of the broken windowpane. A bullet zips by. The Chancellor's furious shout rises up from inside. Guess they're not going to try keeping me alive after that. All my adrenaline rushes forward in a flood of heat.

I shimmy up and out into the evening air. No time to waste. My cap threatens to blow off—I hang out the window for a second and try to adjust it more snuggly onto my head. Last thing I need right now is to have my hair blowing around like a beacon for anyone on the ground to see. When the gusts die down a bit, I pull myself completely out and cling to the window frame. I look up, gauging the distance to the next window. Then I jump. My hands grab on to the bottom ledge of the frame, and with difficulty, I manage to pull myself up. I grunt from the effort. Never would've had a problem with this a year ago.

When I've hopped to a fourth window, I hear the faint sound of something popping. Then, the first explosion.

A tremor runs deep through the entire airship, nearly shaking loose my grip, and when I glance down, I see a ball of orange and gray explode from where the airship is docked to its pyramid base. The Patriots are making their move. A second explosion follows—this time the airship creaks slightly, tilting to the east. Gritting my teeth, I pick up speed. One of my feet slips against a window frame at the same time a gust of wind blows by—I almost lose my balance. For a second my leg dangles precariously. "C'mon," I scold myself. "You call this a run?" Then I throw one arm up as far as I can and manage to catch the next window before my legs give way completely. The effort triggers a dull flash of pain at the back of my head. I wince. No, not now. Anytime but now. But it's no use. I feel the headache coming. If I get hit with it right now, I'll be in so much pain that I'll plummet to my death for sure. Desperately, I climb faster. My feet slip again on the topmost window. I manage to catch myself at the last second, then grab the ledge of the upper deck as my headache explodes in full force.

Blinding white pain. I dangle there, clinging on for dear life, fighting against the agony that threatens to pull me under. Two more explosions follow the first couple in rapid succession, and now the airship creaks and groans. It tries to launch, firing away from the base, but all it manages to do is shudder. If the Chancellor gets his hands on me now, he'll kill me himself. Somewhere far away, I hear a siren sound—soldiers on the upper deck must know by now that I'm heading there, and they'll be ready for me.

My breaths come in short gasps. *Open your eyes*, I command myself. *You have to open them.* Through a blurry veil of tears, I see a glimpse of the upper deck and soldiers running. Their shouts ring out across the deck. For an instant, I lose my memory again of where I am, what I'm doing, what my mission is. The unfamiliarity makes my stomach heave, and I have to keep myself from throwing up. *Think, Day. You've been in bad situations before.* My memory blurs. What did I need up here again? Finally I clear my mind—I need some way to swing down to the bottom of the ship. Then I remember the sleek metal chain railings lining the edge of the deck, and my original plan—my eyes swivel up to the nearest chain. With enormous effort, I reach out and grab at it. I miss the first time. The soldiers see me now, and several of them run in my direction. I grit my teeth and try again.

This time I reach the chain. I grab it with both hands, then yank down. The chain pops free from its hooks. I throw myself off the side of the ship—and let myself fall. I hope to hell this chain can support my weight. There's a chorus of pops as the chain snaps free of hooks on both sides, sending me down at dizzying speed. The pain in my head threatens to weaken my grip. I hang on with every shred of strength that I have. My hair billows around me, and I realize my cap must've fallen off. Down, down, down I fall. The world zips past me at the speed of light. Through the rushing wind, my head slowly clears.

Suddenly one side of the chain snaps loose right as I reach the bottom of the ship. A lungful of air escapes me as I'm vaulted to one side. I manage to grab the remaining chain with both hands and hang on tightly as I swing along the bottom side of the ship. The pyramid base is almost close enough under my feet for me to jump, but I'm going way too fast. I swing closer to the side of the ship, then scrape the heels of my boots hard against the steel. There's a loud, long screech. My boots finally find traction—the force spins me from my swing and sends me twirling. I fight to steady myself. Before I can, though, the chain finally breaks and I tumble onto the outside of the pyramid base.

The impact knocks all the wind out of me. I skid against the smooth, slanted walls for a few seconds, until my boots catch against the surface and I stop there, bruised and limp, convinced soldiers are going to fill me with bullets as I lie vulnerable against the pyramid. Pascao and the others will know by now that I've made my move, and they'll be setting off the bombs all along the naval bases. I better get off this thing before I'm burnt to a crisp. That thought fills my mind and gives me the strength to pull myself up. I slide down the side as fast as I can—below, I can already see Colonies soldiers rushing to stop me. A sense of hopelessness stabs me. There's no way in hell I'll get past all of them in time. Still, I keep moving. I have to get away from the explosion site.

I'm several dozen yards from the bottom. Soldiers are clambering up to seize me. I tense up, push myself up into a crouch, and quickly move sideways against the slanted base. I'm not going to make it.

The instant this crosses my mind, the two final explosions go off under the airship.

A huge roar above me shakes the earth, and when I glance behind me, I see an enormous fireball rise up from where the airship is docked with the top of the base. All along the naval base, orange flames burst from every single pyramid dock. They've gone off in unison. The result is absolutely jaw-dropping. Quickly I glance back to the soldiers who were chasing me—they've paused, shocked by what they're witnessing. Another deafening burst of flame erupts above us and the tremors knock everyone off their feet. I struggle to stabilize myself against the slanted wall. *Move, move, move!* I stagger down the last few yards of the base's wall and fall to my knees on the ground. The world spins. All I can hear are the shouts of soldiers and the roar of the infernos lighting up the naval bases.

Hands grab me. I struggle, but I have no more strength left. Suddenly they drop me and I hear a familiar voice at my side. I turn in surprise. Who is this? *Pascao. His name is Pascao.*

His bright gray eyes crinkle at me—he grabs my hand and urges me to run. "Nice to see you alive. Let's keep it that way."

# JUNE

From the Bank Tower in downtown LA, I can see the giant plumes of orange flame lighting up the naval bases along the coast. The blasts are enormous, illuminating the edge of the sky with blinding light and echoing through the air, the force shaking the glass windows of the tower as I look on. Hospital staff mill around me in a scene of commotion. The lab teams are prepping both Tess and Eden for evacuation.

A call comes in from Pascao. "I've got Day," he shouts. "Meet us outside."

My knees turn weak with relief. *He's alive. He made it.* I peek inside Tess's room, where she's being secured to a wheelchair, and give her a thumbs-up. She brightens, even in her weakened state. Outside the tower, I see the shadow engulfing our building begin to move—the Colonies airship hovering overhead is heading away from us to join into battle. As if our explosions have unsettled a nest of wasps, dozens of Colonies fighter jets are taking off from its deck as well as the decks of the distant, crippled airships, their shapes forming squadrons in the sky. Republic jets meet them in midair.

*Hurry, Antarctica. Please.*

I rush off the lab floor and down the stairs to the lobby of the Bank Tower. There's chaos everywhere. Republic soldiers hurry past me in a blur of motion, while several gather at the front doors to prevent anyone else from getting inside. "This hospital is off limits!" one barks. "Bring the injured across the street—we are evacuating!" The screens lining the hall show scenes of Republic soldiers clashing with Colonies troops in the streets—and, to my surprise, Republic *civilians* wielding whatever weapons they can find and joining in to push the Colonies back. Fires burn along the roads. At the bottom of every screen in bold, menacing letters is the scrolling text: ALL REPUBLIC SOLDIERS TO BREAK SURRENDER. ALL REPUBLIC SOLDIERS TO BREAK SURRENDER. I cringe at the scene, even though this is exactly what we had planned for.

Outside, the noise of battle deafens me. Fighter jets roar past us overhead, while others hover directly over the Bank Tower, prepared to defend the tallest building in LA if— *when*—the Colonies try to attack. I see similar formations over other prominent downtown buildings. "Come on, Day," I mutter, scanning the streets nearby for signs of his bright hair, or of Pascao's pale eyes. A deep tremor shakes the ground. Another ball of orange flame explodes behind several rows of buildings, then a pair of Colonies jets zoom by, followed closely by a Republic plane. The sound is so loud that I press both hands to my ears until they've passed.

"June?" Pascao's voice comes over my mike, but I can barely hear him. "We're almost here. Where are you?"

"In front of the Bank Tower," I shout over the noise.

"We've gotta evacuate," he replies immediately. "Getting some feedback from our Hackers—the Colonies are aiming to attack the building within the hour—"

As if on cue, a Colonies jet screams by, and an instant later, an enormous explosion goes off at the very top of the Bank Tower. Soldiers all around me let out shouts of warning as glass falls from the highest floors. I jump backward into the safety of the building's entrance. Debris rains down in a thunderous storm, crushing jeeps and shattering into a million pieces.

"June?" Pascao's voice comes back on, clearly alarmed now. "*June*—are you okay?"

"I'm fine!" I shout back. "I'll help with evacuations once I see you. See you soon!" Then I hang up.

Three minutes later, I finally spot Day and Pascao staggering toward the Bank Tower against the tide of civilians escaping the area and soldiers rushing to defend the streets. They stumble through the debris. I rush from the entrance toward Day, who's leaning heavily against Pascao's good shoulder.

"Are either of you injured?" I ask.

"I'm fine," Pascao replies, nodding at Day. "Not sure about this guy. I think he's more exhausted than anything."

I swing Day's other arm around my shoulder. Pascao and I help him inside the lobby of a building several blocks from the Bank Tower, where we still have a direct view of the tower and the chaotic, debris-filled square that sits between the two buildings. Inside, rows of injured soldiers are already camped out, with medics running frantically between them. "We're clearing out the tower," I explain as we gently help Day down to the ground. He grimaces in pain, even though I can't find any specific wounds on him. "Don't worry," I reassure him when he glances up at me in alarm. "Eden and Tess are being evacuated right now."

"And so should you," he adds. "The fight's just beginning."

"If I tell you to stop worrying, *will* you?"

My reply gets a wry smile from him. "Are the Antarcticans coming to help us?" Day asks. "Did you tell Anden about the cure—"

"Calm down," I interrupt him, then stand up and put a hand on Pascao's shoulder. "Watch out for him. I'm going back to the tower to help with the evacuations. I'll tell them to bring his brother here." Pascao nods quickly, and I cast one last glance toward Day before running out of the building.

A stream of people is making its way out of the tower, with Republic soldiers flanking them on either side. Some are on crutches or in wheelchairs, while others are strapped to gurneys and being wheeled out by a team of medics. Republic soldiers bark orders at them, their guns hoisted and their bodies tense. I hurry past them and toward the entrance, then push my way inside to the stairs. I hop up the steps two at a time until I finally reach the lab floor, where the door's propped open and a nurse is directing people toward the elevator.

I reach the nurse and grab her arm. She turns to look at me, startled. "Princeps-Elect," she manages to blurt out, hastily bowing her head. "What are you—"

"Eden Bataar Wing," I say breathlessly. "Is he ready to go yet?"

"Day's brother?" she replies. "Yes—yes, he's in his room. We're preparing to move him comfortably. He still needs to be in a wheelchair, but—"

"And Tess? The girl who was under quarantine?"

"She's already on her way downstairs—"

I don't wait for the nurse to finish before rushing into the main lab room and toward the corridor. At the very end, I see a pair of doctors wheeling Eden out. He looks like he's unconscious, resting on a small pillow propped between his head and the chair's back, his forehead damp with sweat.

I give the doctors instructions on where to take him as we all hurry together toward the elevator. "You'll see Day there. Keep him with his brother."

Another explosion rips through the building, forcing half of us to our knees. Some of the medics scream. Dust rains down from the ceiling, making my eyes water—I unbutton my coat, then shrug out of it and throw it across Eden to shield him. "No elevator," I gasp out, heading toward the stairs instead. "Can we carry him down?"

One of the nurses gingerly picks Eden up and holds him tight in her arms. We hurry down the stairs as more dust showers us and muffled sounds of shouts, guns, and explosions echo from outside.

We rush out into a lengthening evening lit completely by the fire of battle. Still no call from Anden. My eyes sweep the roofs as we pause underneath the entrance, other evacuees streaming around us and between Republic guards. One of the guards recognizes me and hurries over, throwing a quick salute before he speaks. "Princeps-Elect!" he shouts. "Get to the adjacent shelter, as quick as you can—we'll send a jeep to take you to the Elector."

I shake my head right away. "*No.* I'm staying here." A spark from the roofs makes me look up, and instantly we all cringe when a bullet hits the overhang in front of the main entrance. There are Colonies gunmen on the roofs. Several of the Republic soldiers point their guns and open fire. The guard who had spoken to me puts a hand on my shoulder. "Then move out," he yells, gesturing wildly for us.

The nurse holding Eden takes several steps forward, her eyes still fixed in terror on the rooftops. I put a hand out to stop her. "Not yet," I say. "Stay here a moment." Not two seconds after the words leave my mouth, I see a bullet hit one of the evacuees—blood sprays, and instantly the people around him flee, screams reverberating in the air. My heart pounds as I scan the roofs again. One of the Republic soldiers finally catches a gunman, and I see somebody in a Colonies uniform fall from the top of a nearby building. I look away before the body hits the ground, but I'm still struck by a violent wave of nausea. *How do we get Eden to safety?*

"Stay here," I command the nurse holding Eden. Then I tap four of the Republic soldiers. "Cover me. I'm heading up there." I gesture for one of the guards to hand me the gun at his belt, and he passes it over without hesitation.

I move into the crowds and make my way toward the buildings. I try to imitate the effortless grace that Day and Pascao have in this urban jungle. As the chaotic evacuations continue and soldiers from both sides face off against one another, I hurry into the shadows of a narrow, nearby alley and start making my way up the side of the building. I'm small, dressed in dark clothes, and alone. They won't expect me to head up here. My mind runs through all of my sharpshooting lessons.

If I can throw them off, it'll give the evacuees that much more of a chance to make it out in one piece. Even as I think this, another Colonies jet zooms overhead and a huge plume of bright red flame erupts on the Bank Tower. A Republic jet tails close behind it, firing as it goes—as I look on, it manages to hit the Colonies plane and ignite one of its engines, sending it careening wildly to one side and leaving a trail of dark smoke behind it. A deafening roar follows; it must have crashed several blocks down. I look back up at the burning tower. We don't have much time. This building is going to come down. I grit my teeth and make my way up as fast as I can. If only I were as good a Runner as Day and Pascao.

I finally reach the top floor's ledge. From here, I get a good view of the battle zone below me. The Bank Tower is under siege from the sky and the ground, where hundreds of Republic troops are pushing back in the streets against a steady tide of enemy soldiers. Patients and medics alike still stream from the tower and down the street toward the makeshift shelter, along with government officials from the higher floors, many of them covered completely in white dust and blood. I peer over the top ledge.

No gunmen here. I pull myself up onto the roof, careful to stay in the shadows. My hand grips the gun so tightly that I can barely feel my fingers. I scan the roofs in the danger zone leading up to the shelter, until finally I see several Colonies soldiers crouched on top of the neighboring buildings, taking aim at the Republic troops heading up the evacuation. I make my way silently toward them.

I take the first one down quickly, aiming at him from behind as I peer over the building's top ledge. It's as if I can feel Metias guiding my gun, making sure I hit him somewhere that isn't fatal. As he collapses with a muffled shriek that's lost in all the chaos, I rush over and grab his gun, then fling it over the side of the roof. Then I hit him in the face hard enough to knock him out. My eyes settle on the next soldier. I press one hand against my earpiece and click my mike on.

"Tell the nurse to keep waiting," I hiss urgently at the guard by the Bank Tower. "I'll send a signal when it's—"

I never get a chance to finish my sentence. An explosion throws me down flat onto the roof. When I open my eyes and look down, the entire street is completely covered in ash and dust. Dust bombs? Through the veil of smoke and dirt, evacuees are running in panic toward the shelter and breaking through the lines of Republic soldiers flanking them, completely ignoring their shouts. The Colonies gunmen have visors on. They must be able to see through all this smoke. They fire down at the crowds, scattering them in all directions. I look frantically toward the tower. Where's Eden? I hurry to my next target, taking him down in the same way as the last. Another gunman down. I lock on to my third target, then spit out a curse as I realize that my gun has just run out of bullets.

I'm about to make my way off the roof when something bright glints from a rooftop. I freeze in my tracks.

Not far from me on a higher building, Commander Jameson crouches on a roof. A chill shakes me from head to toe when I see that she has a gun in her hand. No. *No.*

She's picking off Republic soldiers, one bullet at a time. Then, my heart stops as she catches sight of something that piques her interest. She takes aim at a new target on the ground. My eyes follow the line of her gun. And that's when I see a boy with bright blond hair pushing his way against the stream of the crowd and toward the Bank Tower.

She's aiming at Day.

# DAY

TESS GETS EVACUATED FIRST—I SEE HER LIMP FORM BEING carried in the arms of a nurse as they exit the Bank Tower. I take her from the nurse's arms as soon as they reach ground level, then carry her alongside the stream of other evacuees. She seems only half conscious, unaware of my presence, her head lolling to one side. Halfway to the shelter, I slow down. Damn, I'm so exhausted and in so much pain.

Pascao takes Tess from my arms. He hoists her up to his chest. On the roofs, sparks fly—signs of gunfire. "Get back to the Bank Tower entrance," he yells at me before turning his back. "I'll get her over!" And then he's off before I can argue.

I watch them go for a while, unwilling to look away until I'm sure Tess is safely across the square. When they reach the shelter, I turn my attention back to the tower. Eden should be down by now. I crane my neck, squinting through the crowds for a head of blond curls. Has June come back downstairs yet? I don't see her in the panicking masses either and her absence sends a jolt of worry through me.

Then, an explosion. I'm thrown to the ground.

Dust. A *dust bomb*, I manage to think through the pounding in my head. At first I can't see anything through all the smoke—there's chaos everywhere, sparks flying, and the occasional muffled sound of gunfire; through the floating white dust, I see a blur of people running toward the safety of the

Republic barricades, their legs moving as if in slow motion, their mouths open in silent shouts. I shake my head wearily. My own limbs feel like they're dragging through the mud, and the back of my head throbs, threatening to drown me in pain. I blink against it, trying to keep my senses straight. Desperately I call out again for Eden, but I can't even hear my own voice. If *I* can't hear it, how can *he*?

The people thin out for a moment.

And then I see him. It's Eden. He's unconscious in the arms of a terrified Republic nurse, one who seems to be stumbling blindly through the dust, headed in the wrong direction—straight toward the Colonies troops lining the left side of the square, opposite of where the shelter is. I don't stop to think or shout at him, I don't hesitate or wait for a good interval in the gunfire. I just start running toward him.

COMMANDER JAMESON'S GOING TO SHOOT HIM—THE
direction she's aiming her gun is unmistakable.

Day's sprinting through the dust that blankets the street.
*Day, what are you doing?* He stumbles in his dash, and even
from the roofs I can tell that he's struggling to make his body
move, that every last inch of him is screaming from exhaustion. He's going to push himself too far. I glance in the direction he's going, searching out what has drawn his attention.

Eden. Of course. The nurse holding Eden trips and falls
in the midst of all the billowing smoke, and when she gets
up, fear gets the best of her because she just starts running
away. Fury rises up inside me. Left behind is Eden, slowly
stirring and completely vulnerable in the open street, blind,
separated from the group, and coughing uncontrollably from
the smoke.

I jump to my feet. With the way Day's running opposite
of everyone else, he'll soon be in an area where he's an open
target.

My hand flies to my waist—and then I remember that
my own gun is out of bullets. I sprint back across the rooftop
toward my last target, where I hadn't yet dropped his gun off
the roof. When I glance toward Commander Jameson again, I
see her tense and aim. *No. No!* She fires a shot.

The bullet misses Day by a couple of feet. He stumbles in his rush, throwing an arm briefly over his head out of instinct, but picks himself up and continues doggedly on. My heart thuds frantically against my chest. *Faster.* I take a flying leap from one roof to the next. Down below, I see Day nearing Eden. Then he's there, he's reached him, he's skidding to a halt next to Eden and throwing his arms protectively around his little brother. The dust around them makes them hard to focus on, as if they're both ghosts in faded colors. My breath comes in shallow gasps as I draw closer to the fallen soldiers. I hope the dust is throwing Commander Jameson's aim off.

I reach the downed soldier. I grab his gun. One bullet left.

Below, Day picks up Eden, puts one hand protectively against the back of his brother's head, and then starts staggering back toward the shelter as fast as his broken body will allow him. Commander Jameson takes aim again—I scream in my head and push myself to go faster. All of my adrenaline, every fiber of my attention and concentration, is now focused like an arrow on her. She fires. This time the bullet misses the brothers, but it sparks barely a foot away from Day. He doesn't even bother to look up. He only clutches Eden tighter, then stumbles onward.

I finally near the roof where she is. I leap onto it, landing on its flat concrete surface. From here, I can see both the roof I'm on and the street below. Three dozen yards ahead of me, partially obscured by chimneys and vents, Commander Jameson crouches with her back turned to me, her focus on the streets.

She fires again. Down below, I hear a hoarse shriek of pain from a voice I know all too well. All my breath escapes me. I glance quickly to the street to see Day fall to his knees, dropping Eden for a moment. The sounds around me dull.

He's been shot.

He shudders, then picks himself up again. Hoists Eden into his arms again. Staggers onward. Commander Jameson fires one more time. The bullet makes impact. I hoist the gun in my hands, then point it straight at her. I'm close enough now, close enough to see the ridges of her bulletproof vest lining her back. My hands shake. I have a perfect vantage, a straight shot right at Commander Jameson's head. She's getting ready to fire again.

I aim.

As if the world has suddenly slowed to a million frames a second, Commander Jameson spins around. She senses my presence. Her eyes narrow—and then she swivels her gun toward me, taking her focus off Day. Thoughts flash through my mind at the speed of light. I pull my gun's trigger, firing my last bullet straight at her head.

And I miss.

I never miss.

No time to dwell on this—Commander Jameson has her gun pointed at me, and as my bullet whizzes past her face, I see her smile and fire. I throw myself to the ground, then roll. Something sparks barely an inch from my arm. I dart behind a nearby chimney and press myself as tightly against the wall as I can. Somewhere behind me, the sound of heavy boots approaches. *Breathe. Breathe.* Our last confrontation flashes through my mind. Why can I face everything in the world except Commander Jameson?

"Come out and play, Little Iparis," she calls out. When I stay silent, she laughs. "Come out, so you can see your pretty boy bleeding to death on the street."

She knows exactly how to slice right into my heart. But I grit my teeth and force the image of a bleeding, dying Day out of my head. I don't have time for this bullshit. What I need to do is disarm her—and at that thought, I look down at my useless gun. Time to play a game of pretend.

She's silent now. All I can hear is the soft tap of approaching boots, the steady nearing of my brother's killer. My hands tighten on my gun.

She's close enough. I shut my eyes for an instant, mutter a quick whisper for good luck—and then whirl out from my hiding place. I point my gun up at Commander Jameson as if I'm about to fire. She does what I hope—she flinches to the side, but this time I'm ready, and I lunge straight for her. I jump, then kick her face as hard as I can. My boots make a satisfying sound on impact. Her head snaps backward. Her grip on her gun loosens, and I take the opportunity to kick it right out of her hands. She collapses onto the roof with a thud—her gun flies off to one side, then falls right off the roof and to the smoke-filled streets below.

I don't dare stop my momentum. While she's still down, I swing my elbow at her face in an effort to knock her unconscious. My first blow hits—but my second one doesn't. Commander

Jameson grabs my elbow, snaps her other hand on my wrist like a shackle, and then twists. I flip with it. Pain shoots up my arm as it bends in her grasp. Before she can break it, I twist around and stomp on her arm with the sharp heel of my boot. She winces, but doesn't let go. I stomp again, harder.

Her grip loosens by a hair, and I finally manage to slip out of her grasp.

She hops to her feet right as I put some distance between us and turn again to face her. We start to circle each other, both of us breathing heavily, my arm still screaming in pain and her face marred by a trickle of blood coming from her temple. I already know I can't win against her in an all-out brawl. She's taller and stronger, equipped with years of training that my talents can't match. My only hope is to catch her by surprise again, to find a way to turn her own force against her. As I continue to circle, waiting and watching for an opening, the world around us fades away. I draw on all my anger, letting it replace my fear and give me strength.

*It's just you and me now. This is the way it was always meant to be, this is the moment I've been waiting for since it all began. We'll face each other at the very end with our bare hands.*

Commander Jameson strikes first. Her speed terrifies me. One second she's before me, and the next she's at my side, her fist flying toward my face. I don't have time to dodge. All I manage to do is jerk my shoulder up at the last second, and her fist hits me instead as a glancing blow. Stars explode across my eyes. I stumble backward. I manage to dodge her next blow—barely. I roll away from her, fighting to clear my vision, and pop back onto my feet. When she lunges again, I jump up and kick at her head. It catches her, but she's too fast for it to be head-on. I dart away again. This time I back up slowly toward the edge of the roof, my eyes terrified to leave her. *Good,* I remind myself. *Look as frightened as you can.* Finally, the back of my boot hits the roof's ledge. I glance down, then back up at Commander Jameson. Despite a slight unsteadiness, she looks undaunted. It isn't hard for me to fake the fear in my wide eyes.

She stalks toward me like a predator. She doesn't say a word, but she doesn't need to—everything she's ever wanted to tell me has already been said before. It runs through my head like a poison. *Little Iparis, how much you remind me of myself at your age. Adorable. Someday, you'll learn that life isn't always what you want it to be. That you won't always get what you want. And that there are forces out of your control that will shape you into who you are. Too bad your time ends here. It would've been fun to see what you grow up to become.*

Her eyes hypnotize me. In this moment, I can imagine no worse sight.

She lunges forward.

I have only one chance. I duck, grab her arm, and flip her right over my head. Her momentum sends her sailing over the edge of the roof.

But her hand clamps down on my arm. I'm yanked halfway over the ledge—my left shoulder pops out of its socket. I scream. My heels dig in against the ledge, fighting to keep me from falling over. Commander Jameson flattens herself against the side of the building, grappling for footholds. Her nails dig so deep into my flesh that I can feel my skin ripping. Tears spring to my eyes. Down below, Republic soldiers are still herding evacuees, firing on enemy soldiers on other roofs, shouting orders into their mikes.

I scream at them with everything I have left. "Shoot her!" I shout. "*Shoot her!*"

Two Republic soldiers snap their heads in my direction. They recognize me. As they lift their guns in my direction, Commander Jameson looks up into my eyes and grins. "I knew you couldn't do it yourself."

Then the soldiers open fire, Commander Jameson's body convulses, her grip suddenly loosens, and she plummets like a wounded bird to the street. I turn away so I don't have to look, but I still hear the sickening sound of her body against pavement. She's gone. Just like that. I'm left with her words and my own ringing through my ears.

*Shoot her. Shoot her.*

Metias's words flash through my mind. *Few people ever kill for the right reasons.*

I hurriedly wipe the tears from my face. What did I just do? Her blood stains my hands—I rub my good hand against my clothes, but I can't get it off. I don't know if I'll ever be able to. "This is the right reason," I whisper repeatedly.

Perhaps she destroyed herself, and I only helped. But even this thought seems hollow.

The agony of my dislocated shoulder makes me light-headed. I lift my right arm, grip my wounded left arm, grit my teeth, and push hard. I scream again. The bone resists for an instant—and then I feel my shoulder pop back into place. Fresh tears course down my face. My hands tremble uncontrollably, and my ears ring, blocking out any sound around me except the beating of my heart.

How long has it been? Hours? A few seconds?

The pulsing light of logic seeps into my mind, cutting through the pain. As always, it saves me. *Day needs your help,* it whispers. *Go to him.*

I search for Day. He has reached the other side of the street and the safer areas around the shelter, where Republic soldiers have set up their barricades . . . but even as I start rushing to the edge of the roof, I notice that others have pulled Eden's unconscious form away from Day and are taking him to safety. A few hover over Day as he lies on the ground, momentarily obscuring him from my view. I scramble down the building as fast as I can, until I reach a fire escape and rush down the metal steps. Fear and adrenaline numb my injuries.

*Please,* I beg silently. *Please let him be okay.*

By the time I reach him, a crowd has formed. I can hear one of them shouting, "Move it! Get back, give us some room! Tell them to hurry up!" A lump in my throat chokes me, leaving me short of breath. My boots pound against the ground, keeping rhythm with my heart. I shove people aside and drop to my knees at Day's side. The person shouting was Pascao. He gives me a frantic look.

"Stay with him," he tells me. "I'm going for the medics." I nod once, and he dashes off.

I barely notice all the people crowded around us in a ring.

All I can do is look down at Day. He's trembling from head to toe, his eyes wide open in shock, his hair clinging to his face. When I look closer at his body, I notice two wounds spilling dark blood across his shirt, one wound in his chest and the other near his hip. A strangled cry comes from someone. Maybe it's from me. As if in a dream, I bend over him and touch his face.

"Day, it's me. It's June. I'm right here."

He looks at me. "June?" he manages to gasp out. He tries to lift a hand to my face, but he's shaking so hard that he can't. I reach out and cradle his face with both of my hands. His eyes are full of tears. "I—I think—I've been shot—" Two people from the crowd place their hands over his wounds, pressing down hard enough to force a painful sob from his mouth. He tries to look down at them, but has no strength to lift his head.

"Medics are on their way," I tell him firmly, leaning close enough to press my lips against his cheek. "Hang on. Okay? *Stay with me.* Keep looking at me. You'll be okay."

"I don't—think so," Day stammers. He blinks rapidly, spilling tears down the sides of his face. They wet the tips of my fingers. "Eden—is he safe—?"

"He's safe," I whisper. "Your brother is safe and sound and you'll get to see him very soon."

Day starts to reply, but can't. His skin looks so ashen. *Please, no.* I refuse to let myself think the worst, but it hangs over us like a black shadow. I feel the heaviness of death looming over my shoulder, his sightless eyes staring down into Day's soul, waiting patiently to overwhelm his light.

"I don't want—to go—" Day finally manages to say. "I don't want—to leave you—Eden—"

I shush him by touching my lips to his trembling ones. "Nothing bad will ever happen to Eden," I reply gently, desperate to keep him with me. "Stay focused, Day. You're going to the hospital. They're coming back for you; it won't be long now."

It won't be long now.

Day just smiles at me, an expression so sad that it breaks through my numbness, and I begin to cry. Those bright blue eyes. Before me is the boy who has bandaged my wounds on the streets of Lake, who has guarded his family with every bone in his body, who has stayed by my side in spite of everything, the boy of light and laughter and life, of grief and fury and passion, the boy whose fate is intertwined with mine, forever and always.

"I love you," he whispers. "Can you stay awhile?" He says something else, but his voice trails off so quietly that I can't make out what it is. *No. No. You can't.* His breathing grows shallower. I can tell that he is fighting to stay conscious, that with every passing second, his eyes have more and more trouble focusing on me. For a moment, Day tries to look at something behind me, but when I glance over my shoulder, there's nothing there but open sky. I kiss him again and then lean my head against his.

"I love you," I whisper over and over again. "Don't go." I close my eyes. My tears fall on his cheeks.

As I crouch there against him, feeling his life slowly ebb away, I'm consumed with grief and rage. I have never been a religious person. But right now, as I see medics in the distance hurrying toward us, I send a desperate prayer to some higher power. To what, I don't know. But I hope that Someone, Anyone, hears me. That It'll lift us both into Its arms and take pity on us. I throw this prayer into the sky with every shred of strength I have left.

*Let him live.*

*Please don't take him away from this world. Please don't let him die here in my arms, not after everything we've been through together, not after You've taken so many others. Please, I beg You, let him live. I am willing to sacrifice anything to make this happen— I'm willing to do anything You ask. Maybe You'll laugh at me for such a naïve promise, but I mean it in earnest, and I don't care if it makes no sense or seems impossible. Let him live. Please. I can't bear this a second time.*

I look desperately around us, my vision blurred with tears, and everything is a smear of blood and smoke, light and ash, and all I can hear is screaming and gunfire and *hatred,* and I am so tired of the fighting, so frustrated, angry, helpless.

*Tell me there is still good in the world. Tell me there is still hope for all of us.*

Through an underwater veil, I feel hands on my arms pull me away from Day. I struggle stubbornly against them. Pain lances up my injured shoulder. Medics bend down over his body. His eyes are closed now, and I can't see him breathing. Images of Metias's body flash back to me. When the medics try again to pull me from Day, I shove them roughly away and scream. I scream for everything that has gone wrong. I scream for everything broken in our lives.

# DAY

I THINK JUNE IS LEANING OVER ME, BUT I HAVE TROUBLE making out the details of her face. When I try too hard, the edges of my vision filter out into blinding white. The pain, at first excruciating, is nothing now. Memories fade in and out—memories of my first days frightened and alone on the streets, with my bleeding knee and hollow stomach; of young Tess, and then of John when he first learned that I was still alive; of my mother's home, my father's smile, of Eden as a baby. I remember the first time I met June on the streets. Her defiant stance, her fierce eyes. Then, gradually, I have trouble remembering anything.

I always knew, on some level, that I wouldn't live long. It's simply not written in my stars.

Something bright hovering behind June's shoulder catches my attention. I turn my head as much as I can to see it. At first it looks like some glowing orb of light. As I keep staring, though, I realize that it's my mother.

*Mom,* I whisper. I stand and take a step toward her. My feet feel so light.

My mother smiles at me. She looks young and healthy and whole, her hands no longer wrapped in bandages, her hair the color of wheat and snow. When I reach her, she gently cups my face between her smooth, uninjured palms. My heart stops beating; it fills with warmth and light and I want to stay here forever, locked in this moment. I falter in my steps. Mom catches me before I can fall, and we kneel there, together again. "My little lost boy," she murmurs.

My voice comes out as a broken whisper. "I'm so sorry. I'm so sorry."

"Hush, my baby." I bow my head as she kneels over me. She kisses my forehead, and I am a child again, helpless and hopeful, bursting with love. Past the blurry, golden line of her arm, I can look down at my pale, broken body lying on the ground. There's a girl crouched over me, her hands on my face, her long dark hair draped over her shoulder. She's crying.

"Are John and Dad . . . ?" I begin to say.

Mom just smiles. Her eyes are so incredibly blue, like I can see the entire world inside them—the sky and the clouds and everything beyond.

"Don't worry," she replies. "They are well, and they love you very much."

I feel an overwhelming need to follow my mother wherever she's going, wherever that might take us. "I miss you guys," I finally say to her. "It hurts every day, the absence of someone who was once there."

Mom combs a gentle hand through my hair, the way she used to when I was little. "My darling, there's no need to miss us. We never left." She lifts her head and nods at the street, past the crowds of people who have gathered around my body. Now a team of medics is lifting me onto a stretcher. "Go back to Eden. He's waiting for you."

"I know," I whisper. I crane my neck to see if I can catch a glimpse of my brother in the crowds, but I don't see him there.

Mom rises; her hands leave my face, and I find myself struggling to breathe. *No. Please don't leave me.* I reach out a hand to her, but some invisible barrier stops it. The light grows brighter. "Where are you going? Can I come with you?"

Mom smiles, but shakes her head. "You still belong on the other side of the looking glass. Someday, when you're ready to take the step over to our side, I'll come see you again. Live well, Daniel. Make that final step count."

# JUNE

FOR THE FIRST THREE WEEKS THAT DAY IS IN THE HOS-
pital, I never leave. The same people come and go—Tess, of
course, who's in the waiting room as much as I am, waiting
for Day to come out of his coma; Eden, who stays as long as
Lucy allows him to; the other remaining Patriots, especially
Pascao; an endless assortment of doctors and medics who I
begin to recognize and know by name after the first week;
and Anden, who has returned from the warfront with his own
scars. Hordes of people continue to stay camped out around
the hospital, but Anden doesn't have the heart to tell them to
disperse, even when they continue to stake out the grounds for
weeks and then months. Many of them have the familiar scarlet streaks painted into their hair. For the most part, they stay
silent. Sometimes they chant. I've grown used to their presence now, to the point where it's comforting. They remind me
that Day is still alive. Still fighting.

The war between the Republic and the Colonies, at least
for now, is over. The Antarcticans finally came to our rescue,
bringing with them their fearsome technology and weapons
that intimidated Africa and the Colonies into returning to our
ceasefire agreement, bringing both Anden and the Chancellor
before the international court, imposing the proper sanctions
against us and them and finally, *finally* beginning the process for

a permanent peace treaty. The ashes of our battlegrounds are still here, though, along with a lingering hostility. I know it will take time to close the wounds. I have no idea how long this ceasefire will last, or when the Republic and the Colonies will find true peace. Maybe we never will. But for now, this is good enough.

One of the first things the doctors had to do for Day, after stitching up the horrific bullet wounds, was to operate on his brain. The trauma he'd suffered meant he couldn't receive the full course of medications needed to properly prep him for the surgery . . . but they went ahead with it. Whether or not he was ready was irrelevant at that point; if they didn't, he would've died anyway. Yet, still. This keeps me awake nights. No one really knows whether he'll wake up at all, or whether he'll be an altogether different person if he does.

Two months pass, and then three.

Gradually, we all start to do our waiting at home. The hospital's crowds finally begin to thin.

Five months. Winter passes.

At 0728 hours on an early spring Thursday in March, I arrive at the hospital's waiting room for my usual check-in. As expected at this hour, I'm the only one here. Eden's at home with Lucy, getting some needed sleep. He continues to grow, and if Day were awake to see him now, I know he'd comment on how his brother is starting to lean out, losing the baby fat on his face and taking the early steps into adulthood.

Even Tess isn't here yet. She tends to come in the late morning to work as a medic assistant, shadowing the doctors, and when I catch her on her breaks, we huddle together and exchange conversation in hushed voices. Sometimes she even makes me laugh. "He loves you, really he does," she told me yesterday. "He'd love you even if it destroyed him. He matches you. I guess it's kind of cute." She said this with a shy, grudging smile on her face. Somehow, she had managed to return to the place where I'd first known her, but now as someone older, taller, and wiser.

I nudged her affectionately. "You guys have a bond I could never touch," I replied. "Even when we're at our worst."

She blushed at that, and I couldn't help opening my heart to her. A loving Tess is one of the sweetest sights in the world. "Just be good to him," she whispered. "Promise?"

Now I greet the nurse at the waiting room's window, then settle down into my usual chair and look around. So empty this morning. I find myself missing Tess's companionship. I try to distract myself with the news headlines running on the monitor.

ANTARCTICAN PRESIDENT IKARI, UNITED
NATIONS, SHOW APPROVAL FOR NEW PEACE
TREATY BETWEEN REPUBLIC AND COLONIES

ELECTOR PRIMO ANNOUNCES START OF NEW
RANKING SYSTEM TO REPLACE FORMER TRIALS

NEW BORDER CITIES BETWEEN REPUBLIC AND
COLONIES TO BE RENAMED THE UNITED CITIES,

TO BEGIN ALLOWING IMMIGRATION FROM BOTH
NATIONS STARTING LATE NEXT YEAR

SENATOR MARIANA DUPREE OFFICIALLY INDUCTED
AS PRINCEPS OF THE SENATE

The news headlines bring a faint smile to my face. Last night, Anden had stopped by my apartment to tell me in person about Mariana. I'd told him that I would extend my congratulations to her directly. "She's very good at what she does," I said. "More so than I was. I'm happy for her."

Anden bowed his head. "You would have been better in the long run, I think," he replied with a gentle smile. "You understand the people. But I'm happy that you're back where you feel the most comfortable. Our troops are lucky to have you." He hesitated then, and for a moment he took my hand in his. I remember the soft neoprene lining of his gloves, the silver shine of his cufflinks. "I might not get to see much of you now. Maybe it's best that way, isn't it? Still, please do drop by now and then. It'll be nice to hear from you."

"Likewise," I replied, squeezing his hand in return.

My thoughts snap back to the present. One of the doctors has emerged from the hallway near Day's room. He catches sight of me, takes a deep breath, and approaches. I straighten, tensing. It's been a long time since I've heard any real updates on Day's condition from Dr. Kann. A part of me wants to jump up in excitement, because perhaps the news is good; another part of me cringes in fear, in case the news is bad. My eyes scan the doctor's face, searching for clues. (Pupils slightly dilated, face anxious, but not in the manner of one who is about to break the worst news. There are hints of joy on his face.) My pulse quickens. What is he going to tell me? Or perhaps it's no news at all—perhaps he's simply going to tell me what he usually does. *Not much change today, I'm afraid, but at least he's still stable.* I've grown so used to hearing that.

Dr. Kann pauses before me. He adjusts his glasses and scratches unconsciously at his trimmed salt-and-pepper beard. "Good morning, Ms. Iparis," he says.

"How is he?" I ask, my usual greeting.

Dr. Kann smiles, but hesitates (another oddity; the news must be significant). "Wonderful news." My heart stops for a second. "Day has woken up. Less than an hour ago."

"He's awake?" I breathe. *He's awake.* Suddenly the news is too overwhelming, and I'm not sure whether I can bear it. I study his face carefully. "There's more to it than that, though. Isn't there?"

Dr. Kann puts both hands on my shoulders. "I don't want to worry you, Ms. Iparis, not at all. Day has pulled through his surgery remarkably well—when he woke up, he asked for water and then for his brother. He seems quite alert and coherent. We ran a quick scan of his brain." His voice turns more excited. "We'll need to do a more thorough check, of course, but upon first glance it seems everything has normalized. His hippocampus looks healthy, and signals seem to be firing normally. In almost every aspect, the Day that we know is back."

Tears prickle at the edges of my eyes. The Day that we know is back. After *five months* of waiting, the news is so sudden. One minute he was lying unconscious in bed, hanging on to life night by night, and now he's awake. Just like that. I break into a smile with the doctor, and before I can stop myself, I hug him. He laughs, patting my head awkwardly, but I don't care. I want to see Day. "Can he have visitors?" I ask. Then, abruptly, I realize what the doctor actually said. "Why do you say 'almost'?"

The doctor's smile wavers. He adjusts his glasses again. "It's nothing we can't fix over the course of extended therapy. You see, the hippocampus region affects memories, both short- and long-term. It seems that Day's long-term memories—his family, his brother Eden, his friend Tess, and so on—are intact. After a few questions, however, it seems like he has very little recollection of both people and events from the last year or two. We call it retrograde amnesia. He remembers his family's deaths, for instance . . ." Dr. Kann's voice trails off uncomfortably here. "But he does not seem familiar with Commander Jameson's name, or the recent Colonies' invasion. He also doesn't seem to recall you."

My smile fades. "He . . . doesn't remember me?"

"Of course, this is something that can heal over time, with proper therapy," Dr. Kann again reassures me. "His short-term memory abilities are working well. He remembers most things I tell him, and forms new memories without too much issue. I just wanted to warn you before you see him. Don't be startled that he might not remember you. Take your time and reintroduce yourself to him. Gradually, perhaps in a few years' time, his old memories might come back."

I nod at the doctor as if in a dream. "Okay," I whisper.

"You can see him now, if you'd like." He smiles at me, as if he's delivering the greatest news in the world. And he is.

But when he leaves me, I just stand there for a moment. My mind in a haze. Thinking. Lost. Then I take slow steps toward the hallway where Day's hospital room is, the corridor closing in around me like a foggy, blurry tunnel. The only thing running through my head is the memory of my desperate prayer over Day's wounded body, the promise I had offered up to the heavens in exchange for his life.

*Let him live. I am willing to sacrifice anything to make this happen.*

My heart sinks, turns gray. I understand now. I know that something has answered my prayer, and at the same time has also told me what my sacrifice must be. I have been offered a chance to never hurt Day again.

I step into the hospital room. Day is alert, propped up on pillows and startlingly healthier than the times I've seen him lying unconscious and wan over the past few months. But something is different now. Day's eyes follow me without a hint of familiarity in them; he's watching me with the polite, wary distance of a stranger, the way he looked at me when we first met.

He doesn't know who I am.

My heart aches, pulling at me as I draw closer to his bedside. I know what I have to do.

"Hi," he says when I sit on his bed. His eyes wander curiously across my face.

"Hi," I reply softly. "Do you know who I am?"

Day looks guilty, which only digs the knife in deeper. "Should I?"

It takes all of my effort not to cry, to bear the thought that Day has forgotten everything between us—our night together, the ordeals we've been through, all that we've shared and lost. We have been erased from his memory, leaving nothing behind. The Day that *I* knew is not here.

I could tell him right now, of course. I could remind him of who I am, that I'm June Iparis, the girl he had once saved on the streets and fallen in love with. I could tell him everything, just like Dr. Kann said, and it could possibly trigger his old memories. *Tell him, June. Just tell him. You'll be so happy. It'd be so easy.*

But I open my mouth and no sound comes out. I can't do it. *Be good to him,* Tess had told me. *Promise.*

So long as I remain in Day's life, I will hurt him. Any other alternative is impossible. I think of the way he had crouched, sobbing, at his family's kitchen table, mourning what I had taken away from him. Now fate has handed the solution to me on a silver platter—Day survived his ordeal, and in return, I need to step out of his life. Even though he looks at me now like a stranger, he no longer has the look of pain and tragedy that always seemed to come with the passion and love he gazed at me with. Now he is free.

He is free of *us*, leaving me as the only bearer of our past's burden.

So I swallow hard, smile, and bow my head to him. "Day," I force myself to say, "it's good to meet you. I was sent by the Republic to see how you're doing. It's wonderful to see you awake again. The country is going to rejoice when they hear the good news."

Day nods politely in return, his tenseness unmistakable. "Thank you," he says warily. "The doctors tell me that I've been out for five months. What happened?"

"You were injured during a battle between the Republic and the Colonies," I reply. Everything I'm saying sounds like it's coming from someone else's mouth. "You saved your brother Eden."

"Is Eden here?" Day's eyes light up with recognition, and a beautiful smile blossoms on his face. The sight of it brings me pain even as I am happy that he remembers his brother. I want so much to see that look of familiarity on his face when he's talking about *me*.

"Eden will be so happy to see you. The doctors are sending for him, so he'll arrive shortly." I return his smile, and this time it's a genuine one, if bittersweet. When Day studies my face again, I close my eyes and bow slightly to him.

It's time to let go.

"Day," I say, carefully choosing what my final words to him

should be. "It has been such a privilege and honor to fight by your side. You've saved many more of us than you'll ever know." For a small moment, I fix my eyes on his, telling him silently everything that I'll never say to him aloud. "Thank you," I whisper. "For everything."

Day looks puzzled by the emotion in my voice, but he bows his head in return. "The honor's mine," he replies. My heart breaks in sorrow at the lack of warmth in his voice, the warmth I know I would have heard had he remembered everything. I feel the absence of the aching love that I've come to yearn for, that I wanted so much to earn. It is gone now.

If he knew who I was, I would say something else to him now, something I should've said to him more often when I had the chance. Now I *am* sure of my feelings, and it's too late. So I fold the three words back into my heart, for his sake, and rise from his bed. I soak in every last, wonderful detail of his face and store it in my memory, hoping I can take him with me wherever I go. We exchange quiet salutes.

Then I turn away for the last time.

Two weeks later, what feels like the entire city of Los Angeles turns out to see Day leave the country for good. On the morning I left Day's bedside, Antarctica came calling for both him and his brother. They'd taken note of Eden's gifted touch with engineering and offered him a place in one of their academies. At the same time, they offered Day the chance to go along.

I don't join the crowds. I stay in my apartment instead, watching the events unfold while Ollie sleeps contentedly beside me. The streets around my complex are teeming with people, all jostling with one another to watch the JumboTrons. Their muffled chaos turns into white noise as I watch it unfold on my screen.

## DANIEL ALTAN WING AND BROTHER TO LEAVE TONIGHT FOR ROSS CITY, ANTARCTICA

That's what the headlines say. On the screen, Day waves at the people gathered around his apartment as he and Eden are escorted to a jeep by a city patrol. I should call him Daniel, like the screen does. Perhaps he truly *is* just Daniel now, with no need for an alias anymore. I look on as he lets his brother get into the vehicle, and then follows, lost completely from view. *It's so strange,* I think to myself as my hand moves absently across Ollie's fur. Not long ago, the city patrols would have arrested him on sight. Now, he's leaving the Republic as their champion, to be celebrated and remembered for a lifetime.

I turn the monitor off, then sit in the quiet darkness of my apartment, savoring the silence. Outside on the streets, people are still chanting his name. They chant it deep into the night.

When the commotion finally dies down, I get up from my couch. I pull on my boots and a coat, then wrap a thin scarf around my neck and head out into the streets. My hair blows in the balmy night breeze, wisps catching now and then on my lashes. For a while I wander the quiet roads on my own. I'm not sure where I'm going. Maybe I'm trying to find my way back to Day. But that's illogical. He's already gone, and his absence leaves a hollow, aching pain in my chest. My eyes water from the wind.

I walk for an hour before I finally take a short train ride to Lake sector. There, I stroll along the edge of the water, admiring the lights of downtown as well as the now-unused, unlit Trial stadium, a haunting reminder of events long gone. Giant water wheels churn in the lake, the rhythm of their movement settling into a comforting background symphony. I don't know where I'm going. All I know is that, in this moment, Lake sector seems more like home to me than Ruby does. Here, I'm not so alone. On these streets, I can still feel the beating of Day's heart.

I begin to retrace my old steps, past the same lakeside buildings and the same crumbling homes, the steps I'd taken when I was a completely different person, full of hate and confusion, loss and ignorance. It's an odd feeling to wander these same streets as the person I am now. At once familiar and strange.

An hour later, I pause alone before a nondescript alleyway that branches off an empty street. At the end of this alley, an abandoned high-rise towers twelve stories up, each of its windows boarded up and its first floor just the way I remember it, with missing windows and broken glass on the floor. I step into the shadows of the building, remembering. This is where Day had first reached his hand out to me in the midst of smoke and dust and saved me so long ago, before we even discovered who the other was; this was the start of the few precious nights when we simply knew each other as a boy on the streets and a girl who needed help.

The memory comes into sharp focus.

*There's a voice telling me to get up. When I look to my side, I see a boy holding out his hand to me. He has bright blue eyes, dirt on his face, and a beat-up old cap on, and at this moment, I think he might be the most beautiful boy I've ever seen.*

My wandering has led me to the beginning of our journey together. I suppose it's only fitting for me to be here at that journey's end.

I stand in the darkness for a long time, letting myself sink into the memories we once shared. The silence wraps me in comforting arms. One of my hands reaches over to my side and finds the old scar from where Kaede had wounded me. So many memories, so much joy and sadness.

Tears stream down my face. I wonder what Day is thinking at this moment while on his way to a foreign land, and whether or not some small part of him, even if it is buried deep, holds slivers of me, pieces of what we once had.

The longer I stand here, the lighter the burden on my heart feels. Day will move on and live his life. So will I. We will be okay. Someday, perhaps in the far and distant future, we'll find each other again. Until then, I will remember him. I reach out to touch one of the walls, imagining that I can feel his life and warmth through it, and I look around again, up toward the rooftops and then all the way to the night sky where a few faint stars can be seen, and there I think I really *can* see him. I can feel his presence here in every stone he has touched, every person he has lifted up, every street and alley and city that he has changed in the few years of his life, because he *is* the Republic, he *is* our light, and I love you, I love you, until the day we meet again I will hold you in my heart and protect you there, grieving what we never had, cherishing what we did. I wish you were here.

I love you, always.

# LOS ANGELES, CALIFORNIA
REPUBLIC OF AMERICA

★ ★ ★

# TEN YEARS LATER

# JUNE

### TODAY IS MY TWENTY-SEVENTH BIRTHDAY.

I celebrate most of my birthdays without too much trouble.
On my eighteenth, I joined Anden, a couple of Senators, Pascao and Tess, and several former Drake classmates for a low-key dinner at a rooftop lounge in Ruby sector. My nineteenth happened on a boat in New York City, the Colonies' rebuilt version of an old drowned city whose outskirts now slope gently into the Atlantic Ocean. I'd been invited to a party thrown for several international delegates from Africa, Canada, and Mexico. I spent my twentieth comfortably alone, tucked into bed with Ollie snoring on my lap, watching a brief newscast about how Day's brother Eden had graduated early from his academy in Antarctica, trying to catch a glimpse of how Day looked as a twenty-year-old, taking in the news that he himself had been recruited by Antarctica's intelligence agency. My twenty-first birthday was an elaborate affair in Vegas, where Anden invited me to a summer festival and then ended up kissing me in my hotel room. Twenty-second: the first birthday I celebrated with Anden as my official boyfriend. Twenty-third:

spent at an induction ceremony that placed me as the commander of all squadrons in California, the youngest lead commander in Republic history. Twenty-fourth: a birthday spent without Ollie. Twenty-fifth: dinner and dancing with Anden on board the RS *Constellation*. Twenty-sixth: spent with Pascao and Tess as I told them about being freshly broken up from Anden, how the young Elector and I came to a mutual agreement that I simply couldn't love him the way he wished I would.

Some of these years were spent in joy, others in sadness—but the saddest events were always tolerable. Far worse things have happened, and nothing tragic during these later years could compare with the events from my teenage years. But today is different. I've been dreading this particular birthday for years, because it takes me back to some of the events from my past that I've tried so hard to keep buried.

I spend most of the day in a fairly quiet mood. I rise early, follow my usual warm-up routines at the track, and then head to Batalla sector to organize my captains for their various city operations. Today I'm leading two of my best patrols to escort Anden during a meeting with Colonies' delegates. We may not share the same apartment anymore, but that doesn't change how fiercely I watch over his safety. He will always be my Elector, and I intend to keep it that way. Today, he and the Colonies are deep in the middle of discussions about the smooth immigration status along our border, where the United Cities have turned into flourishing areas with both Colonies and Republic civilians. What was once a hard dividing line between us now looks like a gradient. I look on from the sidelines as Anden shakes hands with the delegates and poses for photos. I'm proud of what he's done. Slow steps, but steps nonetheless. Metias would've been happy to see it. So would Day.

When late afternoon comes, I finally leave Batalla Hall and head to a smooth, ivory-white building at the east end of Batalla Square. There, I show my ID at the entrance and make my way up to the building's twelfth floor. I trace familiar steps down the hall, my boots echoing against the marble floors, until I stop in front of a four-square-inch tombstone marker with the name CAPTAIN METIAS IPARIS embedded in its crystal-clear surface.

I stand there for a while, then sit cross-legged before it and bow my head. "Hi, Metias," I say in a soft voice. "Today's my birthday. Do you know how old I am now?"

I close my eyes, and through the silence surrounding me I think I can sense a ghostly hand on my shoulder, my brother's gentle presence that I'm able to feel every now and then, in these quiet moments. I imagine him smiling down at me, his expression relaxed and free.

"I'm twenty-seven today," I continue in a whisper. My voice catches for a moment. "We're the same age now."

For the first time in my life, I am no longer his little sister. Next year I will step across the line and he will still be in the same place. From now on, I will be older than he ever was.

I try to move on to other thoughts, so I tell my brother's ghost about my year, my struggles and successes in commanding my own patrols, my hectic workweeks. I tell him, as I always do, that I miss him. And as always, I can hear the whisper of his ghost against my ear, his gentle reply that he misses me too. That he's looking out for me, from wherever he is.

An hour later, when the sun has finally set and the light streaming in from the windows fades away, I rise from my position and slowly make my way out of the building. I listen to some missed messages on my earpiece. Tess should be leaving her hospital shift soon, most likely armed with a slew of new stories about her patients. In the first years after Day left, the two of them stayed in close contact, and Tess would keep me constantly updated about how he was doing. Things like Eden's improving eyesight. Day's new job. Antarctican games. But as the years went on, their chatter grew less frequent, Tess grew up and into her own life, and gradually, their conversations dwindled to brief annual greetings. Sometimes none at all.

I'd be lying if I said I didn't miss her stories about Day. But still, I find myself looking forward to some dinner chatter with her and Pascao, who should be heading over from Drake University, probably eager to share his latest adventures in training cadets. I smile as I think about what they might say. My heart feels lighter now, a little freer after my conversation with my brother. My thoughts wander briefly to Day. I wonder where he is, who he's with, whether he's happy.

I really, sincerely, deeply hope that he is.

The sector isn't busy tonight (we haven't needed as many street police in the last few years), and aside from a few soldiers here and there, I'm alone. Most of the streetlights haven't turned on yet, and in the gathering darkness I can see a handful of stars flickering overhead. The glow from JumboTrons casts a kaleidoscope of colors across the gray pavement of Batalla sector, and I catch myself walking deliberately underneath them, holding a hand out to study the colors that dance across my skin. I watch snippets of news on the screens with mild disinterest while skimming through my missed messages. The epaulettes on my shoulders clink softly.

Then I pause on a message Tess had left me earlier in the afternoon. Her voice fills my ears, full of warmth and playfulness.

"Hey. Check the news."

That's all she says. I frown, then laugh a little at Tess's game. What's going on in the news? My eyes return to the screens, this time with more curiosity. None of it catches my eye. I keep searching, looking for what Tess might have been talking about. Still nothing. Then . . . one small, nondescript headline, so brief that I must have been skipping over it all day. I blink, as if I might have misunderstood it, and read it again before it cycles out.

EDEN BATAAR WING IN LOS ANGELES TO
INTERVIEW FOR BATALLA ENGINEERING POSITION

Eden? A ripple glides across the silence that has stilled me all day. I read the headline over and over again before I finally convince myself that they are indeed talking about Day's younger brother. Eden is here to interview for a potential job.

He and Day are in town.

I look around the streets instinctively. They're here, walking the same streets. *He's* here. I shake my head at the little adolescent girl who has suddenly woken up in my heart. Even after all this time, I hope. *Calm down, June.* But still, my heart sits in my throat. Tess's message echoes in my mind. I return to walking down the street. Maybe I can find out where they're staying, just get a glimpse of how he's doing after all this time. I decide to call Tess back once I've reached the train station.

Fifteen minutes later, I'm at the outskirts of Batalla sector; the train station leading to Ruby appears around the corner. The darkness has lengthened enough for the streetlights to turn on, and a few soldiers are heading down the opposite sidewalk; aside from them, I'm the only one on this block.

But when I reach a slight curve in the street, I see two other people headed in my direction. I stop in my tracks. Then I frown and peer closer at the street before me. I'm still not sure of what I'm seeing.

A pair of young men. Details flit automatically through my mind, so familiar now that I hardly think twice about them. Both are tall and lean, with pale blond hair that stands out in the dimly lit night. Instantly I know that they must be related, with their similar features and easy gaits. The one on the left wears glasses and is talking animatedly, brushing golden curls out of his eyes as he goes, his hands painting some sort of diagram in front of him. He keeps rolling his sleeves back up to his elbows, and his collar shirt is loose and rumpled. A carefree smile lights up his face.

The young man on the right seems more reserved, listening patiently to his curly-haired companion while he keeps his hands tucked casually in his pockets. A small grin touches the corners of his lips. His hair is different from what I remember, now short and endearingly unruly, and as he walks he occasionally runs a hand through it, leaving it even more wayward. His eyes are as blue as ever. Even though he's older now, with the face of a young man instead of the teenager I'd known so well, he still shows hints of that old fire whenever he laughs at his brother's words, moments of startling brightness and life.

My heart begins to beat, cutting through the heaviness that weighs on my chest. *Day and Eden.*

I keep my head down as they draw closer. But from the corner of my vision, I see Eden notice me first. He pauses for a second in the middle of his sentence, and a quick smile appears on his face. His eyes flicker to his brother.

Day casts me a look.

The intensity of it catches me off guard—I haven't been subjected to his gaze in so long that suddenly I can't catch my breath. I straighten and quicken my pace. I need to get out of here. Otherwise, I'm not sure whether I can keep my emotions from spilling onto my face.

We pass each other without a word. My lungs feel like they might burst, and I take a few quick breaths to steady myself. I close my eyes. All I can hear is the rush of blood in my ears, the steady thumping of my heart. Gradually I hear the sound of their footsteps fade behind me. A sinking feeling slowly settles. I swallow hard, forcing a flood of memories out of my mind.

I'm heading toward the train station. I'm going home. I'm not going to look back.

I can't.

Then . . . I hear footsteps behind me again. Hurried boots against pavement. I pause, steel myself, and look over my shoulder.

It's Day. He catches up to me. Some distance behind him, Eden waits with his hands in his pockets. Day stares into my eyes with a soft, puzzled expression—it sends an electric shiver down my spine. "Excuse me," he says. *Oh, that voice.* Deeper, gentler than I remember, without the rawness of childhood and with the new elegance of an adult. "Have we met before?"

For a moment, I'm at a loss for words. What do I say? I've spent so many years convincing myself that we no longer know each other. "No," I whisper. "Sorry." In my mind, I beg myself to tell him otherwise.

Day frowns, confused for a moment. He runs his hand through his hair. In that gesture, I catch a glimpse of something shiny on his finger. It's a ring made out of wires. Of paper clips. A breath escapes me in shock.

He is still wearing the paper clip ring I'd once given him.

"Oh," he finally replies. "I'm sorry to bother you, then. I just . . . You look really familiar. Are you sure we don't know each other from somewhere?"

I search his eyes in silence. I can't say anything. There is a secret emotion emerging on his face now, somewhere between strangeness and familiarity, something that tells me he's struggling to place me, to find where I belong. My heart protests, reaching out for him to discover it. Still, no words come out.

Day searches my face with his soft gaze. Then he shakes his head. "I *have* known you," he murmurs. "A long time ago. I don't know where, but I think I know why."

"Why, then?" I ask gently.

He's quiet for a moment. Then he takes a step closer, close enough for me to see that tiny ripple of imperfection in his left eye. He laughs a little, pink creeping onto his cheeks. "I'm sorry. This is going to sound so strange." I feel like I'm lost in a haze. Like this is a dream I don't dare wake from. "I . . . ," he begins, as if looking for the right words. "I've been searching a long time for something I think I lost."

*Something he lost.* The words bring a lump to my throat, a sudden surge of wild hope. "It's not strange at all," I hear myself reply.

Day smiles in return. Something sweet and yearning appears in his eyes. "I felt like I found something when I saw you back there. Are you sure . . . do you know me? Do I know *you*?"

I don't know what to say. The part of me that had once decided to step out of his life tells me to do it again, to protect him from this knowledge that had hurt him so long ago. *Ten years . . . has it really been that long?* The other part of me, the girl who had first met him on the streets, urges me to tell him the truth. Finally, when I do manage to open my mouth, I say, "I have to go meet up with some friends."

"Oh. Sorry." Day clears his throat, unsure of himself. "I do too, actually. An old friend down in Ruby."

*An old friend down in Ruby.* My eyes widen. Suddenly I

know why Tess sounded so mischievous on her message, why she told me to watch the news tonight. "Is your friend's name Tess?" I ask hesitantly.

It's Day's turn to look surprised. He gives me an intrigued, puzzled smile. "You know her."

What am I doing? What's happening? This really is all a dream, and I'm terrified to wake up from it. I've had this dream too many times. I don't want it taken away again. "Yes," I murmur. "I'm having dinner with her tonight."

We stare at each other in silence. Day's face is serious now, and his gaze is so intense that I can feel warmth running through every inch of my body. We stand together like this for a long, long moment, and for once, I have no idea how much time has passed. "I do remember," he finally says. I search his eyes for that same aching sadness, the torment and anguish that had always been there whenever we were together. But I can no longer see it. Instead, I find something else . . . I see a healed wound, a permanent scar that has nevertheless closed, something from a chapter of his life that he has finally, after all these years, made peace with. I see . . . Can it be possible? Can this be true?

I see pieces of memories in his eyes. Pieces of *us*. They are broken, and scattered, but they are there, gradually coming together again at the sight of me. *They are there.*

"It's you," he whispers. There is wonder in his voice.

"Is it?" I whisper back, my voice trembling with all the emotions I've kept hidden for so long.

Day is so close, and his eyes are so bright. "I hope," he replies softly, "to get to know you again. If you are open to it. There is a fog around you that I would like to clear away."

His scars will never fade. I am certain of that much. But perhaps . . . perhaps . . . with time, with age, we can be friends again. We can heal. Perhaps we can return to that same place we once stood, when we were both young and innocent. Perhaps we really can meet like other people do, on some street one balmy evening, where we each catch the other's eye and stop to introduce ourselves. Echoes of Day's old wish come back to me now, emerging from the mist of our early days.

Perhaps there *is* such a thing as fate.

Still I wait, too unsure of myself to answer. I cannot take the first step. I *shouldn't*. That step belongs to him.

For a moment, I think it won't happen.

Then Day reaches out and touches my hand with his. He encloses it in a handshake. And just like that, I am linked with him again, I feel the pulse of our bond and history and love through our hands, like a wave of magic, the return of a long-lost friend. *Of something meant to be.* The feeling brings tears to my eyes. *Perhaps we can take a step forward together.*

"Hi," he says. "I'm Daniel."

"Hi," I reply. "I'm June."

# ACKNOWLEDGMENTS

The end of the path is a strange and wistful place. For the past few years, I've breathed the world of *Legend*; my life became the lives of Day and June, and through them I saw my own fears, hopes, and aspirations play out across their canvas. Now I've reached the point where our stories diverge. They are off to live beyond the confines of the trilogy; I am left waving to them from the sidelines. I don't know where they'll go, but I think they're going to be okay.

I'm not alone on the sidelines, of course. With me are those I started with and those I met along the way:

My inimitable literary agent, Kristin Nelson, and Team NLA: Anita Mumm, Sara Megibow, Lori Bennett, and Angie Hodapp. Thank you, thank you, thank you for standing with me on every hill.

My amazing editors, Jen Besser, Ari Lewin, and Shauna Fay Rossano, who vanquished my Book 3 demons with stalwart battle cries. We made it! I don't know what I'd do without you. Love you ladies.

Team Putnam Children's, Team Speak, and Team Penguin: Don Weisberg, Jennifer Loja, Marisa Russell, Laura Antonacci, Anna Jarzab, Jessica Schoffel, Elyse Marshall, Jill Bailey, Scottie Bowditch, Lori Thorn, Linda McCarthy, Erin Dempsey, Shanta

Newlin, Emily Romero, Erin Gallagher, Mia Garcia, Lisa Kelly, Courtney Wood, Marie Kent, Sara Ortiz, Elizabeth Zajac, Kristin Gilson, and Eileen Kreit. You guys are the most epic teams a girl could have on her side.

The incredible people at CBS Films, Temple Hill, UTA, and ALF&L: Wolfgang Hammer, Grey Munford, Matt Gilhooley, Ally Mielnicki, Isaac Klausner, Wyck Godfrey, Marty Bowen, Gina Martinez, Wayne Alexander, and my fabulous film agent, Kassie Evashevski. Thank you all for continuing to believe in this writer's dreams.

Wicked Sweet Games: Matt Sherwood, Phil Harvey, Kole Hicks, Bobby Hernandez, and of course, the Elector Primo. *Cities of Legend* is a game full of badassery, because you guys are badass.

My incredible foreign publishers for taking *Legend* above and beyond, and sometimes even straight to Pasadena with fans in tow! (I'm looking at you, marvelous Ruth.)

My irreplaceable writer friends: JJ, Ello, Andrea, Beth, Jess Spotswood, Jess Khoury, Leigh, Sandy, Amie, Ridley, Kami, Margie, Tahereh, Ransom, Cindy, Malinda, and the fabulous PubCrawl ladies. Finding one's tribe is a precious thing. I cannot properly express what you all mean to me. Thank you for your friendship.

The fam bam, my friends, Andre, my aunt and uncle, my wonderful fiancé, and most of all, my mom. You are always there, no matter what. Love you.

Finally, I need to give a special acknowledgment at the end of this path: